THE CARNIVAL OF DESTRUCTION

THE CARNIVAL
OF DESTRUCTION

Brian Stableford

Carroll & Graf Publishers, Inc.
New York

Copyright © 1994 by Brian Stableford

Published by arrangement with Simon & Schuster Ltd., London

First Carroll & Graf edition 1994

Carroll & Graf Publishers, Inc.
260 Fifth Avenue
New York, NY 10001

Library of Congress Cataloging-in-Publication Data

Stableford, Brian M.
    The carnival of destruction / Brian Stableford.
        p.   cm.
    ISBN 0-7867-0122-6 : $21.95
    I. Title
PR6069.T17C37   1994
823'.914—dc20   94-22394
                                                                    CIP

Manufactured in the United States of America

For Cymantha, with love

CONTENTS

THE CARNIVAL OF DESTRUCTION

Part One

Guardian Angels

The next war will be the most frightful carnival of destruction that the world has ever seen.

George Griffith, *The Angel of the Revolution*, 1893

1

Anatole tried to close his eyes, but could not do it; nor could he weep for his impotence.

Sight had become a kind of anguish; he wanted darkness.

It was not that he wanted to die, although death would certainly be a *coup de grace*. He wanted rest: rest from pain, from horror, from terror, from war, from ceaseless confrontation with the fragile and tortured world; but he could no more close his eyes by conscious effort than he could raise his hand or move his broken leg. He had lost the power of command over his own body.

He could easily have believed that he was already dead, were it not for the fact that his eyes still blinked, reflexively, at least once in every slow minute. His body still had a will of its own, albeit a miserably weak one. His heart was still beating, and his nerves, unfailing in their unpleasant duty, relentlessly informed him as to the extent of his injuries.

He was mortally wounded; there was no doubting that. Death would come to claim him soon. He had no right to complain. He had been in active service for eighteen months, which was a long time in *this* war: a whole lifetime. It seemed to him now that all his youth, all his growth, all his learning, all his ambition, had been but a prelude, a preparation for that brief lifetime. For men of his time— for *Frenchmen* of his time, at any rate—life was all bombardment and machine-gun fire, barbed wire and short rations, fixed bayonets and gas masks. Life was sighting down the barrel of a rifle with the utmost care, squeezing the trigger with delicate precision, watching some gray-clad figure tumble, knowing that another of the enemy had been struck down by the glad hand of Vengeance . . .

It *was* vengeance, after all. This was French soil; he was a Frenchman. It was the invader who had turned the land into a wilderness, made a black desert where corn and beet once grew; it was the invader who had made a battleground of the honest fields; it was the invader who deserved to die. But for the defenders, too, death followed life as night followed day. No one was safe; no one was protected; no one was favored. Avenger today, carrion tomorrow; that was the world as he had found it, the world as it was. The moment he had fired his first shot he had set forth upon a journey to the moment when he would be the target of just such a shot: the moment when he would be the slain and not the slayer.

The moment should not have come unexpectedly, but it had. Since the Chemin des Dames had been recaptured from the Germans in October it had been a "quiet sector." No one had expected the attack, and intelligence of German troops massing in the woods on the far side of no-man's-land had been discounted by senior officers—but the guns had opened up at one in the morning, drenching the lines to a depth of twelve miles. The attack had begun with gas, and had continued with a mixture of gas and high-explosives. Mortars had taken out the wire with brutal imprecision, and the German infantry had swarmed forth at dawn, obscured—as usual—by the mist. What pockets of resistance remained in the front line had been overwhelmed.

Anatole knew that he should have been dead already. A single bayonet-thrust would have finished him off as he lay helpless in the shell-hole, but muddied as he was from top to toe, with his head bleeding copiously, he must have seemed lifeless enough to the hurrying enemy. In time, no doubt, he would be picked off during the "mopping-up," but there was little dignity in waiting for that.

There was an offensive alien odor in the shell-hole, which stung his sinuses like disinfecting fluid. He wondered if it might be an olfactory hallucination. He could not block it out. His respirator hung uselessly about his neck; he had gladly discarded it when the Germans swarmed forward, fearful that it might choke him. The gas had dissipated by then, in spite of the fact that there had been no wind.

He tried to close his eyes, and could not do it.

There was a dead Britisher beside him. Had Anatole been able to move his right hand he could have removed the pistol from the holster at the man's waist, placed the barrel in his mouth, and blown whatever remained of his brains through the back of his skull. It would only have taken a moment. But his hand would not move, and he understood its reluctance. He did not really want to die. However unavoidable that fate might be, he did not want to meet it yet.

He knew that his head wound must be very bad, but the pain he felt was all in his chest and his leg. Was it possible, he wondered, that the bullet, according to some ironic caprice, had smashed exactly the part of his brain which was supposed to feel the shock of its own dereliction? If only it had pulverized instead the cells whose thankless task it was to tell him, with such an unbearable clamor, that his leg was smashed beyond repair!

He was tempted to pray, but he resisted the temptation firmly. He was an atheist now, and a good communist. It would be a vile weakness to surrender his principles, a pitiful reversion to childishness. His mother had often told him, when he was as young as P'tit Jean was now, that he had a guardian angel stationed on his right shoulder, whose task was to protect him from the traps set by the cunning imp which haunted his left side. Doubtless she said the same to P'tit Jean when she put him to bed, as she had said the same to all his brothers. Did she tell P'tit Jean that Anatole had become a guardian angel of sorts, protecting Paris against the cunning of the Boche? Did she tell the child not to be afraid for his brother's life, because he was still under the protection of the guardian angel in which he had ceased to believe?

Poor Jean! How desolate he would be when the news came of his brother's death! What a terrible way to learn the awful fallibility of guardian angels!

The rattle of the guns was fading in the distance. The French and the British must be in full retreat. Anatole was not in the least surprised. The remnants of the three British divisions which had been sent to reinforce the French-held position had all been sadly battle-weary. The Fiftieth had been hacked to pieces along the Lys, the Eighth had been crushed by tanks at Villers-Bretonneux, the Twenty-First had been blown to smithereens on Messines Ridge. The survivors had been sent to Chemin des Dames to recuperate, not to face the full weight of Ludendorff's next major assault. How could they be expected to give adequate protection to Duchêne's positions?

What now? Perhaps the assault was only a diversionary attack, but if not then the Germans would certainly cross the Aisne, and if they could not be held at the Marne then Paris would lie before them, virtually defenseless . . .

How many times had he heard the generals and the politicians quoted, saying *Paris is France: France is civilization?*

If Paris fell . . .

At long last, Anatole thought, the deadlock would be broken; the slumbering Leviathan which was the war would come fully to life, would yawn and stretch its limbs, and open its avid eyes to see what remained of the shattered world that might still be savaged and devoured . . .

Better, perhaps, to die than to have to live in such a world.

A fragmentary line from one of the frightful songs the English cretins sang in their trenches floated unbidden into Anatole's mind. It was something about the sphinx's inscrutable smile. He tried to cast out the image, but could no more do that than close his eyes.

Why could he not focus his mind on something dignified, something intelligent? It must be the Britisher's presence which made him think of the song: the idiotic expression which death had set hard upon the soldier's face. It was *not* a smile, nor was it inscrutable, but somehow it had triggered the refrain which now repeated in his mind over and over again.

It might have been better if he had known the proper words to the song, but he had only ever heard the mocking, vulgar version. What imbeciles the British were! And traitors, too, to the cause of France. Everyone knew that they had kept back a million able-bodied men, to work their factories and dig their coal, and prepare for the defense of their dreary islands if France should fall—but France had given *all* her young men to the cause, and now there was nothing left to give. Everything was disintegrating, and no help was coming. The American president would not send his troops into a rapidly deteriorating situation; he too was preparing to sacrifice France in order that he might concentrate his attention on other fronts.

Poor France! Poor civilization! Poor Anatole!

Perhaps I am already dead, Anatole said to himself, by way of distraction. *Perhaps the bullet in my head has already killed me, and this is but a dream: a dream whose function is to extend the moment of my annihilation, so that an instant becomes an hour, a year, an eternity. Perhaps that is the eternal life which the illusion-peddlers promise us. Perhaps I will be stranded here in this shell-hole forever: muddy, bleeding, alone, haunted by idiotic lines from childishly dirty ditties formed in a barbarian tongue.*

He had never liked the British, although he could speak their language tolerably well. They were little better than the Germans, after all. They too were invaders, come to spoil the fields of France with their guns and trenches and their arrogantly marching feet.

The British believed with all their hearts that St George had brought a company of English bowmen to cover their retreat at Mons. Now they were in full retreat again, they would doubtless conjure up their patron to wave a second fond farewell. But St George had been a German, had he not? Should he not have been fighting on the other side?

The British, being Protestants, knew little or nothing of the Golden Legend, and should not have had a patron saint at all. A few stupid Frenchmen, caught up in the sad fervor of the moment, had argued that it was St Michael who had come to bear witness to the grand débâcle, and not St George at all. One or two had sworn that they had seen the Maid of Orléans riding into the fray—but the Maid of Orléans had been a witch for several centuries, languishing in Hell while she waited for the Church to change its mind, and loyal Gilles de Rais was there still, hapless victim of the Duke of Brittany's slanders. Why should either of them come to help their treacherous countrymen? Why should anyone?

Reach out and take the revolver! he told himself. *Pluck it out, turn it, and press the trigger! It will only take a moment.*

But he could not do it. In his heart, he did not want to do it.

Perhaps it would be better if his leg hurt even more. Perhaps it would be better if he were more of a coward. Had he lived so long only to become *brave*? He could not believe it. He was only a sniper, after all: a meticulous marksman, not a true warrior. There was no courage in his way of killing. He had never stuck an enemy with a blade of any kind, nor stood face to face with a charging man. He ought to be lily-livered enough to crumble before the agonizing horror of his wounds.

I ought to be able to die. Any man ought to be able to do that!

But he could not do it. He could not take the British soldier's gun. He was lost in time and in space, alive but detached from the levers and sinews of his own body. He was haunting himself, looking down from somewhere else and not *inside himself,* at all.

When death eventually came, he thought, it would not simply be the cessation of his heartbeat and the end of thought; it would be the death of the entire universe whose beholder he was. Infinitesimal as he might be, he was also infinite. When he was gone, so was the universe of his perception, his belief, his understanding.

Still the words of that stupid song drifted through the background of his mind. He hated its vulgarity, its nonsensicality, its Englishness. Surely that was why he could not bring himself to die. He could not possibly die with such absurdities in his brain. He could not possibly quit the earth to the sound of some bizarre doggerel describing the supposedly perverse habits of some comically monstrous animal. He was being kept alive by a dirty tommy song which made no sense. The hell with it! The hell with the camel's hump! The hell with the sphinx and its smile! The hell with everything . . . except, of course, for his soul. He had no soul. He was a humanist, an atheist, a communist. He had no soul at all, and was proud to say so. He was a man, not a pawn of God.

If the world is given to the Devil, he thought, *then I must be given to the Devil too.*

Was that really his thought? It did not sound like a thought of his, but if it were not his, whose could it be? Could the dead Englishman be haunting him, just as he was haunting himself? Was it the dead Englishman who was singing that stupid song, over and over again? Or was it the imp which sat upon his left shoulder, free now to pour its poison into his ear because his guardian angel was in full retreat, fleeing for its life, having deserted his cause for good and all?

He found that his eyes had fallen shut, of their own accord, but no sooner had he discovered the fact than they flew open again. Night was falling, but there was twilight enough to let him see the shadowy forms descending from the rim of the shell-hole. At first he thought they were Germans, come to finish him off, but then he saw that they were Britishers. They were moving furtively, like rats—understandably, given that they were behind enemy lines, marooned by the haste of the enemy advance. There was nothing in the eyes of the one who came toward him but fear and greed.

He thinks that I am dead! Anatole thought. *He takes me for a corpse, and intends to rob me!*

He tried with all his might to move, to signal that he was in fact alive, but he could not do it.

The British soldier reached out to touch his face, and he blinked reflexively.

The Britisher vanished.

The Maid of Orléans was standing on the rim of the shell-hole, looking down at him. It was dark now, but her head was haloed like an angel's.

"If I promised to grant you a single wish," she said, "what would you ask of me?"

He knew that this was witchery and impish temptation. She expected him to ask for his life to be saved, or for entry into Heaven— but he was an atheist, and a man of learning, and a good communist. He was not to be bought by agents of the faith, not even at the moment of death. He knew that the world was too vast a place to be the playground of petty jealous gods.

"If I could be granted a single wish," he answered, boldly, "I would ask that I might share the consciousness of Laplace's imaginary Demon—which, in knowing the exact position and velocity of every particle in the universe, would also know by deduction the entirety of history and destiny. Can you give me that, little saint?"

She smiled, inscrutably. "I never was a saint," she said, as she reached down to touch him with her tender, delicate hand. "I am, and always have been, a soldier, and my trade is death. I will grant your wish—but first, there is something you must see and do in Paris."

2

The pain was gone, and not merely the pain.

For a moment or two Anatole was acutely conscious of being *disembodied*; the bundle of sensations which was the focal point of his sentient being lost all contact with the physical world and drifted in the void. It was not in any way an uncomfortable sensation—the void seemed neither cold nor desolate—but he could not quite bring himself to think of it as a merciful release because he knew, after all, that it was impossible. He knew that there was no such thing as a soul separable from the body, no *persona* capable of surviving death.

He was not at all surprised, therefore, when this benevolently vertiginous interval was abruptly cut short. He recovered the sense of being embodied, of possessing flesh. It seemed so utterly natural and normal to be conscious of inhabiting an organism that he did not at first realize or recognize that his new situation was unfamiliar.

When he did realize that the body he was inhabiting was not his own his instinct was to disbelieve it. He knew that it was impossible for a soul to drift free of the body which it had formerly inhabited, and he knew that the corollary notion of its being able to take up residence thereafter in a different body was simply piling one absurdity upon another. He knew, therefore, that he could not be experiencing what he now seemed to be experiencing. It had to be a bizarre dream.

It did not feel like a dream, but neither did it feel like quotidian experience. *I have been given morphine,* he thought, clutching at explanatory straws. *I was taken unconscious from the battlefield and*

*am now waking up to find my body quieted with drugs; that is why
it feels so strange. All else is . . .*

He could not sustain the delusion. The immediacy of the experience that he now shared was irresistible. He could see, and hear, and
feel, but not as he had ever seen, heard and felt before.

In addition, he was vividly and unprecedentedly aware that he was
not *alone* in what he saw, and heard, and felt. He was privy to the
thoughts and sensations of another human being—or, at least, another
intelligence. The sharing was not mutual; the other was utterly unaware of Anatole's phantom presence.

The strangest and most obvious thing about the intelligence on
which Anatole was eavesdropping—which immediately marked it as
alien—was its sense of well-being. Anatole had never, in his own
body, had any similar sense of his own health and strength. He had
experienced moments of pleasure, joy, triumph and elation, but those
had been peaks of sensation set against a ground-state which was at
best sensationally neutral and often mildly discomfited. This new
consciousness was set upon a different and better foundation. For
this man—if man he was—there was a reward in the mere fact of
life, a peculiar exultation intrinsic to the fact of consciousness.

Is this what the life of other men is like? Anatole wondered, horror-
struck by the enormity of the idea. *Has the fundamental ecstasy of
life been denied to me alone?*

The thought died as soon as it was born, the mystery drowned by
a further torrent of puzzles. Anatole's attention was claimed by the
sense of sight.

He—or rather, the creature whose mindful eyes he now shared—
was looking down at a broad bed, on which lay prone the naked
body of a young boy.

The coverlet which lay upon the bed was quilted, covered in
shades of red and burgundy, decorated with gilded thread. It was
expensive but far from new; it was significantly worn, and some of
the threads were raggedly broken. The boy's body was pale and very
still; the face was turned slightly aside but not to permit breathing.
The child was completely still. Anatole did not have to deduce that
the boy was dead, for his host knew it perfectly well, and Anatole
was privy to that frightful knowledge.

The knowledge was frightful only to Anatole; to the man upon
whose thoughts he was a parasite it was redolent with satisfaction
and an ugly excitement. In fact, Anatole's horror at the knowledge
derived as much from the emotions associated with it in his host's

mind as from the fact that the boy had been murdered by the hand of the man—or creature—who now stood looking down at the cadaver. Anatole knew what it was to take pride and pleasure in knowledge, but not such knowledge as this. This was evil. This was madness. This was inhuman.

The murder had not happened here but in another place: a darker place, high-ceilinged, *before a rapt and fearful audience!* His host's stream of consciousness retained only the barest awareness of what that place looked like, or where it was—although these facts were undoubtedly known to the person, and could have been recalled to mind with the most trivial effort—but the memory of the crowd's reverent and focused attention was very sharp, sharper even than the memory of the movement of the ornamental knife, or of the blood which had spilled from the sliced throat, or of the intensity of the wicked glee which the atrocity had brought forth.

There was no blood now upon the coverlet; that which had been spilled had fallen elsewhere, and that which remained was clotted, undisturbed by the effort of a heart.

The watching creature had no sense at all of the *identity* of the murdered child. The mindful eyes which looked down at the corpse had no sense of his being a particular person, and hardly any sense of his being a person at all. If there was any category to which he belonged it was that of *instrument,* and his murder had been a *stratagem.* It had been a murder committed in a darkly dispassionate fashion, and yet not quite cold-bloodedly. There had been malice in the act; there was malice in its memory. In the contemplative stare of the creature which stood at the foot of the bed there was a kind of hatred, a kind of evil—but there was nothing *personal* in the hatred, nothing intimately human; it was an oddly detached and general hatred.

The self-consciousness contained within the current of awareness was not obtrusive, at first, but Anatole caught one half-deliberately formed subvocalization which threw the whole affair into a very different perspective.

I am Asmodeus, the creature thought, savoring its name. *I am overlord and tormentor of mere mortal men.*

I must be in Hell, Anatole thought, reflexively. *I am in Hell and I have been afforded the privilege of watching a minion of Satan at work. The process of damnation is being laid bare for me, that I may savor its workings. Is this the heritage of all the dead, I wonder, or a lesson reserved for atheists, that they may know their error?*

He knew as he thought it that it was a colorful mistake, a fantasy based in the discarded but unforgotten lumber of his imagination. It was a confabulation, and he knew it. *This* Asmodeus had a human body, and performed before a human audience. If he—it *was* he, and not it—was a demon, he was a demon made in the image of man, able to meet men face to face, to crave their rapt attention and their fear, or to kill as men killed, with a blade and a deadly malice.

Anatole was dizzyingly aware of movement in the body that was not his own, as it climbed on to the bed to loom over the still form of the boy. The boy could not have been more than eight years old, and very slightly built, while the creature who named himself Asmodeus—and continued, now, to relish the name and all the magic contained within it—was both unnaturally old and unnaturally huge.

It was difficult for Anatole to concentrate his own attention on objects at the periphery of his host's vision while his host focused on the child, but it was not impossible. Anatole noted that the hands which were set upon the coverlet to either side of the child's torso were very large, and he deduced from their magnitude and the sensations involved in the positioning of the massive legs that "Asmodeus" must be very nearly two meters tall: a giant among men. This was no amiable "devil on two sticks," but an apparition of a very different kind.

Anatole strove with all his might to distance his own consciousness from that on which he was helplessly parasitic, desperately trying to figure out exactly what manner of being he was dealing with. For this reason, his realization of what the giant was actually *doing* was woefully and horribly belated. He had been concentrating so hard on eyes and hands that he had unwittingly censored his awareness of other parts of his host's body, but the horror of it broke through. Full consciousness of what Asmodeus was actually about burst upon him like a shell; the shock of it was unimaginably savage.

One of the huge hands was holding the little body still, the other was groping between the child's limp buttocks.

Had he a voice, Anatole would have screamed. Had he the power to close the eyes which provided his borrowed sight, he would have done it. Had he any way to shut out the river of physical sensations and their associated responses in thought and feeling, even at great cost to himself, he would most certainly have used it.

In any ordinary nightmare, he might have been able to tolerate what was happening. He was sufficiently inured to the ugliness of death that he would not automatically have woken up, had he truly been dreaming, but this was real. This was unbearable perversity, authentic evil. Asmodeus—the *man* who called himself Asmodeus—was buggering the corpse of a child he had slain.

Of course this is Hell, Anatole thought, bravely using the one power left to him as a defense, sending forth his own barrage of thought and feeling to oppose and confuse that which was descending upon him from enemy territory. *What else is Hell but the worst ugliness imaginable? How could a man like me expect mere lakes of boiling blood? We live in an age of sophistication, of ennui, in which all the old sins have been accommodated, reduced to mediocrity. This is nothing but a moment of macabre theater, of grand guignol, intended to sicken and frighten me. Why should I give way? It is too extreme, too absurd, too revolting. Why should the idea of necrophilia be nauseating if there is indeed a Hell inhabited by none but the dead? Why should a man be horrified by something where there is no earthly reason to do? This is merely an exloration of the limits of imagination. It is not happening on earth, in the actual world. It is a cruel jest of the sinister imp which has claimed me for its own, now that I have banished my guardian angel.*

It might have been more difficult to ignore the sensations which the man who named himself Asmodeus was experiencing had they been more intense, but they were curiously calm. There was a level of erotic excitement there—how, otherwise, could he had performed the dreadful act at all?—but it was not particularly intense. For "Asmodeus," this was a matter of routine; he had done it before. It was, in fact, a kind of private ritual whose reward had little to do with momentary lust. It was not so very difficult for Anatole to adjust his own frame of mind, so that he became a detached, dispassionate observer, uninvolved in the glutinous sensations of tumescence and physical contact.

Anatole's own sexual experience had consisted entirely of infrequent encounters with whores; his masturbatory fantasies were strictly limited in their exoticism. It was not difficult for him to refuse to experience what "Asmodeus" was doing as a kind of erotic stimulation, and to study it instead as a phenomenon of insanity: something to be understood in coolly clinical terms. Anatole was able to do this; he had seen enough of brutal, ugly death to be able to regain his mental equilibrium even in this horrid Hell that had been designed for him alone. He was able to become dispassionate about the corpse and its violation, and he was able to be proud of his capacity to repel the assaults of his personal imp.

With the benefit of this frame of mind, Anatole learned several things while studiously ignoring, as best he could, the disgusting movements of his host's body and the physiological crescendo of his orgasm.

He learned that the man who now called himself Asmodeus had once had another name, whose given part had been Luke. He learned that Luke had been—still *was,* in spite of his aspiration to be a demon—an Englishman. He learned that Luke had long been accustomed to using the bodies of small children for sexual release, and that his malice against them was so amorphous and deep-seated that murder seemed to him to be a trivial modification of his treatment of them. He learned too that Luke-as-Asmodeus took a special delight in piling enormity upon enormity, evil upon evil. He learned that Luke-as-Asmodeus really did dream of being a prince of Hell, and really did desire to do his utmost to please the Satanic majesty which he served—although, oddly enough, he called the Devil "Zelophelon" instead of Satan.

He learned that Luke-as-Asmodeus believed, with the absolute faith of an authentically religious man, that the as-yet-unconquered universe was destined to be ruled by a principle of evil; and that Luke-as-Asmodeus desired, with the absolute commitment of an authentically religious man, that he must strive with all his might to be a faithful and obliging servant of that principle of evil; and that Luke-as-Asmodeus knew, with the absolute certainty of an authentically religious man, that anyone and everyone who thought otherwise than he did was a blind fool fully deserving of any fate which the principle of evil might dictate.

He learned too that Luke, before he had become Asmodeus, had experienced a miraculous vision in which he had communicated directly with the principle of evil which he now served, that he had been *chosen* to do the work which he now did, and that he had been re-created as Asmodeus—huge, strong and immortal—in order to carry out that work.

He learned, in fact, that Asmodeus was the appointed Antichrist—or, at least, believed himself to be that Antichrist with all his heart and all his soul.

Anatole could not have been convinced that his host believed this on the basis of any evidence presented to him in an ordinary way. Had Asmodeus and Anatole met man-to-man there would have been nothing Asmodeus could have said or done to persuade such a cynical and sceptical atheist that he was anything but a liar. Given the supernatural intimacy of their present association, however, there was no room left for doubt or disbelief. Anatole had been given the mysterious power to look directly into this man's soul, to see the world as this man saw it, to *be in the world* as this man *was,* and it was a matter of simple fact that Luke-as-Asmodeus really did conceive of himself as the Antichrist, the ambassador on earth of a principle of evil which intended to conquer all rivals and rule the universe.

One impossibility piled atop another, Anatole said to himself, carefully, but he was *not* an authentically religious man, and had to admit that he did not and could not know where the limits of possibility truly lay. *If this is a nightmare,* he thought, *then it is the ultimate nightmare: the nightmare that does not permit belief in its own unreality, its own impossibility, acknowledging no limit at all in the extent of its horrors.*

There followed an interval when he was able to be glad, for it seemed that the worst was over. Asmodeus had concluded his obscene and ridiculous intercourse with the dead—which had, after all, inflicted no *further* harm upon the murdered creature—and Anatole felt that he had cleverly contrived to minimize his own participation in the careful abomination. He could not feel entirely unstained, or entirely untouched, but he felt a certain pride in the manner in which he had kept the whole procedure *impersonal.*

Even the Great War, he thought, *has been an opportunity to learn, and to make progress. Whatever horrors life has thrown up, whatever threats it has offered, I have functioned as a human being. I have brought my intellect to bear on every passing moment—including the moment of my death, if that is what this is. If I am indeed facing the prospect of Hell and eternal damnation, I am facing it like a man. Alive or dead, I am as yet undefeated.*

At that moment, Asmodeus reached out with his huge hand, and with a casual gesture he flipped the body of the dead boy on to its back, so that the child's face, and the great black gaping wound in his throat, were fully revealed.

Anatole recognized the youngest of his brothers, P'tit Jean.

3

There was barely space for a man to crouch down in the small covert, but Anatole was no stranger to awkward positions and cramped spaces. He knew well enough how to wrap his body around the barrel of his rifle, with the butt wedged between his booted feet. The long wait was no hardship to him; the virtue of patience came easily to one for whom the only peace was to have nothing happening. It was easy enough to drift away into a kind of half-sleep in which he could set the world's troubles aside. His own troubles were not so easily calmed, but he had enough strength of mind to quell the corrosive force of his anger and his hatred.

He had to shift his position occasionally; there was a dull pain in his leg which would not go away, and a tightness in his chest which straitened his breathing. There was a strange sensation in his head, too—not pain, but a kind of light dizziness. More than once he struck the stone wall with his fist, to reassure himself that he was awake, and that the world was solid.

He made no real attempt to listen to the snatches of desultory conversation which drifted up from the main body of the church as the black-clad acolytes lit the candles. The details of the gossip were new to him, but the clichés were always the same. Fifteen German divisions had crossed the Matz. Compiègne would fall by midnight, opening a second route to Paris. The railway stations were jammed solid with refugees. Paris was "a City of the Dead."

Paris had been a City of the Dead for months. The Boche had brought two massive guns to within sixty kilometers of the city, firing huge shells at regular intervals, day after day. Each one burst

19

like the crack of doom, dutifully informing the citizenry that there was nowhere to hide. There was no way of telling where the shells might land. The probability of any particular individual being hit by any such blast was small, but the Terror which had the city in its grip was no master of scrupulous calculation.

At the front, Anatole had learned to tame his fear, and to cultivate a mechanical state of mind in which he did what he had to do with ruthless efficiency. He had made himself over in the image of an automaton, in the valiant hope that he might save the last vestiges of his humanity by hoarding them away.

There was a tune repeating somewhere in the back of his mind, very faintly. He could not place it; nor could he remember the words that went with it. He did not try to bring his concentration to bear on the problem. *Play the machine,* he told himself. *There is naught but pain in playing the man. Pretend that it is all but a dream, or a puppet-show.* Other men, he knew, coped differently with the strain of the everpresent threat of death. Most addressed copious prayers to Almighty God, to Jesus, to the Virgin, and to every hero-saint of the Golden Legend, but Anatole had never been able to believe, even at the extreme of danger, that such rituals were anything but empty. How ironic that he should now be waiting in a spoiled church, intent on deploying his assassin's skill against its wicked desecrators! How the local followers of Christ would applaud him!

The church was cold now that night had fallen. Winter, it seemed, had lingered very late this year—but spring was not always welcome on the battlefield. Spring eased the movement of men, machines and horses, and encouraged the generals in their grand plans. Winter meant short supplies, hunger, debilitation and disease, but spring meant new offensives, new objectives, newly refreshed dreams of victory and conquest. Could the war possibly survive another summer of blood and swarming flies? Or would the time finally come when a cold blast of sanity would reveal to the cannon fodder in the trenches that their true cause lay in union against their masters, the owners and the aristocrats? Russia had fallen to the Bolsheviks; surely it could only be a matter of time before the nations of Western Europe brought their slow suicide to its proper climax.

He peeped over the edge of the balcony which curved above the covert, looking down at the black-cloaked figures moving back to the vestry. The candles they had set in the brackets were white— quite ordinary, save that their smoke carried a slightly disconcerting odor of disinfecting fluid. Only those which decked the covered altar were significantly black.

The first members of the congregation, who were just now entering by the door, also wore a good deal of black, but there was nothing particularly unusual in that. Their manner seemed no more and no less humble than the manner of men and women gathering to hear a true mass. Anatole was not surprised to find the gathering congregation so dull and commonplace. He knew that there had been many active Satanists in Paris in the decades before the war. The greater number must have been cautious libertines in search of abandon for whom the Black Mass was simply one more short step beyond the vulgar thrills of *grand guignol*. It was only for a tiny minority of the crazed and uncontainable that the Devil's Mass offered scope for turning dark fantasy into murderous deed; the rest were only here to watch, and marvel. The self-styled Asmodeus whom Anatole had come here to destroy was, he presumed, a charismatic madman who had taken a license to kill from the fear and awe of his parishioners. Once he was dead, it would be over.

Anatole had not the slightest doubt about his ability to carry through his mission; habit and endurance had made him an expert marksman. The cause of virtue could hardly have chosen a better man.

He watched the preparation of the altar with mild curiosity. The testimony given by the hapless souls tortured in the course of the *Chambre Ardente* enquiry, when the legend of the Black Mass had first taken root, had spoken of masses celebrated over the naked and blood-bedaubed bodies of whores. It was a detail which generations of lifestyle fantasists must have been ardent to duplicate, but there was no sign of any such embellishment here. The black silks which hid the altar were secured by statuettes depicting approximately-human figures with heads like gargoyles. One was wattled and beaked; the other elaborately horned. Both were uglier by far than the central figure embroidered on a tapestry, which had the body of a satyr and the head of a ram, with a radiant third eye set in the forehead. The remaining apparatus seemed orthodox enough; the chalice was silver, and modest in size, as was the paten. Even the crucifix mounted above the tapestry was perfectly ordinary in every detail, save for its inversion.

The ritual has been routinized, Anatole thought, wishing that his leg did not hurt so much. *Sexual perversity has been de-emphasized in favor of a more basic brutality. When spoiled priests made play*

*with naked bodies there were only rumors and suggestions of mur-
dered babes, but now the murders are real they have become the
true focus of attention. The recruitment of so many accessories to
murder must be very useful to a blackmailer, but what does Monsieur
Asmodeus seek to accomplish with the power thus gained? Is he
becoming rich, or merely cultivating power and authority for their
own sake?*

Pride, he remembered, had been the capital sin which allegedly
led to Satan's fall. Not lust, nor avarice, nor gluttony, nor wrath, and
certainly not sloth, but *pride,* alloyed with envy. It seemed absurd
that pride could move a man to the slaughter of innocents, but was
it not pride as much as avarice or wrath which had motivated the
slaughter of so very many innocents at the Somme and Passchen-
daele, at Ypres and Mons? Was Asmodeus really such a monster by
comparison with Clemenceau and Foch, Lloyd George and Haig, the
Kaiser and Ludendorff? Was the Devil really such an appalling object
of worship, given the horrors which were duly perpetrated in the
name of God?

It is no answer to the problem of an emperor God, Anatole
thought, *to turn to some rival pretender. We must have the strength
to confront the fact of a godless universe, in which the only empow-
ering will is that of the community of mankind.*

The thought was sober and sane, but as he voiced it inwardly he
was suddenly possessed by the memory of a dream he had had: a
nightmare, in which he had leeched the thoughts and feelings of
Asmodeus, while . . .

He shied away from the memory, startled by an inchoate horror.

I am a machine, he reminded himself. *I am here to perform a
task. It does not do to think too much about it.*

At long last, it seemed all was in readiness below. Those deputed
to assist in the mass took up their positions. The murmurous whispers
of the congregation died away into a hush of expectation. Anatole
shifted his position, flexing his arms and fingers in anticipation of
lifting his gun. His mouth was dry, and when he tried to moisten it
with saliva he was taken aback by a sharply unpleasant taste. It was
as if he had filled his mouth with disinfectant. The dizziness in his
head increased, but he was in control of himself.

The self-styled Asmodeus appeared for the first time, ascending
the steps from the crypt. He was a striking figure: very tall and
muscular, but graceful in his movements. He was quite bald, and the
shape of his skull was peculiar, being surmounted by two parallel

ridges of bone beneath the scalp, which culminated in projections like tiny horns. Anatole thought that they were probably artificial, but could not see from this distance how the trick had been worked. The Satanist's robes were black, but were marked behind and before in red with two huge inverted crosses.

Anatole was tempted to wait a little while in order that he might study the parody of the mass which was to ensue, but he put the temptation firmly behind him. He was here to carry out a mission, as quickly and efficiently as possible. Curiosity was no reason for delay. Were he to wait for the appearance of the child due to be sacrificed for the sake of the communion of blood he would be just as guilty of theatrical self-indulgence as the assembled worshippers. He did not want that. He was not a player in this game; he was an automaton of justice. Now that Asmodeus had presented himself, there was no reason to delay.

When the tall man turned away from the altar, having made his preliminary obeisance to the effigies positioned to the right, left and center, Anatole lifted his rifle.

He could not balance the barrel on the balcony before him because it was too close, but he rested the upper part of his left arm on its rim, so that he might hold the gun more steadily. He sighted down the barrel, as he had a thousand times before. Although the man who called himself Asmodeus was more than thirty meters away the range seemed absurdly close by comparison with the conditions under which he was normally required to shoot.

The first bullet, Anatole knew, had to be aimed at the heart; it would make sufficient impact to kill wherever on the torso it struck, but he felt that he could hit the heart itself. Then, assuming that his victim fell the way a man shot at this angle ought to fall, he would put a second bullet into the head, to make absolutely certain of his fate.

Would a convinced Satanist be afraid of death if he knew it to be imminent? Anatole wondered, as he put his finger round the trigger, ready to squeeze. *Would he look forward to the prospect of meeting his master in Hell with as much optimism as a good Christian contemplating the judgment of St Peter? Might not his confidence be all the greater, in view of the fact that it is so much easier for a villain to be certain of his wickedness than a saint of his goodness?*

The mock-priest turned slightly, and Anatole paused, waiting for the full expanse of the man's chest to be exposed again.

He had not long to wait.

The words of the mock-mass were clearly audible to him. Asmodeus had an unusually strident voice. He was speaking in French, not in Latin, but his accent was distinctly English. Anatole tried not to listen. The voice was simply a noise, about to be stilled. The misspoken words meant nothing.

He fired.

The sound of the shot echoed eerily from the walls, seemingly magnified into a volley. It was as if an entire firing squad had let loose.

Anatole watched, without emotion, as the Satanist priest was hurled backward by the impact of the bullet, his legs crumpling beneath him while his impotent arms flailed wide of his body. Asmodeus fell exactly as Anatole had expected him to fall. Anatole calmly brought the barrel of his rifle back, following the jerk of the recoil. He reset the hammer, and pointed the weapon at the Englishman's open-mouthed face. He aimed for the gaping mouth rather than the forehead, although the angle was good enough to have allowed him to hit the space between the eyes.

Careless of anything that might be happening in the main body of the church, he fired again.

He should not have had to wait for evidence of the impact, but he found himself waiting, staring at the unmarked features of the stricken man. Three or four seconds went by before he began to ask himself how he could have missed, how his bullet could possibly have gone astray. He felt his senses reel, and there was a crawling sensation about his scalp, as though he had a head-wound of his own which had suddenly began to bleed again.

He fired again, but this time too hurriedly. This time, he was *not* astonished by the lack of any evidence of an impact. He had not been mechanical enough. He had allowed himself to be hurried, and had fallen prey to human error—for which, he knew, there was to be no divine forgiveness.

The stairway which led up from the side-chapel to the covert was narrow and crooked, and the door could not be opened without difficulty, but the time Anatole required to fire for a second and a third time was not wasted by those avid to strike back at him. Already there were racing footfalls on the stone steps, and he stood up, turning unhurriedly to face the arch behind him.

He knew, of course, that there was not the slightest possibility of escape. Had he taken a position down below, near to the main door, he might have fired once, or even twice, and still made a run for it.

He would have had every chance of knocking over anyone who got in his way, but had he done that, there would have been a possibility of his being seen before he had a chance to fire, and prevented from carrying out his mission. The covert had offered him a clear shot and almost certain immunity from premature discovery, and that had been his aim. He had not even tried to make plans regarding what might happen afterward.

Anatole had three bullets left in the gun, and more in his pockets, but he did not intend to use them up. When the face of the first angry pursuer materialized in the archway he slammed the butt of the gun into the bridge of the man's nose as hard as he could, knowing that it would be a crippling blow if not a killing one, and that the heavy body thrown back from the head of the steep stairway was very likely to wreak havoc as it fell. Alas, they were coming at him so thick and fast that the unconscious body did not fall far, and when it came back at him it formed a shield for those behind it. Within half a minute there was a crush in the archway which he could not thrust back; he was pressed back against the balcony himself, and in some danger of falling. He lashed out again and again, striking solid blows which spread confusion among his enemies, but did not force them back. There was no room for the men he had hit to fall down, although one at least howled in anguish as he was thrust forward yet again to meet the force of Anatole's improvised club.

They should be Germans or Englishmen, Anatole thought, *not Frenchmen. But what does it matter, in the end, which particular dupes do the dirty work of which particular masters?*

While he voiced these silent words the man who was in the forefront of the attack let loose a frightful scream, louder by far than the one he had uttered a few moments before, and there appeared such an expression of horror in his eyes that Anatole felt perversely proud. Was it not creditworthy that one such as he should be able to inspire such a reaction in a servant of the Devil! But this time the man was allowed to fall back a little way, for the followers craning to look over his shoulders had seen what he had seen, and were every bit as anxious to retreat from it.

Anatole knew, even as he basked in his petty vanity, that a man wielding the butt of a rifle, however skilfully or dangerously, could not possibly be the cause of such horror. He knew, as he was granted respite from the crush, that there was something behind him—although it was quite impossible that there should be, for he was eighteen or twenty meters above the ground.

Simple curiosity made him turn. He intended no more than a momentary glance, knowing that he must turn back immediately to face his wrathful opponents, but there was no way he could stop at a glance once he saw what was looming over him.

The sheer impossibility of it spun him on his heel, and sent his fingers groping for the trigger of the rifle.

It was thirty meters tall, and although its body was approximately human from shoulder to foot, save for a certain scaliness and misshapenness of the limbs, there was nothing human about its features. It was beaked like a parrot and limply wattled like some exotic cockerel, and its huge glaring eyes were like a big cat's, glowing green in the dim light, with wide-spread lenticular pupils whose darkness radiated wrath.

It was the image of one of the figurines which fixed the edges of the altar-cloth, projected somehow, as though in a phantasmagoria or a cinematograph. Anatole knew that it could not be real. Such things did not exist. There was no Devil for heretics to worship, and there was no legion of fallen angels lurking in the dark caverns of the earth, plotting to storm the gates of Heaven for a second time. Although his enemies saw it too, it had to be a delusion. Even so, he tried to bring up the rifle as the monster reached out for him with its vast talon.

I am a machine, he told himself. *This is a dream, a drama, a hallucination, a trick of stage magic . . .*

The demon reached out for him. He felt its great clawed hand fold around his midriff and pluck him out of the covert, lifting him effortlessly into the air and bringing him ever closer to those huge and horrible eyes. He knew full well that if he fired, and if his shot had any effect, then the monster's fall would very likely kill him, but he fired anyhow, at point-blank range.

No wound appeared in the hideous face at which he had fired, although it was impossible that he should have missed, and even though he should have been so paralyzed by shock as to be incapable of reasoned thought, he remembered that his second shot, so carefully aimed, had had equally little effect on the fallen body of the Englishman who called himself Asmodeus.

It is all a dream, he thought. *It has given itself away; its imitation of reality has failed.*

The talon which held him lifted him higher still, and for a moment Anatole thought that he was about to be hurled down to the stone floor, in order that his bones should be shattered—but that was not to be his fate. The monster now looked up at him, and in spite of the fact that it had no mouth capable of smiling, he felt sure that he caught a glint of black humor in its great green eyes.

It mocks me! he thought. *It mocks the error of my unbelief! But I am right. The poor thing cannot comprehend its own impossibility, its impotence to enter the actual world of matter and mortality.*

Even as he stared into the vast face of a demon which could only have come from a real and literal Hell, his unbelief held firm. The world was still the world, in his considered estimation, and not the fantasy that Churchmen sought to make of it. He wanted to cry out *Take me to your Hell, and let me spit in the face of Satan!* but there was no time.

The clawed fingers which gripped him had begun to squeeze, and the curling tip of one of them had shifted to lie about his throat, so that its horny claw was pressing on his windpipe, choking him. His head must have been scratched, for it was bleeding copiously, and the pain in his broken leg was terrible.

Where is the Maid? he thought, although the thought made no sense. *Where is the savior of France, now that I need her?*

There was no stink of brimstone, nor even of sweat. The only perceptible odors were those of incense and candle-smoke, sweet and acrid at the same time, but his mouth was full of the taste of disinfectant. He wanted to say to himself *I have done my duty! I have killed Asmodeus Antichrist!* but there was no time even for that.

He fell, as if into the dark and limitless Abyss.

4

The ground was hard and icily damp. Arrows of fervent cold had been shot into his helpless body. He was so very heavy that he could not lift any part of himself. His hands were like anvils, his legs like the blackened trunks of massive trees. The darkness weighed down on him like rich black soil, and would have crushed the very soul within him, had he a soul to crush. And yet, when rough hands grabbed him, and rolled him over on to his back, he was as easy to handle as a carved marionette.

What strength they must have, those awesome hands!

The light hurt his eyes, but they held the lantern over him, as steady as the pale winter sun at its humble zenith, and he had no option but to stare into it.

There must have been several faces up there in the darkness, beyond the sun-lantern: huge faces delineated by invisible stars; the faces of the mocking, hidden demons which had brought him to the edge of their parodic Creation. There must have been three or four, perhaps more. Who could number the demons which had been cast into the great Abyss by the Archangel Michael and his battalions of seraphim? Not Anatole, for sure; not poor godless Anatole, who was a stranger now in a world he had never made, nor ever sought, nor ever believed in.

He would have to wait for enlightenment: for *their* enlightenment.

The light which shone into his eyes was not the sun at all, he realized, but the light of the magical eye which shone in the head of the ram whose image decorated the altars of the mages: the inner eye whose sight penetrated the thin veneer of appearance and looked into the caverns of the self, where the loathsome monsters of impulse and appetite skulked and slid. That eye was looking into *him,* to hunt out the wellsprings of his actions, the hatreds which lay at the root of all his noble gestures.

One face, however, moved to catch the light, to show itself to him. Perhaps, if he really were lying on a cold stone floor in a cellar somewhere in Paris, it might only be a man, kneeling down to lean over his injured body, while others stood by, one of them holding a lantern at navel height. On the other hand, were this truly the ante-room of Hell, it might be a recording angel sent to count the credit of his treasonous soul. *But what if this is no-man's-land?* he wondered. *What then? The Maid of Orléans it certainly is not, nor even her dark friend. If it should speak, let its voice be French. Let it not be a Boche or a Britisher!*

"Anatole?" The voice seemed both bitter and querulous, but it was speaking French. "Anatole? Is it really you?"

Oh yes, he thought, *it really is me. Of that, if that alone, I am sure. Wherever I am, and wherever I might be bound, I am Anatole, forever Anatole.* But that knowledge was lost in the explosion of wrath which followed his belated recognition of the voice.

"You!" he cried. He spat the word out. He could not say the word *Father.* He wanted to add a stream of curses, but he had moved his head and the pain caught at his throat, strangling him. He fought for breath.

"Oh, Anatole!"

It seemed that the words came from a far distance, as if the face which floated eerily in the lamplight really were a world staring down like the full moon from the infinite sky. "Anatole, what have you done?"

What have I done? Who has delivered his last born son into the hands of a murderous madman? Who has brought his own infant to the slaughter? Vile Abraham, willing servant of the dark, unmerciful Antichrist who calls himself Asmodeus!

"You do not understand, Anatole." The voice was plaintive, and yet still angry, still complaining. "You should have come to me. Do you think I am a fool?"

Yes.

"Do you think I am a madman?"

Yes.

"Do you think that I would do such a thing as this, without a *reason,* without *proof,* without *knowledge*?"

There was no earthly reason, no possible proof, no conceivable knowledge that might explain or excuse such a deed. At least, that was what Anatole had taken for granted before the demon seized him, and broke his body. As long as that might be a dream, a delusion, a phantom of phosgene poisoning or a fractured skull. If only . . .

"Listen to me, Anatole. The war which you have been fighting is the last war: the war to end war. These are the last days, Anatole; the fallen angels have come to claim their heritage. God is dead; miracles are now the province of the Devil's armies. All hope for the resurrection now rests with the Powers of Darkness. Resurrection can still be ours, my son, if only we have faith, if only we pledge ourselves to the cause of the true Master. *I have seen it done, Anatole!* I would not offer my son as a sacrifice unless I *knew*, beyond the shadow of a doubt, that death is not the end, that it is only the prelude to a new life. *I have seen it done, Anatole!* I have seen the dead returned to life. You should have come to me, Anatole. You should not have done what you have done. Do you not think that the price I paid was for you as well as for me? It was for all of us. This is the Master which has the power of life and death; this is the Master which has command of a legion of demons; this is the Master which will have command of the Earth itself. God is dead, but the Devil lives, and if we are to live we must be his loyal and trusting servants. Oh, Anatole, what a holy fool you are!"

What kinds of vermin haunt these dank cellars, then? Actors in black robes. Rats and mice. Men who bring their lastborn sons to be sacrificed in parodies of the Mass. Slugs and grave-worms. Men who pretend to be demons. Demons who pretend to be men. Fathers who pretend to be fathers. Madmen who pretend. Spiders.

The earth shook. Anatole thought that he could hear the explosion, drawn out in time to a throaty roar of thunder. Number one gun, he thought. Number one gun, aimed at the heart of Paris, to remind the inhabitants of the finest city in the world that theirs was a borrowed life, that death might rain down upon them at any time, that nowhere in God's Creation was safe.

The tremor died. *But you should feel the earth shake in no-man's-land,* he thought, *when the German artillery opens up in all its fury. You should hear the roar of a real barrage, which lasts through the night, which howls and screams and deafens like a legion of demons dancing on the ramparts of Pandemonium . . .*

"You should have come to me." The voice had sunk to a desperate whine. "I could have explained . . . and then, if you could not believe me, you could have put your gun to my head and pulled the trigger, and I could have *shown* you, I could have shown you how easy it is to die when you *know* that you will live again, when you *know* that the Age of Miracles is restored. Damn you to empty Oblivion, Anatole, *you have spoiled everything!''*

Oh yes, I have spoiled everything. I have murdered Asmodeus. I have put an end to a loathsome criminal. I have destroyed a self-appointed magus whose madness demanded the slaughter of innocents. I have spoiled the Devil's carnival. I have done more good in one hour than I have done in a year and more of sniping at the Boche, of snuffing out the lives of frightened young men, of killing the Kaiser's cannon fodder. I have put a stop to one petty kind of madness in a perfectly mad world.

"Oh, Anatole, my son! Why, oh why, could you not *understand*?"

But I do, dear father, I do understand. I am the only one who does.

The face withdrew into the darkness, to join the invisible ones. It vanished into the gloom, as if it were a disappointed god turning his face away from a spoiled Creation. How like a god!

If only this were a dream. If only all of this were a dream. Paris, the war, the pain, the uncertainty. If only I were not in this foul dark cellar; nor in some muddy covert in no-man's-land, nor even in the Year of Our Lord 1918. If only it were summer in a year of peace. If only there were trees in blossom, children playing, vines in leaf, lovers entwining their arms . . . please let the Revolution, when it comes, be calm and glorious, innocent of fire and fury, untainted by gangrene and gas.

Another face descended from the darkness into the uncanny light. It was an inhuman face; an impossible face. It was larger than natural, and quite hairless. It was surmounted by two tiny horns. It was smiling. It was the face of Asmodeus.

"Your father speaks the truth." The voice was deep, authoritative—and yet it spoke with a wretched accent: the accent of an unschooled Englishman. "For those who are servants of my Master, death is nothing to be feared. Your father *knows*. He has *seen*. The child he brought to die is safer by far than those who still live. Look at me, Anatole, and *know the truth!* I am Asmodeus; the World and the Flesh belong to the Devil; the reign of the fallen Angels is about to begin."

It is impossible. There is no God. The world is as we find it, and there is no means by which it can be transformed save the labor of human hands, no means by which it can be perfected save for the desires and ambitions of the human mind. If there are Satanists in Paris offering human sacrifices to their imaginary Lord they are madmen and fools. If there are priests in the Churches and devout Christians flocking to Communion they are poor deluded wretches in search of opium to soothe the pains of their oppression. But men will win their war against the gods of the imagination, because men have hands and hearts and minds, and these are the instruments of conquest, the weapons of victory. This is impossible; the man who posed as Asmodeus was shot dead and the demon which seized me was but a dream. This is not happening.

Asmodeus raised his open hand so that the light caught it, displaying the fingers. Then he slowly reached down toward the stricken man who looked up from the cold stone floor, anchored by the appalling lumpen mass of his broken body. The Antichrist reached down as though he intended no more than a caress, but when darkness claimed the hand again, darkness claimed its intention too, and the touch which reached Anatole's broken ribs—and seemed, thereafter, to pass into the cavity of his chest in order to rake his beating heart—was full of wrath and the avidity of punishment.

"Have no fear, my son," Asmodeus said. "Vengeance is not so very terrible, and the Angel of Pain brings gifts as well as terrors. Nothing is spoiled, except perhaps your own silly illusions. You are ours now, and have only to admit it, to pledge your own soul as your father pledged the soul of your infant brother. My Master looks after his own, and you are his now."

The pain took him away. The tiny sun went out, and there was nothing to be seen or heard or felt but a slight trembling of the earth, which might have been the trembling of his soul before the Seat of Judgment.

5

At first there was nothing of him but an awareness of many pains: a choking constriction at his throat, a tight circlet about his chest, a burning spear in the upper part of his right leg. Some time—perhaps several minutes—must have passed before he began to wonder where he was, and after that, *who* he was.

He found that he did not know the answer to either question, although he knew well enough that he was stretched out on an icily cold stone floor.

He opened his eyes, and found candlelight. It was dim but nevertheless distressing. While he blinked in order to take command of his vision he said to himself, "I have lost my memory!"

He had read of such things, and had been intrigued. Once, he had read the story of a man who set out to investigate a horrid murder with the aid of some seemingly uncanny intuition; the self-appointed detective had been gradually led to the discovery that he himself was the murderer, but had temporarily lost the memory of it by virtue of the horror of its commission.

His remembrance of the story seemed—in the absence of all other acquaintance with his past—awkwardly significant, and he became convinced that he too was a murderer, an assassin so surprised by his own monstrousness that he had hidden away his own identity.

He could see well enough now, and he lifted his head, searching for the candles whose flames provided the gift of light. There were two, set in trays which sat upon the floor some two meters apart. They had been set to illuminate part of a slimy brick wall, into whose face was bolted a wooden cross.

For some insane reason, it did not at first astonish him to see that there was a man nailed to the cross; all that struck him as odd in that first moment of confusion was that the cross was *not inverted,* although he could not quite understand why that should have been his expectation. As that initial confusion faded, though, the horror of the fact did become clear to him.

Atheist though he was, he had spent a good deal of time in churches, both as a child and as a soldier. He had seen many representations of Christ crucified, some of them gruesomely realistic. That, doubtless, was why it had not seemed strange to him that the cross was inhabited; only now did it become wholly clear to him that the man on *this* cross was indeed a man of flesh and blood, who must have been living but a short time ago, and might be living still, although his head had fallen upon his chest and there was no sign of movement in his wasted frame.

The watching man found his lips moving of their own accord, saying *"Pater noster qui es in caelis: Sanctificetur nomen tuum . . ."* He stopped himself, knowing that he ought not to be praying.

"I am an atheist," he told himself, bringing the thought to the very threshold of audibility. "I am a soldier. I am . . ." The momentum of the stream of discovery almost carried him to the point at which his cowering mind let loose his name, but at the critical moment his thoughts froze.

He tried to raise himself further from the inhospitable flagstones, but when he tried to prop himself up on his elbows his chest was flooded with agony. When he shifted his leg slightly the spear of pain which was now its shaft thrust an angry blade into his guts.

"Broken ribs," he said to himself. "Broken femur." There was little enough horror in *that.* He had seen men rejoice in such hurts, feeling nothing but elation at the idea that their release from the field of battle had been signed by kindly fate. There were certain injuries men longed to have, gladly paying the price in pain and disability, refusing to be fearful of the malign forces which could turn seemingly minor wounds into forces of destruction: infection, gangrene, necrosis. He had seen the orderlies in field hospitals deluging ugly wounds with squirming maggots, which would consume the dead flesh to leave the living clean, and had wondered what it must be like to have that boundary between life and death marked out inside the margins of his being . . .

He tried to lift his right hand to his head, to explore his scalp for wounds, but he could not do it.

It was with some difficulty that he brought his eyes and thoughts to focus yet again on the man on the cross. Who was he? Why was he here? Who had driven the nails through his wrists and ankles?

All kinds of rumors had spread like wildfire along the length of the Western front during the time of his service there, increasing with every news of Ludendorff's successes. The Boche, it was said, had such a hatred for enemy machine-gunners that they crucified any whom they captured, nailing them to the blackened stumps of trees that had been killed and shattered by the endless barrages, leaving them to pray for the relative mercy of release by mustard gas or chlorine. Such stories were mere nightmares, of course: ghostly reflections in the mists of fear which threw back exaggerated images of the hatred which Frenchmen had for the German machine-gunners who wreaked such havoc in their ranks.

He knew, though, how crucified men eventually died: strangled by their own muscles, hanged by an inner noose as they dangled from a rope wrought from their own sinews.

Who was the crucified man? Why was he here? Who could have done such a thing? *What spirit of evil . . . ?*

He remembered, then, who he was. His name was Anatole Daumier, and he was a soldier of France.

I was lying in a shell-hole at Chemin des Dames, he said to himself. *There was a dead Britisher beside me. I thought I was done for, but someone came to save me. I thought at first it was a British soldier, but then it seemed to be the Maid of Orléans; that was just a delusion, of course. I must have been taken to a field hospital. It must have been my head-wound that made me lose my mind—but I am sure that I was sent back to Paris. I am in Paris now, am I not? I was certainly sent back, although I have no memory of the journey itself. They said it was a City of the Dead, which soon must fall to the enemy, but surely the Boche cannot be here already. Surely, even if they were, they would not be crucifying honest Frenchmen in the cellars of the churches?*

He discovered other fugitive memories, but thought they must be wayward remnants of some nightmarish dream. He remembered clawed talons clamping his throat, crushing his ribs and snapping his leg. He pictured the awful face of a caricature demon raised from Hell. All that must have been a dream conjured up by the pain of his wounds, which had tried to account for the pain he felt by means of the customary lurid and ludicrous imagery of the dream-life.

Better, perhaps, to fall victim to demons than to be shot by bullets, he thought, ruefully. *In a world where demons were, injuries could be mended by magic. The damage done by bullets is not so easily remedied. In a world where demons were, the Maid of Orléans might lead the host of Heaven to my rescue, and bring me to the Elysian fields. But here, on the battlefield which is France, we really do stand upon the threshold of a kind of Hell, where all hope must be abandoned by those who enter.*

He looked around at the darkness, but he was barely able to see the other walls of the chamber in the ill-lit gloom. He could easily imagine demons issuing forth from every shadowy corner; but even as he conjured up their phantom images a voice somewhere within him told him sternly that there were no *actual* demons, nor any human magicians who could bend demons to their will, nor any fallen angels avid to procure the damnation of innocents.

But if all that were so, why was there a living man hanging upon a cross, in mocking imitation of Christ?

Somewhere in the gloom, a door opened. Anatole turned his head, slowly and painfully, to face the direction of the sound.

A man was coming toward him. He was unusually tall and powerfully built. Anatole looked up fearfully at the new arrival's face, at the angry eyes and the hairless pate with its twin ridges and tiny horns, and he recognized the man who called himself Asmodeus.

Had he not killed Asmodeus? Apparently not. That too must have been a dream.

Asmodeus knelt, to look into his face from a more intimate standpoint, and said, in English: "Ah! Awake again. Good. We will move you soon enough, to better quarters." Then he switched to French, presumably because he could not be sure that Anatole understood him. "Who was it that sent you to kill me, Anatole? Who brought you to the church and stationed you in that covert?"

"The Maid of Orléans," Anatole replied, with a foolish little laugh. "Who else?"

The man who called himself Asmodeus reached out his huge hand, as though to touch Anatole's cheek lightly and reassuringly. At the last moment, however, he whipped the open fingers sideways, smacking Anatole across the face as though he were a naughty child. It was not a hard blow, but the force of the impact seemed to spread upward and across the top of Anatole's skull. He felt as if his head had been split in two. He remembered, although it had never given him the slightest pain before, that he had a bad head-wound.

"You will have to do better than that, Anatole," Asmodeus said.

"Indeed, you will have to do a great deal better than that. Hecate is coming, and I will not have her laugh at me. I am Zelophelon's favorite now, and no one—man or angel—may insult me with impunity. I am immortal, but I do not like to have my mortality put to the test. It smacks of disrespect."

Anatole was perversely glad that as soon as he opened his mouth to protest, the renewal of the pain made his senses reel. He did not understand. He had not the least desire to try. He only wanted darkness, and peace. Mercifully, darkness and peace were coming to claim him. He let himself fall into their tender care.

Perhaps, this time, I shall be allowed to die, he thought.

He was not.

6

When he awoke again his mind, afflicted though it was by many pains, was absolutely clear. He knew perfectly well *who* he was, but he could make no sense of his recent memories. He remembered being in the shell-hole, and the appearance of the figure he had mistaken for Jeanne d'Arc. He remembered sharing the consciousness of the man who called himself Asmodeus. He remembered the church, the attempted assassination, and the appearance of the demon. He remembered the meeting with his father. He remembered the crucified man.

All of these incidents seemed equally real, or equally delusory, but of what had happened in between them he had no notion.

He looked around, hoping to find himself in a hospital, with orderlies and nurses and other wounded men clad in neat bandages. He was actually in a narrow cell with damp whitewashed walls and a stone floor. It was lit by two tallow candles set high in metal brackets. It had no furniture save for two wooden beds. The mattress on which he lay was thin and worn, but it was by no means as unyielding as the stone floor on which he had previously been set, and he had a blanket now, which served to conserve a little of his bodyheat. Had it not been for the pain of his wounds he might have been almost comfortable.

The other bed was occupied too, the man who lay on it being positioned so that his head was no more than a meter away, his face turned toward Anatole's. It took Anatole a few moments to realize that it was the face of the man who had been nailed to the cross. He could not tell for sure that the other man was breathing, but he

41

felt certain that no one would put a dead man to bed. The crucified man must have been taken down while he was still alive, and was probably still alive now.

Some of what he remembered was true, but how much? He put the question aside, unready as yet to face it.

He tried to raise himself, but immediately remembered why that was not a good idea, and tried instead to be very still.

Are there cells in Hell? he asked himself, trying to make a joke of it. *Are its legendary torments no more than the commonplace afflictions of vermin-ridden beds and broken bones? Have the lakes of boiling blood been drained? Is it possible that I am less of a sinner than I ever supposed?*

He could not remember where Dante had placed atheistic Communists in his inferno—or, indeed, whether Dante had been able to imagine that there might ever be such men as atheistic Communists.

Perhaps Hell was not designed with men like me in mind. This might be no more than an antechamber, where I must wait for a century or two, until the eighth and most modern circle has been completed. Who, out of all the famous men condemned to more traditional torments, might be recruited to lay its foundation stone?

He was glad that he had not lost his ability to mock. A sense of humor would surely be invaluable in Hell. He had no difficulty at all in imagining how the newest circle of Hell might be designed. The Great War must have been an education even to the minions of Satan. *"Eh bien,"* he murmured, aloud. "If I must spend eternity in no-man's-land, I have the education for it." He knew, though, that he was letting the haphazard train of thought carry him away from the real questions. Where was he? Who had brought him here? What actual events were embedded in his nightmarish memories?

His whispered words must have been audible. The other prisoner's eyelids fluttered as he struggled to open them. In the end, he succeeded. The eyes were brown and bloodshot. The man who had been on the cross looked into Anatole's eyes with a frank curiosity that was rapidly clouded by suspicion. The thin lips moved as though to pose a question, but no sound came forth. Even such a tiny effort as that recalled a spasm of pain to the man's consciousness, and Anatole watched the distress flare up in his eyes. He wondered how it would figure in the hierarchy of gladdening wounds to have huge nails driven through both wrists and both ankles.

Men at the front quickly became rough-and-ready experts in the effects of injury, and Anatole knew from abundant hearsay that

wounds to the hands and wrists were unexpectedly painful as well
as crippling because of the density of the nerves which controlled
the vital instrument of human labor. He had no doubt that his fellow
prisoner was suffering at least as badly as himself—perhaps worse,
given that he was an older man and noticeably less robust.

"Who put you on that cross?" Anatole whispered, not without
difficulty. "Why?"

The second question was pointless, and he knew it, but the man
who had been crucified tried to answer the first. Anatole watched his
lips form silent syllables, and found it easy enough to guess that
they were "As-mo-de-us."

But Asmodeus should be dead, should he not? He could not be
alive!

Could I really have shot him? Anatole wondered. *Could he really
have lived, if I had? Could he really have murdered my brother?
Could my father . . . my own father . . . ?*

The heavy wooden door opened. It was as if a moment already
lived were repeating itself, and Anatole wondered whether his entire
experience might have been a phantom of *déjà vû.* The man who
called himself Asmodeus came in, and looked down at his prisoners—first at the man who had been crucified at his command, and
then at the man who had been plucked from a high covert by a giant
demon and dropped onto the floor of a church.

"Are you better now?" he asked Anatole. His French was fluent,
but he spoke with a pronounced English accent. He must have observed and understood Anatole's confusion, because he leaned over
and parted the loose shirt which he wore, baring his massive breast.
He pointed to an almost-healed wound, and Anatole saw that it was
exactly where he had aimed.

If a bullet had entered there, Anatole knew, it would have exploded
the heart. Ergo, it could not be a bullet-wound, and he had . . .
missed? He remembered the way Asmodeus had fallen back, struck
down by the impact. What kind of armor could have protected his
heart?

"Who sent you?" asked Asmodeus, again. He spoke softly, as
though fearful that he might alarm his prisoner, and make him faint
again. "Whose *instrument* are you?"

Anatole did not attempt to reply. Asmodeus knelt down on one
knee, beside the bed. "Your name is Anatole Daumier," he said, in
a voice that was still hushed. "Your papers told me that much, and
I recognized the name. I sent for your father immediately. He is very

distressed, Anatole—he believes that you have imperiled his salvation, and the salvation of the child he offered as a hostage to my
master. I reassured him, but not *too* much; anxiety will make him
all the more avid to serve me in the future. What man or angel do
you serve, Anatole? The priests of St Amycus would never send forth
an assassin. Has Mandorla Soulier decided to spare the remaining
werewolves?''

Werewolves, Anatole thought. *Have I been shunted from my own
world into some parallel universe where all superstitions are true?
Have I been displaced by some cosmic jest into a place where everything I have believed is false?*

He did not try to answer audibly, and Asmodeus must have read
the reason in his puzzled eyes. ''I see that this will not be easy,''
the Englishman murmured. ''But you must try, *mon ami.* You must
try with all your might to tell me what I need to know, even though
you believe with all your heart that you have nothing to tell. I beg
you to do that, for I have no wish to do you harm, despite what you
have tried to do to me. Hecate could ferret out the truth, but I would
rather find it for myself. The best alliances are built on strength, and
mutual mistrust—like that between the French and the English.''

Asmodeus stood up straight again, while Anatole tried—unsuccessfully—to find some shadow of sense in what had been said to him,
which might help him to begin to make sense of what had *happened*
to him.

Is it possible, he wondered, *that my present conviction that I am
awake is but one more delusion? Is it possible that I am still in the
shell-hole, dreaming my way to a slow death? Am I so little alive
now that I must create a private universe in which to exist? What
sort of nightmare is this for a good Communist to conjure up, filled
as it is with immortal Satanists, demons and werewolves? I have
stepped through the gate of horn instead of the gate of ivory, and
have lost my way. What should I do, while I try to discover a way
back?*

''I cannot believe that you are a mere puppet of one of the
angels,'' Asmodeus said, reflectively. ''That would not make sense.
It must have been a human being who sent you—a foolish human
being, who doubted my power. There is no magic in you.'' But as
he spoke the last words, he sounded doubtful and uneasy. Immortal
though he seemed to be, he was not immune to anxiety, and he
spoke of angels as though they were as familiar to him as the corpses
of murdered children.

What if there are such things as malevolent imps and guardian angels after all? Anatole asked himself, reluctantly. *What if Satan has indeed bid to become the emperor of the Earth, and has appointed Asmodeus his Antichrist. What if two mighty armies are massing for the Last Days, when the final desperate battle must be fought to win the souls of men for damnation, before the Millennium begins?* He knew, even as he formulated the heresy, that it was a gaudy fantasy. He knew, too, how the seed of such a nightmare might have been planted in his mind. There was a book he had recently read, which might innocently have inspired this horridly perverse delusion by providing a new and cunningly inverted account of all the fantasies which had been visited upon him in childhood.

And yet . . . the world seemed so solid, the pain so real, his consciousness so sharp!

"Fetch food and feed them both," Amodeus said to someone waiting without the door. "Clean and bind their wounds as best you can. They must be able to think clearly, even if they have little enough to say. I want them kept alive and conscious, if you can do it. Tell me when you are done."

The Satanist reached down casually to brush the knee which he had rested on the ground, and then went out. No one else came in, but he did not bother to close the door of the cell. It was unnecessary; neither of the prisoners could walk.

Am I then alive and conscious? Anatole thought. *Can I trust the judgment of one who may be no more than a figment of my dream?* He knew that he had no trustworthy method of determining whether he were awake or dreaming, but as he tried to weigh the possibilities he realized that it did not matter. He had never approved of the moral sophistry of Pascal's wager, which said that one should be a good Catholic because one had nothing to lose if there were no God, and everything to lose if He actually existed, but he could see that there was a similar wager to be made here. If this were in truth a delirious dream nothing would be lost by trying to live in it as if it were real, but if it were real there would be everything to lose by refusing to consider it anything but a dream. However absurd this world of angels and demons was, he must do his utmost to conduct himself as if his life depended on his every decision.

Having reached this conclusion, Anatole immediately set about the task of gathering all his resources, in the interests of becoming a machine. From now on, he decided, he must subject his body and his mind alike to the fiercest discipline which they could bear. He must take as much control of himself as he could. He must stop drifting helplessly, and make every effort to steer himself to whatever further shore awaited him beyond this sea of confusion. It was necessary, if he could do it, to become an instrument of *work,* above and beyond such distractions as *feeling.*

What better ambition could any man have, whatever or wherever he might be?

When a few minutes had gone by two men brought bread and cheese for the prisoners to eat, and water for them to drink. Unfortunately, the meager comfort that this sustenance afforded was more than offset by the pain whose fury was stirred up by their subsequent meddling with his wounds. One of the men washed him with carbolic soap, and the other wound clean bandages around his thigh and his chest. No splint was put on his broken femur, though, nor any dressing on his head-wound. It seemed that they honestly did not intend to increase his hurt, and he was prepared to concede that they were probably doing the best they could to save his life; nevertheless, the immediate result of their ministrations was an excruciation which almost made him wish that he were dead. By the time they had finished with both prisoners and left the cell, Anatole felt that his misery was complete. The mere fact of consciousness had become so awful that for a little while he was hardly capable of wanting anything other than to be rid of it. But his pride survived, and stubbornly refused to let go of consciousness—and in the end, his resolve to be a machine and to steer his course held firm.

He tried to lie as still as possible, in the knowledge that the pain would become gradually duller. In time, the agony did become less intense.

Anatole could hear his fellow prisoner whispering his prayers. He silently cursed the folly of the man, but immediately thought better of it. Why should he begrudge the other his refuge? Any opiate was better than none. He concentrated his own mind, trying to find an opiate of his own in the recollection of better times. How long ago was it that the woods had been decorated with flowers, with birds singing in the boughs? He tried to recall the sweet odors, the gentle sounds, the feeling of well-being which had possessed him, in spite of the fact that no-man's land was so close at hand.

When he thought it safe to do so he moved his head just enough to let him look at his companion, whose prayer had now fallen silent. "Who are you?" he whispered.

The other was lying perfectly still, presumably for the same reason that Ana૮ole was lying still, staring vertically upward. He turned his head as carefully as Anatole had turned his, and their eyes met. "My name is Ferigny," he replied, hoarsely. "I am a priest."

"A priest!" Anatole wondered why the news seemed so startling. Why should Satanists not attack priests? "I am Anatole Daumier," he said, in his turn. "I am a soldier. I was wounded at Chemin des Dames . . . do you know what today is? Is the month still May?"

"I think so," the priest said. "I cannot be sure, but I believe today is the thirtieth."

Three days have passed since the German advance! Anatole thought. *Should I have expected more, or less?*

Aloud, he said: "I believe I tried to kill the man who calls himself Asmodeus. I *think* he murdered my brother. My father . . . I *think* I spoke to my father, and he said, or seemed to say . . .

"Asmodeus would not die. I shot him, and he fell, but . . ."

Take control, he instructed himself, impatiently. *Become a machine.*

"Asmodeus has a powerful protector," said the priest, sourly.

"What do they want from me now?" Anatole whispered, uncertainly. "Asmodeus asked . . . who *sent* me. I told him . . . that it was the Maid of Orléans."

The priest said nothing to that.

"What is it that they want from *you*?" Anatole asked. He understood as he said it that it was probably a foolish question, but it seemed safer to ask questions than to attempt explanations. He did not expect an answer—it was probable that their words could be overheard, and the priest could not know that Anatole was trustworthy—but Ferigny did not hesitate before replying.

"They attacked the house of my Order," the priest croaked. "They sought to take possession of a certain book, but they could not find it. They believe—or hope, at least—that I might be able to tell them where the book is, or the name of someone who knows."

"What book?" Anatole asked, with authentic curiosity.

"A private record." The answer was polite enough, but abrupt and dismissive, implying that nothing further could be revealed.

"Is the man who calls himself Asmodeus really immortal?" Anatole asked, reserving judgment on the matter of whether he would believe the answer.

"All men are immortal," whispered the priest. "You and I have a better immortality than his, for ours is the immortality of the soul, while his is merely of the flesh. No matter what he does to us, we are bound to pity him. He is lost to the love of God."

"Love your enemies," Anatole quoted, bitterly. "Forgive them all, for they know not what they do."

"Yes," said the priest. "That is what you must do, if you can."

"I cannot."

"No matter. God will forgive *you* your lack of forgiveness."

Anatole was tempted to laugh, but stifled the impulse.

"Before today, Father," he said, "I would have told you that no man is immortal, that none has a soul, and that we must find a far better reason for acting rightly than the fear of Hell. Even now, when I have been given reason to believe that the agents of Hell are real after all, I am not yet ready to give up my faith in the hand and mind of man. If Asmodeus is damned, so am I."

"Hell's armies are real," the priest said hoarsely. "Do not doubt it. But that is no cause for despair. Take comfort from the fact that proof of Hell is also proof of Heaven; if you have seen one of Satan's shabby miracles, you may have full confidence in God's. Have courage; have patience; the time is nearly come when all accounts will be settled. Yes, you must forgive your tormentors if you can, for they surely know not what they do, but first and foremost look to your own salvation. Repent your sins and embrace your saviour. No matter what happens, you must keep faith with the fact of your own salvation."

"Because the Maid of Orléans came to pluck me from the battlefield? Was that a miracle, then?"

"Not because of that," answered the priest, "although I cannot tell whether or not it was a miracle. Because of the covenant which God made with mankind. Because of the sacrifice which Christ made of his own frail flesh. Because of the promise that he would come again. These are the Last Days, my son ... we shall not have long to wait."

The priest's voice faded as he reached the end of this speech, as if he were on the threshold of merciful sleep. For the first time in his life, Anatole had cause to wonder whether such words might not be hollow after all; but the thought which came into his mind even now was one that had often come to him before when he heard his devout comrades in arms indulging their fond and fragile hopes.

If Satan is the engineer and overseer of this foul war, which is consuming France and civilization by slow degrees, how can we not believe that God is dead?

Now, he added: *If the Antichrist has indeed come to walk upon the Earth, armored against all weapons of assassination, how can we possibly believe that he will not win, and that his empire will not endure eternally?*

He felt dampness on his face, but could not tell whether it was made by tears or blood. In the pain-filled darkness of his inner being he heard a voice speaking to him. Although he knew that it was utterly impossible, and that the words must be his own, he recognized the voice as that of the Maid of Orléans.

"I cannot soothe your wounds just yet," she said, "but another might do it for you. Promise her anything; it will not matter. You have done what you were sent to do; you have not failed. I am a soldier, as you are; I have been wounded, as you have; I understand your suffering. I will keep my promise to you, in due time. Meanwhile, remember only this: if you were not here, you would be dead, and although you have cause enough now to believe that death might be the better choice, time will prove you wrong.

"In the end, time will prove you wrong."

I do not believe in you, he answered. *Witch or saint or sphinx, I do not believe in you.* But the protest was futile. In spite of himself, he had to believe in her. He did not have to accept that she was exactly what she appeared to be, but he had to think and act as if she were entirely real. *If and when she keeps her promise,* he told himself, *and sets me upon the throne on which Laplace's imaginary Demon sat, to see and know the past, the present and the future in all their awesome complexity, nothing will be hidden and nothing confused. Then, surely, I will understand.*

It was the bravest and most comforting thought he had yet found the strength to entertain.

7

Anatole had no idea how much time passed before the two men came again to lift him from the bed. He had not lost consciousness, but he had lost track of the minutes and the hours. As before, when they had bound up his injuries, the two seemed to have no particular intention of hurting him, but there was no way they could move him without doing so, for his broken leg had not been set and the bandage about his ribs could not protect them from the strain. They did not take him far, and supported him all the way so that his weight did not fall on his broken leg, but the pain lasted far too long.

The room to which they brought him was bigger than the cell, but bare and windowless; it might have been intended for a wine cellar. The walls were dry and the floor had been swept, but it was obvious that no one spent overmuch time here. The chair on which they placed him was an ordinary wooden kitchen chair. The chair which faced it was exactly similar, but the man who was seated upon it presumably felt infinitely more comfortable than Anatole did. The room was harshly lit by two lanterns hung from hooks set in the walls to either side.

While the first of the two men who had brought him placed a gentle hand on his shoulder to bid him be still, the second brought a hypodermic syringe from a leather-lined case that was waiting on the floor. He knelt down in order to take the stopper from a glass phial which he placed on the floor, and then filled the syringe from the phial. He was careful to expel the remaining air from the hollow needle; two drops of clear liquid fell from the needle's point. Anatole hoped that it was a solution of morphine, intended to anesthetize his

51

pain, but he tore his eyes away from it to stare—defiantly, he hoped—at the man who was sitting in the other chair.

This was the first chance Anatole had had to inspect Asmodeus at close quarters and in good light, and he took it. The bony ridges on the hairless skull seemed all the more remarkable now, and the horn-like projections above the Satanist's forehead all the more sinister. His eyes were alarming, in spite of the fact that there seemed to be little or no hostility in his gaze.

The man who was holding Anatole took up his left arm, turning it to expose the inner part, where blue veins were clearly marked upon the pale flesh.

One of the many rumors which circulated freely at the front held that the Germans had a truth serum which they injected into captive officers, not only forcing them to disclose everything they knew that was of military value, but all kinds of personal secrets too: their hopes, their fears, their dreams, their fantasies. With the aid of such drugs, it was whispered, the Boche could steal one's very soul. Anatole did not believe it, of course.

The injection had no immediate effect. The man who had held him still released his arms, while his companion packed the syringe and the phial away in the case. Both left the room without having said a word.

"You came—or were brought—to Paris in order to assassinate me, did you not?" asked Asmodeus neutrally.

"Yes." There seemed no point in denying it, although he felt that he could have, had he wanted or needed to.

"Did no one warn you that it would be impossible?"

Anatole paused for thought, then said: "I would not have believed them."

"Do you believe it now?"

Anatole did not answer, because he did not know what the answer was.

Asmodeus smiled. "You are a soldier," he said. "Your father tells me that you are also a member of the Communist Party. There is no reason why you should be an enemy of ours. You have a famous compatriot and namesake who has had much to say in favor of Satan and the justice of his rebellion against the tyrant God of the devout."

Anatole knew that Asmodeus must be referring to Anatole France, and to the book he had recently read. "*His* Satan is a gentle gardener," Anatole replied, wincing at a random stab of pain which shot through his chest, "who would never require or accept human sacrifice, or sanction torture." He felt a little light-headed, and wondered whether the drug he had been given was beginning to take effect.

"You do not understand," Asmodeus told him. "You are mistaken as to the fate of your brother."

Anatole squinted at his interlocutor, wondering what mistake he was supposed to have made. In the end, he said: "Will you try to tell me that you are innocent of my brother's murder?"

"I slit your brother's throat," Asmodeus replied, unashamedly, "because your father offered him as a pledge of his faith, and I accepted. There is work for your father to do, you see. There is work for all my faithful servants, but they must earn my trust. They must demonstrate their faith that the gift of resurrection is mine—and mine alone—to bestow. What you have done, however disrespectful it might be reckoned, has only served to provide one more demonstration of that truth."

Anatole felt the blood in his veins run cold. He could not feel, as yet, any effect of the injection he had received. Clearly, it had not been morphine.

"Are you surprised that I should try to kill you, then?" he asked, annoyed by the rasp of horror infecting his voice.

"You are twice deluded," said Asmodeus, patiently. "You do not understand the true reason for what *I* have done; and you do not understand the true reason for what *you* have done. It might have been your mother who told you what happened to your brother, I suppose, but you were at Chemin des Dames when Bruckmüller's guns smashed Duchêne's line, were you not? How did you come to be in the church? Was it magic that brought you? If so, whose?"

Anatole could not answer. He did not know.

"Your father is disappointed in you," Asmodeus said. "He fears that you might have damaged his chance of salvation, but I hope that he may be wise enough not to be overly concerned. He has already seen what you have seen: that those who come under the protection of my master need have no fear of bullets or blades, and may come back from the dead if they have his blessing. He would have offered you as readily as he offered your brother, knowing that there was no greater favor he could show you. How else can an honest man prove his faith in the impotence of death and the certainty of resurrection, save by delivering a beloved child to be killed? That is the significance of our rites of sacrifice, Anatole; we do not kill to delight or appease our master, for he needs no such sustenance. We kill to display our faith—our *knowledge*—that death is no end for those who are true servants of Zelophelon. How many followers of Christ would be prepared to do what your father and many others have done?''

"Who is Zelophelon?" Anatole asked, uncertainly. He felt dizzy now, but he did not know whether it was the drug or not.

"It is only a name," Asmodeus said. "Men are ever avid to put names to their guardian angels, and have always manufactured them in needless quantity. The name of Satan has been promiscuously used these last two thousand years and there are too many Satans haunting the human imagination nowadays; although we are not ashamed to be reckoning Satanists, we must have another name for our private use which is less confusing. There are seven fallen angels in all, you see, and Zelophelon is but one of them."

Anatole did not know what to say to that.

"The question we must ask," said Asmodeus, lightly enough, "is whether it was one of the remaining six which sent you forth on your hopeless mission—and, if so, why?"

"I came of my own accord," Anatole said, wishing that his head were a little clearer. "You murdered my brother; that was reason enough. I needed no angel to commission me. I came by the roads, as any man might." He knew that he was lying, but did not know how to tell the truth. Asmodeus had not liked it before when he had named the person who had sent him.

"I am willing to believe that you believe that," Asmodeus told him, in a calculatedly sorrowful tone, "but I cannot content myself with such an answer. Many of those who are pawns of the angels have no inkling at all of what they are, but there are always clues to be pieced together. You must help me to search for those clues, Anatole, for your own sake as well as mine. I do not simply mean that you might save yourself a deal of pain; I mean that it might be to your advantage also to find out who and what you truly are."

"Can you not simply look into my mind, magician?" Anatole replied, belatedly finding the power to mock. "Can your Satanic master not exercise his occult power to divine what he needs to know?"

"Zelophelon can indeed look into the minds of men," Asmodeus answered, with a self-satisfied smile, "but there are so very many men, and the thoughts which occupy their minds at any particular point in time are far less revealing than you might suppose. He could most certainly share your stream of consciousness if he wished, but there would be little enough reward in that, even if you were something far more important and interesting than you seem to be. Zelophelon has more urgent concerns to occupy the foreground of his attention. He dwells in time, and must ration his resources very carefully. He can bend matter and space to his will, but not without cost or difficulty, and must leave the greater part of the work done in his cause to his loyal servants. Do not be deceived, though, none of the fallen angels is omniscient, and Zelophelon's rivals have no advantage over him. They are too blind to all but the tiniest fraction of what is happening in the world and in the minds of men at any particular point in time, and may be taken by surprise. The angels are not so very unlike us, you see.''

''Can they die?'' Anatole asked, with as much curiosity as challenge.

''Oh yes,'' said Asmodeus. ''They are potentially immortal, but they can be injured and destroyed. Who told you I was here, Anatole? Who sent you to the church?''

''I don't know,'' Anatole told him, taking a perverse delight in the unacceptability of the truth. ''I lay dying on the battlefield at Chemin des Dames. It seemed to me that I was rescued by Jeanne D'Arc, but I must have been dreaming. My vision proves, I suppose, that I am a true patriot, Communist or no—just as my namesake is.''

''Sometimes,'' said Asmodeus, ''dreams are as real as anything which happens in the world. There are magicians in the world who can command dreams, and they often wear masks in order to delude mere men. Tell me, Anatole: was there some *other* image or idea which haunted your thoughts when you beheld your rescuer? You must help me to understand this matter, if you can.''

''No,'' said Anatole. ''There was nothing else.''

Asmodeus rose unhastily from his chair, and took two steps forward, so that he towered over his prisoner. Anatole had no option but to look up at him, fearfully.

Asmodeus raised his arm casually, and brought the edge of his hand sweeping round in a descending arc. Anatole had no time to react effectively, although his arms came up reflexively to ward off the blow.

No defense would have been adequate; Asmodeus was a strong man and it did not matter in the least whether he hit his target directly. Anatole intercepted the swinging arm with his own, but the force of the blow knocked him from the chair, and when he fell the injuries which he had already sustained flared up in dreadful agony. He was certain that he could feel the two halves of his fractured femur moving within the flesh of his leg, tearing.

He screamed.

Instead of trying to get up or hit back, Anatole tried to curl up into a fetal ball, intent only on minimizing the pain. He waited to be hit again, or kicked, trying meanwhile to empty his mind of all thought and all feeling.

He could not do it.

Asmodeus kicked him, casually and callously. The Satanist's booted foot connected with Anatole's ribs in spite of his attempt to shield them, and he felt as if a great tide of pain was tearing apart the very chambers of his heart. In spite of his dizziness he could not loose his hold on consciousness. He remained stubbornly awake while the agony of his tormented wounds ran riot through his soul, mocking him with its irresistible force.

Asmodeus knelt down beside him and leaned over.

"Listen to me very carefully, my friend," he said, in a contemptuously confidential fashion. "I will open the door to enlightenment for you, and you in your turn must try to enlighten me. A fair exchange is all I ask. Try not to hate the pain too much, for pain can be a gateway to discovery, and it may be that you will have to go a long way into the unknown territory beyond that gateway in order to find out what you can."

"This is madness," Anatole gasped, fighting hard to get the words out.

"That is a lesson we have to learn," said Asmodeus, sadly. "The world which our grandfathers thought good, and which our fathers thought reasonable, is really neither. There is no omnipotent, generous and loving Father-God to save our souls, nor is there a calm and reassuring absence of divine power which leaves us joyously alone to do what we can and what we please. It was always hopelessly optimistic to think that the number of the gods might be none or one; anyone with the power of sight and thought ought not to be in any doubt at all that the world is a place of conflict and confusion, and that there is no safety at all in what humans call *virtue* or *progress*. The world is certainly mad, my friend, and we must deal with its madness as cleverly as we can. We must entertain the dreams which come from angels and witches, and must assiduously search out the truth which they contain."

When he had finished this speech Asmodeus stood up again, and carefully lifted his huge booted foot. He hesitated for a moment or two, as if spoiled for choice as to where to bring it down. Anatole looked up at the leather sole, wishing that the dizziness which roiled in his brain might carry him away, out of reach, before it fell.

Eventually, Asmodeus let the boot fall—not rapidly, but inexorably—upon Anatole's cracked ribcage. The horror of anticipation amplified Anatole's distress, but when the excruciation began in earnest the horror quickly came to seem irrelevant. It did not take more than half a minute for the pain which seized his anxious heart, squeezing it like an iron vice, to blast his senses away . . . but not to the mercy of oblivion.

It seemed that blinding light filled his head, and a fulminating chaos of images. Anatole could not tell whether it was the effect of the drug he had been given, or simply of the increase in his pain, but he now inhabited two worlds simultaneously: one the brightly lit but utterly enclosed world of the cellar, where he was alone with his torturer and the cruel assaults of matter; the other a blindingly bedazzled and horizonless world, where there was no matter at all, and where he was most definitely *not* alone, but was instead surrounded and shot through with the stuff of angels.

He was possessed by a vertiginous sense of expansion, as though he were the skin of a balloon, as though something within him were *evolving* and *exploding* at one and the same time . . . then the microcosm which was his tiny pitiful self became by miraculous inversion the macrocosm, which contained everything except for God, whose wistful face was the Great Outside, void of power and void of meaning. Anatole-as-God could not look into his own face, for all faces and all masks were inaccessible now, hid from prying eyes in the great cataract of light which was the boundary wall of the infinite universe: a wall made of stars and swarms of stars and plagues of swarms of stars, all crowded together so tightly that they fused into a great crystal sphere, super-dense and yet insubstantial, solid and yet filled with spaces, whose tiny star-cells were so far apart that each and every one was lost in a vast sea of darkness . . .

And yet, swimming in that vast sea, alive and alight in the infinite dark, were the angels. Their serpentine forms coiled around one another, writhing and seething, made of the nothing that was everything, locked together in a ceaseless, irresistible conflict that was also a restless, ecstatic congress, a fission that was also a fusion, an endless war that was also an endless creation . . .

This is what I asked of the Maid, he thought. *This is the station which Laplace made in his imagination, for his allegorical Demon. If only I can see what is to be seen . . .*

Because Anatole-as-God saw the whole of Creation, it became that which he saw. Because it was in him, he became it, and his eyes became huge and compound, seeing not the narrow crack of five-colored whiteness but the whole vast panoply of five thousand colors and more, while his ears caught a distant whisper of the Beginning and a faint foreboding of the End . . .

The one thought which screamed inside his godlike mind was: *Be a machine!* The one vestige of himself to which he clung, fearful to lose everything and not merely his immortal soul, was the resolve to find a pattern, to find a meaning, to find a *plan*, even though the world had gone mad, even though the Age of Miracles had returned to Earth, even though time itself might come to an end, even though he was dead of a bullet in the brain and condemned to Hell for the sins of faithlessness and commitment to Liberty, Equality and the Fraternity of Man . . .

Anatole felt, just for a single instant, that he could never be himself again, that he was lost forever . . .

He heard a voice: a *real* voice, but a voice with the power to cut through sanity and madness like a scalpel blade; a voice of *command.* What the voice said was: "Do you think he will see any more clearly at the moment of his death? Are you not yet free of your petty superstitions?"

The voice spoke in English, but Anatole had no difficulty understanding the words.

All of a sudden, as though the switch in an electrical circuit had been thrown, he was in near-darkness again—or so it seemed, for the first few seconds, until his scarified eyes adjusted to the lamplight.

The first thing he saw was that the man who called himself Asmodeus had snatched him up from the floor, and was holding him face-to-face. He could feel the sweat on the huge hands clamped over his ears. But Asmodeus was already looking away, turning to face the person who had spoken. The expression in his wild eyes was difficult to read, but there was fear in it, and resentment, and envy.

"Was it *you*?" Asmodeus said, bitterly. He spoke in English too. "Did *you* send him to play tricks with me, to test my father's fondness for his pawn?"

"I have better things to do," the voice replied.

It was not until Asmodeus released his head that Anatole was able to turn and look for the source of the voice. It was not easy. When Asmodeus released him he was denied support, and pain rushed through him as he slumped down—but he did turn.

There was a woman standing in the doorway. She was one of the plainest women Anatole had ever seen. Her figure was lumpen, her face fleshy and sallow. She might have been forty years old, or fifty. Her eyes were narrow and her lips were thin. Her hair was dark brown, streaked with dirty gray. She was dressed well enough, but otherwise might have passed for a kitchen servant or a peasant wife. Even so, her voice was the voice of command, and her words had been addressed, with contempt, to a man who had demons at his beck and call.

The woman came forward and bent over Anatole. She touched him lightly on the cheek with a gloved hand.

"You could have killed him," she said.

"I doubt that," Asmodeus replied. "Whoever sent him here does not intend him to die just yet."

"Did you find what you were looking for in his eyes? Did you make sense of his dream?"

Anatole saw Asmodeus drop his gaze. The answer had to be *no*—but if Asmodeus had somehow seen what *he* had seen, it was difficult to believe that there was any other answer to be found.

"Pick him up," the woman said.

"You cannot give me orders," Asmodeus objected—but after a moment's hesitation, he did indeed reach down and take Anatole's broken body in his arms.

"Lay him in his bed," the woman said, and Asmodeus went obediently through the door, and along the dark corridor to the cell where the crucified priest still lay asleep.

Asmodeus put Anatole on the tawdry bed, and covered him with the blanket. Then he stood back. The woman came into the cell, and looked down at Anatole.

"Rest," she said. "Rest, for a while."

He tried to laugh. Rest! If only he could!

She seemed to read the thought, but she surely needed no occult power to assist her. She reached out her right hand again, but this time she caught the glove with the fingers of her left hand, and deftly slid it off. She touched his forehead with her fingers, which were just as ugly and lumpen, in their fashion, as her face.

"Did you know that you have a bullet lodged in your brain?" she asked. She was still speaking in English, and for a moment he thought that he must have misunderstood her, but she picked up his own hand and placed his fingers upon his right temple, where he felt a hole in his skull. The skin had somehow healed over it.

I am dead after all! he thought.

"No," she said. "Not dead, but fortunate: very, very fortunate."

He felt himself slipping away into sleep. He had just time enough to feel glad.

8

Anatole was walking in no-man's-land, across a great sea of mud which stretched from horizon to horizon. The region was crisscrossed by trenches, but none were occupied by troops, and they gave the impression of having been long abandoned. Many had collapsed in upon themselves. Occasional dense tangles of barbed wire remained, but the wire was not deployed to form defenses. Most of it had been carefully compacted into useless aggregations, which were decorated within by plaintive scraps of faded cloth snagged on the wire. These man-made thorn-bushes with their ragged and faded mock-flowers were the only things to be seen that preserved any memory or parody of life. There was not a tree before the horizon that had kept its crown, and every splintered bole was blackened by fire. The sky was leaden and featureless.

"If only the leaders of our nations could see what their war has done to this once beautiful land," Anatole had once heard an English officer remark, "they might awaken from their vile dream and discover the necessity of peace." He had thought the man naïve for imagining that the leaders of nations had any eye for beauty or conscience for its loss, but it seemed that one out of every three English officers was a part-time poet, who thought to make the face of damnation bearable by sad and sonorous scribbling. The British seemed to have no concept of the hard reality of the war; they conducted themselves as if it were merely some legend they were concocting as proof of their eccentricity. Anatole remembered the order going forth which officially forbade British soldiers to use French brothels, on the grounds that the war was a ''sacred cause'' which ought not to be corrupted by immoral behavior; at first he had thought it another silly rumor, but it had turned out to be true.

He was in pain, but could not understand why. He could not see any wounds on his body, and wondered whether he was producing the symptoms himself, by the power of his imagination, in the desperate hope of winning his release. It was said that hysteria could bring forth apparent wounds on the bodies of men who had been too long in the trenches: the stigmata of the Age of Reason; but Anatole's problem was the other way around. He kept lifting his hand to his head, fully expecting to find a bad wound there, but he never touched anything but unblemished skin.

Hurting, he thought, *is such an easy thing to do. If hurting is the price of freedom, why should the war not end tomorrow? Surely there is not one of us who does not ache with fear and grief and the loss of the world that we knew.*

He walked on and on, past a great multitude of dead men who lay unclaimed in the mud. A few were German and a few English, but the vast majority were French. It was, he thought, dreadfully unjust that the soil of France should be fed by so much French blood, and yet no longer be capable of sending forth a single cornstalk. Some of the corpses were without legs, some were without arms and others had great bloody holes ripped in their faces or their bellies. There were, however, many who were untouched by that primitive kind of violence; these had been slaughtered by gas, rent and ravaged inwardly, according to a fashion far more cunning and intimate but no less absolute and final.

Everyone had heard rumors that new gases were being delivered to the battlefields even now, in the desperate hope of halting the German advance. The Americans, reluctant to commit troops to a rapidly worsening situation, were perfectly happy to send medicated weaponry in their stead: chemicals capable of killing in a clinical fashion which no mere human hand could ever have achieved.

"There ought to be men to bury the dead," Anatole said, aloud. "We are civilized, are we not? We should hide our fleshy litter away, with all due care and ceremony." But there seemed to be no one else alive to do what needed to be done, and he could not turn aside from the vital mission which had sent him forth across this godforsaken landscape.

Was it, he wondered, *actually* godforsaken? Or should he rather call it *godreclaimed*?

He paused to rest, but stillness made the ache in his head grow perversely worse. He realized that he had forgotten, just for the moment, exactly what his vital mission was, but he resolved not to let the momentary lapse of memory upset or distract him; he had every faith in his ability to remember it when the time came.

He rubbed his eyes with the heels of his hands. When he looked up again, he saw someone coming toward him, stumbling through a sea of dead men.

He brought his rifle to the ready, but quickly saw that there was no need. The other was wearing a British uniform and had no gun of his own—although he would only have had to pause and pick one up from the mud to make good his loss. The Britisher was considerably older than Anatole—at least thirty, he guessed—but his face was fresh and wide-eyed, and he had fine fair hair that would surely have looked silken had it not been flecked with mud and blood.

The fair-haired man had lost his helmet, too, and had no gas mask, but no sergeant would have screamed at him in wrath; he was an officer. As he drew closer, he began to whistle. Anatole's mind, perversely defiant of his will, insisted on superimposing on the whistled tune the rude and crude version which the conscripts sang, perhaps with the intention of mocking officers. It was odd, he thought, that the British were so fond of silly ditties and petty obscenities. Were they not the men for whom the war was supposed to be a sacred cause? Were they not the men forbidden to enter French brothels lest their minds and hearts be corrupted?

Perhaps they did have a certain innocence, after all—but 606 was a lucky number for them, as it was for everyone else. If the war years had made no other contribution to progress they had produced 606: an authentic cure for syphilis.

As the British officer drew level with Anatole he paused, and looked him in the eyes. "I wish you would give a message to my father, sir," he said, in the kind of English accent which marked him as an educated man, but not as a true aristocrat.

"Of course," said Anatole, also speaking in English for politeness' sake. "What is it?"

"Tell him that it does not matter that my grandfather was wrong, because he is the one with the finer sense of beauty. Tell him that it is not necessary to *love* his enemies, provided only that courtesy is an adequate shield against hatred."

Anatole frowned, but thought it impolite to ask for an explanation, given that the message was intended for another. "For whom is the message intended?'' he asked, instead. ''And where shall I find him?''

''For David Lydyard,'' said the Britisher. ''You will find him at World's End.''

''From whom does the message come?'' Anatole asked.

''Say that it comes from Simon,'' said the Englishman. ''He will not believe it, but he will understand.''

What or where is ''World's End?'' thought Anatole, suddenly, wondering how he had let it go unquestioned. He opened his mouth to ask, but the other gestured him to silence.

''No time,'' said the British officer, in a stage whisper. ''The future is coming: a future we cannot evade, no matter how hard we try. Never despair, though; much that is done cannot be undone, but all history is fantasy. Even the Clay Man has a navel. Eve is innocent, like the Maid of Orléans, although they call her witch.''

''But . . .''

Anatole hardly had time to speak the single syllable. The fair-haired man suddenly collapsed, as if he were a puppet whose strings had been cut. He fell face forward. Anatole went to him at once, knelt down, and turned him over; but when he did so he found that he was looking down at a skull, with so little flesh left upon it that the man must have been dead for months. He could not help casting the uniformed skeleton away from him in horror, and for a moment or two the repulsion he felt almost drowned out the pain that was eating him up inside.

Am I dead too? he asked, no longer daring to believe that because he was capable of thought he must be alive. *Is all of his naught but a nest of dreams, set inside one another like Chinese boxes, spreading through my brain like slow ripples across the surface of a muddy pond as the bullet ploughs through the soft gray matter?*

A faint sound caught his attention and he looked up, scrambling to his feet again. It was the noise of an aeroplane's engine, but he could not see the plane itself, and he wondered whether the great blanket of cloud which masked the sun was closer to the ground than he had thought. The sound grew louder, and he knew that it must be an entire *escadrille,* but he could not see the planes yet, and did not know whether they were French or English or German. He craned his neck, suddenly fearful.

The future! he thought. *The future is coming!*

The dark shapes began to descend from the clouds then. They were huger than any planes he had ever seen before. The sound of

their engines was incredibly loud and deep, and the ground reverber-
ated to its thrumming. Anatole could not count the planes, but there
were dozens, if not hundreds. They were flying east-to-west, and as
they passed overhead they began to release bombs, which fell like a
torrent of rain, in unbelievable profusion.

Anatole ran for the cover of a nearby trench, and scrambled down
into it—but it was only a slit-trench, with no coverts to provide real
cover. He cowered down as the bombs began to burst, and he took
no comfort from the fact that their bursting was neither loud nor
violent. He had no gas mask, and he knew that he was done for. He
cowered lower still, wondering why it hurt so much to compact
himself, pressing his body against the crudely shored-up wall of
earth.

Perhaps he wished that the earth might swallow him up; at any
rate, that was what it did. He passed into its substance very easily;
water would have offered more resistance. It was like stepping
through a doorway. Ghosts, he recalled, were supposed to be able to
drift through solid walls. Evidently he *had* died, and was now a
phantom, free to flee the battlefield in any direction he chose.

The direction he chose was *down*.

There was no light inside the earth, of course, so he could not
see, but his other senses were heightened as if by way of compensation. He could hear the rumble of the bombs falling on the surface
high above him, and feel the seismic ripples sent forth by their impacts—but there were other, subtler vibrations emanating from below,
and there were more delicate touch-sensations. It was cold where he
was, but he could sense a source of heat below him. He still hurt,
but the pain was less acute, and less *unpleasant.* Whatever state of
consciousness he now possessed was in that way much preferable to
the one in which he had previously been becalmed.

As he descended further, in search of comfortable warmth, the
vibrations from above faded to slight background noise, while those
from below swelled into a kind of gentle music.

He passed through a region where all was peace and quiet, but as
the temperature began to rise the sensations flowing up from the
heart of the world grew more intense again, as though the music of
the Earth's molten core were gathering in a slow and majestic crescendo. Anatole felt a curious sense of *belonging,* as if this were the
state of being to which he had always been destined, without knowing it. He realized that he was not, after all, some manlike entity of
shadow-matter moving through the mantle of the world, but some-

thing very solid. The rock was his body now, just as the frail envelope of painful flesh had been, and he was a man of stone—but he was not confined to any particular lump of stone; *all* the earth was his to possess, so long as he had an anchorage. He had the power to be *everywhere,* to extend the level of his thought to the liquid center of the planet or to the smear of slime which was its biosphere.

This, Anatole thought, *is the womb of all human souls, from which they are dragged in order to be made flesh. I nearly remember it now. I know, at least, how foolish I was to forget, and to imagine myself no more than a frail, soft creature of damp flesh and calcined bone. This will be my resting place when the time comes for me to rest: no Hell at all, but a cradle balanced between the infinite peace of bland stone and the restless melody of incandescent iron. This is what I was made for; this is what I really am. For me, this is the ultimate future, the merciful destiny which lies beyond the fantasy of history.*

Somewhere deep inside him, a tiny sceptical voice said, "Alas, it makes no sense!" but he was free to disregard it. Now, he could accept anything. The pain was gone, and he was free to sleep at last.

He relaxed completely, and let himself fall, to the center of the universe and the end of everything.

9

He awoke to dim candlelight and whispered Latin. The priest who had been crucified and then taken down from the cross was still muttering, mouthing the words of the Lord's Prayer over and over, as though to banish all other thought from his brain. Anatole's mouth and throat were very dry but the pain in his chest and leg had become dull. He swallowed hard and moved his tongue, working his salivary glands in order to moisten the dry parts of his mouth. He coughed, and then turned, very slowly, onto his side. He was now facing the man on the other bed.

"How long?" he asked, faintly. He was not certain why he wanted to know, but for some reason it seemed important.

The whispered prayer immediately ceased, and the priest turned his gaunt face toward Anatole.

"How long was I asleep?" Anatole asked again.

"I don't know," said the priest, hoarsely. "Two hours, perhaps three, must have passed since they brought you back." There was something hesitantly expectant in the way he stared, and his brow was furrowed as though in speculation.

"Asmodeus undertook to show me the way to enlightenment," Anatole said. "He injected some drug or other into a vein, and then tormented my wounds. A woman stopped him. Does Asmodeus really have a means to search for mysteries in men's dreams?"

"He has some borrowed power," the priest answered, "but the witch has more. She may be the more dangerous of the two."

"Do you mean the woman who had me brought back? Is she a witch?" *Eve is innocent,* he thought, *like the Maid of Orléans, al-*

67

though they call her witch. But the woman who saved him had been so dull and plain of face!

"She calls herself Hecate," Father Ferigny told him, speaking more comfortably now. "Do not be deceived by her appearance or her manner. The self-styled Asmodeus is more showman than magician, but she is a more intimate servant of those who move behind the scenes, directing the performances of pawns like him. She is the more subtle follower of the Father of Lies."

"If he is the Antichrist, I suppose she is the whore of Babylon?" Anatole said, trying to make light of it.

"Perhaps she is," answered the priest.

The door of the cell opened then, and the plain woman came in. She was quite alone. "Perhaps I am," she said to Ferigny, obviously having overheard the exchange while she paused on the threshold. "Should I be riding, in that case, on a scarlet beast with seven heads and ten horns? Ought I to be carrying a golden cup, full to the brim with abominations? You must have better dreams than that in your secret book. Your brethren, cold-souled men though they be, have surely seen shadow-plays which carried less clouded news of the future, even if they have remained stubborn in their silly conviction that their own protective angel is of a different kind than the rest." She spoke better French than Asmodeus, and might have passed for a native.

"There is but one God," said the priest, "and one saviour."

She reached out to touch his forehead. "I could tell Asmodeus that you do not know where the book is, and make him believe it," she said, softly. "Shall I do that for you, martyr?"

The priest did not answer.

"It would be a lie, of course," she purred, "and you would not like that, would you. *You* may tell him the lie, and reckon yourself a hero, but if I were to do it on your behalf, that would be a different thing. The strangest irony is that the book would be no more use to him than it is to you, for you and he are cats of a more similar stripe than you would ever condescend to admit. Enemies of science both, you cling nevertheless to the notion of a single truth in the one matter where truth is necessarily contingent. Perhaps Asmodeus intends to give it to Harkender, but I doubt it; he is jealous of his former master. You would lose nothing by letting him have it but the chance to be a martyr. Are you really so proud?"

Anatole could still see the priest's face, and he saw how very angry this speech made him. The priest looked up at the woman as any man of God might look at a witch, making a show of spurning her temptations with all the contempt he could muster, although he did not actually pronounce the words *Retro me Satanas!*

He is mad! thought Anatole. *But is she any saner?*

The woman turned to look down at Anatole. Her fleshy cheeks were patchily discolored, her eyes and lips drawn even narrower than usual by the inquisitive expression on her face. She did not look as if she could aspire to be a common whore, let alone the grandiose monster-rider of Revelations.

"Your friend sounds almost virtuous, does he not?" she said. "And yet, the Romans would deem him a vile heretic, because he believes with the Albigenses of old that the material world was created by the Devil as a snare, while the spirit alone is the divine breath of God. The members of his order were hunted by the Inquisition in days of yore, and have treated themselves little more kindly than their one-time persecutors did. His brethren have starved and brutalized themselves for centuries, in the humble belief that the mortification of the flesh is the thorny path to the enlightenment of the soul. He should be grateful to Asmodeus for the gift of such fine stigmata, and will doubtless wear them very proudly indeed if ever they should heal."

Anatole did not know how to respond. It seemed, in spite of her alleged supernatural intelligence, that she mistook the cause of his silence, for she said: "Does it hurt so much?"

She reached out her hand, and placed it on his cheek, then moved it along the line of his chin and over the top of his head, inscribing an oval with her forefinger.

He had not realized how much discomfort he felt until it was abruptly banished. He drew a deep breath, gratefully—but his gratitude was limited by the awareness that if she could do what she had just done, then she might indeed have the powers of a witch . . . and perhaps more. He looked at her more intently, but still she wore the aspect of a slattern, too old and too ugly to be anything but contemptible.

"What are you?" he asked.

She smiled thinly. "You are beginning to believe," she observed. "I had thought you stronger than that in your incredulity—but you will doubtless look back on all of this as a strange interval of delirium, if you are able to look back at all."

"What do you want from me?" he demanded. "If Asmodeus wants his revenge, let him take it—but I have had my fill of taunts and dark ravings. If you are truly able to look into my mind, you know why I came to kill Asmodeus."

"The ability to share the minds of others is less useful than you might think," she replied, sardonically. "Even Asmodeus knows that the authentic levers of human action are hidden far beneath the froth of conscious motives. Puppets are rarely conscious of their own strings, and never find it difficult to supply excuses for their movements. Nor is it easy to read the hidden meanings which surface in dreams; the eye of the beholder is ever ready to impose its own hopes and theories. That is why the loyal dreamers of St Amycus have never quite contrived to perceive the error of their fundamental assumptions. Even though you have tried to kill their Antichrist they would deem you a hapless instrument of the maker of matter, possessed of the Devil."

"Because I am a godless Communist?"

"That too—but I had in mind the fact that you are a magician of sorts yourself. The fugitive warmth in your soul is borrowed, like the warmth which turned cold-souled Luke Capthorn into the mighty Asmodeus, but it is real. You have a bullet in your head, which should have killed you. The power which preserved you would be attributed by the priests of St. Amycus to the Devil."

"I am no friend of that Devil which Amycus worships," Anatole said, coldly. "If you follow the same master you had better kill me and be done with it. If I escape this rat-trap I will surely make another attempt on the life of Asmodeus, with a more destructive weapon."

She smiled. "You might even succeed, in the end," she said. "I cannot imagine why Zelophelon continues to tolerate him—unless, of course, it is true that he is merely acting out a role in a narrative already scripted and determined by some inescapable destiny. I doubt that, as you do."

The future is coming, Anatole thought. *A future we cannot evade, no matter how hard we try . . . but she doubts it, as I do. Is she trying to flatter me or win my sympathy? If so, why?* Aloud, he said, "I thought I knew better once, but I am no longer sure of anything. The world is too strange a place for my comprehension."

"You do not mean that," she said. "You are an educated man, curious and intelligent. Were it not for the war you might be something far better than a soldier. Were it not for the pain of your injuries you would be very enthusiastic to understand what is happening here. You should be grateful to me, not simply for the stilling of your pain but also for my willingness to bring you a calmer kind of enlightenment than Asmodeus offered you.''

''Do not listen to her,'' advised the stigmatized priest. ''She will seduce you with lies.''

She did not turn to look at him. Her stare was still directed, disconcertingly, at Anatole's eyes. ''If I desired to seduce you,'' she said, in a lower tone, ''I would not need mere lies.'' As she spoke, the lines of her face blurred. It was as if she wore a mask of flesh which became momentarily transparent, so that another face beneath it were free to look out: a darkly beautiful face, more delicate by far in the features.

Illusion! he told himself, but the word had a hollow echo.

It was most certainly an illusion, but was such power of illusion to be despised?

''How is it that I am alive?'' he asked her. ''If there is a bullet in my head, how am I here?''

''You were saved,'' she replied. ''Perhaps by an angel, perhaps by something like me. You were presumably sent to shoot Asmodeus in order to attract his attention. He injected you with muscarine and tried to look into your soul, but he has neither the power nor the wit to do that cleverly. Was his soul open to you, I wonder, while he tried to fathom *your* secrets?''

''No,'' he replied—but he remembered as he said it how he had learned of the death of P'tit Jean. Was that the kind of witchcraft which Asmodeus had sought—unsuccessfully, it seemed—to work upon him? Who, or what, then, had worked it on his behalf?

''On the other hand,'' the witch continued, ''you might conceivably have been sent to attract *my* attention.'' Again she reached out, and put her hand on his forehead as though to draw the thoughts from his brain. How could he possibly prevent it, if she had the power?

''I told Asmodeus that it was the Maid of Orléans who sent me,'' he said, ''but he did not like the answer.''

''I have a different attitude,'' she assured him. ''And a different method. Shall *I* tell *you* who might have saved you?''

''I would certainly like to know,'' he answered.

''There are seven beings, which we have learned to call angels although we must be careful not to read too much into the name,'' she said, ''for whom the earth appears to be a crucial battleground. All seven have been quiet for some time, perhaps because they learned discretion when they last sought to defeat and devor one another while using men as their pawns. Lately, the game has begun again in earnest. I cannot pretend to understand why mere men are useful to the angels, but some of them have taken the trouble to possess human servants and some others, perhaps fearful of missing an opportunity, have made shift to do likewise. A few have made magical creatures in the image of men, of which I am one.''

"There *is* a legion of fallen angels abroad upon the earth," the priest put in. "No matter how they represent themselves, they are all servants of the Devil. As the witch says, they have been quiet for a while, but they are becoming active again as the end of the world approaches. There is no need to despair, however, for we have a saviour.''

I must listen to all of this with great care, Anatole thought. *Whether it is true or not, it holds the key to my future.*

"The names of these so-called angels are various," said the woman. "One was named Zelophelon by a man named Jacob Harkender, and seems content with that name. Another is sometimes called Bast by those it has used as instruments, because it was as Bast that a man named David Lydyard pictured it when he encountered it in Egypt. Bast once made a creature which sometimes appeared as a sphinx.''

A sphinx! Anatole exclaimed, silently. *The sphinx is mentioned in that stupid song which has haunted me throughout this nightmare! And David Lydyard is the man to whom I am supposed to deliver a message.* Even as the words formed in the supposed privacy of his mind he saw the woman frown, not in displeasure but in perplexity.

"The sphinx?" she echoed, proving that she could indeed be party to his thoughts. "You believe that your Maid of Orléans was the sphinx? That is difficult to believe. Why should the sphinx send an assassin to attack Zelophelon's minion?''

The message, Anatole thought, helpless to prevent himself. *Perhaps the key lies in the message . . .* He stopped, mildly surprised to find that he *could* stop, and had the power to refuse to vocalize any more.

"Tell me about the message," she said, though not in any threatening fashion. "I am not your enemy, Anatole; I may be able to help you understand it. Tell me, please.''

If the dream was only a dream, Anatole thought, *it can do no possible harm to reveal what I dreamed. If it was not, she is infinitely more likely to be able to unriddle it than I . . . and if she is my enemy, she surely has the power to force me to tell her.*

"When you bade me rest," he said, "I slept. I dreamed that I met an Englishman on the ruined ground which had been the Chemin des Dames. He said that his name was Simon, and asked me to deliver a message to his father, David Lydyard, at World's End."

"Ah!" said the woman. "Now that *is* strange. Will you tell me what the message was?"

I would be breaking a confidence. Anatole thought. *She clearly believes that the dream was real—and if she thinks so, should I not behave as if it were?*

"That would not be right," he answered. She withdrew her hand from his brow, as though respectful of his diplomacy. She did not object to his refusal, nor did she try to persuade or threaten him.

"The third of the beings I was describing named itself Machalalel," she said, picking up the thread of her own story as if the interruption had been of no importance. "Long ago, it molded an imitation man of clay, and formed a company of creatures which have lately been known as the werewolves of London; by these means it may have learned much that its rivals have only recently begun to learn, but that advantage will probably count for nothing in the long run, because Machalalel seems to be conspicuously weaker than the others. The fourth is my own maker. The fifth is revered by this poor fool beside you, and is credited by allegorical legend with the sanctification of one Amycus, whose name and nature you might recognize. That one might also have been the mysterious maker of Jesus Christ, if Christ was indeed a creature like me, and not a man like you—the priests of St. Amycus certainly believe that to be the case."

"She seeks to diminish Almighty God, to make Him the equal of the fallen angels," said the priest, stung by her evident contempt, "but that is diabolical pride in all its idiocy."

"Of the two that remain," the woman went on, imperturbably, "we know next to nothing. They remain mute, and perhaps blind—but it is possible that one of them brought the human race into being, or discovered it even before Machalalel, and might have used its instrument more cleverly than the rest. If there is any vestige of truth in the more fundamental beliefs of the Order of St. Amycus, the last might conceivably be the author of matter itself, or at least creator of the earth. If you were an instrument of one of these, that would be very interesting."

The earth itself, Anatole thought, *became my refuge when the airfleet began to rain destruction upon its surface. Perhaps* ... He looked up immediately to catch her reaction.

"Perhaps," she echoed. After a moment's reflection, she went on. "Yes, it is possible. The two hidden angels can hardly remain hidden indefinitely if, as seems probable, some climax in the angels' affairs is fast approaching."

"What do you want from me?" Anatole asked her, uneasily.

She glanced briefly at the man on the other bed, smiling slightly. "I am a witch," she said. "What else should I want but to make a pact with you?" He knew that she must have chosen the word *pact* deliberately, to tease the priest, and that Ferigny must have known it too.

"What do you offer?" asked Anatole. "And what do you want in return?"

"I offer you life, and freedom from pain, at least for a while," she replied, succinctly. "In return ... I want you to consent, now, to grant a single request which I will one day make of you—whatever that request might be and whenever it might be made."

"You ask me to consent to something without knowing what it is?" he said, frowning. "To sign a promissory note which might be applied to any commission whatsoever?"

"Certainly," she said. "What I offer you is a chance to live, when otherwise you might have none. Asmodeus will probably destroy you if I leave you to his care, and not cleanly. Is any price too high to pay for the avoidance of that fate?"

"Yes," interposed the priest. "There *is* a price too high."

"A *chance* to live," Anatole echoed, warily, "and freedom from pain *for a while.* You are not over generous."

"You are a soldier," she said. "You understand the nature of alliances. A bargain made with me is made with me alone. I can help you to escape from Asmodeus, but if he chooses to pursue you, I cannot prevent him. All I can possibly offer you is a *chance* to live. I cannot offer unlimited future protection from Zelophelon's agents—or, for that matter, from German bullets—but a chance is better than nothing. Asmodeus will certainly want to make an example of you, when he tires of his torture games. He is, at heart, a simple man with a limited imagination. The Maid of Orléans might come to save you again, of course, given that she seems to intend that you should search out David Lydyard ... but I do not know how much trust you ought to put in her. To win my help, you only have to promise to grant me a single wish." She was taunting him as well as tempting him, and he wondered whether she might have dealt more pleasantly with him had he not refused to tell her what she wanted to know. He had an uncomfortable feeling that if he gave her the promise she desired she might not settle for anything as simple as the betrayal of a message that had been entrusted to him.

"I thought that witches were the ones who offered to grant the wishes of ordinary men," he said, sarcastically. "I never heard of one who demanded the right to have a wish granted."

"I only ask for one," she said, unsmilingly. "The traditional three smacks of reckless greed."

"This is no mere jest," said the priest, ominously. "Do not let her make light of it."

"But I must ask for two," Anatole countered, thinking that if the mad game had to be played, he might as well make his authority felt.

"What do you mean?" she asked. She was obviously unable to read *all* his thoughts.

"You must give Ferigny the chance to escape too," he said. "I will not go if it means leaving another man here."

"No!" said the priest. His anguish seemed sincere. "I will not see my freedom bought at such a price. I refuse!"

The woman laughed. "Done!" she said, with a promptness which made Anatole think that he had not made the bargain hard enough.

The priest groaned.

"I still have a broken leg, my lady," said Anatole. "Can you heal the splintered bone as easily as you stopped the ache in my head? And the priest's wounds too, of course."

The witch moved a little further into the room, and leaned over to place her hands upon his injured leg. Although she was kneading the flesh and moving the ends of the broken femur he felt no pain. She worked for a minute or more before straightening up. He did not feel the ends of the bone meet, let alone knit, but when he tried to move his leg he found that he could. He breathed deeply while she placed her hands upon his breast; again he felt no pain as her hands roamed, not too delicately, about his torso. He could not feel the bones becoming whole, but he did not doubt that they had.

"You have such gifts," he muttered, in annoyance, "and yet you league yourself with murderers, hatching vile plots. If you could turn this talent to a *good* cause ..."

"Do not mistake me for a human," she said, speaking more coldly than she had before. "I do this for my own advantage; it is no part of my life's mission to haunt the hospitals of Paris, or to raise the dead who have fallen on the battlefields of Europe.''

She turned to the priest, and threw to the floor the blanket which had been covering him. Anatole sat up, extremely glad to be able to do so. He was anxious to watch the effect of her touch on the savage wounds left in the man's wrists and ankles by the huge nails. The priest could not draw away from her. She took his wrists in her two hands, and held them up while she looked back at Anatole.

"I promised the opportunity of escape," she said. "Once he is whole, he has it. If he refuses to move, it does not affect our bargain.''

When she released the thin man's hands, the wounds in his wrists were gone, save for faint scars. She moved immediately to his ankles.

If all this is real, Anatole thought, *then what we fighting men have done in the battle lines these last four years has been a farce! All the wounds we have taken, all those that we have inflicted . . . none of it was necessary. The dead could have been made to walk again, as Asmodeus was; every dreadful injury could simply have been undone. If only we had the trick of it. There are angels and witches in the world, which have the power to work miracles—but what do they do with that power? They send forth men like Asmodeus, to say to the fathers of little children, "Give us your lambs to be slaughtered, as evidence of your faith in our power!" They make tantalizing pacts, bartering their favors for unspecified future advantages. What kind of beings are these, that care so little for their fellow creatures?*

Even as he voiced the thoughts, his mind conjured up replies. He had been eighteen months on the Western Front, and knew that men did not hesitate to inflict death and horrific injury on their fellows, while quite convinced that death was eternal and severe injury irreparable. Even if there had been no wars, would there not still be slaughterhouses and prisons, factories and mines?

While the witch soothed away the gaping holes that had been torn in the priest's feet as he struggled to raise himself while hanging on the cross, Anatole began to see the import of her words. *Do not mistake me for a human,* she had said—but he had. He had not been able to look beyond her appearance, although he knew it to be deceptive. He had not been able to exercise his imagination upon the problem of what she truly was, and what Asmodeus might be, and what the *beings* which empowered them both might be.

He began to see why it was that the crucified priest had clung so desperately hard to his optimistic faith that these beings, despite their power, were unimportant in the true scheme of things. *If this is the true nature of the world in which we live,* he thought, *perhaps we need a redeemer after all.*

It was a terrible thought for an atheist like himself to entertain.

The witch brought the priest upright, to demonstrate that he could stand on his two feet. "You have no power over me," the priest said, with a sob in his voice. "I am not to be tempted by gifts of the Devil. I promise you nothing, save that I will do all that is in my power to save this man's soul, and cheat you of your prize."

She laughed. "Had I a creator as deceptive as the one you have chosen to worship," she said, "I would be an unfortunate creature indeed."

10

The corridor outside the cell was empty, but the witch blocked the passage which led to the room to which Anatole had earlier been taken. "Go that way," she said, pointing in the opposite direction, to a narrow downward flight of steps. "In the wall of one of the deeper cellars they have made a passageway into the sewer which runs beneath the house; they use it to dispose of things they had rather not discover to the world above. If you try to go up through the house you will surely be seen, but the sewer should provide an avenue of escape."

"You might protect us with witchery," Anatole said sharply. "Could you not blind them to our passage, if you cannot simply spirit us away?"

"Miracles are not worked without cost," she answered flatly. "Magic requires cleverness, and effort. When an effect can be achieved without disruption of the ordinary course of events it is reckless to waste soul-warmth. I have kept my part of the bargain well enough."

"Oh my son!" said the priest, clutching at his arm. "You do not begin to understand what you have done. She did not promise you escape; she promised you a *chance*. She has already betrayed you."

Anatole narrowed his eyes as he looked at the complacent features of the woman. She stood quite at ease, waiting for them to go.

"I doubt that," said Anatole. "She needs me alive, if I am ever to make good my promise—and I will make sure that we both win free, or die in the attempt."

The priest shook his head, but even as he dismissed the objection he was urging his companion to proceed in the direction the woman had indicated. "Go, then!" was all he said.

Anatole realized, with a sinking heart, that what he had said must not be as obvious as he had thought. Perhaps, after all, it did not matter overmuch to the witch-woman whether he escaped or not. Now that he was in her power, committed to her cause, even death might not put an end to their contract. Had he not been repeatedly assured that in the affairs of these mysterious angels, death was *not* an end? He went back into the cell in order to take the two candles from their brackets. The priest and he had no trays in which to carry them, but Anatole found a piece of rag to wrap around his hand, protecting it from spilled wax. He was still wearing his uniform, but the priest had only the loincloth which he had worn while he was fixed upon the cross. Anatole picked up the blanket from the priest's bunk and wrapped it about the man's scrawny shoulders.

"Can you move quickly?" he said. "More to the point, do you know of any place where we might find effective sanctuary?"

"There is no sanctuary for those who have sold their souls to the Devil," Father Ferigny replied, unhelpfully. "Go, I beg of you, while we still can!"

They moved off together. As they began the descent Anatole glanced back to see if the woman was still watching them, but they had brought the light with them, and the gloom had already swallowed her up. Already Anatole's mind was crowded with questions he had not asked, mysteries he had not begun to penetrate.

They found the entrance into the sewer easily enough, and squeezed through it without difficulty. Anatole did not pause to wonder why the Satanists had thought it desirable to make the opening, or what they usually cast through the hole. The water in the sewer was not deep, although it was all the fouler for its shallowness, but long months in the trenches had inured Anatole to all kinds of filth, and the priest did not seem overly fastidious.

They had not gone a hundred meters, though, before they heard the sound of pursuit. They had turned corners enough for their lights to be invisible but it was difficult to move on without making so much noise as to signal their position.

"Curse her!" said Anatole. "Surely she could have won us more time!"

"Did you expect fair dealing?" asked the priest. His voice was still uncomfortably hoarse; the wounds in his wrists and feet had been healed but his throat had not been properly eased. "She told

you herself that she has no compunction at all. She is playing a game
with us, Monsieur Daumier, and Asmodeus is another player—or
pawn—in the same diabolical game.''

It was evident that they must outrun their pursuers if they could,
or hide if they could not. Anatole looked about for a way up to the
surface, but could find none nearby. "Keep going!'' he urged, as his
companion faltered. "Whether or not you have the information that
Asmodeus wants, they will certainly murder you in trying to get it.
Or was the witch right about your enthusiasm to be a martyr?''

Ferigny did not answer immediately. Anatole forged ahead,
wishing that he might go even faster. The priest was trying as
hard as he could to keep up, but he was by no means a strongly
built man and he was inconveniently dressed. Anatole wondered
whether it had been altogether wise to insist that the two of them
must join forces.

"It will have been no bad thing to have been a martyr,'' the
priest said, eventually, breathing meanwhile in an awkwardly labored
fashion, "when all men stand before the seat of judgment.''

"But no good thing, perhaps, to have been a heretic,'' Anatole
retorted. The filthy water had filled his boots and soaked his socks.
His legs felt heavy, but he forced them on, grateful for every intersec-
tion they came to, at which their pursuers might have to hesitate. He
had ceased to take account of direction—his main hope was that
their pursuers might lose themselves in the maze.

"The only unforgivable heresy is diabolism,'' countered the priest,
"and I owe no debt to the Devil, even though I have accepted
your help.''

Nor do I, Anatole thought, *for it was a bargain wrought under
sore duress. Anyhow, she did not let me go because she needed
or believed my promise; there is some resentment between her and
Asmodeus. Asmodeus thought that it might be her who had sent me
to kill him, and it seems that she has little sympathy with his ambitions or his methods. The priest would doubtless count all that decep-
tion, or the petty squabbling of quarrelsome imps, but even if I must
accept that the world lies under the dominion of supernatural things,
that is no reason to embrace his religion. He sees the world through
the lenses of his faith, and fits everything to his axioms. I must not
do that; if I am to understand what has befallen me I must doubt
everything except my own experience, and even that I must not take
too much for granted.*

The sound of splashing feet grew louder. Their pursuers were gain-ing, and could not be far behind. The sewers were not mazy enough; there were too few opportunities for them to take a wrong turn. Anatole and his companion were slowing down with every step they took. It was not entirely the priest's fault; Anatole was whole now, but he was extremely tired, and his head was beginning to ache again.

"Damn her to Hell!" he muttered aloud. "This was but half a chance, if that. I should have asked for better guarantees."

They were in a long tunnel now, downwardly inclined but otherwise straight. The water was very sluggish in its flow, and it was deepening every step of the way. When Anatole looked back he saw the lights carried by Asmodeus's men for the first time: they were bright lanterns, not pitiful candles. Their pursuers were still in shallower water and were catching up with every stride they took. The drag about Anatole's calves was brutal enough to make him wonder whether there were imps in the water snatching at his legs, determined to slow him down.

Where is my guardian angel? he complained, no longer knowing or caring what kind of angel it was whose absence he regretted.

The priest's candle had burned so low that he could no longer hold it in his naked hand, but instead of dropping it into the water Ferigny took care to set it down on a narrow ledge which ran along the left-hand wall of the tunnel, where its light continued to flicker. The two of them went on, leaving it behind.

"We *must* get up to the surface," Anatole said, breathlessly—but there was no obvious way to do that, and even as he finished speaking a gunshot rang out. The noise was multiplied as it echoed from the walls. The bullet went wide, but the fact that it had been fired provided disturbing evidence of their pursuers' intent. They obviously had no orders to capture their prey intact. Anatole instantly abandoned his own candle, setting it aside exactly as the priest had set his before rushing on into the darkness—but it was hard to rush now that the sticky stream was about his thighs, and he was uncomfortably aware of the fact that he had never learned to swim.

Because it was so difficult to move quickly against the cold drag of the water, and because he was so much younger and stronger, Anatole soon drew ahead of the floundering priest. He was desperate to reach and turn another corner, to get out of range of the pistolier as well as out of his sight—but then he stumbled over something massive and unseen, and fell full length into the foul water. He floundered, thinking for a moment or two that his head would go under, but then his feet found bottom again, and his groping hand met the wall. He managed, somehow, to right himself.

The priest was beside him in a matter of seconds, helping him to haul himself upright, but Anatole, drenched and stinking as he was, could no longer imagine that they would be able to attain their objective. Nor could he imagine that they had any chance at all of fighting off the men who were chasing them. Their pursuers had not yet drawn level with the first of the two abandoned candles but he could count their lanterns now. There were three. He knew that there must be more men than that—perhaps five or six.

As the two of them staggered on, trying with all their might to accelerate their pace in spite of the fact that they could no longer see their way, Anatole felt his heart pounding madly, and his head too. He felt strangely dizzy, as though he were once again in danger of stepping outside the mainstream of events into some crazy half-world. He had grabbed the arm of the priest to make sure that they stayed together, and had drawn far enough ahead to be pulling the other along—but as another shot rang out he felt Ferigny's body hurled forward by the impact.

Half-turning, he caught the older man as he fell, and instantly picked him up, cradling him in his arms as he exerted all his strength in the attempt to stumble on.

The priest made no sound at all; the scream which suddenly rent the air was not his.

Anatole spun around, not so much in astonishment as because he felt that he could go no further; the scream offered him an excuse to halt, and he took it reflexively.

He looked back at the bobbing lanterns, which had been moved to an astonishing agitation. They were no longer coming forward, and one smashed against the tunnel wall, spilling burning oil over the bricks and on to the surface of the turgid stream. Anatole could not make out the shadows of the men who held the remaining lanterns, or those of their companions; everything seemed to have dissolved into a chaos of violence. The first scream was not the last by any means, and the tenor of the screams told Anatole that whatever had attacked the men—presumably from the rear—was as fearful to them as the huge demon which had seized him in the church.

Has the witch kept her bargain after all? he wondered. *Has she sent some imp to cover our escape?*

The priest stirred in his arms, and put a hand up to grip Anatole's shoulder. Anatole was glad to have evidence that the man was not dead. He moved sideways to slump against the wall of the passage, breathing deeply. He heard splashing sounds as one or more of his pursuers was bowled over, cast down into the filthy stream. Another shot rang out, and then a fourth, but no more; the pistolier must have been struck down before emptying his weapon.

The sounds of hand-to-hand fighting continued, but there was no more gunfire. All three lanterns had gone out now, and the burning oil was producing far more smoke than light. The two candle flames which still burned on the ledge at the farther side of the tunnel were far too weak to cast any useful illumination upon the battle.

The shouting continued for a while, but then died. As the last echoes faded, leaving an ominous silence to compound the darkness, Anatole found time to wonder whether whatever unexpected force had attacked his pursuers would be inclined to treat him any more benignly.

Anatole let his body crumple slowly against the slimy wall, and he set the priest down as gently as he could.

"Can you stand?" he whispered, wishing that the words did not seem quite so loud.

"I think so," Ferigny answered. "The shot . . . my back."

Anatole knew better than to grope with his hands for the wound the bullet had made. *In a minute,* he said to himself, *I will walk back to recover one of the candles, that we might have its benefit while it lasts.*

Only the nearer one of the two candles was still burning. It was less than a dozen meters away, its wan yellow light reflecting eerily from the sluggishly moving surface of the murky stream which flowed constantly past its station.

Because it was the only thing he could see, Anatole fixed his eyes on that uncertain patch of light, and began to move toward it. *Have I reached the end of my strength so soon?* he thought.

He was only half a dozen steps away from the candle when the head of an animal floated into view at the far end of the lighted slick.

At first he thought the beast was dead, but then he saw that it was trying desperately hard to keep its head out of the water. It was a huge dog, and his first thought was that it must have been brought by his pursuers to track the fugitives—but there was blood on its jaws. He reached out immediately, intending to help the beast if he could. It was an unwieldy creature, and he could not pick it up in the way he had picked up the priest, although it certainly weighed no more than Ferigny. Once he had his arms around its body, though, he could at least keep its head well above the water.

Anatole knew as soon as he embraced the creature that it was badly hurt, and deduced that at least one of the last two bullets fired by the gunman must have struck its target at point-blank range. Even so, the beast had followed through with its purpose. No one had emerged from the gloom to chase it.

After a brief pause, Anatole made a supreme effort to lift the creature out of the stream, and finally managed to do it. The candlelight showed him that a bullet had gone into its belly just below the ribcage and had gone clean through, ripping out a terrible exit wound beside the spine. Blood was still gushing from the wound, and there could be no doubt at all that the animal was dying. Anatole looked into the darkness whence it had come, but there was nothing to be seen or heard. If any of the pursuers was still alive, he was not moving.

Anatole lifted the dog a little higher, and looked down into its eyes. He could feel its panting breath on his face. Its features were blurred; some unnatural kind of change was overtaking them.

So inured was he by now to the marvelous and the miraculous that there was never any chance of Anatole's losing his grip on the beast. As the weight distribution of the body which he held shifted, almost as if its flesh had become fluid, he simply adjusted his hold upon it. Long before the transformation was complete he knew that what he had held was a wolf, and that what he would end up holding was a naked woman.

She had pale skin and flowing blonde hair. She must have been very beautiful when she was younger, but she was old now. Oddly enough, that astonished him more than the fact of the transformation. Somehow, one did not expect werewolves to be middle-aged.

The wounds in her torso were no longer bleeding, but they were as bad as they had been before. The entry wound was above and to the left of her navel; he was holding her in such a fashion that he could only see the edge of the larger and uglier hole in her back. She was already near to death but her lips were moving even as they formed, with the urgency of communicating something.

"Siri," she said. "I am Siri ... If you can ... tell Mandorla ... where my body lies ..."

She spoke in English. The witch had mentioned the werewolves of London, and Asmodeus had spoken the name Mandorla. The web of his delirium seemed to be enfolding him ever more tightly, but he was calm and composed. He was a machine, and it no longer mattered whether the things that happened to him made sense or not.

"Yes," he said, feeling a compassionate compulsion to ease her last few moments. "If I can, I will."

Did she really rip the throats out of five or more men in a matter of seconds? he wondered. *Werewolves must be very artful in the business of murder . . . but for them too, I suppose, death is but a temporary interruption of a never-ending destiny.*

He contrived to take up the candle again, although it was by no means easy while he had the dead weight of the woman's body in his arms. Then he carried his burden back to the place where the priest waited.

Father Ferigny's wound was not as bad as the werewolf's, but it seemed likely to be mortal. The bullet had hit him near the shoulder. It had smashed the scapula and passed through the wall of the pleural cavity, which was slowly filling up with blood. The priest could hardly breathe, but he too had a message to impart, and no time to listen to Anatole's account of the peculiar nature of their saviour. Ferigny was uncannily steady and controlled, as if the certainty of his impending martyrdom had given him an abundance of inner strength.

"The book," he whispered, very faintly, "is hidden beneath the floor of an attic room . . . at thirteen, rue Marcassin. Take it, if you can and if you will, to the London house of my Order. It is in Wheel Street, in Bromley-by-Bow."

Anatole could not resist the temptation to say: "Why tell me? Am I not possessed by the Devil?"

Ferigny did not try to smile. "You asked the witch for my freedom," he said, very faintly. "That is how I would have used it. The members of the London house know David Lydyard; they can tell you where to find him."

The name Lydyard was more firmly fixed in Anatole's memory than any other. Somehow, the fact that the priest knew his name, just as the witch-woman had, did not surprise him in the least. *Do I really need to search out this man?* Anatole thought, ironically. *Destiny has made an appointment for me to meet him at World's End—how can I possibly avoid it?*

Nevertheless, he said: "I will do what I can." *For you,* he added silently, *for the creature which I hold in my arms, for the young Englishman who visited my dream, and for the Maid of Orléans— and perhaps, if ever she should ask me to redeem my promise, for the enigmatic witch. If I am to be a piece in this mad game, I might as well play my part as well as I am able. If this is real—and how can I possibly doubt it now?—there is surely no other game in all the world worth playing.*

His candle guttered suddenly, and went out, leaving him in total darkness.

First Interlude

The Age of Fool's Gold

After this I looked, and, behold, a door was opened in heaven: and the first voice which I heard was as if it were of a trumpet talking with me, which said, Come up hither, and I will shew thee things which must be hereafter.

Revelations 4:1

1

The Age of Gold was in the final phase of its languid decadence when Machalalel took it upon himself to educate his favorite sons in the ways of the common men in whose image they had been created. In order to do this he took them up to the crest of a high hill, from which they watched a little battle, in which a company of men drawn from farms and villages tried, unsuccessfully, to halt the murderous advance into their land of a tribe of marauding nomads.

At the end of the little battle some thirty-five or forty men lay dead, and a dozen horses with them. All but a few had first been felled by spears and arrows, but many of the defenders lay helpless and bleeding while the battle ran its course, until their victorious adversaries had the leisure to finish them off with swords and cudgels.

"This is the beginning of a war which will be long drawn out, although in essence it is already won and lost," Machalalel explained. "The loss of this battle by the tillers of the soil leaves the entire valley at the mercy of the invaders, who will advance across it, claiming for themselves whatever the farm folk leave behind when they flee. Any men who stay to defend what they held will be killed and their womenfolk made captive, either to be raped and killed or raped and enslaved.

"In time, however, the nomads will go on with their hungry herds, to afflict other valleys in other regions. Then, those who fled from their land will return, to begin the work of rebuilding their houses and replanting their fields. By hard labor and gradual accumulation they will replace all of their stolen wealth, and hold it safe until the nomads come again.

"There is a pattern of continual recurrence here, for the two ways of life which came into conflict here today are fundamentally opposed. There will always be crop growers who settle the land, and adapt it to their purposes; and there will always be herdsmen, who drive their animals from place to place in search of pasturage. It is in the nature of their way of life that crop growers should accumulate and hoard considerable wealth, and defend it with all their might. It is in the nature of *their* way of life that herdsmen should be rootless predators upon their own kind and plunderers of laid-up treasure. There will always be men of these two kinds, and all men will inherit one or the other inclination.

"In time, the crop growers will be the founders of cities and the builders of walls, while the herdsmen will be adventurers and conquerors, against whose assaults no walls can stand forever. As the numbers of men grow and grow, and as the strength of their labor becomes organized in greater and greater companies, the cities which contain them will grow larger, the walls which confine and protect them higher, and the destructive forces arrayed against them ever more ambitious and ever more powerful; and so the cycle of recurrence will become ever broader, ever more extravagant. With each turn of the great wheel, the defenses will become more difficult to overcome, and the forces of destruction more difficult to resist.

"That is the future history of the human race in a nutshell. I call the process of escalation which converts the cycle into an ascending spiral *progress*. Its primary products are armor and armaments, but it has some interesting by-products. Far the best of them, in my estimation, are curiosity, knowledge and the scientific method. Alas, these by-products have further by-products of their own which are worthless phantoms of the imagination: conceit, faith and dogmatism. By virtue of these complications, the path of progress will never be smooth, and human wisdom will be forever tripping over its own eager feet as it reaches out into the unknown."

Machalalel wore a semblance of human form at that time, in order that he might address his favorite sons face to face, but his handsome human face was merely a mask which hid his true nature. He did not condescend to divulge the reason for his intimate interest in humankind, or the significance of the lesson which he took such care to teach the creatures he had set to dwell among men.

One of the two pupils on the hill had been a wolf before he was remade in the image of a man; the other had been molded out of glutinous gray clay. Neither of these two knew what form Machalalel had worn before he adopted human form and gave himself a name, but each had a conceit of his own which he invented as a substitute for explanation.

Pelorus, who had been a wolf before Machalalel made him nine parts man, imagined the real Machalalel as the ultimate shapeshifter: a reservoir of raw, archetypal matter capable of projecting any appearance at all. The Clay Man, who knew well enough that his intelligence and sense of self were essentially intangible, arbitrarily imposed on a material matrix, imagined the real Machalalel as a kind of vast soul which existed outside and beyond matter, which might more realistically appear upon the earth as an infinitely glorious blaze of immaterial light.

While they descended from the hilltop to inspect the sad legacy of the battle at closer range, it happened that Pelorus and the Clay Man fell to arguing over this question, and Pelorus asked Machalalel to settle their dispute.

What Machalalel said in answer to this plea was: "All creatures are prisoners of their senses, which give them very limited intelligence of the world in which they live; none is created with the means to envisage or comprehend the real nature of its Creator. Perhaps none ever can; but who knows what cleverness *progress* might generate if only the continual cycle can sustain itself long enough? So long as the forces of destruction do not become so great as to break the great wheel and interrupt the ascending spiral, there remains a possibility that curiosity, knowledge and the scientific method will reveal the true history of the world, the true nature of the universe and the secret identity of the intelligences which shaped its evolution."

"But what will they see?" Pelorus asked, unsatisfied with the answer. "If creatures like these—like us—learn what their Creators are, what will they and we actually *see*?"

"I cannot tell you," Machalalel replied, "because I do not know myself. Creators have no eyes of their own with which to see their real selves. Only manlike creatures with manlike bodies and manlike senses can make mirrors with which to study their own appearances, and even they can only see their faces and not their souls. When Creators make eyes for themselves in order that they might look into mirrors, they can see nothing but their masks; they can no more see their true substance than they can see their souls. Behind this mask I wear there is no recognizable face."

"If we cannot ever see you," said the Clay Man bitterly, "how can we ever hope to comprehend what you are?"

"I cannot tell you that either," Machalalel said, sadly. "I can only suggest that you interest yourselves in the unfolding pattern of human progress. If some Creator was responsible for the quirk of *clinamen* which set in train the process that produced human beings from hairy apes, it was a clever trick. You might be witness to the forging of an instrument which will one day tell us all what we are and what we may become."

"On the evidence of this day's work," said Pelorus, surveying the bloody and broken bodies stretched out on the muddied ground, among which they had now arrived to stand, "the perfection of the instrument might take a long time."

"One thing which my kind have in abundance," said Machalalel, "if only they care to claim it by their quietude, is time. It is a gift I have granted to you both, in what I hope will be an adequate measure."

"Let us hope that time does not hang too heavily upon us," said the Clay Man. "If Pelorus is right, it might turn out to be as much a burden as a gift."

"It is a burden which *they* would have been very glad indeed to bear," answered Machalalel, pointing one by one at a few of the corpses which littered the field all around them. "If you grow impatient, you must do what you can to smooth the path of progress for the mortal beings who must lay it down, and exert your best efforts to sustain the spiraling ascent of human wisdom."

"Is that a suggestion, or a command?" asked the Clay Man sourly.

"It is a necessity," replied the angel.

2

Mandorla looked up into the human face which her Creator had chosen to wear. It was a handsome face, in a masculine sort of way, with its jutting jaw and its craggy cheekbones, its thick, high arched eyebrows and its pointed beard. It looked back at her with approval, perhaps even a hint of affection.

This human form which he gave me was designed to delight his eye, she mused. *Because he chose that the desires of his own eyes should be male; males being the active and powerful sex among humans, he naturally chose a female wolf to be the object of desire, even though it is the females among wolves who lead and govern packs. I suppose it is in the nature of Creators that they should order things in such a way that creatures must look up at them—but it ought to be in the nature of all creatures to resent the fact.*

Machalalel's mask was more beautiful, after its fashion, than any actual human face. Its skin was smoother and more evenly colored; its features were more symmetrical; the gaze of its eyes was more commanding. But Mandorla, who had looked into mirrors with her human eyes, knew that her own human face was more beautiful still, after a fashion which permitted the female greater beauty than the male. She was no more grateful for this gift than she was for any of the others he had bestowed upon her.

"I do not understand," she said to her Creator bitterly, "why you created me at all. Your favorites are your sons; it is to them that you address your questions and explain your hopes, and it is their cooperation you seek in your perverse quest for self-knowledge. Why did you take the female cubs from my mother's litter as well as the male? Why did you extend your curse to my sisters and myself?''

Machalalel smiled at her, indulgently. ''You would have been lonely, little wolfling,''' he says, ''had I taken all your brothers and left you with no company but your sisters. And your brothers would have been lonely too.''

What about you? asked Mandorla silently. *Would you have been lonely too? And if so, why should you not say so, vain deceiver?* Aloud, she said: ''But you have not made a woman of clay, to keep the Clay Man company. It seems to me that you apply your principles of fairness rather haphazardly.''

''The Clay Man is fully human, at least in his appearance,'' Machalalel said negligently. ''He may seek solace in the company of human women. Pelorus and his brothers, on the other hand, are wolves at heart and will always remain so; although they may consort with human women when the whim takes them, the wolf in them will need a certain recompense.''

''And is that my function—the reason for my being? I am *recompense!*''

Machalalel seemed amused by her annoyance. ''And beauty too,'' he added, with an ironic smile upon his full and handsome lips as he spoke in carefully honeyed tones. ''For Creators, beauty is its own justification, and needs no utilitarian purpose.''

''If you think that a creature such as I could be content with that,'' Mandorla told him, mocking by mimicry that ironic smile, and speaking in tones more honeyed and silken than her Creator's human voice could ever achieve, ''you are mistaken.''

''Contentment,'' said Machalalel, ''has never been one of my goals, for myself or my creatures.''

''Your goals are no concern of mine,'' she retorted. ''Among wolves, it is a female who is the heart and mind of the pack. It is *my* will, not yours, that will determine what the pack becomes. I shall not prostitute myself or my sisters to your plans and your purposes; I shall find goals of my own, and if I choose to place contentment high among them, I shall.''

''You will doubtless find your own amusements,'' Machalalel observed unrepentantly. ''It is of little consequence what they are. But in any contest of *will*, you are bound to lose. Whichever is the best of the pack will hear my will, and be bound by it forever—and you will never be able to set that will aside, no matter how you try. In the end, you cannot help but serve my plans and my purposes, for you are and always will be *my* creature."

"I may be a creature reshaped by you," Mandorla said, her defiance becoming fiercer by the minute, "but I am a true wolf at heart, and the moment my remaking was done I became my own creature again. Whatever I do with the eternal life which you have forced upon me I will *never* serve your plans and purposes, and I swear that I will strive to the utmost to undo whatever will it is that you bind into the unluckiest of my brothers."

"How well I did my work!" Machalalel said, oblivious to the insult he offered her. "How very *beautiful* your anger is! What a delight to the human eye! Be angry often, Mandorla, and be beautiful always. You will never lack for human love."

"Love! Do you think I want *human love*? I am a wolf, Machalalel, no matter how your interfering hand has polluted my soul. I am a wolf, with a wolf's desires and a wolf's needs, and I will keep and treasure those desires and needs through all eternity, if necessary. I do not want human beauty and I do not want human love. I want the pure joy of the hunter in the hunt, the unalloyed triumph of the killer at the kill. You may order things so that I must look up into your face, but you cannot make me call you *master*."

"I would not wish it," he assured her. "I make creatures, not slaves. I make creatures which are ambitious to be other and better than what I have made of them. I make creatures who have some power to remake themselves. Even so, I make them with certain goals in mind—goals which I could never achieve unaided. What, otherwise, would be the point of Creation?"

What could Mandorla do but turn away to hide the face of her fury? What could she do but resolve to keep the promises she made in anger, and to do her utmost to undo the will of Machalalel, whose instrument would be the best of all her brothers and lovers? What could she do but determine to discover her own purposes, her own ambitions, her own ways of dealing with the world of men?

She turned away from her Creator, therefore, and never again consented to look up into his loving mask.

Even as she turned away, though, and forever afterward, she was haunted by a dark and dire thought. What if Machalalel were playing with her? What if her reaction were exactly the response he intended to produce? What if his negligent contempt were merely one more in the infinite series of his masks? What if his true and secret purpose were to make her into the defiant rebel she was now determined to make of herself?

Of all the unforgettable words which he had spoken to her, one taunting sentence in particular burned in her memory like a tormenting puzzle: *In the end, you know, you cannot help but serve my plans and my purposes, for you are and always will be my creature.* How was she ever to know, even ''in the end,'' exactly what that purpose was, and exactly what she must do and be in order to refuse to serve it?

Mendorla knew even then in her secret heart, and knew throughout the long millennia which followed as the Age of Gold gave way to the Age of Heroes and the Age of Heroes to the Age of Iron, that she simply did not know why she had been made, or what she truly was, or what she might become. Machalalel, the not-so-vain deceiver, had certainly told her lies aplenty, and in so doing had kept the truth of the matter very carefully hidden.

3

"There is no more interesting creature in all the world than man," Machalalel told his favorite creatures, as the process of their education extended toward the end of its first, painstakingly didactic, phase. "Man's is a slow method of discovery, but a rewarding one. The mills of his wisdom grind slowly, but they grind exceeding small."

"But his life is nasty, brutish and short," objected the Clay Man, "and he is perpetually at war with his fellows. Whatever dreams he claims, there is something in his baser nature which craves self-destruction."

"Cruelty, brutality and brevity are subjective," said Pelorus. "Men might judge the life of a wolf nasty, brutish and short, but the lucky wolf who has never known human intelligence is possessed by a wondrous joy and sense of rightness which is utterly uncorrupted by any awareness of death or empathy with the misery of other creatures. I dare say that the life of the Creators themselves might seem nasty enough, brutish enough and short enough to some higher being."

"It might," said Machalalel, with a bleak sigh. "And perhaps to lesser beings too, had they only better eyes to see with, or better minds to imagine with. Sometimes, I think the world of men is a curious kind of shadow-play, a theater in which the Creators might see allegories of their own existence. Sometimes, I think the entire universe of matter might be simply a reflection of the reality in which angels live—a dim and murky reflection, to be sure, but a reflection nevertheless."

"Like those masks that some tribesmen wear," suggested the Clay

Man, "which are huge and garish, and make them seem twice as tall and twice as fearsome as they really are."

"They make those huge masks to simulate their gods," Pelorus commented. "Little do they know that their gods must make little masks to simulate humanity, in order to inhabit and see the world of matter."

"Little is all they do know," observed the Clay Man. "There are ten thousand tribes, each with its own gods, its own image of the world, its own account of Creation; but what do they truly *know*, outside the making of a few primitive tools and implements, and the domestication of a handful of plant and animal species?"

"Almost nothing," Pelorus agreed, "except for ten thousand different ways of killing one another."

"There are some of the tribes of men," Machalalel pointed out, "which have discovered concepts of honor and fairness. They have begun to regulate and control their internecine fighting by strict rules."

"Rules can make little difference, however strict," Pelorus said. "In fighting, the strong win and the weak perish."

"The observance of rules usually serves to *ensure* that result," the Clay Man observed, "by carefully excluding the kind of cunning tricks which may enable the weak sometimes to take the strong unawares. Human laws invariably forbid the weak to murder the strong while they sleep, or to kill them with sly poisons. Laws are for the protection of the strong."

"It is by no means so simple," Machalalel objected. "Rules and laws are fascinating things, which often have a logic of their own. Sometimes, the manner of their working out is not exactly what was intended or expected." He waited for his pupils to demand an example, but they showed not the slightest interest in following his chain of reasoning further. In the end, he shrugged his broad shoulders and went on anyway.

"Imagine," he said, "a tribe in which disputes are settled by the casting of javelins. Whenever two men enter into a formal duel, they must draw lots to decide who makes the first cast; if the better man loses he must survive his opponent's first throw before making his own. The rule ensures that the weaker man always has a chance of victory."

"Not as good a chance as he would have if, knowing himself the less accurate thrower, he decided to stab his enemy in the back instead of fighting a formal duel," said the Clay Man.

"The better thrower always has the better chance," Pelorus observed. "If the drawing of lots is honest he has an equal chance of being allowed to throw first. He is more likely than his opponent to make his throw count if he does take his turn first, and more likely than his opponent to survive if he does not."

"Quite so," agreed the Clay Man. "None but a reckless man would go into such a fight against a better opponent, even if he had an even chance of winning first throw."

"But suppose," Machalalel said, carefully, "that there were *three* combatants instead of two. Each would have an equal chance of being allotted the first throw, but each would then have to decide which of his opponents to aim at. The best thrower would doubtless aim at the second best, and the second best at the best. Neither would take aim at the weakest until the stronger of his two opponents had been slain, but once a killing blow had been struck the next man to take his turn would be the man who had not struck it. The weakest of the three, if he had any sense at all, would not try to kill either of his opponents even if he drew the first shot; he would wait until one of his opponents killed the other, and take his own throw next as a matter of right. In such a contest the weakest thrower would be the most likely to win."

"It is an amusing prospect," admitted Pelorus, "but I cannot believe that there is any human tribe which regularly stages three-cornered duels governed by such silly rules."

The Clay Man was more intrigued. Of the two, he was more ready to begin the second, heuristic, phase of his education. "The rules of engagement are of no particular significance if there are three combatants rather than two," he pointed out. "Whether there is to be a predetermined order of throwing or not, the situation remains the same. The two strongest contenders must each attack their more dangerous opponent first—which is to say, they must attack one other. The weakest of three contenders can always stand aside until one of the others is struck down—and then, if he is quick enough, will always be able to strike at his surviving opponent before the other is fully recovered. In a three-sided conflict, the advantage would always lie with the weakest combatant, would it not?"

Machalalel smiled.

"That cannot be true," said Pelorus, frowning. "It makes no sense."

"On the contrary," replied the Clay Man. "It makes perfect sense—always provided, of course, that the combatants know who among them is the weakest. An even greater advantage would be possessed by one whose opponents *believed* him to be weak, but was in fact strong.''

"Suppose," said Machalalel, "that there were more than three combatants. Suppose that there were four."

"That is much more difficult," said the Clay Man, after a pause for thought. "While the first and second strongest attacked one another, the third strongest would presumably have to attack the weakest . . . but then, no one would have the advantage of standing by, ready to strike as soon as one opponent struck another down. I cannot see who would be most likely to emerge victorious from *that* situation, rules or no rules. But if there were *five,* the advantage would surely swing again to the weakest, who would not come under attack . . . it might make a considerable difference, might it not, whether the number of combatants were even or odd?''

"Yes it might," Machalalel agreed. "And if *five* is an interesting number, think how much more intriguing *seven* might be. Is it possible, do you think, that the *weakest* of seven might actually be the likeliest to survive a war of all against all?''

"No," said Pelorus. "I cannot believe it. And in any case, I cannot imagine any such situation, whether it involved human individuals or whole human tribes."

"I believe he might," the Clay Man said to Machalalel, disregarding his friend's dismissal. He nodded his head thoughtfully. "I really believe he might."

"Except, of course," Machalalel pointed out, "that if there were seven combatants, the temptation to make *pacts* would be very strong, and that would introduce a further dimension of complexity. Much would depend on who entered into alliance with whom . . . and at what point the partners in any such treaty would choose to betray one another. Do you think, taking *everything* into consideration, that the weakest of seven might still stand a chance?''

"No," said Pelorus.

"Oh yes," said the Clay Man. "A chance, certainly. But the best chance of all would surely fall to the *cleverest,* provided that he could delude the others as to the truth of his strength and the value of his friendship."

"That was my conclusion too," said Machalalel, proudly. "That *is* my conclusion."

"An entirely pointless conclusion," said Pelorus, tiredly, "given that there is no real situation to which it could possibly apply."

"In time," the Clay Man said, "the ever-changing human world might throw up all manner of strange situations. And if, as Machalalel says, the human world is a kind of shadow-play, murkily reflecting another ... should we be overly hasty in judging the relevance of this little flight of fancy?"

The Clay Man looked up at his Creator then, expecting praise for his cleverness; but Machalalel was lost in thought.

"If only there were rules," Machalalel said, more to himself than his companions. "If only there were laws. Or, if there *are* rules and laws, if only it were possible to find out what they are! Then, the battle might not be to the strong, nor even the race to the swift."

"I know which I'd support if I had the choice," said Pelorus, cynically.

"You don't," said Machalalel, coldly, "and you never shall."

Part Two
In No-Man's-Land

And the stars of heaven fell unto the earth, even as a fig tree casteth her untimely figs, when she is shaken by a mighty wind.

And the heaven departed as a scroll when it is rolled together; and every mountain and island were moved out of their places.

And the kings of the earth, and the great men, and the rich men, and the chief captains, and the mighty men, and every bondsman, and every free man, hid themselves in the dens and in the rocks of the mountains;

And said to the mountains and rocks, Fall on us, and hide us from the face of him that sitteth on the throne, and from the wrath of the Lamb;

For the great day of his wrath is come; and who shall be able to stand?

Revelations 6:13–17

1

David Lydyard no longer dreamed of the guardian angel which he had once identified with the goddess Bast; he had seen none of her many faces in five-and-twenty years. Nor did his dreams any longer allow him to share the private thoughts of others. He was tempted to conclude from this that the angel, having no further use for him, had set him free to live as other men lived and to dream as other men dreamed, but he could not be sure. Once a man has found revelations in his dreams he can never cease to search for them, and David still dreamed. He required no angelic inspiration to carry forward the various dream-odysseys and dream-images which had begun in his first delirium, when he was bitten by a snake in Egypt.

In David's recent dreams, Satan lay crucified upon the floor of the seventh and ultimate circle of the Inferno which is Creation. No molten magma burst from the surface beneath him to blister and burn his back; here was nothing but an infinite field of deep-laid, translucent ice whose dire and dreadful chill had long since seeped into every corner of his being to freeze the blood within his veins and extirpate the warmth of his heart. Only his soul was denied the implacable grip of the ice, and the feverish appetite of his soul was made all the more avid by the frigidity of his flesh.

At one time this particular arena of David's dreams had been reserved to the *vargr*-folk: the restless ones; the wolves accursed by Machalalel. In recent years, however, the wolves had learned too well to wear the mask of humankind. In David's dreams their howling was mournful still, but they no longer mourned their consciousness of their identity and their immortality. This was not because they had

107

learned wisdom, but because they had learned *hope*. Theirs was now the subtler torment of Tantalus or of Prometheus. David-as-Satan had changed places with them, having been condemned to know at least a few of the secrets of eternity, and hence to stare interminably into an infinite black sky whose countless stars formed only the *illusion* of the face of the ultimate Creator.

Sometimes, even now, David-as-Satan's imagination drew that Face from the formless cataract of light, in order to study its particular sadness and its unique sorrow: the pitiful gaze of Divine Impotence. David had long known how fruitless it was to look for a God outside and beyond the cosmos, when all the gods there were or ever could be dwelt within it, woven into its fabric, part and parcel of its form; and yet, how could the eye of a *human* being—for Satan inevitably made himself in his own image, however contorted—do anything other than search for some ultimate order in that glorious confusion? He knew too well that the nature of the mindful eye requires it to search, and hence to find; he knew too well that sight is action, not reflection. For that reason, and for that reason alone, the Satan of David's dreams sometimes saw the imaginary God which made the angels, mirrorless and desolate, utterly lonely and utterly lost.

David's Satan had been beautiful once, believing himself to be an Angel and thus entitled to beauty if not to truth, but he knew nowadays that he was only a man, albeit without the consolation of mortality, and he knew that he was neither beautiful, nor young, nor party to the truth of things. He was pale, shriveled and innocent; but he knew that the corruption which worked within him had no vestige of a beginning, no prospect of an end. He knew, in spite of his innocence, that he had begun to die even before he was born, and that his unconcluded dying would last—alas!—forever. Once, the earth had hung above his station, cocooned and haloed with a cool and comforting darkness which shielded it from the fiery fury of the sky; but now he could not see the earth at all, lost as it was in that incalculably vast wilderness of stars, and he knew that the darkness which clothed it was no longer a shield but a confining cage. His repentance and regret were meaningless now, for his right arm was no longer capable of reaching out, and he would not have known where to direct it if it could. The disease of damnation was beyond treatment or cure, amenable to amelioration or to anesthesia.

Once, in his vanity, David's Satan had dreamed that there was another in his Private Hell, who could and might reach down to free his redeeming hand, and bring it to the earth, so that the work of healing might at least begin and deliverance from evil might at least become conceivable. It had not been *only* a dream; but it had nevertheless been a dream that died, or had been murdered, and it was impossible now for him to believe in its resurrection, for he had lost his faith. David-as-Satan, who had seen the face and served the purpose of a true and actual god, had lost his faith in humankind and human kindness.

David always knew, even in the dreams which visited him in his deepest sleep, that he had been uniquely privileged among men. He had walked past the place where the souls of common men were chained, past fire which cast the enigmatic shadow of *matter* on the wall for all to see and feel, past the road where the gods themselves walked, to the mouth of the cave that was Creation; and there he had looked out into the furious blaze of light which the gods themselves had no eyes to penetrate, and had *seen*, for a fleeting instant, what lay beyond. He knew full well that this had been the one crucial moment of his life, the moment which had made him more than man. After that, what kind of life was left to him? Small wonder that his faith had shrivelled with his flesh, to be lost forever in the wilderness of his desolation. Even the *vargr* now had hope, but Satan in the Hell of ice and darkness had none. Satan, whose one and only name was David, now had none.

The Face of God, made and contained in the eye of its beholder, was the only face which David's Satan ever saw, but it was not the only face which his dreams *remembered.* In his dreams, he remembered many faces, actual and imaginary. One face, however, constantly eluded the questing net of his dream-memory, stubbornly refusing to be caught: the face which the Angel of pain once wore.

Awake, David suffered still the agonies and inconveniences of arthritis, but his dream no longer worked the alchemical transformation which transmuted that pain into angelic sight. For David, the Angel of Pain no longer had a face; she had ceased to be his guiding spirit, and had entered instead into the secret coverts of his flesh. He felt her presence in the seven nails which pinned him to the ice—the two which were driven through his ankles; the two which were driven through his knees; the two which were driven through his wrists; and the one which was driven through his throat—but he was no longer party to her glory, her beauty, or her soaring flight. He no longer beheld the black, sleek wings which cloaked her with darkness when they were furled; she no longer marked with her talons in sweet, red human blood the track of her affection; she no longer shed her poisonous tears upon his cheek to lament her loneliness.

Perverse though it undoubtedly was, David could not help but regret, sometimes, the loss of this dangerous acquaintance. He was so very lonely now that the Angel of Death in her gaudiest and most vivid aspect might have provided a welcome distraction from the deadness of his days. Instead, it seemed that she had become his dark *doppelgänger*: a sulky shadow within him; his shameful secret self. Whenever David-as-Satan tried to remember the loving face of the Angel of Pain, it was another face entirely that stared back at him from the deepest recess of his wounded heart: the face of his one-time wife Cordelia.

2

Jason Sterling carefully drew back the plunger of the hypodermic syringe, and watched the barrel fill up with dark red blood drawn from a vein in the Clay Man's arm. The two catkin looked on; although their faces were not human enough to bear recognizable expressions their manner suggested intent curiosity. Sterling did not know whether that was illusion or not. Perhaps they *were* curious, avid for knowledge and understanding in spite of the fact that their poor half-human brains could not retain it.

The Clay Man bore the ordeal bravely enough, although his expression was not without resentment. "It must be the fortieth draught I have let you take," he observed, through gritted teeth. "I'd swear that you have had the blood out of me three times over."

"Blood regenerates constantly," Sterling told him, as he turned away with his prize. "Even a common man can donate a pint at regular intervals without suffering the least harm. How else am I to find out why you have begun to grow old save by scrupulous analysis?"

"Twenty-five years of scrupulous analysis has not served to give you a means to duplicate the angels' magic," the Clay Man pointed out, with more sorrow than complaint. "Master of mutation you may be, but are you any closer to the secret of immortality?" The Clay Man stared as he spoke at the silent catkin, which stared mutely back at him. Their arms were folded across their naked and almost hairless chests, as though to hide from view the hands to which they had no right, and which they had not readily learned to use even for the simplest tasks.

111

"Yes," said Sterling, assertively. "I am far better informed than I was before regarding the secrets of *mortality*, and that is a vital step on the way. I have a fuller understanding than anyone else alive of the chemistry of aging." Sterling did not think of the catkin as a failure, but merely as another small step on the path of progress. In giving them the shadow of human semblance he felt that he had come at least half way toward the miracle by which Machalalel had made men out of wolves. They stood erect and walked as men, and he was convinced in his own mind that they had the inbuilt *desire* to think and act as men in spite of the fact that their feline brains could not cope with such ambition. They were mortal too, alas, but Sterling did not doubt that if he only continued to experiment he would one day stumble across the trick that he was so ardently desirous of mastering.

"You have made progress," agreed the Clay Man. "If only there were a thousand men to do as much, you might be far nearer your goal. If you were more enthusiastic to publish what you know, the burden would not rest entirely on your shoulders."

"I would be called blasphemous and mad if I published the half of it," said Sterling sourly, as he connected a circuit to an electrical current to the blood in order to maintain its liquidity while he proceeded with his analyses. "The unwelcome attention which I attract from my neighbors would be increased tenfold. I came to Ireland to escape the worst effects of the war; I would rather avoid the worst effects of rumor too."

"If you published what you can *prove*," said the Clay Man, obstinately, while he rolled down his sleeve, "whispers concerning blasphemy would not intimidate others from following in your footsteps, and you know it. The trouble is that you have the secretive bent of the magician where you should have the communicative instinct of the scientist; you revel in being the one and only man with half an understanding, when you ought to be avid to be one of a million possessed of a whole understanding. You cannot do this *alone*, Jason, even though you might have all the time in the world to attempt it."

"I will not need *all* the time in the world," Sterling replied, scornfully. "Nor would my work benefit from the collaboration of a legion of fools. I know how anxious you are now that you have lost the best of the gifts which your Creator bestowed upon you, but you must trust me. I will not fail you."

The door behind them opened, and Hecate came in. The catkin stirred restlessly, although she was hardly a stranger. Sterling frowned. He did not like to be interrupted when he was in any of his laboratories, and he preferred it when she deigned to knock before doing so. "What do you want?" he asked. "I must work with the Clay Man's blood while it is fresh; I have no time for your news or your intrigues." He brought out a set of clean slides, and a small pipette.

"Let your hands do what they must," she replied, calmly. "Your ears can listen in the meantime."

"Is the war really over now?" asked the Clay Man, who evidently did have an appetite for news of the greater world.

"It depends what you mean by *over*," she said. "The English and the Germans have come to a settlement over the withdrawal from France, but the fate of the Low Countries hangs in the balance. Even if the English withdrawal is total, neither side can regard the conflict as concluded. The Russians, who would rather have fought the Germans than made peace with them in the spring but could not because the Americans would not help them, are now forced by circumstance to fight the Japanese; they might forge firmer ties with the Germans if the Americans still refuse to help them, but if the Americans do offer assistance the Eastern Front will be renewed as the Western Front is dismantled. Whatever happens, the Bolsheviks will surely lose control. Further east the Arabs and their allies, who were on the point of victory, are now staring defeat in the face. The Arabs will surely continue to fight even without Allenby's aid, but the Turks may now prevail. Sheer exhaustion will probably bring about a pause while the Germans tally their gains, but the munitions factories will not be still for an hour; the forces of destruction continue their implacable advance."

"Still," said the Clay Man uncertainly, while Sterling curled his lip in mute derision, "it is good that the worst of the killing has stopped. Perhaps the pause may yet turn into a peace. Perhaps half a victory will satisfy honor on all sides."

Honor! thought Sterling. *It is 1918 and still the man can speak of honor! How slow immortals are to adapt to changing times. He is three-quarters of the way through his new book, which is supposed to overturn all the ideas in the one he wrote more than a century ago, but at heart he remains Lucian de Terre, gallant champion of the hoped-for Age of Reason.* He was already at work preparing a series of slides, placing a drop of the Clay Man's blood on each one. The various reagents and stains which he intended to use were neatly arranged in a line, ready for recruitment.

"It would have been better for the cause of peace had the Germans been comprehensively defeated," said Hecate. "That may be why Zelophelon set Luke Capthorn's agents to strive in their cunning fashion to prevent that eventuality—if it was indeed the angel, and not the man, who formed that intention." The catkin cowered away from her, retreating to the alcove where they slept on quilted mattresses.

"What does it matter?" Sterling asked. "The future will be born here, not in the melting pot of Europe's myriad wars. As long as I can continue with my work, it cannot matter how Luke Capthorn uses Zelophelon's gifts, or why." He was still preparing the slides with mechanical precision.

"I wish that were true," Hecate said, with a sigh. "But what Zelophelon's instruments do affects us all. The self-styled Asmodeus is undoubtedly mad, and Harkender, for all his charm and arrogance, may well be mad too. Can the angel which equips them so liberally be any saner—and if not, are we not entitled to be anxious?"

"What is sanity or insanity in an angel?" said Sterling, with an airy wave and a brief laugh. "You of all people should be careful of anthropomorphic thinking. Capthorn and Harkender were mad long before they were given back their youth and increased in stature; madmen make useful tools, by virtue of their capacity for obsession. I am mad myself in the eyes of many of my fellows, but I am the clearest thinker in the world, and the only man who can hope to unravel the secrets of living flesh. Leave the generals and politicians to fight their wars and the angels to fight theirs—at least until your maker decides to conscript you once again."

Hecate turned to the Clay Man, who had finished adjusting his clothing. "Can you not take *them* outside?" she asked, pointing to the watching catkin.

Sterling permitted himself a secret smile. Hecate liked the catkin as little as they liked her. In some strange and subtle way they disturbed her, although she was no more a child of nature than they were. In some ways she was all too human, and all too feminine. The Clay Man, on the other hand, was much more at ease in the presence of Sterling's chimeras, and they had a naïve trust in him.

The Clay Man did as he was asked, and led the two catkin to the French windows so that they could go out onto the lawn. The day was cloudy and cool; a fresh wind blew steadily from the Atlantic across the treeless land to the west of the estate, sending a breath of air into the room. The chill of it made Hecate shiver before the Clay Man clicked the latch behind him.

"That was pointless," Sterling said. "You and I are no better able to keep secrets than anyone else, given the angels' talent for spying. Anyhow, the Clay Man and his maker are quite harmless. We know that Machalalel is the weakest of the seven."

"The Clay Man's irrelevance is something I had rather not take for granted," she answered, curtly, "and there are far too many secrets which have been successfully kept, at least from the likes of you and I."

Sterling shrugged his shoulders. He had little sympathy with her anxieties. Was she not a magical creature, with powers for which common men would have paid the highest price if they could? "I still have work to do," he said, dismissively. He carefully sealed a slide-cover in place with two thin lines of wax.

"We need to consider the situation," said Hecate, insistently. "You have an intelligence I cannot match, for all my magic, and I need your insight. Luke Capthorn has achieved more than once seemed likely; human history is falling under his control, at little cost to his guardian's reserves of power. He has acquired an unexpectedly efficient grasp of the patterns of cause and effect which operate in the community of nations; the single act his minions inspire *here* unfolds into vast consequences *there*. I cannot understand why Zelophelon allows or encourages it—or, if the angel is the true architect of the scheme, what the ultimate object of it is."

Sterling sighed, leaving his slides for the moment. He stared at her impatiently, wondering why she chose to be so very plain and unappealing to the eye. "Perhaps human civilization has served its purpose," he said in a deliberately bland tone. "I dare say that all we *need* of it is here." He tapped his head. "If Zelophelon cares to waste time in contriving the wreck of the superfluous, let him. While our own guardian protects us, nothing is lost." He was not as confident as he sounded, but he could not see any profit in debating the matter.

"Something strange happened in Paris a little while ago," she continued, obstinately. "Luke was shot down by a soldier. He was instantly brought back from the dead, but the fact that the shots were fired at all must be significant. I talked to the assassin, who was undoubtedly angel-inspired. When we reckon in the fact that Luke's men have wrecked the Order of St. Amycus and all but exterminated Machalalel's werewolves—upon whom the curse of aging has lately fallen—we must recognize that the war between the angels is entering a new phase. We are very likely to be caught in the crossfire.''

"It is as well, then, that we have a protector as powerful as the angel which guards my once-faithful servant,'' Sterling said impatiently. He could see that she was becoming impatient with his refusal to engage in the game of speculation, but he was unrepentant. He moved away and began scrubbing his hands at the sink, preparing for the next stage in his preliminary investigation of the aging Clay Man's blood. He checked that all his bottles were neatly capped again, and that everything was in its proper place. When he had dried his hands he went to unlatch the door of the wooden case where he kept his best microscope.

"We are running out of time, Jason,'' Hecate said. "Something strange is happening, and we do not know what it is.''

"Something strange is always happening,'' he complained, "and we never know what it is. Curse your melodramatic sensibilities! *We* are doing something strange—and vital—and we must be allowed to see it through. There is a secret *here* to be penetrated: a secret more valuable than anything to do with the petty squabbles of men or angels.'' He was only too keenly aware, though, that the progress of his work depended upon the continued interest of at least one angel, and his own fate upon the possibility of some eventual revelation which that angel might consider precious.

He connected the microscope to the electrical power supply and switched on the light beneath the platform. He reached for the first of the slides. As he picked it up, it exploded in his hand. Tiny, dagger-sharp slivers of glass flew in every direction, striking deep into his flesh and lacerating his fingers.

Sterling screamed, as much in shock and frustration as in pain, and it seemed—although it must have been an illusion based in coincidence—that the sharp note of his scream cut through the room like a shock wave, shattering the glass of all the other slides as it went. All the bottles arrayed on the bench exploded too, and all the beakers and burettes and retorts. The glass in the French windows, as if by way of contrast, imploded into the laboratory. There was flying glass everywhere; the air in the room was filled with it. The shards flew in every direction, with frank disrespect for Newton's first law; they followed curving paths, gathered into swirling vortices, and they struck and struck again and again at Sterling's hands and face, blinding him with his own blood and turning the whole surface of his body into a white-hot sheet of agony.

Even then his terror was swamped by anger: anger that this could be done *to him*, that some cackling imp of the perverse could be allowed to destroy *his work*. Why had his guardian permitted this? Why had he not been properly protected?

He knew that he was not dying—that none of the tiny missiles had struck deeply enough into him to puncture his vital organs—but he knew too that this was no trivial assault. He was blinded, and his skin had been ripped to shreds. Although he had remained young and healthy these last twenty-five years he was uncomfortably aware of the fact that his guardian angel's determination to protect him had never been tested to the full. Unlike Luke Capthorn, he had never been mortally wounded.

Help me! he cried, although he could not shape his scream to pronounce the actual words. *Make me whole again!* It was a demand, not a plea. In his dreams, which he trusted absolutely, Jason Sterling was the most important man alive; he was the only one who could plumb the alchemical secrets which—he firmly believed—even the angels ardently desired to know.

He felt his body jerk erect, and then begin to run. It did not seem that *he* was running; there was no conscious control in what he did. His body was running without the least regard for the authority of consciousness and choice. It was as if someone had drenched him with oil and set him alight; his response was pure reflex, pure panic, pure madness. He felt his body speeding toward the shattered French windows, bursting through into the open air, while the laboratory continued to disintegrate around and behind him.

He must have fallen on to the grass, but there was no identifiable sensation to inform him when he hit the ground. The cascade of pain reached its frightful climax within a few seconds, and then began swiftly to decline. He felt the merciful force of his guardian close in on him, like a great hand protectively enfolding his soul.

He felt the shards of glass being dragged out of his scarified flesh, which healed behind them. He felt relief and release as his flesh knitted. His blood-filled eyes became whole again, although he could not open them immediately. By the time he came to his knees, and raised his knuckles to wipe the rivulets of spilt blood away, his hands were once again uninjured. His fingers were sensitive to every touch, despite being wet with blood.

When he was able to open his eyes and look he saw Hecate coming unsteadily to her feet. She was some three or four meters away. Her face and hands were as red with blood as his must be. It seemed that no permanent injury had been done to her—but the same could not be said of the two catkin. Their semi-humanoid forms lay stretched out on the earth, more grotesque in death than they had been in life. The flying glass had not come forth in a deadly stream to cut them to ribbons; they had simply been rent apart by some careless magical force whose sole purpose had been to murder and spoil them.

There was no sign of the Clay Man; he had vanished without trace.

Sterling wasted no time in contemplating the corpses of his creatures. He turned immediately to look back into the laboratory. There was little enough to see; the destruction had been comprehensive. A fire had started in the wreckage and was already burning fiercely. Alarms were going off in other parts of the house, and his servants had already begun to evacuate their quarters. He was tempted to howl curses at them, to urge them to fetch buckets and form a chain, to fight the fire as best they could, but his eyes told him how pointless that would be.

He realized, belatedly, that he was more vulnerable than he had imagined. His person could be protected from harm easily enough, and his body brought back from the dead if necessary—but his work was something else. His instruments, his books, his experimental materials . . . everything, he now saw, could be reduced to dust and ashes with little expenditure of effort or power. To put it all back together again, on the other hand, would severely tax the power and ingenuity of an angel. Flesh, he knew, had its own capacity for self-repair and its own innate structure; there was an intrinsic process of nature with which magic could ally itself. Glass, wood and metal—even when wrought by the hand of man into something cleverly useful—had no such intrinsic organization. Destruction was so much easier than creation that his guardian angel could not defend his little empire of reason and inquiry against attack by another of its kind.

"If *you* did that to make a point," Sterling whispered to Hecate, "it was a vile and stupid thing to do."

"Don't be a fool," she retorted, sharply. "This was the work of an angel. It might have been Zelophelon . . . but I fear not. Something there is, dear Jason, that does not care for your precious work, and which has the power to confound it. We are caught up in a war, and we do not know what our enemy's objectives are."

Sterling looked down at his bloody hands, wondering how much he had lost. Little more than the pint he had taken from the Clay

Man, he supposed—but it seemed a great deal. The loss made him slightly dizzy.

"I am only a man," he whispered, more to himself than his companion. "I can do a man's work as well as any, perhaps better than any, *but I can only do a man's work.* You are the witch, the creature made by magic. You have no right to come to me with warnings and complaints. *What can I do?*"

"Nothing," she replied in a whisper. "Nothing, save to make what effort you can to understand. What else can any of us do?"

"Ask your maker!" he replied, bitterly. "What advantage is there in your existence, if you have not your maker's ear?" He struggled to get a grip on himself, knowing that his fury was not helping.

Sterling had always known, since the day he was transported from his house in Richmond to Hecate's strange Eden, that the ordered world of men existed on sufferance, but he had managed to put the ominous thought aside, to disregard the destructive potential of the power which the angels had even while he accepted the benefits gifted to him. Now that some brutal magical whim had smashed everything he owned, he could no longer set his anxiety aside. "It wasn't supposed to happen like this," he whispered. "I could have penetrated the most intimate secrets of life, if only I had been given time . . . if only I had been given *time!*"

Hecate did not reply. She was still uncertain, still lost. She had no more understanding of what was happening than any creature of common clay. She came to him, and put a consoling hand on his shoulder, but he shrugged it off. "No," he said. "It isn't over. We have to go on. There's nothing else to be done. The work has to continue. If it was worth destroying, it has to be worth completing." He lifted his eyes to the leaden sky, although he knew full well that the angels were no more *up there* than they were in any other identifiable place. "Hear me!" he shouted. "If it was worth destroying, it is most certainly worth remaking, and carrying to its end, no matter what the cost. Dare you leave it undone, now that an enemy has tried to rob you of its rewards?"

The sky was silent, as it always was. His guardian angel had never condescended to speak to him, even in his dreams. Whatever answer he received, if he received any, would arrive by some other means.

"We have lost a little blood," he said to Hecate, "but we have blood to spare. We have to go on. You do see that, don't you? We have to go on, even if the world disintegrates around us."

''Yes we do,'' she answered, softly—but he could see, now that she stood so close, that there was a fear in her eyes which he had never seen there before: a fear so innocent and kittenish that he could almost have believed her mortal.

3

Pelorus trudged wearily along the rough and rutted road. The sound of his too-heavy footfalls was muted, but seemed more than loud enough in the absence of any wind to rustle the hedgerows. The fields behind the hedges were preternaturally quiet, as if the mice and voles froze at the noise of his approach, somehow knowing who and what he was.

It was easier to move by night, although his poor human eyes were less than adequate to the task of penetrating the darkness. At night he attracted no attention, and was free of the need to answer questions. As a wolf he could have moved with ease through the problematic world, his wolfish sight thriving on the faint light of the half-moon and the stars; as a wolf he could have run, filled with joy, free of the least atom of conscience, but a handless wolf could not have carried the burden he bore. Only a man could perform the task which had fallen to Pelorus; only a man could achieve his present purpose. When had it ever been different for the wolf who was the Will of Machalalel?

Pelorus had never found it comfortable to work under the *geas* which Machalalel had placed upon him in what he remembered as the dawn of time, but he had never before found it as painful as it had lately become. He had remained young through many lifetimes, but he was young no longer. The strength was ebbing out of him, year by year and day by day. He had no idea why. Perhaps Zelophelon or some other malevolent Angel had contrived to plant a seed of destruction in his once-imperishable body; perhaps the undead but quiescent Machalalel no longer had the power or the inclination to preserve his immortality; perhaps by virtue of too much thinking and too much compassion he had simply become *too human*. The last hypothesis, at least, seemed unlikely; if that had been the case he would have begun to age and decay long before Mandorla, and yet it was Mandorla who was his burden now: a thin, faded Mandorla who seemed less than a shadow of her former self. He hugged her close to his breast as he walked on, anxious that if he could not bring her to a safe haven she might suffer the kind of death that humans suffered.

Mandorla had died many times, sometimes very violently, but the Mandorla who had gone arrogantly to her destruction before was not the Mandorla who lay unconscious in his arms now. *This* was a Mandorla who feared extinction, a Mandorla who had all but lost her faith in the permanence of resurrection, a Mandorla who felt the full horror of her wounds. This was a Mandorla who had begged him to save her dwindling life, whatever the risk or cost.

He might have refused, of course. The will of Machalalel had commanded him to serve and protect *human*kind, and had made no mention of his own, but there had been no real question of refusal; however anxious Mandorla had been to kill him in earlier incarnations, and however ready he had sometimes been to retaliate in kind, he and she were bound by blood. There was, in any case, a unique and glorious freedom in the ability to decide what he would or would not do in the cause of her salvation, which would have been utterly spoiled and betrayed by refusal. For the first time in his long life, Pelorus felt like a hero. How paradoxical it was that the feeling should come upon him while he skulked in English country lanes, avoiding towns and villages whenever he could: a predator acting the part of timorous prey!

He felt the rhythm of his footsteps falter, although he had made no conscious decision to pause. His body had always had its own powers of decision, but this was not the work of the will of Machalalel; this was the pressure of exhaustion. Wasted though she was, Mandorla was still heavy in his weary arms, and he had to pause at regular intervals in order to rest. He had no food but dry bread, which he could not make her eat and which added hardly at all to his own strength, but he had not taken wolf form for a long time and he doubted that the energy required for transformation had been adequately replenished. Even to attempt it might be a risk he could not afford. He came to a halt, and gently laid Mandorla's body down, in the shadow of a stately oak whose bulk interrupted the hedgerow.

Her thick black cloak was wrapped around her to protect her from the unseasonable cold, and he took care to gather it more tightly about her. He pushed the hood back in order to wad the cloth into a crude pillow, allowing her silver-blonde hair to spill out. Her tresses had been glossy once, wonderfully silken to the touch, but they seemed desiccated now. By everyday human standards they would have been pretty enough in a woman of her apparent middle-age; to Pelorus, accustomed by the habit of centuries to her super-natural beauty, it seemed that her crowning glory had been reduced to little more than a mass of coarse cobwebs.

He positioned her so that she lay on her side, in the moon-shadow of the oak's branches. A casual observer, knowing nothing of the wounds hidden by the cloak, would have assumed that she was merely asleep and might wake at the slightest sound or touch, but Pelorus knew that only magic would rouse her and make her whole again. He sat down, leaning his back against the bole of the oak and stretching his legs out horizontally. He broke a few fragments of bread from the half-loaf which was his only sustenance, chewing each piece assiduously before swallowing. The bread was slightly stale, and its sojourn in the pocket of his travel-stained suit had not improved its taste, but his hunger was sharp enough to make him relish it, and it took an effort to put the rest away when he had taken his ration.

He looked up at the sky, squinting at the stars. He usually had an acute sense of time, but the endless plodding drumbeat of his walking had detached him from the faster tempo of the seconds, and he did not know whether midnight had passed or not. Nor had he any real idea how far he had come since sundown, or how far he might still have to go before he reached his destination. He had faith in his sense of direction, and knew that the road on which he traveled led as straight as any toward his goal, but he could not estimate the extent of his progress with any real accuracy. All he knew for sure was that he was not near enough to Lydyard's cottage to reach it tonight. Fifteen or twenty miles still remained to be traversed.

"It was easier by far to come to you, my friend," he murmured, "when you lived in London. The streets of London are so very easy to navigate, and there are so many ways to travel them."

It was not only for his own convenience that Pelorus regretted David Lydyard's decision to remove himself to the remoter regions of the East Anglian coast; he could not believe that such wilful isolation was good for the man. No matter what contact Lydyard had with the wide world of men by means of the books he read and the letters he wrote, the loss of actual human contact had not worked to his advantage; it had become a form of self-punishment as ruthless in its fashion as any to which the luckless man had been subjected by his tyrannical and ever-mysterious guardian.

Pelorus let his eyes fall closed, knowing that he was doing it but reassuring himself that it would only be for a few luxurious moments, only for the briefest pause . . .

He dreamed of the Golden Age; of light and gaiety; of verdant hills and trackless forests; of the teeming angel-spawn; of the mask which had been the temporary face of Machalalel, his adoptive father . . .

"Bring up the lantern, man! Let's have a light here!"

The words brought Pelorus to with a shock, and it was not until he felt the texture of the shock that he realized how deeply asleep he had been. His first thought was a curse, directed at himself for his criminal carelessness. He was not ready for the light, which blinded him, and he added a second silent curse, directed at his poor human eyes. When he *could* see, he found the tip of a bayonet before his face. As soon as he focused his gaze upon it the rifle to which it was attached changed its angle, so that the cold metal was pressed to his throat.

"Move nary a muscle, Cuddy," said the harsh voice which had called for the lantern. "Be still as carven stone." The voice was rough but not entirely uncultured, and the accent had more of the northern counties in it than rural Suffolk.

Deft hands were rummaging around in his coat, and they had already found his own pistol. He had no choice but to let it be drawn out.

"What gun's *that*?" said a second voice. "Not army issue, for sure."

"Not *our* army," said the first man. "A Yankee gun—but he's no Yankee. Didst ever see eyes so blue, lads, e'en in the yeller lamplight?"

There were four of them, all told. Two of them carried rifles, though only one was bayoneted; one of the others had a cudgel. Three wore military uniform—or parts of uniform, at least; had they been in barracks they would certainly have been deemed improperly dressed.

Deserters, Pelorus thought. *Men allowed home on leave, who de-*

cided that the life of a scavenger would be preferable to the trenches.
Ever since the war began there had been dark rumors of a "fifth
column" of German agents lurking secretly in England, but it was
only in the last few months that a real secret army had begun gradually to reveal itself: a rough and ragged army of the disaffected, who
thought it safer to turn predator against their own kind than return
to the wilderness of Belgian mud and wire which was civilization's
slaughterhouse. Since the spring, when France had fallen, the heart
had gone out of England's fighting-men. The generals no longer
knew where best to deploy them—if they ever had—and while they
wriggled on the horns of their dilemma the army had begun to disintegrate. In the end, Pelorus thought, the Low Countries would have
to be abandoned, and Fortress Britain would have to prepare for a
century of siege; but if the defense of the island citadel could not
be organized and set in place very soon, it might find the cancers
within as difficult to combat as the enemies without.

Pelorus could not help but stir himself as the hands returned to
their work, but his movement brought a swift response.

"Still, now!" said the warning voice of the man with the rifle.

"No pocketbook," reported the owner of the greedy hands. "No
money, no papers. Nothing."

"These are dangerous times in which to have no identity," said
the second rifleman. "One who cannot demonstrate his friendship is
likely to be taken for a foe." This was clearly an educated man,
although his accent was Lancastrian, or perhaps Cumbrian.

"I've nothing more for you to steal but the remains of a loaf of
bread," Pelorus said, fixing his eyes upon the man who had spoken
last, on the assumption that he must be the ringleader. "Take the
gun and go." But while he spoke, the furtive hands of the man who
carried no weapon were already at work parting Mandorla's cloak.
Pelorus watched from the corners of his eyes, but did not look away
from the half-shadowed face of the man.

"Nothing," reported the searcher, when he had done. "No papers.
Nothing at all."

"Heavy sleeper," commented the man with the cudgel. His tone
was speculative, but it was not the reason for Mandorla's unconsciousness that was exercising his thoughts.

"She's badly hurt," said Pelorus. "For mercy's sake, let her
alone." Cold anger was working in his hungry belly, sharpening his
senses and tensing his muscles. He did not know if he could change,
or whether he could free himself from the prison of his clothing if

he did, but he wanted to be ready. The wolf in him always woke when danger threatened, eager to be free.

"How can we hurt her," asked the leader, ironically, "when she has no papers? Does she even exist? If she does, can she be anything but a spy? She's no fenland farm-girl, that's for sure. We're all strangers here, I think—all castaways from the ship of state. Can you pick her up, Billy?"

The man with the cudgel, who was half a head taller and three stones heavier than the one with the inquisitive hands, passed his weapon and the lantern over to his slighter companion, and bent to test Mandorla's weight.

"Let her be!" said Pelorus sharply. The point of the bayonet was pressed insistently to his Adam's apple, pinning him down; he could not rise or start forward without hurting himself.

The second rifleman, holding his weapon at the ready, knelt down beside Pelorus as the man addressed as Billy lifted Mandorla in his arms.

"Easy," Billy said confidently.

"Perhaps you do not know it," the ringleader whispered to his prisoner, "but the *real* war has begun now. The war of all against all. There is no property now, in food or guns or women, and so there is no theft. Nor is there any longer a tribe or society of men called *England*, and hence no law to say that killing you would be an act of murder. Things have changed, my nameless friend."

"We are not nameless," Pelorus replied, refusing to speak in a whisper. "I am Paul Shepherd, and my sister's name is Mandorla Soulier. You must let us go." He could see the face of the other man quite clearly now, illuminated by the lantern. It was dirty and bearded, but the eyes shone brightly with malign intelligence.

"Must?" the bearded man echoed, dressing the echo in a sneer of contempt. "There is no *must* any more, except that which is won by force of arms. You do not realize how fast the world is changing, how rapidly the order of things decays. What kind of a name is Mandorla? Not a Christian name, for sure."

"You had best be careful," said Pelorus, looking up at the man who held Mandorla. "If she wakes she will tear your throat out, for she is one of the werewolves of London." It was a desperate move. He had hoped to cause, at the very least, a stir of surprise, but he was disappointed. They did not even laugh.

"Though thou art abandoned, be not waylaid," the ringleader quoted, in a voice that was acidly soft. "Advice which you, my nameless friend, forgot to follow. But we are *real* wolves, not children's fantasies."

"You are *vargr*," Pelorus admitted, steeling himself for the desperate spring which he knew that he must make very soon, in whatever form. "You are numbered among the restless ones. If only you knew, *human*—if only you understood!" He tried to concentrate all his attention on the problem of knocking the bayonet aside. Unless he could first do that, all other options were null and void.

What he said was enigmatic enough to generate a flicker of doubt and unease in the malign stare of the ringleader, peculiar enough to puzzle the man who held the blade at his throat and draw his thoughts away for a brief second. Pelorus brought his arm across swiftly and savagely, knocking the bayonet away from his throat. He did not try to rise to his feet but squirmed sideways, lashing out with his right leg in the hope of tumbling his erstwhile captor to the ground. But they were not unready enough, nor was he strong enough or fast enough for the task which fate had set him.

The ringleader brought the butt of his rifle round in efficiently brutal fashion, smashing it into the side of Pelorus's head. The instant the blow struck home, Pelorus knew that he was finished. He tried to change, knowing that he had no time to accomplish his transformation, and that his clothes were far too cumbersome and tight, but knowing also that there was nothing else to try, nothing else which could possibly help.

He could not do it.

As his senses reeled he felt the awful ignominy of his failure, of his entrapment in human form, in merely human being.

A booted foot crashed into his midriff, driving the breath from his lungs. His mouth filled with bile as he tried to stop himself vomiting, and the fear flooded over him that this time might be the last, that this time there might be no awakening. Would there even be a world, he wondered, in which he might otherwise have awakened? Or was the bearded fanatic right, for all the wrong reasons, in thinking that the Last Days had already begun, and that history had nearly reached its end?

His body curled up reflexively, in futile anticipation of the blows that were to come, and the callous blade that would put an end to him . . .

What ignominy! he thought. *How could Machalalel have dreamt that his will would come to this?*

While the thought flickered and died, the dark and silent night was split and filled by a hideous scream. *Mandorla!* he thought, exultantly, even though he knew it to be impossible.

Both rifles went off, the two shots merging into one, but the sound of screaming went on. One voice was cut abruptly short, as if the throat which carried it had been unceremoniously torn out, but the eerie crescendo went on as Pelorus rolled over and opened his eyes, trying to see through the dizzying waves of pain which still confused him.

He saw that the lantern had crashed to the ground, and that its oil had spilled out, giving birth to a lazy rivulet of fire. The rivulet was coursing toward him, and he had to roll over again to be out of its way, but the ribbon of firelight displayed to him the shadow-show of what was happening, and he drank it in during the course of a long and startled glance.

The shadows of the four men were like ragged paper dolls, casually tossed about by something far larger and infinitely more furious: something massive and majestic, awesome in its power and its grace. Balanced on its huge hind legs, his rescuer towered high above the road, its clawed forepaws lashing out with casual precision. Two shots had been fired, perhaps at its gargantuan head or perhaps into the bulk of its body, but they had not had the slightest effect. The creature was nothing which could be stopped by mere bullets. He had threatened them with a werewolf and they had not even condescended to laugh, but this was something far worse, far more terrible. As he rolled over yet again, Pelorus saw that Mandorla's body lay on the ground, very near to the place where he had carefully arranged it when he stopped to rest. The man who had picked her up had dropped her, and he now lay beside her with his head caved in, spilling blood. Pelorus immediately began to squirm in her direction, anxious to give Mandorla what protection he could.

He ducked his head as he moved and by the time he looked up again, not one of the four was left standing. One—the man with deft fingers—had tried to run, but his back had been broken before he had taken a dozen strides. The two gunmen had been struck down where they stood. The ringleader had been rent from breast to belly; the other had no face. Their conqueror, having disposed of them with casual contempt, was slowly sinking down on all fours. Its clawed forepaws moved back and forth, ready to lash out again at the slightest provocation.

Perhaps you do not know it, the bandit had said, *but the real war has begun now. The war of all against all ... things have changed, my nameless friend.* Doubtless the bearded man had thought himself a man ahead of his time, a man who had reasoned out the future and wanted to be at its forefront. If only he had possessed a little more understanding, or a little more imagination!

The huge shadow took two steps forward before finally coming to rest. Pelorus looked up curiously at the face of the sphinx, dimly lit by the flames of the burning oil. Pelorus did not recognize the face; it was not the semblance of anyone he knew. It was, of course, beautiful, at least by human standards: beautiful, *and young.* The angel which had fashioned it—or resurrected it—clearly had not suffered the same depletion of its powers as Machalalel.

Oddly enough, the first question which sprang to his lips was: *"Why?"*

"I owe you one life," said the sphinx. The voice, like the face, was female. "Had it not been for you, I might have killed Tallentyre in Egypt half a century ago—and that would have been a sad mistake."

His senses were still confused by the blow to his head, but he could think straight enough to know nonsense when he heard it. "There are no debts of honor between angels," he said, "let alone between angels and their humbler instruments."

"We live in the world of human understanding now," the monster replied, still peering down at him as he came to his knees and crawled to where Mandorla lay. "Even angels may make pacts and contracts now, and must not hesitate to do so, while time presses."

She is deceitful, he thought, as he felt for the pulse in Mandorla's neck, and found it. *If she has come to save me, she has a good reason of her own. But if time presses, even for the angels, there may be desperation here. Might she need friends so badly that she is eager to court Machalalel?*

"What ... ?" he began—but she was not inclined to let him frame a question, let alone to answer it.

"We will take you to Lydyard," she said. "We will give you twenty-four hours, and not a moment longer. Mandorla may stay there, but you must go on your way."

"We?" he said, cautiously, although he knew that the question that most needed answering was *Why?*

She glanced sideways, and he saw that there was another man on the road now, incuriously looking down at the corpses. Pelorus recognized William de Lancy, who had been the appointed companion and servant of the sphinx a long time ago. Unlike the sphinx, de

Lancy looked almost as old as he really was; his hair was white and
his face was wrinkled. He looked lost, almost as if he were asleep
and dreaming; there was something strange about the way his gaze
passed over the dead men and came to settle on Pelorus's face,
turning into a hard but vacant stare.

"What is happening, de Lancy?" Pelorus asked.

De Lancy was no more inclined to answer him than the sphinx
had been. That did not surprise him. The sphinx was, after all, the
sphinx—her role was to pose riddles and punish those who answered
them wrongly—and de Lancy was her consort and slave.

"You could have saved us a deal of tiredness and trouble," Pelorus said drily, as his eyes moved from the man to the monster and
back again, "if you had come to us three days ago—or even three
hours."

They made no reply to that, either. The sphinx nodded her head
to de Lancy, issuing some silent command; then she crouched down
and stretched herself out in the road. "Lay Mandorla's body across
my shoulders," she said, "and climb up behind."

Better to obey, Pelorus thought, than to goad her into picking
Mandorla up in her teeth, as a lioness might carry a cub. "I have
not been offered such a ride since the Age of Heroes ended," he
said. "Was that seven or eight thousand years ago?" While he lifted
Mandorla up, he told himself that the sphinx could not have intended
to show herself at all, and would surely never have allowed him to
know that her angelic mistress *wanted* him to bring Mandorla to
Lydyard—to bring *Mandorla*, for he himself was evidently not
wanted—had she not been forced by circumstance to do so.

David might be able to guess why, he told himself, *if there is any
reason beyond the mere habit of secrecy.*

The smell of human blood was strong in the still night air, and
Pelorus could not help but feel the thrill of it. Even though he was
the bearer of the Will of Machalalel, eternally forbidden to do men
harm, and even though he had lost the power to change, he felt a
flicker of honest and joyous wolfishness in the shadowy depths of his
burdensome consciousness. *Not the end of us, after all,* he thought, as
the sphinx turned on her heels far more gracefully than any well-
schooled horse. *We have a function left to serve, it seems, and one
which warrants a generous sacrifice of human blood. Oh, Mandorla,
if only you might yet awake, how you would love the scent and
the sensation!*

4

The wood which surrounded David Lydyard's cottage was noticeably denser than Pelorus had last seen it, and the pathway which led to the door was more intricately curved. The boughs of the trees to either side extended over the pathway in such a fashion as to make the pathway into a tunnel which was pitch-black by night and would doubtless be gloomy even by day.

The place where the cottage was had been named World's End in the distant past, when it had been a low hill rising from a salt marsh which extended for several miles to the seashore. In the course of the intervening centuries much of the marshland had been drained, its brackish waters diverted into channels so that beets and turnips might be grown in the reclaimed fields; but during those same centuries, the sea's erosion of the coast had brought the tides to the toe of the hill, so that a mere hundred yards' walk now separated the cottage from a crumbling and sandy cliff which looked out over the gray and often mist-shrouded North Sea. It seemed more like World's End now than it ever could have when it won its name, and the ominous enclosure of the wood enhanced that appearance.

In respect to the thickness of the wood Pelorus did not doubt the evidence of his eyes and memory. He was well used to more gradual changes which overcame the world, imperceptible to all but those who were—in essence, at least—outside it. He saw that the cottage was changed too. Its substance had become darker, its walls more solid. It stood in a clearing of sorts, allowing space for the moon and the stars to shine upon the tiles of its precipitously inclined roof, but the boughs which clustered about its eaves seemed ambitious to enclose it in a smothering embrace. The cottage was an ancient edifice; according to Lydyard the foundations were at least four centuries old, although the walls and roof had been renewed within the last hundred years. It looked more ancient still as it basked in the shadows cast by the cold white light of the moon and stars, like some remnant of that quiet and placid era which men of Lydyard's stripe called the Dark Ages.

Pelorus hoped that the cottage had been moved to the margin where even the most lumpen matter became vulnerable to the whims of those beings whose intelligence operated at a more fundamental level, in order that it might be better protected from invasion or corruption. He shifted Mandorla's weight so that he could reach out with his right hand to lift the heavy iron knocker. He rapped three times, then paused to redistribute his burden once again. No more than a few seconds passed before he heard the sound of footsteps within. No inquiry was made as to who might be there, nor did any bolt have to be withdrawn, before the door opened.

Lydyard was fully clothed. The light which he carried was a low-burning candle in a tray, by no means bright enough for reading or writing, but his eyes were alert. He looked old and weary, as befitted a man of nearly seventy years. There was not an ounce of spare flesh on his lean frame, but he did not seem unduly frail. Indeed, his features gave the impression of having been carved from age-hardened ivory. "Pelorus?" he said wonderingly. Pelorus knew by Lydyard's tone that the less expectable marks which time had made on his own features must be very obvious.

"Yes," the werewolf replied. "I have Mandorla with me, sorely hurt."

Lydyard immediately moved aside to let him pass, and closed the door behind them. "I was in the kitchen," he said. "The warmth of the stove is usually oppressive at this time of year, but the nights have been cold of late. Summer never arrived, in any proper sense. Go to the left. Set her down on the sofa."

While Pelorus gently laid down his burden, Lydyard used the candle flame to light the wick of an oil lamp, which cast a much brighter light once the glass was in place. Oil was evidently in short supply, not to be burned except when bright light was needed. Lydyard brought the lamp to the low table which stood near the end of the sofa where Pelorus collapsed into an armchair. The flickering lamplight cast unsteady shadows on the pale walls; Lydyard's swayed and blurred like some eager and attentive spectre.

"How she has aged!" Lydyard whispered, when he eventually turned to face Pelorus. "You too! What has happened to you both?"

"Nothing in particular," Pelorus told him, tiredly. "It seems that while other angels have granted their seers a better measure of immunity from time's afflictions, the schemes of your guardian and mine run in a contrary direction."

"What happened to her?"

Pelorus scowled. "Luke Capthorn's zealots got through to her at last. I suspect that the whole pack has been consigned to the long sleep, save for the two of us. Perris, Arian and Siri took the fight to Capthorn's base in Paris, trying to disrupt his web at its center, but it was hopeless. We have heard no news from them in months. I hope that the Clay Man is safe with Sterling. Hecate might condescend to shield him, as the sphinx shielded us when we might have been killed an hour ago."

The flicker of surprise which showed in Lydyard's eyes was momentary. He had lived too long as an angel's minion to be astonished by anything. "So the sphinx lives again," he murmured. "But why should she help you?"

"I think she would rather we had made our way here without her help," Pelorus said hesitantly. "I dare say that she might have kept Zelophelon's agents away from us without our ever knowing, but we were unexpectedly menaced by others. Had she not intervened . . . you might be more careful answering your door, David; there is ordinary human evil abroad, as well as other kinds."

"Who was it that attacked you?" Lydyard asked.

"Renegades. Deserters or dilatory conscripts, I suppose, who calculated some time ago that living wild in England was preferable to facing the might of Ludendorff's armies, and now find themselves facing the equally unpleasant prospect of the British army's return."

"Are we definitely to withdraw from Flanders? I didn't know— even rumor has difficulty reaching the villages in these parts." He did not seem unduly depressed by the news; no doubt he was optimistic that Teddy and Nell might soon be home if an orderly withdrawal were to be effected.

"I doubt that anyone knows for certain," Pelorus told him, fearful of feeding false hope, "but morale has plummeted since the French capitulation. If the tattered remnants of the British armies cannot be brought home to preserve order here, England itself may soon collapse into virtual anarchy." Lydyard shook his head. "That can't be true," he said.

"It can be, if enough people believe it," Pelorus told him.

Lydyard perched on the arm of the sofa, looking down at Mandorla. "How she would have loved to see that happen," he murmured. His shadow, cramped by his change of position, crouched down as if it were a predatory beast ready to spring. The air inside the cottage seemed unusually thick and stifling, palpably hostile—but only to Pelorus.

"No more," said Pelorus, wishing that he did not feel so utterly exhausted, so completely *human*. "She has changed of late, David—very rapidly, by the standards of our kind. Had you seen her during the last twenty years you would have seen the difference. As she began to age it became more and more exaggerated. After millennia of stubborn resistance, she has consented to grow a little fonder of her human self, and she has quite lost her faith that the Golden Age might one day be restored. If she wakes, you might find her almost contrite."

"*If* she wakes?" Lydyard echoed.

"I thought her chances slender," said Pelorus, "but not hopeless. They may be better now that the sphinx has touched her. It was on Mandorla's behalf that the sphinx was commanded to interfere. I have been instructed to leave again as soon as I am rested. The angels may have other plans for me, which will become clear in due course."

Pelorus knew that Lydyard had been left alone by the angels for nearly half a lifetime, but still the man showed no evidence of astonishment at what was happening. "What plans?" he finally asked, after a long pause.

Pelorus shook his head. "What Machalalel requires of me I cannot imagine. You are probably better able than I to guess why the sphinx or her maker might want to bring Mandorla to your house. The angels have given and taken hostages before, have they not? It is possible that the battle-lines are being drawn for the angels' final conflict."

Lydyard's shadow was still now but the room remained oppressive.

"Where will you go?" Lydyard asked, with genuine concern.

"I will try to find the Clay Man," Pelorus said. "I will go to Sterling's house in Ireland, if I can. If the sphinx can make Mandorla welcome, perhaps Hecate will do the same for me."

"Be sure that I will do what I can for Mandorla," Lydyard assured him, perching beside her on the sofa and reaching out to touch her forehead, testing its temperature. "However she tried to use me once, it was nothing compared to the ways in which *others* have used me. I no longer bear her any ill will.''

''She has done far worse to me than she ever did to you,'' Pelorus said levelly, ''over a much longer period of time. She and I are blood kin, it is true, and that makes it easier to forgive and forget— but there is a sense in which you too are kin to the werewolves of London. We are all *vargr*-folk now. We dwell in the borderlands of the world.''

''I know,'' said Lydyard, with a humorless smile. ''When I dream of my Satan-self nowadays I no longer find myself in the traditional Hell of fire and brimstone. I see myself committed to *your* kind of damnation: cursed to remain in an infinite wilderness of ice, eternally desolate and deprived.''

''I have never thought myself damned,'' Pelorus said mildly. ''Even Mandorla, who felt the curse of humanity far more keenly, has almost become reconciled to her second self. Were we condemned to be human forever, never to be wolves again even for the brief intervals which have long been permitted to us, I think we could bear it. For myself, I could even welcome it.''

''For myself,'' Lydyard countered, taking back his hand, ''I think I could welcome the innocence of the hunting wolf, even if it were but a tenth as joyous as Mandorla claims. I sometimes feel that there is a wolf-self in me which longs for the freedom it has never had.''

''Not in you, David,'' said Pelorus. ''I could believe it of almost any other man, but not of you. According to Mandorla, all men are wolves in the most secret depths of their hearts, but if she were to permit an exception, it would surely be you.''

''You overestimate me,'' said Lydyard, dully. He gestured idly with his right hand, and his shadow on the wall extended a limb which seemed to Pelorus to be a great sweeping wing. ''I am too old now,'' Lydyard continued, ''to be all man and all mind. Even Tallentyre became a lesser being in the years before he died. What might have become of him had he lingered longer I hesitate to think.''

Pelorus found his eyelids drooping, and knew that he could not remain awake for much longer. He forced himself awake, reminding himself that he had ridden the last few miles of the journey, whereas he might have been forced to walk—but the air seemed to have thickened about him oppressively. The house was haunted by something that did not want him here, and would not give him pause to relax even while his day of grace lasted.

"Have you heard from Nell?" he asked, anxious to maintain the flow of the conversation in spite of his discomfort.

"She wrote a week ago that she hoped to be coming home," said Lydyard. "Like everyone else, she was awaiting developments. With luck she might be in Boulogne by now, waiting for her turn to cross the channel. Teddy is less likely to be released immediately. I am with them constantly in spirit, and often wish that I might be permitted to visit them in my dreams. I fear for them so desperately."

Pelorus was awkwardly aware of the fact that Lydyard's younger son, Simon, had to be left unmentioned. He had fallen victim to the war in its earliest stages, one of tens of thousands caught up in the awful catastrophe of Mons. Pelorus could not quite imagine the effect of that kind of grief, or the fear Lydyard must feel for his remaining children.

"Whatever happens, it will not be the end of the world," Pelorus said, attempting to be resolute even though it was not in him to be cheerful. "Whether the Germans drive the British from the continent or the slaughter continues for another ten years, it will only be one more chapter in the human story. Mere men do not have the power to destroy their species or their world."

"The Clay Man would disagree," Lydyard said dourly. "The establishment of an uneasy stalemate, however it might be formulated, will subordinate the human imagination entirely to the business of preparation for war, diverting the march of technology conclusively from the path of progress to the path of destruction. Zephyrinus, the superior of the English House of the Order of St. Amycus, told me long ago that this would happen. I could not believe him then, but were I to tell Teddy or Nell now what Zephyrinus said to me in 1872 they would not entertain a moment's doubt. They have seen the effects of machine guns and the new gases, and they have watched aircraft fighting in the sky. They know that what has begun will be very difficult to end now that it has failed to reach an absolute conclusion. Lucian de Terre's celebration of the collective power of human intelligence and human hands was premature, as he now knows. The Age of Reason was stillborn and an Age of Madness is emerging in its place.

"Mandorla was over-optimistic to hope that *magic* might one day put an end to the world of matter and men, but there is no need now for magic to accomplish the latter aim . . . and though the infinitesimal strength of the human hand is impotent to put an end to the entire cosmos of matter, I cannot help but fear that human intelligence might somehow plant a seed in the mind of an angel which would enable it to be done. We have already begun to unravel the mysteries of the atom, and I see no reason to believe that we will not succeed in reaching a full and final understanding.''

Can that really be the purpose for which mankind was made? Pelorus thought. *Was its function simply to discover certain principles determining the organization of matter, in order that the angels could learn the secret of its disintegration?* His tongue felt thick and huge in his mouth, and he could not muster the energy to debate the point. In any case, he knew no argument powerful enough to contradict Lydyard's pessimism. Sir Edward Tallentyre would not have tolerated it, of course—''However we find the world,'' Tallentyre would have said, ''we must live in it as best we can''—but Pelorus was not Tallentyre. He had been following the dictum, tacitly, for ten thousand remembered years, but he was not equipped to defend and extrapolate it as Tallentyre would have done.

Lydyard realized how reluctant his tired silence was. ''I tell myself over and over again that what Tallentyre made Zelophelon see half a century ago is as true now as it ever was,'' he said, with a sigh, dutifully playing devil's advocate against his own despair. ''I tell myself that the universe is a huger *and finer* place than the angels imagined. I tell myself that although they thought themselves gods when first they borrowed human sight they are only alien beings, with limited bodies and even more limited minds. I tell myself that Sir Edward always understood that, and that no matter how fiercely they hated him for it, they could never deny it. I tell myself that although the angels have the power to torment and tyrannize tinier creatures they too stand naked, afraid and immeasurably tiny before the immensity of Creation . . .''

Lydyard paused for a moment, while his shadow trembled upon the wall, as though shaking with suppressed laughter. Then he went on in a darker vein, switching sides yet again. ''I wish I could be sure of all that. I tell myself that it is true, but I cannot help doubting. The angels may beg leave to doubt it too, I suppose. I sometimes think, and often fear, that science may yet reveal to us the awful truth that Sir Edward's vision of the universe is only a little less primitive than the older ideas he so righteously despised—and if that is true, the question of what the angels are, and what they might do if they only knew what they are, has yet to be properly asked, let alone answered. It is, I suppose, a privilege to have been selected as one of those charged with the asking and the answering, but even if

I believed that my destiny was to find a better and more hopeful answer than the nightmarish one which threatens me now, I could not bring myself to be grateful. When I look back over my life, I cannot even *begin* to be grateful.''

Nor can I, Pelorus thought, feeling a dismal echo in his own heart of the cold, brooding horror which had touched Lydyard and seemed to have saturated the very atmosphere of his dwelling. *Nor, any longer, can I.*

5

Pelorus had helped David carry Mandorla upstairs to one of the bedrooms before setting forth on his travels again. Modesty had led David to leave the task of removing her clothes to the werewolf, but he had to overcome that embarrassment in order to tend her injuries. He pushed the blankets down so that he could see the ugly dagger wound which extended from her shoulder to her navel, but was glad to see that it appeared to be healing well enough. It had not been stitched, and might leave a nasty scar, but it was free of infection.

When he gently touched the skin beside the wound, Mandorla stirred. Her limbs twitched and her head rolled from side to side upon the pillow with increasing violence, until David felt moved to grip it and hold it still, but she did not recover consciousness. He left her alone again, but her presence in the house made him so uneasy that it was impossible to read or concentrate his thoughts. He busied himself with cleaning and cooking for an hour or more, and then went back upstairs to see how she was.

This time Mandorla groaned as soon as he entered the room, as if she were dreaming that someone or something was hurting her. She writhed from side to side, in such distress that he sat down awkwardly upon the bed and pulled her toward him, cradling her head in his arms as best he could. He held her thus until she suddenly thrust away from him violently, and opened her eyes.

Alas, there was no spark of intelligence or recognition in her gaze. David's heart sank as he met her stare and found no real power of perception in it. She did not cower away from him but she was rigid

139

with incomprehension. She did not know what or where she was, and had no ready instinct to guide her reaction.

"Mandorla," he said softly. He hoped that the sound of her name might bring her to her senses, but it had no immediate effect. She looked wildly around, holding her body rigid. It was as though she longed to poise herself for a predatory leap, but could not work out why she had such unwieldy limbs, or how she came to be imprisoned by heavy bedclothes.

David had once seen Pelorus in a similar state, which had lasted for several weeks. It had been no mere disorientation; Pelorus had been disabled by Bast's newborn sphinx creature. Mandorla had been injured by perfectly ordinary means, but she too had been touched by the sphinx. David could not be sure that she would come to herself soon, given the extent to which her magical nature had been degraded.

"Wait," he said, rising from the chair. He raised his arms in a placatory gesture as he began to move toward the door.

She watched him, uneasily, as he backed away.

"I'll bring you some food," he said, stressing the final word in case it should have the power to strike a chord in her brain. She kept her eyes on him while he moved to the door, but her expression was utterly blank.

When he returned, in due course, with a bowl of rabbit stew and a spoon with which to feed her, Mandorla had not moved from the bed. She was staring at her own hand, as though astonished to find herself equipped with such a thing. David set the soup down on the dressing table and took a hand mirror out of the drawer. He held it out to her but she could not take it, and he had to place it before her face so that she could look at her reflection. She did not recognize herself. Perhaps that was not so very surprising; the face she wore now was not the one she was used to seeing. In any case, to Mandorla mirrors had long been magical devices for the deployment of visions rather than instruments of commonplace vanity and reassurance.

David took the mirror back, and laid it to one side. He brought her the bowl instead. She regarded the spoon with caution, but consented to be fed; this at least she understood. The stew had been simmering on the stove for some time, but its aroma was still rich, and it had enough meat in it to recommend itself to her palate. She was in dire need of the sustenance, but there was nothing avid about the way she ate. She watched him all the while with anxious, lackluster eyes.

"Pelorus brought you here," he told her, while he fed her. "He thought that you might be safe here—safer than elsewhere, at any rate—and that my medical skills might be of some use. Whatever I can do for you, I will—but you must recover your senses, for I shall need your help. You must remember me, Mandorla. I am David Lydyard, Pelorus's friend."

It was not until she had finished eating that she tried to speak, and when she did it was to say: "Pelorus?" She pronounced the syllables as though she were uncertain of their significance, but he took it as a hopeful sign that she had found her human voice.

"He had to go," David told her. "He has gone to search for the Clay Man. The will of Machalalel has weakened its grip upon his soul, I think, but the bond of friendship and loyalty is as strong as ever. He fears that Luke Capthorn intends to destroy all Machalalel's progeny, and that Machalalel is no longer able to prevent it."

The speech evidently made no sense to her, but the simple fact of his speaking began to recall a little of her precarious humanity. Her expression gradually changed, and her eyes began to look at him in a different way. He could see that she knew him some moments before she spoke his name.

He reached out a hand again, intending to touch her brow, but she took it in her own, and brought it instead to rest upon her cheek.

"David?" she said, shivering slightly. "is it *David*? How *old* you are!"

David ran his other hand through his milk-white hair, and wished that the wrinkles around his eyes had set to that mahogany hardness which had possessed and preserved Sir Edward Tallentyre's handsome face until the day he died. "I never thought that I should have to say so," he said, sadly, "but even you, Mandorla, have lost the bloom of youth."

She frowned, and lifted her delicate fingers to touch her throat, and then her cheek.

"Even so, you are still the handsomest woman I ever saw," David added, by way of awkward recompense.

She did not reply immediately, and when she did he was genuinely surprised by what she said. "But you never loved me," she murmured forlornly. "You ought to have loved me, and never did."

He did not know what to say to that.

"There was a man with a knife," she said, dreamily, looking down at herself as if she were amazed to find that she still wore solid flesh. She saw the wound in her breast, and frowned. "I had not time, nor strength," she murmured. "The blade . . . did the blade do that?"

"You were stabbed," David confirmed. "Pelorus saved your life."

"And brought me to you," she said, still speaking as if she were in a trance, "so that you might love and cherish me, as you should."

"The first time we met," he reminded her drily, "your only purpose was to taunt and torture me. I had not understood that you intended me to *love and cherish* you. Later, to be sure, you proposed an alliance—but there was an element of mockery even in that."

She moved her pillows so that she could lie back upon them while keeping her head upright. She was clearly very tired, but she was alert now, and in full possession of her human self. He was glad to see it, although it robbed him of the authority which he had briefly exercised over her. She looked at him now as she had long before, as if he were her plaything, to do with as the whim took her.

"Make love to me now, David," she said softly. She was still holding his hand, but only lightly, and he was easily able to take it back.

"I can't," he said, wishing that his voice sounded less gruff, less timorous.

She frowned. "I never found that human love was weakened by confrontation with cruelty," she said, as sardonically as her weak voice could contrive. "My experience has been that beauty has more power to cleave a way through the heart of a man if it has a razor's edge. I promised to come back one day, did I not, to steal you away from your beloved Cordelia when she had grown old and over-familiar? Here I am, at last. You should be grateful."

An expression of mild perplexity crossed her face as she watched his reaction, and David knew that his own face must have darkened considerably. It must have taken her a moment or two to realize why. She had been delving deep to recover her memories of him, and had not quite connected them with what Pelorus must surely have told her during the intervening years.

"Ah!" she said, softly. "She never did become over-familiar, did she? But she *has* grown old, has she not?"

"I haven't seen her for twenty years and more," David said, trying hard to keep his voice perfectly steady. Confrontation with Mandorla always seemed to require such efforts of him.

Mandorla was silent for a few moments, during which she looked around the room, doubtless finding it narrow, dreary and drab. Although she had never liked her human form she had long indulged and cultivated its taste for luxury. She touched the exposed part of her wound, and David saw that its condition had further improved, as though weeks of healing had been compressed into an hour and a half. She pulled the blanket up again, not out of modesty but as armor against the cold; she was shivering slightly. She made an evident effort to gather herself together before meeting his eyes again, and succeeded.

"I never thought I should have to say it to a mere mortal," she confessed, with an affected sigh, "but I feel that a long time has passed since last we talked. Time was when twenty years was a mere eye-blink to me, but time seems to have slowed in its paces since I became reconciled to my humanity. Now that I have begun to age, my youth—although it lasted ten thousand years and more—seems like a fleeting dream. You must take your share of the blame for that, David. Can you honestly say that you would not rather have found me inhuman and unrepentant? Can you honestly say that you did not love me at all, when I was the dangerous guiding light of the werewolves of London?"

"I always liked the human in you better than the wolf," David said. "I hesitate to declare myself an exception to your wide experience, but I have always found more to love in gentleness than mere glamour."

"*Mere* glamour!" she echoed. The timber of her mild laughter assured him that she was quite well again. But the laugh died away, and she became contemplative. She looked at him with what seemed to be genuine concern.

"How are you, David?" she asked him, in an absurdly conventional way. "Does your unkind angel still rack your joints and sinews with merciless insistence?"

He found it difficult to choose an appropriate tone in which to frame his reply. "Not so much," he said, carefully. "I have arthritis still, but it has developed very slowly and I have adapted to it. The human brain has the capacity to do that. It is a direly difficult thing to achieve, but with schooling and determination it really is possible for the physical aspects of pain to be reinterpreted by consciousness. Given time enough, even the most hellish of tortures can be accommodated. I still take laudanum but less often than I used to, as much for the wings it lends to my dream-self as for its anesthetic qualities. I never contrived to turn pain into a species of pleasure, but I have managed to dull its effects on my senses and my spirit. I cannot honestly say that I am *well*, but I could be worse."

"And what about the other kind of pain?" she asked.

He frowned.

"You know what I mean," she said. "I have read your work, as you know." She was certainly recovered now, and the rapidity of her reversion had left him slightly confused.

"I have never found a way of adapting myself to *that* kind of pain," David said reluctantly. "Simon is dead, and Teddy and Nell have long been under constant threat of injury and death in this appalling war. I have no barrier at all against the fear and despair which haunt my all-too-lucid dreams." He did not dare to mention Cordelia.

Mandorla reached out again with her right hand, and placed it over his for the second time. It seemed to be a reflexive gesture, and a human gesture at that. "I think I understand," she said. He was not certain that she did, or that she ever could. He knew that she had never cared at all for any of her human lovers, regarding them as mere prey, while her genuine and wholehearted affection for the members of her pack had never been threatened by the possibility of their irredeemable loss—until now.

"I may be oversensitive, even by human standards," he admitted, ashamed of his unkind judgment of her inability to feel true sympathy. "I suppose it's merely my weakness that makes me hurt so much. Tallentyre would have borne it far better, had he a son to lose." *But he had a daughter,* he added, silently, *and Lady Rosalind, and his beloved Elinor.* "You must think me very feeble," he continued, aloud, "to complain so bitterly of something so slight."

"Once," she said reflectively, "I would have thought so. Now . . . there are many things about which I am not so certain."

She is trying to be kind! he thought. *Mandorla Soulier is trying to be kind. Of all the omens and portents of the end which have been brought to my attention, this is surely the most eloquent!*

"Pelorus asked that I keep you here for a while," he said, abruptly deciding to be businesslike. "I told him that you could stay as long as you please."

"Why?" she asked.

He blinked, taken by surprise. "Because he asked me, as a friend," he said.

She shook her head, as though it were the wrong answer. She released his hand again, and used her own to take up a few of the long hairs which hung down from her head, rolling them between her slender fingers. Something about their texture was evidently not to her liking.

"Perhaps I ought to tell you," he said hesitantly, "that it was the sphinx who brought you here, and she who sent Pelorus away. I cannot be certain that you are *free* to leave, if the sphinx desires that you stay."

She looked at him sharply. "Oh, I am free," she said. "Make no mistake about that. If I do not wish to be here, no power on earth can force me to remain. But why should the sphinx act on *my* behalf? She seemed only too eager to thwart me when last we met."

David remembered the way Mandorla had stood beside him when Tallentyre had been appointed by the sphinx to confront Harkender in Zelophelon's little theater of hell. She had whispered ironic asides in his ear. She had not *met* the sphinx at all—and she had been a mere pawn then, as she was now, no matter how keenly she sought to become a player.

"I shall be very glad to have you stay, Mandorla," he said, with a faint smile. "I had not realized how dull life had become, until I saw your eyes open, and heard your voice."

"In that case," she said, "I will stay, for a little while at least. And what you ask of me, as a friend, I will grant. Is that a mirror lying there?"

He took it up again, and passed it to her. "You have looked into it once already," he told her, "but you could not see yourself."

"I cannot see myself now," she muttered, as she peered into the glass. "I can only see a human—and a stranger. If only I had a little magic left, I could change the reflection, and the flesh too."

"If only," David echoed, feeling slightly embarrassed by the perverse pang of satisfaction that he felt to see her so reduced. But when she looked up at him, reproachfully, it was all too plain that she had not lost all of her glamour, nor her power to disturb the paces of his wounded heart.

"Perhaps I am a gift," she said whimsically. "Perhaps I was summoned here to relieve your endless misery. Perhaps it was always fated, from the moment we first met, that you and I should love one another."

"You can't love me, Mandorla," he said stonily, "because I'm not a wolf. And I can't love you, even a little—because you are."

She laughed—and then she smiled.

"Not any more," she said, putting a far braver face on her distress than he had ever put on his. "Not any more."

6

The upper lounge had been reserved to officers and civilians, but still it was full of noise, hardly less raucous than the lower deck where the enlisted men were crammed in like cattle. Whiskey and cheap gin were flowing in some abundance, but there was something forced and false about the celebration. Nell could feel the bitter undercurrent beneath the mask of joviality, not only in her own group but throughout the vast smoke-filled space. While she and her companions laughed and joked with the young men in uniform, their hearts were anchored by doubt and haunted by anxiety, and Nell had no doubt that the suave masks which the captains wore and the subalterns aped hid dolor and confusion. She was continually losing track of the conversation, her rudderless and somber thoughts drifting helplessly away while her incurious eyes roamed back and forth in objectless quest.

The ferry was bound for Southampton, and the great majority of those it carried had not set foot on English soil for some time. The relief of their homecoming was, however, offset by the knowledge that this was by no means a triumphant return, whatever the politicians might say about peace with honor. The war was not really over; still less had it been won. No amount of diplomatic bluster could hide or disguise that fact.

All these men—and women too, Nell was careful to add, even in the privacy of her own thoughts—had been sent to wage a war to end war. They had been assured that it was worth fighting, and vitally necessary, for no less a cause than the salvation of civilization. Millions of their comrades had laid down their lives for such slogans, but in the end they had succeeded only in fighting to a weary stale-mate which no one believed permanent. These people were not re-turning to civilian life, but to a Britain which must now become an island fortress, perpetually under threat of invasion. All the nations involved in the war had been severely impoverished, because the economic heart had been ripped out of Europe, and all their people would suffer in consequence; but the munitions factories would have to be kept busy, to lay in supplies and stockpiles for the next flare-up of hostilities.

The only winners of the war, it was widely said, had been the Americans, who had procrastinated so long over the commitment of their troops as not to have to fight it. There were numerous American officers in the lounge, fraternizing freely with the English, but there was more than the usual English reserve keeping them at bay. The Alliance which had, in the end, failed to stand firm against Luden-dorff had been rotted and corroded by mistrust and recrimination.

Nell's aimlessly wandering gaze was intercepted, and briefly held, by that of a young man in civilian dress: a young man with dark, brooding eyes and an impression of such intense and honest seri-ousness that he seemed to her to be the only honest man in the crowd. Although he was moving in her direction, and looking directly at her, it did not immediately occur to her that he had any particular purpose in mind, so she looked away again almost as soon as their glances had locked—but when he came to stand before her she could not help but meet his eyes again, uncertainly. He was nineteen, per-haps twenty, and quite handsome in spite of the melancholy cast of his features. Her practiced eye noticed the scar of a bullet wound high on his right temple, partly obscured by his neatly combed, dark brown hair. It must have been a bad one, she judged; he was lucky to be alive. He was slimly built, although this was by no means obvious, because he wore a heavy and ungainly overcoat beneath which something rather bulky was concealed.

"Excuse me," he said. "Miss Elinor Lydyard?" He spoke in English but his accent was unmistakably French.

"Yes," she said. "Have we met?" She had met a great many Frenchmen in the last four years, and the patients she had tended—for obvious reasons—often remembered her far better than she re-membered them.

"No, never," he replied, punctiliously. "My name is Anatole Dau-mier. I wonder if I might speak with you, in private."

In private! She looked around at the bustling crowd. The lounge was far too full to permit the existence of a quiet corner or uninhabited alcove.

"I fear that I have no cabin," said the Frenchman—had anyone aboard this floating madhouse a cabin of his own, save for her master?—but I believe that we might find a place to talk on deck, if you do not mind the cold too much. The rain has almost stopped."

Almost! she thought. "Why do you want to speak to me?" she asked. One or two of her companions were casting curious glances at the newcomer, wondering why there was suddenly a Frenchman in their midst. The French, close allies for four years, were seen differently now that they had come to terms with the Germans; amity had turned to uneasy mutual suspicion.

"It is difficult to explain," he said. "If I spoke to you of angels, in connection with your father, would you understand what I meant?"

Nell felt a sudden chill in her veins. This was not something she had expected—not *here*, in mid-channel, surrounded by the jetsam of the war, and not *now*, after a quarter of a century. She had put away such fantasies with other childhood things, although she knew full well that her father had never been able to forget. "What do you want with me, Monsieur Daumier?" she said, sharply.

"I have a message for your father, from your brother Simon. I need your help in delivering it."

The chill was renewed, but quickly controlled. "Simon is dead," she said, in a carefully neutral tone. "He was killed at Mons."

"Yes," said the young man, imperturbed. "I know that."

She rose immediately from her seat, taking up her cape, and squeezed past the people who were hemming her in. Daumier offered to take her arm but she declined; he followed her to a door which let them out onto the deck, hurrying to keep up as she deftly threaded her way through the drunken company.

The rain was no more than a fine drizzle, and they found shelter easily enough in the lee of one of the lifeboats. There were men moving back and forth on the deck, but none spared them more than a desultory glance.

"You had better explain," she said.

"You may be better placed to explain much of what I have to say than I am," he told her sadly. He reached into his overcoat, and exposed the corner of a bulky volume, not unlike a ledger of accounts. "I was asked to bring this to England," he said, "by a priest who claimed membership of an order named for a nonexistent saint."

"Amycus," she said. How had she remembered the name, when

she had not heard it for so many years? She would rather have forgotten it.

"I understand that your father has had some contact with the English branch of the order?"

She did not want to discuss obscure heretical sects. "You mentioned Simon," she said coldly. "How is it that you claim to have a message from him?"

The Frenchman looked down, embarrassed by her hostility. "I met him in a dream," he said. "I can only hope that my saying that seems less ridiculous to you than it sometimes seems to me."

"You are unlikely to have met him anywhere else," she replied coldly. "What makes you think that the dream ought to be taken seriously?"

"Among other things, this," he said, touching the book again. "It is a record of visions, whose makers clearly believed them to be meaningful and prophetic. In any case, the world itself seems recently to have taken on the semblance and logic of a dream, at least so far as I am concerned. I can no longer draw the boundary between actuality and illusion with any confidence. Do you see the wound on my forehead?" He pushed back his hair as he spoke.

"I see it."

"A German bullet went in there; it is still inside. I should have died, but something prevented my death. Something intervened, and kept me alive . . . at a price. I have been its puppet ever since; my actions and my dreams are no longer my own. It is a fearful thing, the scriptures tell us, to fall into the hands of the living God; I never thought to feel the truth of that threat, but I have lately learned that it is not as empty as I believed."

"What have Simon and my father to do with all this?" she asked impatiently.

"Your father, I think, is—or has been—in a similar situation. I have met others: one who calls himself Asmodeus, and one who calls herself Hecate. I was made prisoner by the first after trying to murder him; the second procured my release—but not, I think, for any noble reason. Under the influence of a drug given me by Asmodeus, perhaps also with the aid of Hecate's magic touch, I had a surpassingly strange dream. At one point I met an English officer, who asked me to carry a message to his father—to *your* father, Miss Lydyard—and to say that it came from Simon. I do not for a moment believe that it *does* come from your brother's shade, but the real sender doubtless has some reason for the pretense, if only a desire to be heard. Your father will certainly be better able than I to guess the true source of the dream and the message, for I am still a stranger in the world of these wayward angels, and a novice in their ways. Will you tell me where I might find him?''

Nell stared past the Frenchman at the gentle rain drifting down from the pitch-black sky, the tiny drops glistening in the glow of the ship's lights. The channel was so calm that there was hardly any rolling or yawing movement to signify that the ship was afloat, but there was a certain *latent unease* in the pit of her stomach: a visceral awareness that she was not, after all, on dry land, and that nothing stood between herself and the Abyss but a thin hull of painted steel. The relief which she had contrived to feel on embarking at Cherbourg, like that which she had felt on hearing of the signature of the peace treaty, had been measured and provisional; she had known all along that she could not feel safe until she stepped on to the solid mass of England. Now, she wondered whether she could feel safe even then, given that she was one of the unfavored few who knew of the war beyond the war. She had never wanted to be part of that stranger conflict, having seen only too well what it had done to her father—and, for that matter, her mother. She had always wanted to live a fully *human* life, even if that meant years of service behind the lines, surrounded by the maimed and the dying; but she had always feared that no one was beyond the reach of the angels' mysterious games.

She had a curious sensation of being *watched*, and looked around at the gloomy shadows crowded about the deck. There were people lurking here and there, some of them half-hidden, but the source of the feeling was no peripheral perception of their fortuitous presence. It was the knowledge that there were indeed such things as angels, even though the Church had grossly mistaken their form and function.

"If you tell me what my brother is supposed to have said to you," she said tiredly, "I will make sure that my father hears it."

"That would not be right," the Frenchman said. "It was intended, I think, that I should be the one to deliver the message."

"It may have been intended," she retorted, "but that is no reason why you or I should consent to the intention. Even the possessed retain the freedom of their will."

"True—but the scope for its exercise is limited in so many ways that it is more a curse than a privilege."

"Do not say that, Monsieur Daumier," she said tiredly. "Despair is a sin—perhaps the deadliest one of all, although it does not appear on the traditional list of seven. The angels may have the power to make pawns of us, to mold our flesh and corrupt our dreams, but we are in the end *ourselves*, and we must cling hard to everything that they cannot take away."

"Do you have bad dreams of your own, Miss Lydyard?" he asked. His compassion seemed sincere, and she was prepared to believe that it was more than a mask for curiosity. She had begun to like him. He seemed so very young, so very forlorn. She herself was thirty-six years old, perhaps not *quite* old enough to be his mother, but she felt that the last four years had aged her by half a century.

"Oh yes," she said, in a low voice. "I do not believe that they are demon-sent, but I certainly have dreams of death and destruction. Do you think that anyone could have lived through that hideous tumult and *not* be beset by nightmares? The world is a nightmare itself, as you know to your cost."

"Still we must live in it," he said. "Your grandfather's saying, I believe."

She was unimpressed by the extent of his research. "Why come to me, Monsieur Daumier?" she demanded. "Can you really not locate my father without my help?"

"I can probably locate him," he answered, readily enough, "but I am not sure that I could reach him. To tell you the truth, I tried to find your brother Edward before I came in search of you, but there has been such chaos in Belgium since France capitulated that it was not possible to track him down. I came to you because the opportunity arose."

"The son was unavailable, and so you reluctantly settled for the daughter," she said, with a hint of bitterness. "No wonder you quote my grandfather with such evident approval. Did you say that you had tried to murder Luke Capthorn?"

"I had good reason."

"So has everyone who has ever had the opportunity to meet him. I never have, but I have met his master—his human master, that is, not the monstrous angel which squats at the heart of the web which has entrapped them. Jacob Harkender is his name." She did not care to explain when and how she had met Jacob Harkender. There had only been the one occasion; she had never visited her mother since.

"I mean no harm to your father, Miss Lydyard," he said, earnestly.

"If my father needs to be guarded against your coming," she said, hoping that it might be true, "you will not be permitted to penetrate his defenses, even if I offer my assistance. I am a mere old maid, beloved by none and respected by none; I have no authority in the world of the angels."

He was, of course, compelled by gallantry and Gallic temperament alike to deny it. "I cannot believe that, Miss Lydyard," he said. "I am sorely in need of a friend to help me grope my way through the murk of this mad adventure, and I think that you would be a very valuable friend to have. I wish you would consent to help me. I wish that you would tell me what you know of these matters, for I am in desperate need of understanding."

He looked so very young, so very helpless, like hundreds of other young and helpless men who had needed her help desperately, and had come to depend on her ministrations. He was just one more in the vast company of walking wounded, stumbling bravely on toward the grave and the gate of Hell, not daring to ask for anything more than an arm to lean on and a kind word. The force of ingrained habit made her want to reach out to him, to give him whatever he thought he needed.

What he needed most, it seemed, was not to be alone in this dreadfully transfigured world which had seized him in its grip. Still she felt obliged to hesitate, lest she unwittingly play traitor to her luckless father.

"I will think about it," she promised. "Can we go back inside now? The rain is beginning to seep inside my collar."

"Yes, of course," he said hastily. He turned abruptly, determined this time that he should lead the way, at least to the doorway. Nell was more than ready for a scalding taste of whiskey, to take away the bitterness that had crept unbidden onto her thick tongue and into her desert throat. But the young Frenchman's progress toward the door of the lounge had been blocked by another lumpenly dressed figure, and Nell had to pull up short to avoid bumping into him. The newcomer did not move aside. She had barred their way on purpose. To Nell she looked extremely ordinary, but Daumier's sharp intake of breath testified that he knew her, and was afraid. Nell realized that her feeling that she and Daumier were being watched had been more accurate than she had been prepared to credit.

"Miss Lydyard?" the woman said, in a dull and distinctly English voice.

"I am very popular tonight," said Nell, trying hard to be flippant. "What do you want of me?"

"The same as Monsieur Daumier. I need to deliver a message to your father."

"She is the one who set me free in Paris," said Daumier quickly. "The one who calls herself Hecate."

"Given that," said the woman quietly, "there seems little need to fear me now." She certainly did not look fearsome; she was shorter than Nell by an inch, and the doughy flesh of her features hung tiredly from the bones of her skull. She looked like a scullery maid defeated by the rigors of mean existence. But Nell remembered the name Hecate as easily as she had remembered Amycus, and remembered her father had called Hecate a murderer by magic.

"The Royal Mail is very efficient," said Nell. "If you address a letter to my father it will certainly reach him, even at World's End."

"Perhaps," the woman replied. "But I strongly suspect that nothing can reach him at present without some deliberate relaxation of the invisible barriers which have grown up around him. Something destructive is abroad in the world, and we are all in danger. The barriers which protect your father are not under his control, but I think he may be more important than he knows. He will be permitted to make you welcome, and if you can persuade him to invite us into his home . . . his curiosity is a very precious thing, and his guardian angel ought to be anxious to assuage it."

"Do you not have the power to reach into his dreams to ask him for an invitation?" Nell asked. "You are a witch of sorts, are you not?"

"I have magic," the woman agreed unenthusiastically, "and there was magic in my making, but I was born of a woman, as you were. I have a mind of my own, and interests of my own. I am neither my maker's mask nor my maker's helpless slave. If the angels' war has brought the world to the brink of destruction, I have my own fate to settle."

Nell shook her head, well aware that her question had gone unanswered. "I am in no position to judge these matters," she said. "I will tell my father what you have said—what *both* of you have said—but I will not bring either of you into his house until he tells me that I may."

The woman immediately nodded in agreement. "I ask no more than that," she said. "I will do what I can while we are *en route* to convince you that I am not your enemy."

"Could you not transport us to my father's house in the blink of an eye?" Nell asked sarcastically. "Are you not accustomed to traveling by broomstick, or magic carpet, or by mere whim?"

"Miracles are not worked without cost," the witch replied evasively. "The greater the miracle, the greater the cost. Even the angels exert themselves to be as clever as they can in making the minimum of effort produce the maximum effect, and even the angels fear that their awkwardness and artlessness might lead them to disaster. It would be foolish to reduce myself to a shadow, though time presses. Trains will serve our purpose well enough."

"It is an uncomfortable world in which we all have to live," Nell admitted, not pressing the point although she strongly suspected that the woman had something to hide. "What burdens and embarrassments matter, space and time must be to those who live outside them."

"We all dwell in *time*," Hecate corrected her. "Even the angels." The fine rain had wetted her features so much that they glistened palely with reflected light, but she did not seem at all like a witch or any supernatural thing. She still wore the guise of a servant or a slattern, and Nell wondered whether the appearance might be more honest than its wearer intended—but she knew that she too must seem misfortunately plain and sadly dishevelled.

"We should go in now," Nell said. "There is a long way to go before we dock in Southampton, and a long journey ahead of us once we are disembarked. The time will weigh heavily enough on all of us."

7

In the days which followed her arousal from the deathlike trance which might have held her in its grip for centuries, Mandorla hardly slept at all. Nor could she settle into comfortable stillness for more than a few minutes. She wandered from place to place, fretting over the narrowness of the cottage's rooms. She went out a dozen times a day, walking through the gloomy woods to the broken shore where the sea was gradually consuming the slowly tilting land. Usually she went alone; David's presence sometimes increased her restlessness, adding a further irritant to whatever unquiet spirit moved within her.

David had never seen Pelorus like this; it was by no means a normal aspect of the lycanthropic condition. Even so, he could not help interpreting what he saw in terms of her unruly animal soul raging against imprisonment. He had seen big cats in Regent's Park Zoo endlessly pacing back and forth in their narrow cages, spurred to action by deep-set instincts which could not adapt their motive force to claustral captivity.

When Mandorla could not bear him to be near her David scrupulously stayed out of her way, but he watched her carefully, partly to study her and partly because he feared for her. At other times, however, the restlessness within her had a different effect. Then she looked to him for distraction and amusement, requiring his attendance and his attention. She would not leave him alone, plaguing him with all kinds of arbitrary inquiries and requests. He felt himself sadly inadequate to meet such demands. It was never sufficient to answer the specific questions which she posed or meet the particular requests which she made; what she wanted was never that for which she actually

157

asked, because she never knew herself what it would take to soothe her wayward heart.

David knew that he had always been a dull companion, even to those he loved best, but he was more acutely aware of it now than ever before, partly because Mandorla made more prolific demands than Cordelia or his children ever had, and partly because there was not the least vestige of dullness in *her*, even though her pale skin was lacklusterly creased and her violet eyes had faded to a ghostly lilac hue.

One day she walked with him into the nearest village. It was not strictly necessary for him to go—he had already sent messages to the local tradesmen *via* their delivery men to ask for an increase in the goods which they supplied—but it was his habit, and the prospect promised a brief release. He always felt better once he had passed through the oppressive woodland which separated his tiny realm from the greater world; there was an odd kind of comfort in being a man among men, which persisted even though he had a werewolf by his side. News of Mandorla's presence had already spread far and wide—others beside the delivery men had seen her abroad—and her progress down the winding main street was observed with a good deal of attention by the local women. She ignored them all, gracefully rather than contemptuously; it had long been second nature to her to pose as an aristocrat.

David had long since ceased to care about the whispers that were forever abroad concerning his many eccentricities, but he took the trouble to listen carefully to a few of the conversations which went on around him, curious to know if any evidence had been left behind of the sphinx's murderous intervention in Pelorus's adventure of the previous week. There would certainly have been a healthy measure of horrified gossip had four dead men been found on any road within the county, even after a lapse of some days, but he heard nothing, and concluded that the bodies must have been stealthily removed.

He had hoped that Mandorla might be a little less ill-at-ease while they were away from the house and its too-solid walls, but it was impossible to detect any considerable benefit. Once they were at home again her restlessness returned in full force. He offered her laudanum but she would not touch it; she preferred agitation to drugged oblivion. She took wine with the evening meal, but intoxication did not relax her in the least, and when David tried to read she prowled around so excitedly that he could not concentrate at all.

Eventually, he laid his book down, lit a candle and blew out the lamp, hoping that quiet light might calm her.

It did not.

He began to wonder, after a while, whether it might have been a mistake to rouse her so soon from her unnatural sleep. Perhaps, he thought, she might have recovered herself more completely if she had been allowed to rest a little longer.

In the end, she asked him again, forthrightly, to make love to her, and became annoyed when he said again: "I can't."

"You need not fear that I will turn into a wolf," she told him waspishly.

It was on the tip of his tongue to reply that it was no compliment to be asked to make love as though he were being asked to scratch an itch, as a means of relaxation, but there was no point in any such evasion or pretense. "It matters not who or what you are," he said in a low tone. "When I say that I cannot, I mean just that."

She had the grace to be a little sympathetic. "Has your jealous mistress robbed you of that, too?" she said. "Her rivals are much kinder, if rumor is to be believed."

"I know that," he replied bitterly.

She was sufficiently careful of his feelings not to pursue the point. Instead, she said: "Talk to me, then. Tell me what we are doing here together. Tell me what it is that we are waiting for."

Oddly enough, it was not until she said it in so many words that he realized that they were indeed *waiting*. David suddenly felt completely isolated from that world of men which he had visited only a few hours before. He was glad, then, that he was not alone.

"We *are* waiting, are we not?" said Mandorla. "We have been placed here in readiness for *something*, but nothing is happening and I cannot penetrate the veil of ignorance. My dreams are nothing but confusion and the recapitulation of ancient memories—fragmented, momentary things. I used to be a far better dreamer than that, although the pollutions of hope and ambition betrayed the accuracy of all but the best of my visions."

"I wish I still had hopes and ambitions to pollute mine," said David.

"Sometimes," Mandorla said, looking deep into the flame of the candle which was all the illumination they had or needed, "I think that my entire existence as a human has been a dream, and that my transformations have been but a dream within a dream, a phantom echo of my true self. Sometimes, I think that my real body lies sleeping somewhere, sleek and white and patient, and that one day I will rouse myself, scratching at my fur and licking my teeth, and will discover that these ten thousand seeming years have been but a few greatly magnified moments, that the Golden Age never came to an end, and that Machalalel—if he ever existed at all—found far better occupation for his meddlesome powers of creativity than the making of false men. But I can only end by reminding myself, sadly, that even if the world is but a dream, it is the world in which I must live, and that if I have already lived ten thousand years in the space of a few brief moments of real time, I might have to endure a hundred thousand more while my true heart beats half a dozen times.''

"I know the feeling," said David, uncannily sure that he did. "There have been many times when I have wondered whether I ever really recovered from the delirium into which I fell when I was bitten by that tiny snake in Egypt. I have often thought that my apparent awakening might have been one more in the series of visions which afflicted me as I lay in the hammock. Those other visions never released me; still I dream of myself as Satan; still I dream of an impotent God; still I dream of the werewolves of London; still I dream of the allegorical cave which Plato described. Each of those images still encages me, forms and shapes my understanding of the world . . . and if three of the images are purely symbolic, why not the fourth? Why should I not believe that the werewolves of London too are mere actors in some allegory, and that the real world which I believed incapable of containing such things has no such things within it. Why should I not presume that the world of werewolves, which I have inhabited for nearly fifty years, is but a tissue of dreams from which I might one day awake, if only the serpent's venom could be leeched from my flesh?

"In the end, though, I too remember what Tallentyre used to say so boldly and unrepentantly, once he had been forced by circumstances to admit that Acts of Creation were indeed possible: that if the world has, in fact, the texture and the logic of a dream, then we must live in it and strive all the harder to understand what limited order it has. You are right, Mandorla: if we have lived so long in a world which is naught but a dream, we might live here longer yet . . . perhaps for all eternity. And if, one day, we should happen to awaken, and find the world as it was when you were cursed and I was bitten, how could we ever know for sure that we really had returned to our true selves, rather than moving into one more deceptive phase of the infinite illusion?''

She was staring at him, as if astonished to find so close an echo of her own thoughts in his. ''We have dreamed too long,'' she whispered, after a while. ''It is true, David. We have dreamed too long to pledge our faith to any apparent wakefulness. And yet . . . perhaps that is what we are waiting for: an awakening.''

''Men are overfond of writing stories which conclude with awakenings,'' David said, shying away from the question of their *waiting*. ''The better ones are those in which the awakened dreamer finds some token which tells him that the dream was not a dream after all, but an actual disturbance of the scheme of things.''

''Perhaps our story will end like that,'' she said. ''What proper ending can a story have, after all, but a restoration of health and harmony?'' He knew that she was thinking wistfully of the Golden Age, and of the state of innocence which she had enjoyed when she was a wolf whose consciousness had never known the taint of thought.

How simple the vexatious business of ambition and hope would be, he thought, *had I such a clear goal before me.*

''Every story ends with a return to reality so far as its hearers are concerned,'' he said dourly, ''but the story which *is* reality cannot bend back upon itself; it must go on forever, changing into something new with every day that dawns.''

''Then I must hope that we are dreaming after all,'' she muttered.

''It is an unworthy hope,'' he told her. ''We have had our share of misfortune, you and I, but if we are to resist despair, we must find a better hope than *that*. Better to hope for the extinction of the angels than the restoration of their gaudy empire.''

''What are we waiting for, David?'' Mandorla asked, abruptly. ''And why should it be necessary for us to wait, if the angels can do anything upon a whim?''

''I can only guess the answers,'' he said. ''I could easily be wrong.''

''Guess,'' she bade him.

''I can only explain it in the form of an allegory,'' he said. ''It is the only way I have ever been able to think about the true nature of the world.''

''I am educated now,'' she told him stiffly. ''I understand what an allegory is.''

''Do you know the allegory of Plato's Cave?'' he asked.

She shook her head. This, he recalled, was the Mandorla who had once demanded that he dream for her: that he journey forth with the dark Angel of Pain and bring back news of the actual angels and the future of the world. How had she hoped to understand the news he brought back, when she knew so little about the vocabulary of ideas on which his dreaming had perforce to draw?

"In the *Republic*," he said, "Plato imagines that the human condition might be likened to that of prisoners tightly chained within a cave, with a great fire burning behind them. Because they cannot turn their heads they can see nothing but the wall before them, on which shadows are cast by beings which move back and forth along a road whose course lies between them and the fire. Seeing nothing but these shadows, all but a few of the prisoners cannot help but believe that the shadow-play is the whole of existence, and even the favored few must stretch their imagination to the limit if they are to catch the faintest comprehension of the greater reality, and of the nature of the beings which cast the shadows. If one man were to break the chain about his neck, so that he might turn and see the beings on the road directly, and the fire behind them, he would see what a mistake his fellows had made—but how could he convince his companions that his sight was not a kind of dream, or a kind of madness?"

"Once," Mandorla said, reflectively, "all men respected the kind of sight which the Others had, and were ever anxious to seek truth in their own dream-sight. It is only in recent times that such visions have come to be called *madness*."

"There is more," said David. "I dreamed, of course, that I was the man who turned around, and saw the entities which paraded themselves upon the road *directly*. Because I was in Egypt, and my head was full of the images of ancient Egyptian gods, those were the forms which my questioning sight imposed upon them; and the one which looked back at me—the one which had broken the chain about my neck—I saw as cat-headed Bast. I knew even then, I think, that what I was seeing was a product of my own mind—that the reality of what I was looking at could only become imaginable by the arbitrary establishment of a set of signs and symbols. How else can a connection be made between a human being and an entity which has no material body?"

"This is not so very complicated," said Mandorla, with a frown. "You turned away from the shadow-world of everyday experience and beheld the reality whose shadow it is. You became the pawn of one of the beings which inhabit that greater reality. I understand all that.''

"You must understand more than that,'' David insisted. "You must understand that looking into the world that lies behind and beyond the world of appearances is very difficult. We can only do it by building a further set of appearances. Even ordinary sight is not passive; the eye and the brain collaborate in the complicated processes of attention, recognition and interpretation. Any sight which tries to grope for the greater reality, whether through the medium of scientific theories or revelatory dreams, must be more active still. If these entities we call angels are to be seen and understood, they must be given names, and perhaps faces—but we must not fall into the trap of thinking that we have captured their true nature with our tentative descriptions.''

"I understand that too,'' Mandorla assured him.

"But that is not the whole of the allegory of the cave,'' he told her patiently. "The fire which casts the shadows is not the *ultimate* source of light, nor are the beings whose shadows are cast the ultimate constituents of reality. There is a narrow passage beyond the fire, which leads upward to the outer world. In order to see the universe in all its complex majesty, it is necessary for the prisoner to cast of *all* his shackles, to walk past or through the fire, and to pass through the narrow corridor. Only then may he stand at last on the threshold of his prison, and look out into the glory of the *true* light.

"The entities which walk upon the road, you see, even if they be gods or angels by comparison with mere men, are still inhabitants of the cave; and the fire which warms their souls is but a fire. When the angels pass along the corridor, to look out upon the world as it truly is, they too go forth as ignorant strangers who must *learn* to see—and in order to do that, they need the borrowed sight of men as much as men need the borrowed sight of magic.

"Twenty-five years ago, three angels consented to approach that threshold, bringing six lesser creatures with them to act as collaborative seers. By that means they snatched a momentary glimpse of the prospect which lay before them. To this day I can only speculate about what *they* found in the chaos we beheld, but I know that I saw far too little. I was dazzled, and was snatched intemperately back from the edge when I had hardly *begun* to see or understand. Since then, I have tried as hard as I might to improve my understanding, but I have always known that unless I could go back again to the mouth of the cave, far better forearmed, I would never know the truth.

"Perhaps I never shall know the truth. Perhaps the human mind is too feeble an instrument, even with the aid of the angels, to penetrate the glare . . . but I suspect that I shall be given a second chance. One day, I will be asked to be an oracle again. I do mean *asked*, for no man can be forced to an understanding he does not desire . . . but Bast and I both know that I cannot and will not refuse. What else matters to me, now?

"That, Mandorla, is what we are waiting for."

He did not expect her to be content with that, and she was not. "But *why* are we waiting?" she repeated, yet again. "And why must *I* wait with you?"

"The difficult we do at once," he said, quoting an advertising slogan he had read, "but the impossible takes a little longer. The angels dwell in time, as men do, but they experience it very differently. Angels have no hearts to beat time and measure out their lives. They have some power to alter the appearances of the world, including the appearances of the past, but they are bound by the arrow of time to move ever forward. Sometimes they have the facility to move very quickly, but sometimes they must slowly feel their way. Last time, the preparation of the oracle took far longer than the vision itself. Whatever the angels are trying to do, it is difficult for them, perhaps because it involves their active collaboration. They are undertaking careful maneuvers, in order to achieve something unprecedented and delicately contrived. It may be that they are under fire the while, from others not involved in the collaboration. We see none of this, not even in our dreams, but we are like little insects lost in the no-man's-land which separates forces beyond our comprehension. We may easily become casualties of the war, but not true combatants.

"As for you, Mandorla . . . perhaps you too have a vital part to play. Perhaps, unwillingly and unwittingly, you have been forged by long experience of life on earth into an instrument capable of adding to our understanding of what lies beyond the cave."

"If you are right," she said, after a few moments, somehow seeming more human now than she had ever seemed before, "the angels don't know, any more than we do, what might be necessary to that understanding. How can they possibly prepare us, if they don't know what they're preparing us *for*?"

"They have used us for a long time," he said. "They have used your kind as well as mine, but it is only in the recent past that our true potential has become evident. If they do not know by now how best to use us, they must at least *believe* they know. I only wish I knew whether I ought to hope that they are right or wrong.''

8

Mercy Murrell watched herself in the mirror that was mounted in the ceiling above her bed. The greater part of her body was obscured by Jacob Harkender's as he moved back and forth with his customary stately rhythm, but that did not matter to her. It was her face that she watched with delight and fascination: her dark, provocative eyes; her full, sensuous lips sliding back to reveal the tips of her even, pearl-like teeth. Her tawny hair cascaded across the pillow like a framing aureole.

All that is mine, she thought.

She never tired of watching her face as it softened and flushed in the grip of the dull tide of sensation which swelled inside her, but she always felt a curious sense of detachment while she did so. She always thought *that is mine,* never *this is me*; she had no doubt that her body belonged to her, and that it was entirely at her disposal, but there nevertheless remained a sense in which it was not really *her*. It was something given—or perhaps only lent—by another. That sense of the precariousness of her ownership was one of the reasons why she never tired of watching herself in mirrors.

There had been a time, many years ago, when she had tired of almost everything. She had been bitter then; her soul had been knotted with wrath and resentment. She had hated beauty because she found it only in others and never in herself. In her earlier incarnation she had never taken pleasure in sexual intercourse; as a whore she had suffered it and as a mistress of whores she had taken pride in the fact that she need suffer it no longer. All that had changed when Harkender found the fount of youth, and invited her to share in its

167

rewards. Youth was a powerful antidote to the kind of heart-sickness which had spoiled her life. In that former incarnation the joys and privileges of youth had evaded her, but she was young now. She never took it for granted that she would be young forever, in spite of Jacob Harkender's confident assurances. She had heard too many assurances given by boastful men to place any credence at all in their judgments of probability, let alone their honor and honesty. Harkender was a better man than most, in her estimation, but he was still a devoted servant of the Father of Lies. The delight she took in mirrors was sharpened by a lurking anxiety that the time would one day come when she would look into one and see her true self instead of the lovely mask that she had been given to wear.

Because Mercy could not assume that her renewed youth and beauty would last forever she had not the least fear that it might become tedious in its perfection. Every new day found her enthusiastic and determined to make the most of her opportunities, and she pursued her customary pastimes with relentless vigor. She was, as she had always been, a whore and mistress of whores, but she no longer dabbled in mere brothel-keeping. The transactions in which she engaged were far more subtle and far more lucrative; she had not lost her love of the theatre but she now had pride enough to think of the world itself as one more stage.

She had not lost all her contempt for the ludicrous business of sexual intercourse, nor had she learned to take the abundant pleasure from it of which some women were evidently capable. Blind Tiresias, having been privileged to experience sexual congress as a man and as a woman, was reputed to have said that the pleasure a woman obtained far outweighed that of a man, but the woman Tiresias had been must have mastered secrets that Mercy, for all her vast experience, had never penetrated. Even so, she had found some capacity to revel in erotic intoxication, and was not altogether displeased with her attainments. Of all her lovers, she reckoned Harkender the best, not because of his physical enhancement but because there was a special bond between them. Unlike the rest of her acquaintances, he knew what she really was and what she really thought, and did not care at all. She did not *love* him in the glutinous fashion that his beloved Cordelia appeared to do, nor did she any longer feel much gratitude for the fact that she owed her present condition entirely to him, but she respected and admired him. She obtained little pleasure from the contemplation of his body, handsomely Dionysian though it was—whenever Harkender turned her head away from the mirror, forcing her to look into his eyes so that he could look into hers, she remained indifferent—but he assisted her, after his fashion, to glory in the one she owned.

Harkender paused briefly in his endeavor now, and demanded her attention. Obediently, she looked into his sea-blue eyes.

He had nothing to say to her; he desired only to remind her of his claim upon her soul, and perhaps to take pleasure in contemplation of his achievements. Whatever the expression in his eyes might be, as he studied her features, she was perfectly certain that it was not love. Harkender loved no one but Cordelia, who had been Cordelia Tallentyre and Cordelia Lydyard but was now simply Cordelia.

Mercy knew that Harkender thought of his love for Cordelia as something pure and wholly good, but she felt free to be cynical about its perversity. Could he have loved Cordelia, she thought, had she been anything other than the most precious possession of his adversaries? Probably not. Could he have loved Cordelia if he had not been forced by Zelophelon to share her defiantly brave, coquettishly self-loving, shamelessly sentimental consciousness for so many years, contrasting it all the while with Luke Capthorn's petty viciousness and Mercy's own adamantine hardness? Surely not. Could he have loved Cordelia if Zelophelon had not restored her luminous youth and porcelain prettiness to a peak of perfection she had never quite achieved without angelic aid, and maintained it so very carefully? Absolutely not.

Mercy was equally cynical about Cordelia's love for Harkender, which he thought of as something honestly won and honestly retained. Although she suspected that David Lydyard would never be able to shake off his own doubts, Mercy had none at all; she was certain that it was by Zelophelon's irresistible command and not by the force of her own free will that Cordelia had deserted her husband and children, and that Lydyard's own guardian had for some perverse and secret motive consented to the theft and to the treason. In Mercy's eyes, Cordelia was no less a whore than any of the girls she herself bought and traded daily.

Harkender released her gaze, and she returned it gratefully to the mirror. She met her borrowed eyes, and exchanged a luxurious conspiratorial smile with her *doppelgänger*. She knew that mirrors were often used by magicians as visionary windows, through which they could look into other worlds, but she was satisfied with the very ordinary magic of reflection. In the long-gone days when Harkender had tried to tutor her she had never shown the least talent for his kind of magic.

Sometimes, when she looked at herself in this way, Mercy could not help but wonder whether there was some other presence behind her eyes. She had been told that Harkender was not the only one who had used her as a seer—that Lydyard had done likewise—and she had observed that sometimes, when Harkender spoke to her, he seemed to be addressing others as well as or instead of her: angels as well as men. It was a disturbing thought, in its way, but it carried a curious kind of thrill. She was, after all, a whore, and had she been required to set a price on her soul she would have offered it as readily, and at no greater price, than her body.

Harkender came smoothly to his climax and then gradually relaxed, letting the weight of his body descend smotheringly upon her. There was no sharp climax to her own pleasure, merely a heat which tentatively waxed and gradually waned, fading by languid degrees into a half-hearted drowsiness. She waited, patiently, until Harkender condescended to withdraw. When he had done so he lay face down, luxuriating in his self-induced fatigue, but Mercy shook off her incipient torpor, got up, and quickly sponged herself before putting on her clothes. By the time she had finished he had turned onto his side, and was watching her.

"There is no urgency," he said. "You must try to become accustomed to the fact that we have all the time in the world. You should put away your old habits, Mercy dear, and cultivate some which would be better suited to your station."

"I have a certain affection for my habits," she told him drily. "I feel comfortable when I indulge them. In any case, you are so fond of your own habits and addictions that you have made them into sacred rites."

He laughed, although she had not intended the insult as a friendly jest. "*That* is no mere habit," he said. "It is art, it is transcendence, it is heroism and it is indeed *sacred;* it is not an addiction. You ought to try it, as you take such little pleasure in more mundane excitements. You have seen for yourself that it is perfectly safe."

"I have no talent for vision," she told him, "nor any other compensation for the ill-effects of pain. As for safety, I am not so sure that your guardian angel loves me as well as he loves you, and I hesitate to make reckless demands upon his protective magic."

Sometimes, Mercy wondered if Harkender's sole reason for making a mistress of her was to preserve and complete her role in those private rituals in which she had always been his assistant. It seemed unlikely; preliminary intercourse did not seem to be necessary to the ritual. In any case, there was nothing intrinsically odd in the fact that a man like Harkender should desire more than one mistress, even though he loved his first wholeheartedly. Pride was infinitely more precious to him than fidelity.

When Harkender rose from the bed and shuffled off into the adjoining room, Mercy turned to the mirror on her dressing table and inspected her face casually, satisfied with its symmetry and its agelessness. She waited patiently. This was but an interval; the second and more important phase of the drama had yet to begin. She felt hardly any sense of anticipation; her mind easily evaded contemplation of what was still to come. She had never been able to cultivate a level of fascination adequate to make it personally rewarding.

There are others more fitted for this work than I, she admitted to herself, meeting her own frank stare with brutal honesty, *but I ought to be grateful that he never had the inclination to seek out one of them—and doubly grateful, I suppose, that he would never dream of inflicting this duty upon his beloved Cordelia. It is at least possible, if not probable, that my renewed youth hangs upon the thread of this peculiar service. It is as well that I have lived in such strangely interesting times, and have adapted to them with such determination. What right has he to mock my habits or to advise me to change them? I have served myself well enough, and need not hunger for novelty. He may yearn with all his desperate heart to see what the world might become were its present dour appearances to be set aside, but I cannot. I can more easily imagine worlds that are worse by far than worlds that might be better.*

Harkender had often told her that the story of mankind would not be long delayed in reaching a suicidal climax and a subsequent period of transformation. It was easy to believe his prophecies of destruction—who could doubt them, while the war had raged so fiercely in France?—but she had no faith in his hopes for the aftermath of the Apocalypse.

Five or ten minutes passed before Harkender came back. He was still naked, but he had washed himself carefully and had doubtless made mental preparation for what was to come.

"Let's go," he said brusquely. "I am ready."

Mercy looked up at him; there was no pleasure in the anticipation which she could no longer help but feel, but there was no horror in it either; she had become inured to horror, at least where Harkender was concerned. Anyhow, she did not doubt that he would be preserved from lasting harm. His guardian angel had punished him once by abandoning him to blindness and dreadful injury for twenty long years, but cherished him very carefully now. Harkender had boasted to her that were he to imitate the Wandering Jew in that strange German poem, and cast himself into the maw of an active volcano, he would rise again from the scorching lava like the glorious Messiah rising from the harrowing of Hell, with some new prize of wisdom nestling in his heart. He had not learned to *like* pain, still less to consider it a species of pleasure, but he had learned to live productively within its utmost fury, and to value the treasures he brought back above all else.

Mercy preceded Harkender into the corridor, and led him to a door through which they passed into an open space totally enclosed by the walls of the sprawling house. She shivered as she met the cold air, even though she was fully dressed. The weather had been unseasonably bad for several days. The servants who had prepared the arena had withdrawn some time before and were forbidden to return; she alone had the duty of bearing witness to Harkender's ordeals.

The apparatus which awaited them was familiar; there would be no attempt today to make progress toward some new extreme. Ritual recapitulation had its own function in such matters, and Harkender was just as unhurried and as self-controlled in this more vital kind of exploration as he was in his desultory exploration of Mrs. Murrell's pliant body; that was his invariable style.

She watched, numbly, as Harkender lay down and extended himself upon the St Andrew's Cross which lay horizontally on its carefully constructed bed of straw and logs. She picked up the hammer and one of the nails which awaited her on the oak-topped table with wrought-iron legs. She placed the point of the nail in the center of the palm of Harkender's right hand, and drove it through, embedding it deep in the wood with half a dozen practiced blows.

Harkender made no sound, although he convulsed reflexively as the agony ran through him. Mercy felt no pang of sympathy, but concentrated all her attention on her work. She had done this too many times to be sickened or hurt by it; it was as if she were reading a passage in a book for the thousandth time, hardly able to find any meaning in the oft-repeated syllables, or any shock at all in whatever vestige of meaning there was.

She drove the second nail through his left hand.

Mercy did not know whether this service was *required* of Hark-

ender as the price for his eternal youth, health and vitality, or whether
it was entirely self-inflicted, as a voluntary tribute or testament of loyalty. It hardly mattered; the effect was the same. Thirty or forty times
a year Harkender set forth upon these odysseys; thirty or forty times
a year he returned, having allegedly enjoyed an unholy communion
with the world of the angels, quite unembarrassed by the petty distractions of the human condition.

The third nail was driven in through the heel of the right foot;
then the fourth through the heel of the left. Harkender maintained
his silence throughout. *Is this courage,* she wondered, *or commitment? Could I do the same, if it were demanded of me as the price
for my rejuvenation? Would I agree to pay such a price, or be able
to go through with it if I did agree?*

She could find no answer. She could not tell. "The point is not
merely to *enter* the world of the angels," Harkender had told her,
on one of the many occasions when he had tried to explain and
justify his actions, "but to see as clearly as a mere man can what
is there to be seen when one arrives. In order to achieve that end, it
is necessary to drown out *all* distraction. Petty hurt and sore humilia-
tion can only take a man so far, and any ordinary man would be
claimed by death long before he could reap the rewards of his destruction. The werewolves and the Clay Man would be dismally im-
perfect instruments for work of this kind, even if they were able to
find the courage for it, and I have no reason to believe that Lydyard
or Hecate is any better equipped. I have been more cleverly remade,
of sterner stuff. I am the one man in all the world who can look
into the light and *see*. I am the one man in the world who dares to
do it."

Whenever he made such speeches, Mary heard other, unspoken
sentences that he would not condescend to say aloud. *This is proof,
is it not, that I am a better man than Lydyard? This is proof, is it
not, that Sir Edward Tallentyre was nothing at all, while I am the
messiah who will lead mankind to the glorious Millennium? This is
proof, is it not, that I and I alone deserve to stand alongside the
angels, and bask in the warmth of their love and admiration?*

To all of which inquiries her own unspoken reply was *Who is to
judge what is proof and what is not? And who is supposed to care?*

She doused the pyre and Harkender's naked body with paraffin.
She was very careful to spill none on her own clothes. When she
struck the match that would set it alight she stood well back, holding
the light well away from her own body. She drew her dress tightly

about herself before flinging the match, and instantly retreated lest she be singed by the first eager gush of flame.

By the time the black smoke began to billow up into the gray sky, its dark turbidity inconstantly riven by avid flames, the last vestiges of her post-coital contentment had worn off. She felt utterly cold, in every sense of the word, and the leaping flames were impotent to warm her.

Why should the gods require martyrs, she wondered, as she watched Harkender's unconsumed flesh sear and blister in the heat, *and why should they require their favorites to be martyred again and again? There is no sport in it, nor does it seem a useful test of faith. Why should the angels bother to be cruel or kind to human creatures, when they surely have their own affairs to conduct? If the universe really is as huge and dark and empty as Harkender now admits, this comedy surely makes no sense at all.*

While she was wondering, Harkender began to scream.

The mere fact of his screaming was not unprecedented, but the timbre of the scream seemed unusual, and she peered into the smoke and flame, trying to see what condition he was in. Normally, his flesh was rebuilt as fast as it was melted and scorched away; the process of burning was continuous but balanced. Like some damned soul in the Hell of awful legend, he burned and yet was not consumed.

This time was different.

This time, the process of regeneration seemed less powerful, less easily able to combat the effect of the flames. An unaccustomed dagger of horror stabbed her heart as she saw Harkender writhing upon the cross, the outer layers of his flesh stripped away to leave a horrible red mass, seemingly all bone and red slime—but somewhere in there he still had lungs, and enough of a throat to scream.

That Harkender's guardian angel was still active Mercy could not doubt; he would otherwise have been quite dead. But she could not doubt, either, that something was opposing its action, fighting against its attempted regeneration of Harkender's body. Nor was it only Harkender who was the focus of the fight, for the flames of the fire were becoming ever more fervent, far whiter with heat than any flames which ordinarily sprang from paraffin-soaked wood. She was forced to step back, raising her arms before her face to ward off the terrible heat. She was tempted to flee, but the temptation was quelled by a contrary impulse which told her that she must stay, to see what would happen.

She saw Jacob Harkender raise his right arm, and knew that the nail which held it must have been drawn out of the charred and crumbling wood of the cross. The limb was unnaturally thin, pitch black in color. It was as though the residue of molten muscle and sinew had hardened into something like obsidian. The arm moved like something mechanical, as if it were controlled by levers or wires.

The hand reached out, and as it emerged further and further from its prison of flame Mercy realized that the other hand must also have been torn away, and that Harkender was leaning over as far as he could, stretching out toward her.

The sound of his screaming was twisted into the shape of a single word: "Mercy!" She could not be certain that he was calling her name, but the word struck terror into her regardless. Fear told her that he was reaching out to grab her, to draw her into the inferno to share his fate. Fear told her that the term of his Faustian pact was complete, and that the time had come for him to be taken down to Hell.

"Mercy!" he screeched again, forming the word with the utmost difficulty.

She stepped back another pace, but the hand kept coming. Both his feet must have been free by now, although the steel nails must have been buried in the vitrified flesh, if they had not entirely melted. Harkender was free now to step down from the bed of straw and logs, if only he had the strength of will to do it—and it seemed that he had. The black claw which had been his hand was still reaching out for her.

"Mercy!" he howled. "Mercy!"

She wanted to yell back at him, to tell him that there was neither Mercy nor mercy to be had, but she could not find her voice. Her throat was taut and desiccated, scorched by heat and smoke, and she was not sure that she could take another step back, for her limbs felt just as taut, just as dry, just as feeble, just as *old* . . .

She wished, desperately, for a mirror.

"Mercy!" screamed Harkender, so violently and so exhaustedly that she could not believe him capable of repeating the word again.

The talon of smoked black glass was still reaching for her, still moving. He had come down from the pyre now, but the flames had followed him. It was his own flesh that was on fire, burning far more fiercely than it ever had before. All that his guardian angel could preserve of him was a black mock-skeleton dancing on invisible strings, but whatever the skeleton was made of, it could still feel pain. Mercy could not doubt that the pain which had Harkender in its grip now was worse than any he had ever felt before.

Are you glad, now, to be in the company of the angels? she cried, silently. *Are you proud, now, to be the one man in the world who can enter their world? Are you vain enough, now, to be ringmaster of the carnival of destruction and bawd of the harlots of Hell?*

Mercy! he cried, voicelessly. *Mercy! Mercy! Mercy!*

He had asked for mercy before, she knew, when he had passed through the fire that had destroyed his house, and when he had suffered the slow and partial regeneration of his nerve-endings while he lay helpless in the asylum. He had asked for mercy before, and had been forced to wait for many long years while it was parsimoniously eked out. Cowardice told her that he could bear it. The same cowardice told her that *she* need not.

Her back was to the wall now, and there was no door there. The devil's black claw was still reaching out for her, reaching out to pull her into Hell. Conscience told her that she deserved no better. Conscience told her that the lie she had lived these last twenty-five years was an injustice whose price would have to be paid. *Not now!* cried the voice of her terror. *Please, God, not now!*

She had never called upon God before; she could not believe that He would answer now.

She had not the courage to reach out and take the proffered hand, but something else reached out and took it on her behalf. Something else which *truly* owned her body reached out and took Harkender's horrid hand, clasping it as a merciful ally might.

As soon as she touched the hand, she saw Harkender's face—or what was left of it—very clearly. She saw the tar-black skull and the burning eyes, and the gleaming teeth set in the eternal lipless grin of the damned. She did not doubt that it was Harkender's face, but even as she saw and recognized it the image changed and dissolved, and became another face, very different in its form and aspect.

The new face looked at her, softly, with sky-blue eyes. It was a beautiful face, but she had refused once before to see it as the face of an angel, and she refused now to see it as the face of an angel. Even so, she recognized it readily enough.

The hand drew her, gently and not without courtesy, into the inferno. She began to burn, and needed no mirror to tell her what she had become.

9

Nell left Hecate and Anatole Daumier, and the bulk of her luggage, at the public house in the village, promising to send for them when she had obtained her father's permission so to do. She set out to walk to World's End but was soon overtaken by the baker's cart. The baker knew her, and invited her to ride with him.

It was not a comfortable ride; the road was badly rutted and they frequently had to duck under overhanging branches, which should have been cut back two or three years before. The baker apologized on behalf of the landowner, whose laborers had all gone to the war, leaving no one to mend the road or coppice the wood or clear the offending branches. "The great garden of England's been left to run wild," he reported morosely. "Weeds're springin' up everywhere."

"Better that," she told him, "than to be battered and blasted into a sea of blood-stained mud."

Little daylight filtered through the canopy of the wood, but it did not seem to Nell to be an unduly gloomy place. It was green, and peaceful; "gone to sleep," she thought, might be a better analogy than "run wild." She could imagine that the clustering shadows might have made others feel unwelcome, but they had no such effect on her, and the baker was evidently content to make the trip as often as might be necessary; the milkman and the postman presumably felt the same way. If the cottage really were under close protection, as Hecate had suggested, its guardians were discreet.

Nell took the bread from the baker as she descended from the cart, and bought two extra loaves in anticipation of receiving further guests. The baker made no comment as he scrawled a note in his book regarding the probable scale of future orders. Nell watched him go, saluting him as he turned the cart, before she passed through the wrought-iron gate.

By the time she had latched the gate again her father had come out to greet her. She put down the bread in order to embrace him, and did not immediately observe that someone else had come out of the cottage to pick it up. It was not until she released her father and stepped back that she looked the second person up and down. Nell did not recognize the woman, although there was something about her that was familiar, and her curiously colored eyes were very distinctive.

"Well," said Nell, as pertly as she might have done had she been eight years old, "here I am again."

"Nell," her father said, "this is Mandorla Soulier."

Nell started in surprise, partly because of the revelation itself and partly because she had not expected to see evidence of aging in a werewolf. She could muster no more articulate reply than "Oh!"

"There's nothing to worry about," Lydyard said quickly. "She means no harm to anyone. She came to me for help."

"And received it," the pale woman said. "Pelorus brought me; there is no more enmity between us."

Nell nodded her head to indicate that she had no objection. "There are other petitioners in the village," she said. "Suddenly, the world is enthusiastic to beat a path to your door, anxious meanwhile lest permission be refused?"

"Who?" her father asked, sharply.

"A man named Anatole Daumier. You do not know him; he says that he was commanded to seek you out in a dream. He says that he was given a message to deliver, by someone claiming to be Simon. The other you have met; she calls herself Hecate."

"Hecate?" He sounded as though he could not quite believe it. "*Hecate* waits in the village for permission to approach, sending you as her intermediary?"

"She claims that other methods of communication have been blocked," Nell told him. "She seems to be afraid to use whatever powers she has, and I suspect that she may have very few. I doubt that she has begun to feel the enfeebling effects of age, but some supernatural process of erosion seems to be chilling her soul." As she spoke the last sentence she glanced sideways at the retreating figure of Mandorla, who had turned away to take the bread indoors.

"I had better go to the village," Lydyard muttered.

"No need," Mandorla called back, pausing in the doorway. "Stay here with your daughter. I will be your messenger."

Lydyard frowned, dubiously. Nell supposed that he wanted the chance to hear what the two visitors might have to say before he invited them to his home.

"They seem meek enough," Nell said, although she felt uncomfortable about claiming the competence to make such a judgment, "and I have a suspicion that they too might need such help and protection as your guardian can provide. According to Hecate, something destructive is abroad, but you are precious enough to be shielded from its random wrath."

"Hecate once had the power to make an otherworldly haven of her own," her father said, uncertainly, "or stood in such favor with her maker as to have it made for her."

"We have all lost favor since then," Mandorla said, still listening from the threshold. "All, that is, save Zelophelon's pets."

"They too seem to be under attack," Nell said, wishing that they had not proceeded so quickly to this kind of talk. "Daumier was sent upon another mission before the one that brought him here—to shoot Luke Capthorn. Capthorn's protector resurrected him, but his powers may have been crucially limited. Hecate believes that *no* exercise of angelic power now goes unopposed, and that none any longer proceeds in an unproblematic fashion."

It was Lydyard's turn to shake his head. "Come inside," he said to her. "We should not be standing in the cold, discussing such matters. Are your bags in the village?"

He moved off as he spoke, linking arms with her and drawing her along. She consented to be drawn, and was glad that the matter of the would-be visitors was set aside for some little while. He took her into the kitchen and sat her by the table, explaining that the range kept the room reasonably warm while the rest of the house was too cold for comfort. He set about making tea, which Mandorla politely refused so that the two of them could be together.

Nothing further had been said about who should go to the village and when, but Mandorla took the decision into her own hands. When they heard the door close behind her, both Nell and her father looked up, but neither said anything about it. They were too engrossed in one another.

Gladly and impatiently, the two of them set about asking one another all the mundane and intimate questions which they had been storing up for months, whose mostly irrelevant answers they dearly wanted and somehow needed to hear.

Nell, observing that the warmth of the kitchen did not extend to the flagstoned floor, soon set her sturdily shod feet on another chair, glorying in the opportunity to be unladylike while she and her father chattered on: a stable atom of community, unbreakably bound by unconditional affection, in a great sea of fissile confusion.

"And so," said Nell, eventually, by way of concluding a rambling and oft-interrupted account of her recent exploits and new prospects, "it is not yet over by a long chalk. I shall probably be reassigned to a hospital in England—one not so far from here, I hope. There are casualties aplenty requiring continuing care, and I dare say that it won't be long before the supply is renewed. The darker rumors say that if we withdraw entirely from Belgium and the Netherlands now we'll be invaded before the end of next year."

"We'll have a more reliable estimate of that when Teddy comes home," Lydyard said. "He's a good judge of such matters, although the censor makes it difficult for him to express his judgments. Once he's safe in England he'll be able to write more freely."

"I'll visit him if I get the chance," Nell said. "I may go to see Alice and the children very soon, even if Teddy's not there. I have a duty to play the maiden aunt."

"Perhaps you might think of marrying now," her father said luke-warmly. He had never been able to feign enthusiasm for any such prospect.

By way of reply she shook her head dismissively. The war had provided her with a perfect excuse, but she had had plenty of time before its outbreak to marry, had she wished, and no dearth of oppor-tunities, but she had firmly set aside the idea of marriage in the months following her mother's departure from the London house, and had never found any reason sufficient to make her reconsider. She had only once set eyes on her mother from that day to this; Teddy, so far as she knew, had not condescended to see her at all. Simon had gone to see her at least twice, before going out to the battlefield where he had fallen, but what had passed between the two of them Nell had no idea.

"Do you think I was wrong to have children?" her father asked, apparently in response to the frown which had quietly taken posses-sion of her brow. She knew that he was far too careful with his words to be unaware of the fact that the query was tantamount to asking her whether she would rather not have been born.

"You were right," she told him. "You were right to lay claim to an ordinary life, no matter what poison was injected into you by that snake in Egypt." She had heard the story of the snake often enough, from her grandfather as well as her father; she knew exactly when and how her father's tribulations had begun.

"He that hath wife and children hath given hostages to fortune," Lydyard quoted. "But he that has none . . . I have never regretted it, Nell, in spite of everything."

She realized, belatedly, that he was trying to offer her conscience-driven advice regarding her own decision to remain a spinster. He was trying to say, in spite of his own reservations, that it might be worth her while to offer her own hostages to fortune . . . as if fortune had not demanded enough of her already.

"England is full of maiden aunts just now," she said quietly. "It is no cause for shame. Husbands are in direly short supply, and no one who has rested content on the shelf for as long as I have can possibly entertain expectations. Teddy's David will carry forward the family name, provided that future wars will give him space to do it."

"The name means little enough," he said. "The name of Tallentyre meant more, and if that has been eclipsed what right have I . . . ?" He did not finish the sentence.

"Every right," she said softly. She wanted to say that it did not matter a jot which of them had been the better man, but she could not. Simply to have raised the question would have been an insult of sorts, overriding any protest as to its irrelevance. The expression on Lydyard's face was difficult to read, and the task was not made any easier by the sombre light, which seemed to be growing dimmer with every minute that passed.

"I am in danger, Nell," he said, in a voice even softer than her own. "I can feel it now. We are *all* in danger. Should I be ashamed to be glad that Pelorus brought Mandorla here? I *am* glad, even though you have come now to save me from loneliness. I do not know what enemy it is that seeks to diminish me, but I feel sure that Mandorla is its enemy too, and that lets me take comfort from her company. Even Hecate . . . Nell, the angels themselves are afraid! Can you begin to understand what that means?"

"By all accounts," said Nell, having had the opportunity during the last few days to bring various fragments of knowledge into some kind of whole, "they have never been anything else but afraid. Everything you and my recent companions have told me about them declares that they are arrant cowards."

He blinked in evident surprise, but then he smiled. "Your grandfather would have said the same," he conceded. "He died without resenting the fact that he might have been made immortal, preferring to believe that the angels were too nervous of his opinions and insights to tolerate him any longer than was necessary. Sometimes, it is is difficult to be proud of the fact that I was thought worthy of being kept alive."

"You would have lived as long by your own unaided efforts," she told him. "You have not the slightest reason to feel grateful."

"Perhaps," he said. His head was bowed, and his features seemed unnaturally gray.

"Father," she said uneasily, "why is it growing darker when it is not yet noon?"

He looked up, faintly startled but not alarmed. "Darkness never seems to be far away," he said. "The nights are growing longer in any case, but the shadows always seem to be in a hurry to enfold World's End. The trees seem to soak up the light, and even the whitest clouds draw a curtain across the face of the sun." He got up and went to peer out of the window, as if to confirm his suspicion that windblown clouds were responsible for the changing light; but when he got there he turned around abruptly. She watched his eyes as his gaze flicked back and forth about the room.

The white walls were already gray, and turning blacker. It was as if an entire army of conscript shadows were marching to occupy them. Nell did not know what to do. Her instinct was to flee, but where was there to go? She maintained her no-longer-comfortable position, keeping her feet quite still as they rested on the chair.

"Don't worry, Nell," her father said calmly. "The angels love to play tricks with light, but it is petty conjuring even at its best."

"I'm not afraid," she lied. "I doubt there is a safer place in all the world than this." To herself, she said: *I have endured shellfire and gas attacks, and have kept constant company with all manner of agues and fevers. If the angels have any interest in me, it is protective.*

The walls were as black as pitch now, and it seemed that they soaked up almost all of the gray light that struggled through the window. The dresser and the cupboards had been claimed by the unnatural night, but Nell was close enough to the range to see its outline and feel its warmth, which seemed all the more welcome now. The floor had become a well of darkness, like a bottomless pit, although the invisible flagstones were still solid enough to support the chairs on which she rested. She was glad that her feet were not on the floor, where the rising dark might have seized and trapped them.

Her father moved quickly to her, and stood behind her, with his right hand resting on her shoulder and his left gripping the back of her chair. The fingers of his right hand stroked her neck lightly and reassuringly.

"It's a kind of waking dream," he told her. "It's only light, not substance. We're perfectly safe." He sounded as if he believed it.

She raised her right hand and placed it on his, but took care not to force his fingers to be still. She only wanted to touch him, not to stop his absent-minded caress.

The darkness beneath them shifted and surged, as if it were some heavy and turgid gas stirred by dull convection currents. It was leeching the warmth out of the air; Nell could feel a cold blast on the backs of her horizontal calves, and she wished that her skirt did not hang down so loosely.

She caught her breath as something extended from the pit of shadow: something black and slender. Because it was black against a black ground, and because the light from the window was so weak, it was almost impossible to see what shape the thing was, but once her mind had seized upon the idea that it was a hand she felt sure that she could trace the desperate movements of the groping fingers. The point of emergence was no more than three feet away from each of the chairs on which her body rested, about equidistant from both. It must have been very close to the front of the range, just in front of the door of the lower oven.

For a few seconds she thought that the hand would begin to move toward her, reaching for her legs, but it did not. Its movements were limited, as though it were anchored. She could not possibly see sufficient detail to know whether it was a right hand or a left, but it was sinister enough regardless. It was, she thought, as if a damned soul were reaching up from some icy underworld, hoping against hope that some living person might have the courage to grab hold and haul.

It was not until the voice sounded that she thought there might be an invisible face behind and beneath the arm, but the moment she heard the first spoken words she became convinced that there was. She could not make out the least suggestion of human features in the eddying shadow, but she knew they were there, beneath the surface, constricted by agony and desperation.

"Lydyard!" said the voice, in a feeble, quavering whisper. "Lydyard! Take my hand! Lydyard, *for the love of God, help me!*"

How little she knows him, Nell thought, *if she thinks that the best appeal she can make.* She had not known until she formed the word "she" that the voice was female, but now she did.

Her father's hand continued to play with the nape of her neck. If he recognized the voice he gave not the slightest indication.

The shadow-hand was already being withdrawn, the fingers groping madly in futile protest. It was as if the owner of the hand were being dragged down, taken away.

Another hand, larger and sturdier, began to emerge as soon as the first disappeared. This one was calm; it was as though the shadow were inviting her father politely to shake hands.

"Lydyard!" said a new voice, deeper and calmer than the other. "I wish you would take my hand. There is nothing to fear. However much you hate me, you know full well that we are in this together, stronger in union than apart. Something is working against us, not wisely or with any trace of strategy, but with no shortage of raw power. Come now, lest it be too late. Take my hand."

As the words "however much you hate me" were spoken her father reacted. When he heard that phrase his hand clutched convulsively at Nell's shoulder and his fingernails dug into the flesh beneath her collarbone. She knew immediately what construction he had put upon those words. But he did not move and he made no reply while the strange speech continued. The room was still growing darker. The window was a dark gray rectangle now, cut into four by the wooden frame which held the panes.

"Get out!" Lydyard hissed, when the shadow had completed its plea. "Damn you, Harkender, *get out of my house!*"

"Lydyard!" sobbed the other, weaker voice, so faintly that it seemed to come from an extremely remote distance. "For mercy's sake! For mercy's sake!"

Nell felt the ripple of a helpless and humorless giggle course through her father's body, although no sound of laughter escaped his lips.

"Lydyard, please take my hand," said the calmer voice. "There is some urgency in this, and common hatreds mean nothing by comparison with the task which faces us now."

"Please," Nell remarked to herself, *has the advantage over "For the love of God," but it is equally impotent.*

"Lydyard!" keened the other voice, as if from the very edge of Creation. "Help us! Help *me!*"

"Were I to find you both burning in Hell," Lydyard retorted, clearly rejoicing in the strength of his own voice, *"I would not give you a single drop of water to drink!"*

My God! Nell thought. *He thinks . . . !*

"You do not understand . . ." the calmer voice interrupted; but it was already fading into nothing, and the reaching hand was dissolving into inchoate darkness. The unnatural shadow began to drain away. The outline of the window grew steadily brighter.

Within half a minute Nell could see the flagstones again, and the cupboards, and the ranks of plates and bowls on the shelves of the dresser. Within a minute and a half, the natural order had been completely restored, at least to the world of appearances.

Her father released his grip on her shoulder, and went back to his chair, only a little unsteadily.

"Ghosts!" he said when he was seated. "Only ghosts. No need to be afraid, Nell."

"Phantoms of the living, if you guessed correctly," she said, succeeding somehow in keeping her own voice relatively level. *The other could not have been my mother,* she said to herself, secretly. *My mother would never have called him by his surname, and would surely have called out to me as well, or instead.*

"Perhaps I did not," he said, with wry hopefulness. "Perhaps I was wrong."

Nell's legs had grown stiff, and she took her feet down from the other chair, settling them gingerly upon the stone floor. It felt reassuringly solid.

"If they come back by night," she observed, "they might contrive to be more frightening." She felt proud of her cleverness in implying that because they had come by day they had not been frightening at all.

"Ghosts which renew their hauntings time after time eventually become tedious," he said. "The cleverest are those which show a measure of discretion." Like her, he was avoiding all the real questions. Why had the shadowhands reached out for them? Were the warnings they had given true? Should Lydyard, in spite of everything, have consented to take the hand of his enemy?

"You are more in demand than I thought," Nell said casually, trying with all her might to be Sir Edward Tallentyre's granddaughter and David Lydyard's child. "Is there anyone among the devil-led who does not need or want your help?"

"I wish I knew what help I had to give," he said bitterly. "I know of nothing I can do for the likes of Hecate and Harkender. I suppose I must hope that Hecate might be able to tell me what is going on, insofar as she can guess or divine it."

"She will do that," Nell confirmed. "But I fear she may know less than you suppose, and may be under the false impression that you know or can deduce, much more."

"If she wants advice," he replied, "she surely has access to better sources. But I may be more fortunate than I know. Perhaps my guardian angel is exerting far greater efforts on my behalf than I suspected. Perhaps you arrived just in time. Your friends may yet find it difficult to accept my invitation."

"I hope not," she said, not realizing how sincere the sentiment was until she spoke the words. "Indeed, I hope they will arrive soon." *If we are to be besieged by shadows,* she thought, *it may be as well to be five instead of two. If one must go to Hell, better not to go alone.* She thought that her father might resent her hope, but she saw in his eyes that he did not. Whether or not he was anxious to meet Hecate and the Frenchman, he had clearly grown used to Mandorla's company.

And why not? she thought, defiantly. *Why not, when werewolves are more honest than those human hypocrites who hide their wolfish nature away until the fire of battle or the rage of rape lets it so extravagantly loose?*

10

Anatole would have been content to rest in the public house but Hecate preferred to walk abroad, and he thought it best to stay with her.

"They probably will not send for us immediately," she told him, by way of reassurance, as they went out into the street. "You need not fear that we will miss the message, even if we miss the messenger. The landlord will tell us if anything happens during our absence." She spoke in English, presumably because they were in England, although she had occasionally spoken to him in French during the time they had been traveling together. Nell understood French, but did not speak it well.

"Your powers of divination seem very weak, for a sorceress," he observed, also speaking English. "Almost as weak, in fact, as your power to assist our passage here."

She looked at him sharply, but did not trouble to repeat her formula regarding the reckless use of magical power. A group of women chattering by the empty post which had once borne the name of the village fell silent as they passed by, and stared after them in the frank manner of country-folk everywhere.

"Something has sapped your strength, has it not?" Anatole said, trying to sound sympathetic rather than glad.

"In a manner of speaking," she conceded, evidently feeling that there was no point in denial. "It is as if the world has become stubbornly resistant to certain kinds of magical operation. If any have become easier, by way of compensation, they are ones I have never mastered. Perhaps I was always weaker than I thought, and what I mistook for my own power was really that of my maker.''

"But why should your maker withdraw that power now?"

She shrugged her shoulders, to indicate that she was not privy to her maker's schemes. He was inquisitive enough to be unsatisfied with the evasion.

"You and I are mere instruments," he said. "You even more so than I. Why should the beings which hold our lives and minds hostage wish to weaken us, or allow us to become weak?"

"There is less difference between us than you might suppose," she said resignedly. "Your human life was about to come to an end when you were adopted by your guardian, while I was in thrall to mine from the moment of my conception, but I lived a human life—of sorts—for almost as many years as you did. I discovered my true self in a moment of revelation, but I remain, like you, the inheritor of my unmagical past as well as the product of some arbitrary miracle. I am myself as well as my maker's catspaw, with my own ideas, my own understanding, my own ...''

She stopped. Whether it was a half-reasoned guess or a flash of divination Anatole could not tell, but he suddenly felt sure that he knew what word she had omitted, and why. "Your own motives," he finished for her. "But that is our difficulty, *n'est-ce pas*? We do not know what our own motives might or ought to be. Given that we exist by the sufferance of our mysterious guardians, and have no power to rebel against them or to dissent from their command, it is impossible to make real plans of our own. How can we know what we might be allowed or forbidden to do?"

"We are not mere puppets," she replied stubbornly. "We are free to choose. I do not understand *why* we are free to choose, but we are. Perhaps if we were to rebel and refuse to do what our guardians want us to do, we would simply be discarded—allowed to die—but I am not so sure. I suspect that our guardians do not know exactly what they want us to do, or what else we might do for them in addition to the missions which they appoint us to carry out. David Lydyard is more intelligent and more knowledgeable than you or I, and he is also less obsessive than Jason Sterling, less arrogant than Jacob Harkender; he might be better able to bring reason to bear on the situation than anyone, including the angels themselves. Let us hope so.''

"Whatever he has to say," Anatole persisted, "the fact will remain that we cannot and do not know what motives we might entertain, what ends we might work toward.''

''Were you in any better situation when you were a mere human?'' Hecate countered.

''Most certainly,'' he told her. ''I was a soldier, with a part to play in a war that needed to be fought; and I was a Communist, with a part to play in a transformation of society which needed to be achieved. My goals were very clear.''

''I was an ugly whore,'' she said flatly, ''with small parts to play in a series of lewd and petty dramas, as a pathetic grotesque, afterward to be abused in more ways than one. My goals were far from clear.''

They were far beyond the village boundary now, and Hecate had left the road to follow a footpath which led into a wood. Anatole did not know whether the path led toward Lydyard's cottage or in a different direction, but the matter did not seem particularly important. The sun was shining brightly, although drifting cumulus clouds sometimes hid its face for a few moments, and the temperature was quite comfortable even in the shadow of the trees. Many of the trees seemed ancient, and their heavy boughs sagged under the weight of their own leaves and those of parasitic ivy. They were mostly oaks, as one would expect of England, but there were beeches and birches too. The occasional slopes and clearings which interrupted the trees were full of tall ferns and grasses, which encroached upon the path but could not obliterate it.

Hecate seemed to be reveling in the calm of the wood; her face seemed a little less plain in this context, and there was nothing in the least witch-like in her demeanor. Her mood seemed so conducive to confidentiality that Anatole asked her a question he had not dared to ask before. ''Why did you ask me for a promise to grant you a wish when you helped me to escape from Asmodeus? What service did you think I might one day be able to perform for you?''

She had not met his gaze since they had left the public house, but she turned toward him now and looked him in the face for a few seconds. Her ugliness was somehow disturbing in direct confrontation, perhaps because he knew that it was a mask she had calculatedly chosen to wear. She smiled, very slightly, but the awkward configuration of her features made all such smiles seem ironic and humorless.

''I wanted you to escape,'' she said, turning away again and marching on without pause. ''I knew that your guardian could have released you, had it cared to, but it seemed to me that a courteous gesture of amity might not come amiss. The opportunity was there to ask a price, and so I asked the only one which you could possibly offer. I have little or no idea what service you might one day be able to render in return, or whether I shall ever have occasion to demand it, but I am happy to have the promise, just in case. Nothing has changed, of course—I shall expect you to honor the debt if ever I ask you to do so.''

''Perhaps I should be grateful that you are so vague about your motives and goals,'' he said sarcastically. ''While you know not whence you are bound, you are unlikely to demand any self-sacrifice on my part to ease your way.''

''True,'' she admitted. ''But I would dearly like to discover a goal, and some viable means of working toward it. I will be sure to ask David Lydyard what his goals are, and how he tries to further them. I respect his opinion.''

''That might not help,'' said a second female voice, cutting into the conversation from behind. ''I had clear goals once, and a sharp hunger for the means of their attainment—but ever since I deigned to listen to David Lydyard, and learned to respect his opinions, I have been cast into dire confusion.''

Anatole turned a fraction of a second sooner than Hecate, that much more anxious to see who had spoken. He had to shade his eyes from the sun, whose light was temporarily uninterrupted by cloud or branch. He saw a tall woman with silvery blonde hair and violet eyes, wearing a dark cloak that was surely too heavy for such temperate weather. She seemed to be forty-five or fifty years of age, but was exceptionally handsome for such an age. She stopped as soon as he turned to look at her. Hecate stopped too.

''I apologize,'' said the newcomer, in response to their startlement. ''I did not think my approach had been so quiet, given that I am condemned to wear this unwieldy body. Indeed, I am surprised that I managed to track you so well, lacking both the nose and the instinct.''

Anatole guessed who she was. He had read the book which he had delivered to the house in Bromley-by-Bow, and had found the name which the werewolf named Siri had spoken before she died. He could not tell whether his certainty was a leap of faith or a flash of supernatural inspiration, but he did not doubt the intuition.

''Are you Mandorla Soulier?'' he asked.

Her pale eyebrows arched in astonishment—or perhaps in mock-astonishment.

"You have the advantage of me, sir," she said negligently. "Nell mentioned your name, I believe, but I have quite forgotten it."

"My name is Anatole Daumier," he said stiffly, feeling slightly stung by her studied carelessness. "I met one of your sisters in Paris, albeit very briefly."

The tall woman's manner changed immediately. The amusement which she had displayed after overhearing what he and Hecate were saying to one another vanished in an instant.

"Which sister?" she asked, evenly.

"Her name was Siri. She asked me to tell you, if I ever got the opportunity, where her body lay. I did not understand at the time, but I do now. She was mortally wounded while attacking men who were pursuing me, and might well have saved me from being kiiled. I am as much in her debt as in Hecate's, and thus in yours. If there is anything you need of me, now or in the future, you have only to ask." He did not glance sideways as he made this undertaking.

The pale woman nodded. "You must tell me exactly where Siri is to be found," she said. "I can do nothing about it now, but the time might come when the pack can be united again, and I must be prepared. That goal, at least, I must keep firmly in mind however far away its attainment seems."

"Have you come from Lydyard?" Hecate asked the newcomer.

"Yes. You may come to the cottage. It might be best to come quickly."

"Why?" Anatole asked.

"Do you not feel the unease in the air?" Mandorla asked. "It is in the cottage too, but while we are all together we have its walls about us. I hope we can be allies." As she spoke the last few words she looked directly at Hecate, as if challenging her to demur.

"I hope we can," Hecate answered quietly. "Shall we return to the village first? Our luggage is there, and Nell's too. It would be as well to find someone to drive us in a cart."

Anatole guessed that Mandorla might have smiled at that, taking it as a confession of weakness, but the tall woman merely nodded. Hecate took a step forward—or tried to. She stumbled, and gasped in annoyance. Anatole reached out reflexively to take her arm, and took a step forward himself—but he too found himself impeded. A fern frond leaning over the path from his left had somehow wrapped itself around his calf. It did not seem to be gripping him hard, so he tried to pull away, bracing himself with his other leg, but it was not so easy. The frond would not come loose. Hecate was similarly entangled, although the werewolf was evidently free; she was already coming toward them to help.

Having taken the shielding hand away, Anatole was unsurprised to be blinded by the sunlight and did not realize for a second or two that the light was fiercer than it should have been. He looked down at their feet, where there seemed to be no particular cause for alarm despite the odd behavior of the ferns.

It was not until Hecate reacted with a wordless cry that he looked up again, and saw that something appeared to be coming *at* them, straight out of the sun: a bolt of golden fire.

Anatole put up both his arms as if to ward off the bolt, but the gesture was impotent. The strange light was suddenly all around them, bathing them in searing heat and surrounding them with a vivid yellow aura. There was a hesitant moment when he thought that he had actually caught fire, and that he was really burning, but the sensation which flooded him was not like that at all once it had taken possession of him. The heat was as much within as without, and he did not feel that he was being hurt or *consumed,* but rather that he was undergoing metamorphosis into some other kind of creature: something birdlike, or perhaps "angelic" according to the stereotyped imagery of Christian art. He was seized by the idea that he could simply leave his inconveniently anchored body behind, and soar aloft into the sunlit sky. He was convinced that with only the slightest of efforts he could tear his true self free from his lumpen body and find a freedom which he had previously glimpsed only in his bravest and most ambitious dreams.

Then, without pause, he felt hands grappling at his shoulders, trying to force him down and hold him in, trying to make him prisoner. He struggled against their insistence, vainly but hopefully, feeling that if only he had the knack of it he could slip through their grasp like a luminous gas. Alas, he could not quite master the trick. He fought with his own arms, knowing that the strain of muscle against muscle was only a sham, a displacement of the true battle, which was magic against magic, art against art.

He fell, sick with the consciousness that his *true* self need not be falling with his awkward body, if only he had the sleight of mind that would enable it to wriggle free. He raged and cursed, but still he fell, crashing backward to the hard ground.

The wind was knocked out of him, and he felt a tight pain in his chest as he strained to draw more air into his collapsed lungs. The pain drowned out his misery, focusing all his attention once again on his frail and stupid flesh. By the time he managed to draw breath, he was completely in the grip of mundanity again, and he knew—or felt that he knew—what a fortunate escape he had had.

He sat up, with his head between his knees and his eyes closed, and took three or four deep breaths. Then he opened his eyes and struggled to his feet. His booted feet were free; nothing curled around them as he stood up. Hecate was likewise struggling to her feet, while Mandorla Soulier stood over them, arms akimbo, shading them from the light of the sun.

"What was that?" he asked forlornly. "The world was supposed to have become impervious to magic, was it not?"

"Reluctant, not impervious," Hecate corrected him. "The angels still have power, if they care to use it."

"There must be easier ways of preventing us reaching Lydyard's cottage," he said. "Magic and its users may be capricious, but . . ."

"That was not the objective," Hecate said positively. "As you say, there are a thousand ways by which we might be destroyed or rendered incapable. That was no attempted murder."

"I think one or more of us might simply have been caught in crossfire," the pale woman said, as she relaxed and tried to draw them both forward. "The question is, which of you was the actual object of that . . . shall we think of it as an *invitation?* Not I, for sure!"

"No," said Hecate, readily consenting to be hurried now that she could move freely. "Not you." But she did not venture to suggest whether she or Anatole, or both, might have been the true target of the problematic assault. Anatole caught up with her easily enough, shielding his hand again as he peered upwards, half-expecting another petty firestorm to come hurtling out of the sun.

The poor priest whose book I took to that house in London might have thought that a goal to be desired, he reflected. *He would surely have seen it as a chance for the divinely sculpted soul to escape its devil-made prison of flesh. But I have not his faith in Heaven, nor any other reason to hope for such a conversion.* He longed to feel walls about him again, not because they offered any secure promise of safety, but because they would map out a familiar and thoroughly humanized space. His thoughts ran on, unstoppably, in helter-skelter fashion. *These are mere omens, mere flashes of anticipation. The real event is yet to come, and it will be awesome. We are being urged on, physically and psychologically, so that we might arrive at the threshold anxious and curious. Something is waiting for us—*

something stranger than any mere end of the world, and something more momentous.

Still he could not tell, though, whether all of this was but a bold guess born of reason and imagination, or some well-directed shaft of enlightenment darted into his skull from the world beyond the world, where the Maid of Orléans dwelt in glory with her patient guiding voices.

11

David lay still upon the narrow bed beneath the slanting beams of the attic ceiling, staring at the round window whose panes were dimly lit by the last vestiges of a dour gray twilight. This was not the room in which he usually slept, but he had given the best bed to Nell and had left Mandorla to distribute his other guests as comfortably as she could contrive.

He lay as still as he possibly could, because any move he made was excruciating. His arthritis had always tended to flare up if he came under unusual stress, and the invasion of his house by shadows which were at best unwelcome and at worst malevolent had triggered a massive reaction within his traitorous flesh. He could not be surprised that his condition had become suddenly worse, but he nevertheless regretted it deeply, and felt perversely ashamed that his visitors should find him thus. His right hand was virtually useless, and the arm so nearly paralyzed that he had not strength and skill enough to strike a match and light the candle by his bedside. He felt empty, drained of all resource.

How undignified it is to grow old! he thought. *Better by far to have been struck down by some lightning-bolt from beyond, or to have stepped into that pit of shadows, than to be failed and felled by my own careworn and exhausted tissues.*

Nell came in. She was not tall, but she had to duck in order to pass through the low doorway, and she had some difficulty closing the awkward door behind her.

"You should not be here," she complained. "Far better to hide

195

the Frenchman or the witch up here, if you had too much pride to ask me to bear a little discomfort.''

"Too late now," he told her, anxious to cut short the recriminations. "It would hurt me too much to move."

He watched her take a match from the box and strike it. He stared into the heart of the tiny flame which fluttered into life at its terminus while she held it to the candle's wick. As soon as the candle caught, however, he looked away.

"Your guests are anxious to see you," she said gently, "although I told them that you were as yet in no fit state to receive them. Hecate says that she will gladly exert what feeble magic remains to her, in the hope of healing you, but she dare not make any promises."

David did not want to be seen by anyone while he was in his present condition, but he knew that he must overcome his reluctance. He ought not to indulge his feebleness. Time was pressing.

"I want to see the Frenchman first," he said colorlessly. "I want to hear this supposed message from Simon—that is more urgent than any mere physical discomfort. Hecate can come in afterwards, to say what she has to say and to exert whatever soul-warmth remains to her."

Nell did not question his judgment. Nor did she venture to suggest that she ought to stay and listen. She moved towards him, but she must have known that any touch, even hers, would be more painful than productive. She hesitated, momentarily frozen by helplessness, then smiled as bravely as she could. She moved a chair close to the bed, and blew him a kiss before going out again.

He contrived a smile of sorts by way of reply.

He listened to her dwindling footfalls on the short flight of stairs which connected the attic to the first floor, and the longer one which descended to the ground. Hardly a minute passed before he heard heavier footsteps ascending.

The newcomer bumped his head on the low wooden lintel, but did not curse, then wrestled with the recalcitrant catch as he tried unsuccessfully to close the door behind him. He did not linger long at the thankless task before coming on into the room, warily dodging the slanting beams. Somehow he found space enough to stand upright and make a sober bow before seating himself in the chair which Nell had moved.

"My name is Anatole Daumier," the young man said formally, although he had been briefly introduced already. "I was at Chemin des Dames in May, when the Germans broke through." His English was accented, but otherwise flawless.

"So I understand," said David faintly. "Please continue."

"I was stationed as a sniper, and could not immediately retreat when the line broke. When I descended to the ground it was too late to make a gateway—the Boche were all around me. I tried to take shelter in a shell-hole, but I was hit three times, in the leg, the chest and the head. I would have died had not something moved to save me."

He paused, as if expecting a challenge, but David simply said: "Go on."

"I do not know, even now, what it was that saved me. I had begun thinking of what my mother used to say about the guardian angel which sat upon my right shoulder, countering the evil influence of the imp which sat to the left, but it was nothing but idle fancy. I was too good an atheist to pray, or even to wish that the fantasy might be true. I drifted into unconsciousness and I began to dream. I am not sure that I ever awoke. I believe you know what I mean."

"I do," David said. "You dreamed of my son, I believe—my son Simon."

"Yes I did. That was later, after I had tried to kill the man you know as Luke Capthorn. He tried to question me, and gave me a drug, and then Hecate came to help me. She soothed my wounds, and put me to sleep. I will try to tell you as precisely as possible what happened in the relevant part of the dream, because you will probably be better able than I to judge what is significant and what is not.

"At first, I found myself walking across a deserted battlefield, torn by shellfire and turned into a sea of mud. I was in pain, but could not locate my wounds. There were many dead men, all mutilated. I did not know what I was doing there, but I had the feeling that there was something I must do. I stopped to rest, and heard the sound of a man whistling a tune." The Frenchman paused, blushing slightly, then continued. "The approaching man was a British officer. He was fair-haired, perhaps thirty years old. He said: 'I wish you would give a message to my father, sir.' I asked him what it was, and he said: 'Tell him that it does not matter that my grandfather was wrong, because he is the one with the finer sense of beauty. Tell him that it is not necessary to love his enemies, provided only that courtesy is an adequate shield against hatred.' Those were, I think, his exact words."

"Was that all?" David asked.

"No. I asked him who the message was for, and he gave me your name. 'You will meet him at World's End,' he said. I did not understand that at the time. 'Say that the message comes from Simon,' he went on. 'He will not believe it, but he will understand.' Then, without giving me a chance to speak, he said: 'No time. The future is coming: a future we cannot evade, no matter how hard we try. Never despair, though; much that is done cannot be undone, but all history is fantasy. Even the Clay Man has a navel. Eve is innocent, like the Maid of Orléans, although they call her witch.' Again, those were his exact words. Then he fell down, and became nothing but a skeleton.''

"And that was the end of the dream?"

"No. A huge fleet of aircraft then appeared, dropping bombs by the thousand. I tried to hide in a trench, but I knew it was hopeless— but then I fell *into* the earth, descending to its center. The molten core of the planet received me warmly, and there I went to sleep, peacefully. After that ... I assume that time passed, before I awoke again into *this* world. Does the message I was asked to bring make any sense to you?"

"It makes a sort of sense," David admitted, "but it certainly does not come from my son, and it is not clear who the true sender was, or why it was sent."

"I would not describe the dream to anyone else, not even to Nell and certainly not to Hecate," the Frenchman said, matter-of-factly, "but I have gleaned some relevant information while I have been in their company. I gather that the grandfather mentioned in the message is Sir Edward Tallentyre, the famous philosopher."

"He would have been gratified to hear you describe him thus," said David drily. "Less so to hear you allege that he was ever wrong. But yes, he *was* wrong, at least in part, when he tried to explain to an angel what the universe is really like. I would like to think that it did not matter, as the message says, but I fear that it might ... and I have no reason at all to think that I have a finer sense of beauty than he had. As for extending courtesy to my enemies ... perhaps that part of the message comes too late." He looked down as he spoke at the numb and useless right hand which he had failed to extend to Jacob Harkender's shadow.

"Nell told us that you had been visited by ghosts," the young man said. "She did not elaborate."

"It was the shadow of an enemy, which begged for help," David told him tiredly and not altogether accurately. "I offered none. I do not regret it. Something struck at me thereafter—I don't know what it was. I believe that something struck at you, too, at much the same time."

"It did no damage," the Frenchman said awkwardly—almost as if he were embarrassed to have suffered no harm. "It did not *feel* like an attack. It felt . . . more like temptation. The imp upon my left shoulder, I suppose. In any case, my guardian angel remains with me, as jealous and as enigmatic as ever."

David tried to smile at the joke. "I also once dreamed that I fell into the earth," he said. "I thought at the time that I was taken there by the angel which claimed me for its own in Egypt, but now I am not so sure. I have been visited by other angels in my dreams: by Hecate's maker, and—once at least—by Machalalel. Perhaps I too have been touched by the one which interested itself in you."

David had begun to find the conversation relaxing. Talking was not painful—his jaw was one of the few joints in his body unaffected by his illness—and it provided a distraction from his discomfort. In any case, he liked the Frenchman, and was beginning to feel more comfortable in his company.

"I think I know enough about your father-in-law's work to see the double meaning in the allegation that all history is fantasy," Daumier went on. "He referred, if I understand it correctly, to the act of imagination which historians must employ when they try to reconstruct the thoughts and motives of the men of the past."

"His view was that such reconstructions are never provable," David said, "least of all by the statements which the men of the past made regarding their thoughts and motives. He was of the opinion that we cannot always know what the true reasons are for our own actions, even when we feel certain that we do—and he believed that to be true even in the absence of any interference from the beings we learned to call angels. He was also of the opinion that men are inveterate liars, whose explanations of their conduct are merely excuses in disguise."

"That is true," said the Frenchman flatly. "Nor is it merely history which is a fantasy of that kind; the same applies to the society in which we live our daily lives. Were we not to make assumptions about the motives and intentions of other men we could not organize our own behavior . . . and yet, we can never know for sure that our assumptions are true, and must often suspect that they are not. We are gamblers all, *Monsieur* Lydyard."

"Call me David, Anatole. Yes, we are gamblers all. But you and I know that Sir Edward did not tell the whole truth about the lottery of fate. We know that humankind's legacy of myth and legend, which connects it to a world of magic and godlike Creators, has a kind of truth in it, even if it is not the kind of truth which religious men believe. And we know that the seven angels which have fallen into the world of matter have some power to reconstruct the world, much as if it were indeed their fantasy. Does that seem to you to be a delightful prospect, Anatole?"

"Never despair," the Frenchman quoted. "That was what your dream-child said."

"So he did," David agreed, with a slight sigh. "It is advice I have tried to follow."

"Hecate claims that the Eve to whom your son referred is herself, and she has also told me who the Clay Man is, but she seems unsure of the significance of his navel."

"It is an odd remark," David agreed. "I think I know what it means, but not why it was said. The Clay Man was not born in the normal way, but he nevertheless has a navel; as with the Adam of legend, whose name he has often borrowed, spurious evidence of a history was incorporated into his creation. The werewolves and the Clay Man believed until recently that the universe changes continually as a result of angelic Acts of Creation, and that the earth really did once resemble the world represented by myth and legend, but they were wrong. What they took to be memories of the Age of Gold and the Age of Heroes were as false in their implication as the Clay Man's navel.

"Yes, the angels do have the power to work miracles, but when they change the world in the present the changes they make incorporate an imaginary history which makes it seem that they have done much more than they have. They are not gods, but merely alien beings; they can manipulate matter, move objects back and forth across some strange dimensional border, and play elaborate games with human and other minds, but they too are subject to the fundamental laws of physics, and they too dwell in time. They can only create the *illusion* of omnipotence, by supplying false evidences of a glorious past which never actually happened.

"The angels somehow made a similar error of over-estimation in evaluating their own capabilities, and Zelophelon at least seems to have been unaware of it until my father-in-law made it clear to him.

Your guardian angel presumably wished to remind me of this. I don't know why."

The Frenchman nodded thoughtfully. The serious expression on his face suggested that he was striving hard to come to terms with all of this. "Nell has told me what she knows about her grandfather's confrontation with the angel Zelophelon," he said uncertainly. "She claimed that he confounded Jacob Harkender's schemes by confronting Zelophelon with indubitable truth—but you agreed with the sentence in the message which says that he was wrong. Is there not a contradiction here?"

"Sir Edward's revelation was not so much *wrong* as incomplete," David said. "It was true in respect of the crucial point I have just cited, but in certain matters of detail it has been superseded. Sir Edward's vision—which he rightly thought far better and far more beautiful than anything imagined before—was the vision of nineteenth-century science. It displayed an infinite universe filled with stars of many different kinds, aggregated into clusters and nebular clouds, millions upon millions of them, serving as suns to worlds like the planets of our own solar system. This was a universe which had always existed, operating according to its own inherent principles, needing no Creator to have made it, nor any paternal God to oversee it; a universe containing countless worlds where the molecules of life were stirred into being by the warmth of suns, producing beings of many different kinds, all different and yet all hopeful, all making progress, all attaining and exploring new levels of complexity, continually adapting to new circumstances and constantly learning new strategies, ever driven to improvement by the motor of ceaseless competition for resources.

"It was a fine, *brave* dream, awesome in its majesty. Some men have, of course, been intimidated by it. Some have thought it terrible, because it makes the planet on which we live seem so very tiny and insignificant, and humankind so trivial and unimportant; but Sir Edward did not see it that way. He found a certain sublimity in the notion that the solar system and humankind were merely instances of patterns far greater, paradigm examples of a grand adventure which extended throughout the infinity of the universe. Humankind is but a single example of life, of sentience, of intelligence, of rational being—but we contain, in Sir Edward's view, an image in miniature of an unimaginably vast whole. In Sir Edward's vision, the Medieval idea of the macrocosm and the microcosm as reflections of one another is further reflected; when he contemplated the universe of his

Brian Stableford

belief he did not feel insignificant and he did not feel lonely, for he conceived of humankind as part of a vast community which extended forever and would endure forever.

"Having accepted a universe of that kind, Sir Edward felt no particular fear when he was forced to see that there were beings more powerful than men abroad upon the earth. To him, they were simply other members of that great community of beings, other creatures which could and should be helped to share his vision. He went to them demanding respect and recognition, never doubting that he deserved a kind of courtesy which they were too stupid, or too churlish, to offer him. For just a moment, he gave them pause, and made them hesitate; for just a moment, the angels themselves believed that he must be right, not merely about their own limitations, but about *everything*.

"The truth is, however, that universe is stranger than Sir Edward imagined it to be. Albert Einstein has demonstrated that, and others are already extending his insights. It seems probable, too, that the angels are stranger than Sir Edward imagined *them* to be. There never was a man with more common sense than Sir Edward Tallentyre, but the universe is so peculiar that *common* sense can hardly begin to get to grips with it. The ultimate truth may be so esoteric that the human imagination is doomed to fail in the attempt to comprehend it; nevertheless, I think that some of us will soon be given an opportunity to try. We must do our utmost to get as close to that ultimate truth as our limited senses and their augmentary intelligence will permit, not merely because our own future depends on our success, but because the future of the angels—and the future of everything the angels have the power to affect—might well depend on it too.

"That, my friend, is the hidden significance of your message, so far as I can unravel it. I suspect, though, that there is a sense in which what you were intended to bring here was yourself. A company has been gathered here for collection, although it may not yet be quite complete. The new oracle—the *ultimate* oracle—must be nearly ready, in spite of the best efforts of whatever it is that threatens to subvert the process."

Anatole was silent, and David knew that he would need time to absorb the information he had been given—more time, probably, than would be allowed to him.

"Thank you for bringing the message," David said. "My son is dead, alas, and the angel which used him as a mask was a liar—but you did what was right, as well as what you had to do. I am glad that you did."

"But at the end of the day," Anatole replied haltingly, "I have told you nothing that you wanted or needed to hear."

"Let me be the judge of that," David said, as softly as he could. "Will you send Hecate to see me now? If she has any magic left, I would like to have its benefit."

The Frenchman blushed again, embarrassed at the thought that he had prolonged his host's suffering, and conscience-stricken in consequence, although it was David who had asked to see him first. David wished that he could reach out a reassuring hand, but dared not move.

Anatole rose from his seat. "I will send Hecate," he promised. As he struggled through the still-unfastened door he bumped his head again—but still he did not curse.

Poor boy! David thought. *He is no older than I was when I was bitten by the snake, and he has been thrown into the deep end of this pool of chaos with no time at all to learn the art of swimming.*

12

The world beyond the fire was an airless void. There was nothing left of her but *shadow*, which clad her, body and mind alike, in empty darkness. She had neither blood nor bones nor flesh, and yet she maintained a kind of presence and a kind of shape. She had neither hand nor heart nor eye, and yet she could feel the flow of time, and touch the glassy wall of the world, and see into the world as if through a distant, dimly lit window. The void in which she was suspended had no temperature at all, and thus no power to chill her, but she nevertheless felt robbed of all her native warmth.

There is nothing left of me, she said, although she could make no sound, and hardly any sense. *I am condemned to be nothing, and nothing but nothing; there is nothing left of Mercy, and nothing left of mercy.*

It was not entirely true; there was mercy of a kind in the fact that she was not alone. To be outside the world and made of shadow was bad enough, but to have been alone would have been terrible. While she was not alone, she could not be reduced to absolute zero, and it was only terror which made her protest that she was.

She was not alone because Jacob Harkender was with her. She could neither see nor hear him, but she was aware of his presence. Like her, he was a mere shadow imprinted on the emptiness of the void, but the nearness of him was palpable. She might have taken greater comfort in his presence—in spite of the fact that it was he who had drawn her into this nightmare—had there not been something very strange about his shape, which seemed to have far too many *folds* to be describable. She knew who and what Harkender was, but she knew too that he had undergone some unimaginable metamorphosis. He was neither beside her nor within her, but was nevertheless inextricably linked with her, and although she knew that she ought to be glad of it she could not help but feel a certain horror and disgust.

When Harkender moved, Mercy moved with him. They *did* "move," after a fashion, although it was not really movement because they were not in space. They did not pass through space, but simply changed their relationship to the particular spaces which touched the vitreous skin of the world from which they had come. It was almost as if they did not need to move in any true sense because they were already everywhere; they merely had to change their *point of view,* by means of some trick of their own impossibly convoluted geometry.

Mercy had only the dimmest apprehension of all this, but she had to hope that if anyone could understand what and where they were, it was Jacob Harkender. She tried to tell herself that of all the people in the world, he was the one best equipped to operate competently here. She tried to tell herself that she would be safe as a mere passenger, that she must be content to drift in his wake, and that she had no alternative but to trust that if ever there was a chance to return to the world, Harkender would recognize it and know how to take it. Alas, it was not so easy to convince herself when everything was so utterly alien, and terrifying. Mercy did not have to cling to Harkender because she could not have let go had she tried, but she could not shake off the fear that he might in the end be no more than a straw, and she a drowning woman.

Harkender seemed to have some purpose in the shifts and sleights which took the place of true movement, but Mercy had no idea what that purpose might be. If he had some mission to perform, or some goal to attain, she was not privy to it. Nor did she understand why there was such haste and urgency in his exertions. She could only assume that although they no longer dwelt in space they still dwelt in time, and that time was desperately short.

She did not know that she was capable of action, or what actions she might be capable of, until panic galvanized her. She had no plan to reach out into the world because she had no inkling that such a thing was possible, but when her eyeless sight caught a glimpse of David Lydyard beyond the mysterious window through which she looked into the world, she could not help herself. It required every last ounce of her strength—for she still had "strength," and was still capable of exertion, and over-exertion, and failure—to form a phantom hand and a phantom voice, but the combination of terror and hope drove everything else from her fugitive mind.

When Lydyard recoiled, disappointment brought her to the brink of desolation. She did not understand why Harkender also reached out to his enemy, but she understood the urgency with which he did it, and she understood that there must be some dire necessity in his invitation. There was no vestige of satisfaction in seeing that Lydyard would no more take Harkender's hand than hers, merely an amplification of her anxiety.

Have I spoiled his approach? she wondered. *Have I betrayed his purpose with my anguish, my desperation, my cry of "For the love of God!?"*

"You do not understand . . ." Harkender was saying, as the sight of the ancient Lydyard and his wretched old maid of a daughter faded away like some decaying after-image. He was trying to play the voice of reason, trying to play the strategist. But had he any idea, really, of what they were about? Did he know what they were doing, and why?

There was no time for angry sorrow or lachrymose contemplation. Harkender had twisted himself around, to face some other windowed surface of the world of space and matter. He was already extending a shadowy hand to someone else.

I am no help in this stupid quest, Mercy thought, *which is not mine in any case. I must control myself, at least to the extent of being quiet. Let him strain his own imaginary sinews to the limit, let him exert his own stubborn presence of mind.*

She was able to stick to the decision now; panic had released her. It was Harkender alone who spoke to the man who sat at a desk, furiously scribbling. It was Harkender alone who extended a hand of shadow to Jason Sterling.

"There is only one way now to understand the mysteries, sacred or profane," Harkender whispered to the alchemist of life. "You have done it before, Jason, and you know how little there is to fear. You have been five-and-twenty years a dreamer, but now is the time to dream in earnest. Come now, and join the company of angels— and come quickly, for destruction is abroad and hungry chaos is snapping at our heels!"

Mercy could not quite make out the expressions which passed across Sterling's face as he threw down his pen. She did not hear him speak, if he spoke at all. But she saw him reach out, tentatively,

to take the spectral hand which Harkender proffered. She saw him
dissolve into a kind of darkness, and she felt him take the step which
carried him out of the world and into the convoluted cradle-knot
which she and Harkender made for his security. She felt better once
he too was part of the knot, because she knew how strange it would
be for him, and felt that she had an advantage of sorts.

We are three now, she thought, as they fell through the fabric of
eternity, knowing even as she pronounced the silent words that she
was wrong. *No,* she said to herself, carefully, as if by concise concentration and patient argument she might tease out the whole of the
truth which she had unaccountably divined. *We were already three,
for the face—it was a face, was it not?—which smiled to welcome
me was not Jacob's face, but rather the face of a seraph. We are
four-in-one now, intimately woven into some unimaginable shape
which extends into more dimensions than the three I know . . . and
we will soon be more.*

She felt her fear diminish as she became mistress of this item of
knowledge. The fact that she had recognized it made her feel that
she was not utterly lost and helpless after all—that this peculiar
realm, however alien it might be to her frightened consciousness,
was a place where progress was possible.

Harkender was already extending another spectral hand, already
whispering another invitation and issuing another temptation. This
time, it was Sterling's voice he used, although the mind behind the
words was certainly his. Whether or not he had Sterling's blessing
for this imposture, Mercy could not tell.

"Heed me, werewolf," the voice said. "Will of Machalalel, the
time has come. If you desire to be free, if you desire to understand,
if you desire to see the face of the one who made you and made
you what you are, *come now!* Take my hand, and come into the
darkness for the last time. Your destiny is at last at hand; this is the
end for which you have devoutly hoped."

Within an instant they were five. Mercy knew that much, although
she could make little enough sense of the datum or the sensation
which gave it birth. She was not aware of the individuality of Sterling's presence, nor of any discrete mentality that might have belonged to Pelorus. It had been difficult to conceive of herself as half
of a pair with the only man she had ever loved—if she had ever
loved anyone—and even that had been self-deception, for there had
been a third with and within them even then . . . the shape which

they *now* had, now that they were five, was more peculiar still, even further beyond the grasp of her dizzied imagination.

Can these others conceive of it? she wondered. *Do they have intellect enough to picture the kind of creature we are and are becoming? Am I the only one who cannot figure the fourth and fifth dimensions? If so, why am I part of this at all?*

"Reach out to us," Harkender said, using a voice which was a kind of composite, with hardly any character of resonance. "Reach out, chimera, and reclaim that which was stolen from you, for want of which you are restless and incomplete. This is the moment for which you were made, the purpose for which you were sent to haunt the earth. Reach out, and be *reunited.*"

Through the darkling glass which was the mercurial wall of the world she saw a living sphinx, whose handsome, haunted face bore a curiously tender expression. The sphinx did not hesitate before answering the tempting voice, and Mercy felt its arrival as a sudden torrent of emotion. The intelligence which the creature added to their composite being was sharply and unexpectedly perceptible; to Mercy it seemed strangely mechanical, strangely obsessed and strangely detached, stuck in a rut so narrow and so feverish that it could not remember its own name. Mercy would never have believed that a sphinx was capable of fear, but she discovered now that the sphinx felt fear so intensely that its mere presence in their midst was briefly nightmarish.

The flare of the nightmare faded away as the six-in-one took flight again, no longer seeming to be twisting and tumbling but *soaring,* as if on angelic wings. The window through which Mercy had looked upon the world dwindled to a crack; it seemed to her that the being of which she was a part was no longer haunting the surface of the earth, preferring to keep company with the stars.

The creature that they were still did not feel *complete,* but it seemed to Mercy that in bringing the task of fashioning itself to a proper conclusion it had only to return to some alien anchorage; it had no further need of pleading, of cajoling, of tempting, of demanding, of deceiving, of persuading; it only needed to *fold in* upon itself. It was almost as if the six became seven by mere sleight of hand.

Mercy had only the briefest and slightest sense of the identity of the seventh; it was nothing that she could put a name to. As the climactic moment of consummation arrived, though, she finally remembered whose face it was she had glimpsed *and recognized,* as she had been drawn into the divine and all-consuming fire. She remembered the angel which she had not recognized before simply because she had not believed in angels.

"Gabriel Gill," she said to herself, while she still had a voice of sorts with which to speak, and a self of sorts to which she might report. "It was Gabriel Gill, not dead or gone at all."

She would have laughed to think that something as utterly bizarre as the being which had snatched her out of the world, to become a mere cog in a fatefully complicated wheel, could possibly have been born from the womb of a shabby whore, but she had no time. There was no time left. They were in full flight now, no longer soaring but diving, and they were not diving for the joy of it. Something was pursuing them: something dark and vast and infinitely more nightmarish than the alien cast of the sphinx's mind.

Whatever the pursuer was, she knew with a dreadful certainty that if it had any mercy at all, it had not the mercy to let Mercy or her companions be. She did not know if she could see it, for she had no eyes and the window of the world was shuttered now, but she felt that if she contorted herself just *so* she could turn and look "behind," or "up," or whatever the direction might be called from which the danger came.

She did it.

She did not know what she did or how, but she did it. She looked back, not with any kind of sight that a human might have used, but with the sightedness of an anxious, fearful and hunted angel. There were no words to describe what she "saw." It had no face and it had no shape. There was nothing in its "appearance" to trigger any ordinary phobic response. Even so, she knew that it was the worst thing in or out of the world: it embodied death, pain, Hell, loss . . . everything that was not life, not hope, not existence.

She wanted to scream, but could not.

Something that was with and within her felt her distress and moved its angelic wings to cover and cherish her.

"Don't be afraid," it said to her. "We are on our way to Heaven, and it cannot catch us now." It was not Jacob Harkender who spoke, nor even Gabriel Gill. It seemed to her to be the entity for which she had mockingly been named: Mercy itself.

Gladly, she fell asleep.

13

Hecate studied Lydyard's pale features, determinedly held rigid against the threat of pain. He was old, but not broken. His protector had done him no favors, and met none of his demands, but he might be all the stronger and wiser for that. She hoped so.

"Was the message which Daumier brought important?" she asked, delicately.

He shook his head, in puzzlement rather than denial. "It must have been important that it was brought," he said, "but the significance of its contents is not obvious."

Hecate was not surprised. She could not pretend to understand the steps of this peculiar dance, but she knew that it was more a matter of form than meaning. There were hidden connections between these strange and disparate incidents, which the angels could perceive, and which somehow constrained their actions. She had no illusions about her own part in the unfolding drama; free though she was to act as she pleased, there was a script of sorts for her to follow—and she had so far done what was expected of her.

"How is Sterling's work?" Lydyard asked. "Has he found the secret of mutation? Is the science of immortality within his grasp?"

"He has run out of time," she answered. "As have we all, unless our guardians can work new miracles on our behalf. The final battle in the war between the angels has already begun, and I cannot believe that they were prepared for the fray."

"No one ever is," he said. "Even those who may choose their moment to attack invariably move too soon, lest they sacrifice the element of surprise. Those who make wars are careless of their cannon fodder. They operate in a dream-world of maps and strategies, of Great Wars and sacred causes. We are mere conscripts, you and I, never to be favored with consultation or explanation. Orders are issued; we follow them. We do not even have the options of mutiny or desertion.''

She picked up his useless right hand while he was speaking, and proceeded to stroke it gently, trying to ease its distress. It seemed, on the contrary, to make him feel oddly uncomfortable. He was evidently not used to being caressed. She presumed that no one but Nell had touched him in any tender fashion for many years—not since his wife Cordelia had deserted him. Perhaps, she thought, he might be better able to bear it if she were a prettier woman: the kind of person whose caresses he could have accepted with sensual pleasure.

If any magic remained in her touch it had no immediate effect. She felt dead inside, and wondered if this was what it was like to be only human. That made her think of the long-gone days when she had not known that she was anything more, but she promptly put the thought out of her mind. After three or four minutes she frowned and laid Lydyard's hand on the counterpane.

"I'm sorry," she said. "I truly am."

"I don't doubt it," he replied.

"This will not last. For the time being, we are in a kind of no-man's-land, but one or other of the angels will soon come to take us away."

"We are, it seems, already exposed to sniper fire," he said wryly. "At any moment we may become targets of a full-scale barrage. We have no power to retaliate and no bunker or shell-hole in which to hide. We must rely on the angels of Mons, or Daumier's Maid of Orléans, to spirit us away—but they will only send us to another front."

"I dare say that the angels which have taken an interest in us need an oracle now more desperately than they ever needed one before," she said. "They will surely do whatever they can to keep us alive and well."

"Until we have served our purpose," he said. "We shall have to hope that ours will not be a suicide mission. Do you have *any* idea which of the angels might be winning the war, or where the lines of their alliances are drawn?"

"I wish I had," she told him. "All I can confidently say is that this is a war which involves them all, and that any victory which is won might easily be Pyrrhic. We can deduce, I suppose, that your guardian and mine are at least loosely allied with Daumier's and Mandorla's—but I cannot say what they are allied *against*. Not Zelophelon, I think, nor the angel whose eyes and ears have been the Order of St Amycus. Perhaps the mysterious seventh is the would-be destroyer, but it is possible that there is something even vaster than angels, which does not love any of their kind.'' She moved to the little window as she spoke, and looked out. The dark wood seemed impenetrable; its canopy formed a seamless black ocean beneath the stars. Nothing moved.

"There would be a certain ironic propriety in that," Lydyard admitted, "but no hope for the likes of us." He paused, and then said: "Do you think I was right to refuse Harkender's invitation? He, after all, is the man best equipped to understand the ways and ambitions of the angels."

"You do not need him," she said. "You are the man of science; you have your own means of understanding, which has advantages that his has not. If Harkender had not made an enemy of you, he might have learned from you, but he was too proud, or too self-indulgent. What moved him to do what he did I cannot tell, and what moved your wife to collaborate I cannot imagine, but in isolating himself from you so comprehensively he denied himself the one critical voice which might have checked the growth of his delusions."

"Flatterer," he said. He meant it as a compliment of sorts, but the implications of the term were not entirely comfortable. She had not said it to be kind.

"You must rest," she told him. "Conserve your strength."

"I have little alternative," he retorted drily.

She had begun to move toward the door, but she turned as she remembered something else that she had intended to tell him. "At the risk of adding to your melancholy," she said reflectively, "Jason Sterling is convinced that this is not the first time all of this has happened. He believes that other intelligent beings must have evolved on other worlds, and must have been used as we have been used. If neither you nor Harkender can succeed in finding a way to end the angels' conflict, the whole story may have to be recapitulated yet again, perhaps interminably. When Jason told the Clay Man this, the Clay Man remembered some parable which Machalalel supposedly related to him about endlessly repeating cycles and the precariousness of progress, and wondered aloud whether Machalalel had had the angels in mind as well as men. It was all to be in his new book, but I fear that he will never be able to complete or publish it now. He disappeared without trace when Sterling's laboratories were destroyed.''

This news startled Lydyard, and deepened the frown of anxiety which possessed his brow, but he seemed to lack the energy to make any appropriate response. ''I fear that I'm very tired,'' he said apologetically. ''The spinning of any further webs of speculation is beyond me for the moment.''

Hecate looked down at her useless hands—hands which, in former times, could have restored him to health and alertness with a casual flourish. ''Never mind,'' she said, but could not in all honesty add that there would be time enough. She went to the door. Her clumsy, lumpen hands could not even contrive to close it properly behind her.

She went down to the kitchen, where Nell was sitting with Anatole Daumier. There was a bright oil lamp on the table, and the two of them had brought their chairs close together in order that they might bathe in the full glory of the light.

''What will you do now?'' Nell asked the Frenchman, as Hecate moved a chair for herself. ''Your message has been successfully delivered; you are free.''

''I doubt that I shall have much choice in the matter,'' Daumier replied tiredly. ''If I have not outlived my usefulness—and I can hardly imagine that the moment of my death was worth interrupting for the sake of what I have so far done—I will doubtless receive some kind of instruction or inspiration. What does it matter, given that the alternative was to die and rot in a filthy shell-hole? All this is profit: every breath I take, every sip of water or wine, every mouthful of food.''

''You do not seem excessively grateful for it,'' Hecate observed.

''Do I not?'' he said. ''I ought to, I know. If I were able to go back in time, to visit myself as I lay in that shell-hole, and say *In a little while, Jeanne d'Arc will appear to you, and offer to give you life instead of death, if only you will pledge your soul to be the stave of some nameless and formless entity which will use you to perform meaningless missions in the furtherance of some incomprehensible conflict,* the only reply I could make would be: *Only produce the contract, and I will gladly write my name in my life's blood.*''

Nell smiled. ''What could any of us say? None but the devoutest of fools would ever refuse such an offer.''

''I thought she offered you more than that,'' Hecate said.

"Much more," he agreed. "She offered to grant me a wish, and I asked to be seated on the throne which the philosopher Laplace devised for his allegorical Demon, which would know the position and direction of every atom in the universe, and could thereby extrapolate its entire past and predestined future. Do you think the promise will soon be made good?"

"Soon enough," said Hecate pensively, "but I dare say that the result will surprise you."

Daumier, like the Frenchman he was, made only the most cursory acknowledgment of her remark before turning again to the prettier woman. "It is a pity that you have to return from a long and grueling war to *this*," he said. "Would you not be safer and happier at your brother's house, with his wife and children?"

"Do you think I would desert my father?" she retorted, with unexpected asperity. "Do you think that I would simply *abandon* him, when he is in such distress?"

"No," he said quickly. "No, of course not." Hecate could not suppress a grim smile.

"I am not permitted to *take up arms*," Nell went on, apparently having not yet expended the bile that she had somehow stored up inside herself, "but that does not mean that I must hide like a coward. I have been in France throughout the war, never far from the front, doing my utmost to preserve the lives of men whose bodies and minds were bloodied and blown apart. Do you think I would retreat *now*, while my father lies hurt, at the end of his tether?"

"No," the Frenchman said again. "I did not mean . . ."

"I know," Nell answered, swiftly but less softly than she probably intended. "In any case, I have no reason to think that I am any freer than you. I too may have an allotted role in this: a part to play in *Götterdämmerung*."

She has already played a part, Hecate thought. *All her life she has been playing a part, voluntarily if not under compulsion. What attempt has she ever made to live as other women do? She has been content to be her father's child, even though she knows full well what her father is.*

"Your dead brother told me never to despair," Daumier said awkwardly. "I am trying to follow that advice, although I dread to go to sleep for fear that I might dream."

"There are no dreams any more," Hecate said sourly. "Everything now is possible, everything now is real. There is no sleep, no rest, no solace. We are confronted with Hell, and yet we are denied death. There is no mercy left in all Creation.''

He condescended to look at her. ''If everything is possible,'' he said, ''we may hope that something better will emerge from all this wreckage. Something solid and actual: a world in which men may live with the hope of making things better, with the hope of bringing order out of chaos, justice out of oppression.''

''You sound like the Clay Man,'' she said.

''We are all made of common clay,'' he told her, seemingly anxious to score a point. ''While we live, we cycle a dozen bodies through our phantom selves, atom by atom, changing and renewing our material form piece by piece and pattern by pattern. We are clay, but we are also hope; mind as well as matter; ambition as well as resignation.''

''Good,'' said Hecate, miming silent applause. ''Eloquent, even, given that you speak in a foreign tongue.'' *Why are we quarreling?* she thought. *Is it mere tiredness, or some insidious unease which has crept into our souls?*

The light of the lamp seemed to have grown brighter, and Hecate frowned in puzzlement—but then she saw that Anatole Daumier was staring past her, at the window behind her. She turned around, reflexively shielding her eyes. *It is happening again,* she thought. *It is the same thing, happening again.*

But it was not.

She came to her feet and looked out. The trees nearest the house were darkly silhouetted by fierce yellow light; the surrounding wood was afire, burning so fervently that a great wall of flame had leapt up in seconds, extending high into the sky. She moved closer to the glass, peering leftward and rightward in order to see how far the wall extended. There was no limit that she could see.

Daumier had thrown open the door and vanished through it, but she already knew what he would see, no matter which room he went into. The fire was a circle all around them; the column of heated air thus circumscribed would ascend with alacrity, creating a wind which would blow from all directions simultaneously, drawing the ring of flame tighter and tighter, like a noose . . .

She watched the dancing flames, rampant with fury, and sensed that something was holding them back, that there was a battle here which matched magic against magic, heat against heat. She knew, though, that if the assertive magic of the imp which had lit this blaze were simply being nullified by the guardian which was determined to protect the cottage, natural law would be the decider. The radiant heat streaming through the glass was already becoming oppressive, and she flinched as she moved backwards—but she could not tear her eyes away from the hungry conflagration. Among the silhouetted trees something moved: a human form, frail and slender. It was not running away from the advancing flames. It could only be Mandorla.

Her restlessness must have tempted her out, Hecate thought. *She is trying to change: to become a wolf for the last time.*

The unretreating shadow remained stubbornly human.

Hecate heard Daumier shouting that there was no way out, and the clatter of Nell Lydyard's shoes on the wooden stair as she raced to her father's side, but inside her own body she felt utterly numb, utterly empty. The room was filled with wrathful yellow light, the walls and the ceiling reflecting it so vividly that it was impossible to make out the shape or colors of anything within. Hecate could see nothing dark but the silhouettes of the nearest trees and the wisp of shadow which was Mandorla. The whole world seemed to have become a cocoon of light enclosing her and them, and the branches were already bursting into flames like fireworks as the searing heat bore down upon them, and bore down likewise upon her . . . but there was no actual *pain* in this supernatural heat, she realized, unless exultation and exaltation were to be reckoned species of pain.

Hecate felt, perversely, that it was she and not Mandorla who was on the threshold of some awesome metamorphosis, which would not be in the least unwelcome. If only she could surrender to the heat and the light, she thought, Heaven would be hers: infinite joy, eternally extended. She felt that she was being *hunted* by some awesome predator which, in spite of its clear intention to consume and digest her, meant her no real *harm,* but was in some strange fashion trying to *save* her, to make her one with the fire forever, so that she too might dance away eternity as an ecstatic and conscienceless flame . . .

Only a few minutes before, the Frenchman had waxed rhapsodic on the subject of the common clay which was cycled through a man's body, replacing it over and over again, atom by atom, while the patterning mind followed its own path of progress and maturation; now he, like Hecate, must have been invited—so *temptingly* invited—to leave that common clay behind, in order to enter the world beyond the world as a creature of light, or something even brighter and even more mercurial than light itself . . .

She was aware that Daumier, driven by confusion, had come back into the room. It was to her that he turned now, not to Nell, because

she was the witch and Nell was only human—but she did not immediately turn to face him. Instead, she stared into the heart of the
flames which were rushing upon her from the other side of time.

Why not? she cried, silently. *Why be an ugly whore when I might
be primal fire?*

She felt herself carried upward even as the thought formed, and
knew that this time there was nothing to entangle her ill-shod feet
and anchor her to the sullen earth. Through the melting window she
saw the last sliver of darkness which was Mandorla rise upward from
the ground to become . . . not a wolf, but a soaring bird. She felt
herself floating toward the ceiling, and had no doubt at all that she
could pass through it, and the next one above it, and the slanting
roof . . .

Then she saw the shadow-bird which was Mandorla flutter downward, as if the feathers of fire which were her angel-wings had been
burned to the bone, and she saw something like a black hand reach
up from the scorched earth to seize and crush her . . . and her own
thoughts were suddenly convulsed by doubt.

"Anatole!" she howled, twisting in mid-air to face him, writhing
in the grip of the force which had claimed her. "Take my hand!
Make good your promise and take my hand!"

He would not have done it, save that he was a man of his word.
He had given her an undertaking, and she had the right. She had
almost reached the ceiling but she never passed through it. She felt
the groping fingers of Daumier's right hand close upon her left, and
in that instant the shadows came to claim her. They erupted from
the floor in appalling profusion, crowding together to form a great
greedy whirlpool of darkness whose maw extended into the abyssal
depths of a cold and storm-tossed ocean.

Her right hand, unaccountably rebellious, reached out for the light,
but it was too late. That hand was also seized, its revolt nipped in
the bud—not by Daumier but by another, whose other hand joined
with Daumier's to knit the three of them together into a tiny ring.
The whirlpool had them securely in its grip, and it dragged them
down with irresistible force, spinning them around and around so
quickly that Hecate's senses reeled. The only crumb of comfort left
to her was that she was not alone. The vortex of shadow had claimed
her so completely that her hands were becoming shadows too, incapable of grasping or gripping, but she and her companions were too
securely bound by now to need any mere hand-clasp . . . and in

any case, they were dissolving into the whirling liquid walls of the bottomless pit.

Even as the walls of David Lydyard's cottage at World's End splintered and collapsed into dusty calx, Hecate and her companions were buried deep in the fluid bowels of the illimitably dark and womb-like earth. They were a teardrop lost in a great and silent sea.

Where are we going? she wondered, as the shearing forces of the vortex tore the teardrop apart and folded its molecules into some unimaginable shape, whereby she was more intimately united with the others, made pattern of their pattern and mind of their mind. *What are we becoming?*

There was no answer, and the question itself was folded up, and twisted out of shape and out of meaning. But she knew who "we" were, and who had been excluded.

Poor Mandorla! she thought, while she still had time for one more thought, and while there was still a thinker to think it. *And poor abandoned, clay-bound Nell, left to die and decay and never to see what there is instead of Heaven!*

14

Nell dreamed that she was in a huge house with many staircases and many corridors, all of them ill-lit and cobwebbed. The rooms were cluttered with heavy furniture and velvet drapes, and the air within them was thick with cloying dust. There were clocks everywhere, with polished oaken cases and huge brass pendulums. The sound of their ticking was oppressive. There were many mirrors, but even when she stood directly in front of them she never saw her face or figure reflected there. All that could be seen in their imaginary depths were the chairs and cabinets, clocks and curtains, carpets and ceilings.

She wandered through the house from floor to floor, room to room, passage to passage, utterly lonely and utterly lost. She felt that she had been here for a very long time, since she was a little child, and that she would remain here until she was too old and frail to walk.

She found one of the rooms which had a huge brass bed, and lay down upon it. It was difficult to go to sleep, but she eventually dozed off, at least for a few moments, and awoke again to find herself lying in a silk-lined coffin. Her eyes were open but she could not move them from side to side, nor even blink. Her arms were folded upon her breast, but she could not uncross them, nor could she twitch a single one of her fingers. She could not feel the beating of her heart, and knew that the blood had been taken from her veins and replaced with some preservative fluid.

While the coffin remained open a series of faces appeared above her, looking tenderly down into her dead eyes. Some of the visitors leaned over to kiss her lightly on the cheek but she could not feel the gentle pressure of their lips. Each of them whispered a brief message of love or reassurance in her ear, which she heard with perfect clarity.

"Don't worry," her brother Simon said, "it's not so bad being dead. Grave earth is surprisingly soft, and the worms unexpectedly tender. Decay isn't unpleasant at all; it's like lying back in a warm bath after a hard and dirty day, peacefully and luxuriously *dissolving.*"

"You were the best of us, dear Nell," her brother Edward said. "The kindest, the most patient, the most loyal. You never took anything *for yourself,* and I wish you had. You should have had something of your own, instead of sacrificing yourself for others. You were a saint, an angel, and you deserved far better. I'll miss you, terribly."

"Pain is part of the price we pay for being able to think," her father told her. "To be able to think and talk, we have to be conscious, but we can't just decide what to be conscious of, or we'd surround ourselves with lies. Pain is just part of the package; it reminds us that the world wasn't made for our convenience, that life itself is a struggle against hostile circumstances. Pain is a spur which urges us to see more clearly, to understand more fully. Fear of death—not just our own death but the death of others near and dear to us—is just a species of pain; it's a gift as well as a curse, which ennobles as well as degrading us. To dream of dying isn't the same as *actually* dying; it's scary but it's a kind of enlightenment. It's a kind of foresight; it shows us that mixture of possibility and certainty which is the future."

"Pull yourself together, Elinor," her grandfather told her. "Concentrate hard. Look and learn. Even a girl can do that much. The past is dead, but the present can always be remade, if only the future will allow. Dead or alive, we all have a part to play in this; you must play yours as best you can."

"I didn't deserve to be abandoned," her mother said. "I don't say that your father did deserve it, but even if he didn't, two wrongs don't make a right. You ought to be more understanding, more tolerant. Do you think it didn't hurt *me* to do what I did? But I had the right; we *all* have the right, whether we're born men or women or wolves. Each and every one of us has to find her own destiny, and sometimes we can't help hurting others by doing what we have to do for ourselves. I don't need your forgiveness and I don't ask for it, but I do ask for your understanding. I want you to see that I had *reasons* for doing what I did. I don't regret it and I don't repent it, but I demand to be *understood.*"

Nell could not answer any of them.

When they nailed the lid of the coffin down she was left in darkness, but she was able to keep track of what was happening. She knew when they put her onto the funeral cart, and she felt every rut in the road as the horses drew her to the church. She heard the hymns being sung, although she could not find the slightest hint of meaning in the words, and she was aware of being carried out to the cemetery and lowered into the grave.

It was not until the sound of the clods falling on her coffin from above finally faded away that she was left in peace.

Simon was quite right. Decay wasn't an unpleasant experience at all. In fact, it was the most sensuously rewarding experience of her problematic existence, infinitely less tedious than anything she had felt while still alive.

It doesn't matter that I died an old maid, she thought. *It doesn't matter at all. I didn't miss anything important.*

She would have been content to decay forever, but she was not left alone for long. Two half-angels came to her resting place and took hold of her hands. One was almost but not quite a man; the other was almost but not quite a woman. They drew her soul from her body, and made it into a shade; then they breathed enough life into her phantom form to give it the power of movement. Then they led her away, and took her to a dark river, which they were to cross by means of a ferryboat.

"I don't have the fare," she told the ferryman.

"That's all right," he said placidly, "you can owe it to me. Pay me double next time."

"I thought no one ever came this way twice," she said.

"Not many do nowadays," he told her philosophically, "but it's always been possible. If you have the trick of it you can look into the future before you live it, and if you learn from what you see, you may be able to live it differently. It's not easy, though, and it's a dubious privilege at the best of times. This isn't the best of times."

Beyond the dark river was a dark land, across which the three of them trekked for many miles. Had the sun shone here they would have been walking for many days and many nights, but the darkness was eternal. She saw thousands of other shades, many of whom looked at her curiously, as if they knew that she was different, but none of them spoke to her.

The ferryman was right, Nell thought. *This isn't going to be easy.* She wondered what the ferryman had meant when he told her that this wasn't the best of times.

In the end, Nell was brought by her companions to the Seat of Judgment, where Hades sat. There was a second throne beside his, but it was empty. The Underworld had—as yet, at least—no queen. Hades wore the face of her father, but she doubted that he really *was* her father. He was an angel, or an angel's puppet.

"Well," she said, "here I am."

"Don't worry," Hades told her. "If you wait long enough, someone will probably come to take you back again. This isn't bound to last forever. Never despair."

"Where exactly are we?" she asked, not hopeful of receiving a sensible answer.

"It's difficult to say," he answered, stroking his chin just as her father always used to do when she was a little girl and she asked him one of those deceptively simple questions that required an adult explanation. "Where I am, you see, the notion of *where* is rather elastic. In a sense, we're *everywhere,* but that doesn't really help, because we're not actually occupying any space in the sense that matter does. And if your next question relates to *what* we are, the answer's much the same."

"Actually," she said, "I was thinking of asking how long I might be here, if not forever."

He shook his head wearily. "Ordinarily," he said, "that would be easier. Even angels dwell in time. But this is new to us, too. I really don't know. It all depends how the war goes, and whether any resolution is possible other than mutual annihilation. That's what we have to figure out."

"Isn't there an easier way to do it?" she complained.

Hades shrugged his shoulders, the way her father often used to do when he was arguing with her grandfather and losing, even though he was right. "If not us, who?" he said. "If not now, when?"

"Who exactly is *us*?" she asked.

"All of us," he replied, unreasonably cryptically. "Angels and men alike. There are no bystanders now; no one is hidden any longer. Hopefully, we now have the power to see all the way to the beginning and all the way to the end—but it won't necessarily do any good, unless we can figure out what end we need to reach, and which beginnings might unfold to produce it."

"Are you the angel which my father calls Bast?" she asked, curiously, wondering why, if so, it now presented a very different face to her.

"No," Hades replied, with refreshing frankness. "I showed myself to Daumier as Jeanne d'Arc, but Hades is more appropriate, and not just for you. I know your father and the werewolves well enough, although they probably don't know that they ever met me. I was observing the world of men even before Machalalel. You might say, I suppose, that humankind is my discovery."

"But not your creation?"

Hades shrugged, the way her father often used to do when he was displaying false modesty. "Not exactly," he said. "But if I'd ever had a name, I think I'd be entitled to have the species named after me."

My own mind is forming these ideas and images, Nell reminded herself. *I really am dreaming, although it's real. I have to supply some of the imagery which enables me to do it, but I really am standing face-to-face with an angel. How grandfather would have envied me this moment!* As that thought crossed her mind, though, she became anxious lest she should fail dismally to take as much advantage of the situation as Sir Edward Tallentyre would have.

"This is a desolate place in which to wait out a war," she said. "Couldn't you design something a little less tedious?"

"The human imagination is our only resource in creating these marginal spaces," Hades told her. "If this isn't to your taste, you have only your ancestors to blame."

"They imagined Heavens as well as Hells."

"Not very clearly, alas. That's part of the problem. But this isn't Hell—it's simply a place beyond life."

"It can't be very comfortable for you either," Nell observed. "Don't you find it rather boring and dispirited?"

"Boredom is not something we suffer from," he told her. "Our nature doesn't allow us to be conscious of doing nothing. We're capable of consciousness only when we act, and even then . . . it's always easier to act unconsciously, and if ever we cease action we cease to be conscious even of our own existence. Memory is a problem for beings like us; we forget easily and rarely pause for recapitulation and reflection. The fact that humans are capable of experiencing tedium is a marvel and a mystery to us. You live so briefly that we find it almost impossible to understand how time could ever weigh heavily on your consciousness. You can have no idea how ficrcely and how minutely we must concentrate in order to intrude into your lives and your thoughts.''

Nell looked around. The two half-angels had already gone about their business. There were other shades visible in the far distance, but they seemed to be very wary of approaching the two thrones. The surrounding wasteland seemed to her to be utterly bleak and desolate. She wondered how it looked to beings who were unaccustomed to the concepts of bleakness and desolation. "Do angels ever feel lonely?" she asked.

"Never," he answered curtly—but after a moment's thought added: "or perhaps always. Material organisms have choices that we don't have. You can remove yourselves from the company of your fellows with the aid of walls, or mere distance. There are no walls in our world, and as for distance . . . The manner in which we're separated one from another is very unlike the manner in which human beings are bounded and enclosed. In one sense we're never apart. In another we're incapable of coming together."

"In one of his more cynical moments," Nell said, "my grandfather told me that Hell is being eternally locked in a narrow room with all the people you ever loved."

"There is no necessity," Hades told her darkly, "for the room to be narrow."

"I suppose you have no sense of beauty either," she said, studying the dreary twilight and the ugly thrones.

"That's quite a different thing," he told her. "Beauty we understand, perhaps too well." He was becoming enigmatic again. Nell formed the distinct impression that he now wanted to cut the conversation short. He might not understand boredom but he understood urgency. Before she could ask another question he said: "Do you think you can play *your* part in this adventure, Nell? You have to coperate willingly, or it won't work. You have to consent, or it will all be confused."

"What *is* my part, exactly?" she asked.

"You'll provide a kind of anchorage," he told her. "We have to gather information from different sources—different worlds—and it will help enormously if we can form a kind of *focal point*. That's what this place is—and what you and I are. That's as clear as I can make it. Are you ready to do it?"

"I'll do my best," she said bravely. "After all, what else would I be doing but rotting in my grave?" She tried not to let the Lord of the Underworld see what a sacrifice it was to give up the languorous ecstasy of decay in favor of the stern call of duty.

What am I after all, she thought, *but common clay and Tallentyre blood and Lydyard pain? He is right, is he not? If not us, who? If not now, when? How can we be content with sweet decay, and the lovely safety of where and what and when, if our guardian angels are gracious enough to open the windows which look out upon the worlds beyond the world, and humble enough to ask us what we see there?*

The Age of Fallen Heroes

And the woman was arrayed in purple and scarlet color, and decked with gold and precious stones and pearls, having a golden cup in her hand full of abominations and filthiness of her fornication.

Revelations 17:4

1

The Age of Heroes had by no means ended before its histories were being rewritten, fantasized and allegorized so that they might serve as warnings and inspirations to generations of heroes yet to come.

Prometheus, the first and greatest of the heroes, became a veritable demigod credited with all manner of presumptuous miracles. His name was chosen to signify *forethought,* in celebration of the triumphant power of human reason. The ambitious sensibility which men learned to call tragedy provided him with the archetype of all Satanic tales, while the subversive sensibility which men learned to call comedy provided him with an ironic counterpart in the form of an unlucky twin. The name allotted to his brother was Epimetheus, signifying *afterthought,* in sad recognition of the frequent belatedness with which human reason was invoked.

The Age of Heroes was an excessively masculine era. The lusty lads who wrote its histories were so reluctant to admit the true value of their women folk that they refused to admit that any females of the human species had even existed until the gods became jealous of all the marvelous achievements of Prometheus. At that point, according to these primitive archivists, the gods hatched a cunning plot to get their own back on mankind.

The first woman, these zealous chroniclers dutifully reported, was designed by Zeus, fashioned by Hephaestus and conveyed to Earth by Hermes, who talked unwary Epimetheus into accepting her as a bride. The name which the historians gave her was Pandora, meaning *all gifts.* Her dowry was a box from which—out of foolishness or recklessness or malice or some combination of the three—she released all the evils which would afflict mankind throughout future history: famine, plague, war and pain. The authorities remained divided as to whether the last item in the box, hope, ought to be reckoned a perverse compensation for these disasters, or simply one more evil to be added to the list.

Pelorus, who knew Pandora well and might have loved her just a little, remembered things differently. He reckoned her the first of the many female heroes who would never be given their due while history remained the fantasy of men-at-arms. He knew that while she was known by the alternative name of Eve she had gone to some trouble to steal fruit from the twin trees of knowledge, despite that they were watched over by a jealous angel which considered them its own property, aided only by a clever Serpent and a nimble Spider.

"If only the men to whom I gave the fruit had realized their value," she told him, some time afterward, "things might have been very different. But some idiot named Adam took one bite from the first fruit, condemned it as bitter, and threw the rest away. His fellows were stupid enough to trust his judgment, and flatly refused to make their own trials—with the result that the wealth of wisdom rotted on the ground, untested and disregarded. The Serpent, the Spider and I had to bear the full weight of the angel's vengeful wrath. The Serpent was condemned to an eternity of legless squirming, and the unreasonable contempt of men. The Spider was condemned to an eternity of thankless spinning, and the unreasonable contempt of men. I was condemned to an eternity of sweated labor, and the unreasonable contempt of men."

"Angels are not known for tempering their justice with mercy," Pelorus admitted. He added as an afterthought: "In fact, whatever reputation they may claim, there is no conspicuous evidence of their ability to temper their jealousy with justice."

Some later historians suggested that Eve-as-Pandora released the host of evils upon the world in order to get her own back for this earlier incident, citing as their authority the universally acknowledged opinion that Hell hath no fury like a woman scorned, but they might have thought differently had their ancestors only had the sense to eat the forbidden fruit which she stole on their behalf. Pelorus knew the truth, which was that she had opened the box in order to give the ungrateful crew a second chance.

"Every evil is a two-edged sword," she explained to him, when he consulted her as to the true reason for her action. *"Of course* the fruit of the tree of knowledge is bitter, but that doesn't mean to say that it isn't nutritious; man does not live by honey alone. Yes, it has to be admitted famine and plague, war and pain will wreak vile havoc upon the descendant generations of humankind, but can you possibly imagine that without such threats hanging over them people would ever learn *anything*? In the fullness of time, people have the means to win their own salvation from all these evils, if only they have the heart and mind to do it. In the fullness of time, people will have knowledge enough to feed themselves lavishly; to cure all diseases, not excepting death itself; to live together in peace and harmony; and to conquer pain. All they need in order to accomplish these ends is the will, the wit and the wisdom—and, of course, a few thousand years of concerted effort.

"They might easily destroy themselves first," Pelorus pointed out. "If only war were a trifle less seductive . . ."

"If only," she agreed.

"What about hope?" Pelorus inquired. "*Is* it the redeeming virtue, do you think, or just one more evil, calculated to make people add to their own torment by struggling on against overwhelming odds?"

"Every redeeming virtue is a two-edged sword," she told him. '*Of course* honey is sweet, but every sweetness is a temptation to lethal excess. Hope, pleasure, love . . . not one of them can fulfil its tempting promise unless it be sensibly rationed, according to a proper sense of moderation. In the fullness of time, people won't have such a desperate *need* of hope, nor any other redeemer, and that will be all to the good."

"I don't suppose for one minute," Pelorus said sympathetically, "that the avenging angel condescended to turn a blind eye to your second attempt to improve the lot of mankind."

"Hardly," she replied. "My sentence was increased, even though it was already limitless in time. It was decreed that I must bleed excessively with every waning of the moon, and that my children would grow so big-headed that the pain of their birth would torment me throughout eternity, and that the milk of my breasts would always be inadequate to their sustenance. In addition, all the warriors of the world were given an unlimited license to rape me."

"That takes account of plague, pain, famine and war," Pelorus acknowledged, with a sigh. "Were you at least forgiven for letting out hope?"

"What do *you* think?"

"So how were you penalized for that?"

"I was condemned to love men, immoderately, *in spite of all their faults.* But as I said, every evil's a two-edged sword. Just imagine how strong and patient I'll be after a few millennia of *that* sort of treatment. One day, my time is bound to come—and that's not just hope talking; it's sound common sense. One day, the avenging angel will fall upon its own flaming sword, and the fruit of those twin trees will be ripe for anyone to pluck. Then we human beings can *really* start cooking. I'm already saving recipes.''

Throughout the age of heroes, Pelorus never met another who had such afflictions to bear, nor one who bore them more bravely, nor one who was more stupidly misunderstood by those who came after her.

2

Of all the heroes, only Orpheus was a peacemaker. It was not true, as some later commentators reported, that even stones and trees followed him around, nor even that he charmed very many wild beasts, but the music of his lyre certainly soothed the hearts and minds of human beings. The human part of Pelorus loved him for that, and even Mandorla in her wild heyday was reduced to near docility on the one occasion when she was unwary enough to listen to his playing.

Pelorus was not a member of the *Argo*'s crew, and never knew how much faith to place in the oft-told tale that Orpheus out-played the sirens and saved his companions from their fatally seductive song, but he thought it not too improbable, given that the song the sirens sang was probably overrated by rumor and reputation. Orpheus, of course, swore by all the gods that the tale was true, but that meant nothing. All heroes are not liars, but the narcissistic effects of fame are such that it is quite impossible to detect the rare ones who decline to embellish the truth.

Pelorus was, however, present when Orpheus undertook his most celebrated adventure. In fact, it was Pelorus who guided Orpheus when he went into the Underworld in search of his beloved Eurydice, so he was certainly qualified to testify to the absolute truth of that particular story. While he was in Hades' realm Orpheus did indeed play and sing so beautifully that the damned forgot their labors for an hour or so, and the shades did indeed flock to hear him in their tens of thousands.

"Orpheus was always at his best when he was deeply sad," Pelo-

rus reported, many years later. "He could play merrily enough for
the dance, if people begged him to, but he could never put his heart
into that kind of strumming. Nothing brought him out of himself like
grief; his best compositions and improvisations were all keening,
mourning and yearning. It was hardly surprising that the dead loved
him even more than the living, or that Hades and Persephone themselves found their hearts melting. Orpheus himself had no idea how
he did it, of course; he wasn't theoretically inclined. He didn't know
how it came about that music had meaning, in emotional terms, and
he didn't have to think about producing his effects. He just plucked
away at the strings of his lyre and if he was in the mood it all just
poured out of him."

No one knows why Hades imposed the condition that Orpheus
should not look back until he and his beloved had actually left the
Underworld. Perhaps Hades didn't know either; any man who as-
sumes that the gods must know what they're doing is overestimating
their competence. Some said, of course, that it was a spiteful trick,
and that Hades knew perfectly well that Orpheus would look back,
but that seems unlikely. If Hades had been sincerely moved by Orpheus's music, why should he be spiteful? In any case, how could
he know that Orpheus wouldn't be able to observe such a simple
condition?

"Hades seemed to me to be perfectly willing to let Eurydice go,"
Pelorus said, when asked his opinion of the matter. "My impression
was that the condition wasn't an arbitrary imposition of his own, but
an honest warning. I think Hades was actually trying to help Orpheus
by letting him know the ground rules. It wasn't his fault that the
ground rules didn't make sense, was it? He didn't expect Orpheus
to look back. Neither did I. It just goes to show that you should
never underestimate a hero's capacity for fouling things up."

Some historians suggested that Orpheus looked back because he
was overcome with anxiety that Eurydice might not be following.
Others inclined to the view that it was a simple mistake—that he
thought it was safe to look back because *he* was clear, not realizing
that she was so far behind him as to be still within the bounds of
the Underworld.

Pelorus remembered it differently. "Orpheus wasn't a coward,"
he said, "and he wasn't a *complete* idiot. Whatever impulse made
him turn, it wasn't fear or simple foolishness. It was something
deeper, more convoluted. I'm not sure he'd ever have admitted it,
even to himself, but I think he learned something terrible about him-

self when he played to the dead and won such an enthusiastic response. That was his finest hour, you see—the best performance he ever gave, to the only audience capable of appreciating it fully. I think he realized, while he was playing in the Underworld, that nothing he experienced in the future would ever measure up to that moment. And I think he realized, too, that what he was doing was far more an expression of his own innate capacity for feeling grief than of the *particular* grief arising from the death of Eurydice. I think he came to believe, rightly or wrongly, that the loss of his only beloved had been a kind of trigger, an *excuse* for his descent into Hell, whereas the true *reason* for that descent had been the opportunity to play at his very best for an audience which truly understood and appreciated his art. One way or another, though, he convinced himself that he neither truly deserved nor truly desired the reward that he was offered. That's why he decided, in the end, that he couldn't take it. That's why he looked back.''

The ever scrupulous historians were even more puzzled as to the reason why Orpheus was torn to pieces by maenads when he returned to Thrace. The chroniclers couldn't understand their motive for doing it, and they couldn't understand why Orpheus hadn't beguiled and confounded them with the music of his lyre.

''*They* knew well enough what had happened at the mouth of the Underworld,'' Pelorus explained, when he had fully formulated his theory. ''They knew that he'd had the chance to redeem his wife, and had failed to follow through. And he still felt badly enough about it, whether he understood it himself or not, to let them exact their revenge. Because, you see, he *should* have cared more about Eurydice than he did about his art. She may have been only a naiad, one water-spirit among a thousand, hardly distinguishable from the rest, but she was his *wife,* and he was supposed to do his utmost on her behalf. Even his mother, Calliope, and her fellow Muses, left his head to float down the river and out to sea when they gathered the rest of him together for burial. They all knew, you see, what a traitor he was to Morality and Reason.''

None of this, however, compromised Orpheus's claim to heroic status in Pelorus's eyes.

''Perhaps his music *was* a process of exaggeration,'' he said, ''but that doesn't take away anything from the *effect* it had. You can have no idea how utterly beautiful it was, how consummately stylish, how irresistibly moving. The songs which Orpheus sang calmed wrath, awakened empathy, and made men yearn for a world without war and death. They were born of pain, and they expressed pain, but in the end they were an enemy of pain. The echoes of them which survive in the music of mankind are some of the finest achievements of which the human imagination is capable. Without music, men would be less than they are—and if they are ever to be more than they are now, music will surely be one of the instruments which saves them from damnation."

Pelorus first met Odysseus on Aeaea, the island where Circe lived. It was actually Pelorus—not Hermes, as later commentators alleged—who warned Odysseus about Circe and gave him the antidote to her drugs. Pelorus had made it his business to find out everything he could about Circe because she was so friendly with Mandorla, who was at that time very enthusiastic to send Pelorus to sleep. It was also Pelorus, not Circe, who guided Odysseus into the Underworld, as he had earlier guided Orpheus. In fact, it was Pelorus who persuaded Odysseus that he might do well to learn something of his future from the seer Tiresias.

"You must be careful about taking what he says *too* seriously," Pelorus told the hero. "Men who put too much trust in prophecy are too often enslaved by their conviction, but a little foreknowledge can be a very useful thing."

Odysseus was either unable to take this advice to heart or too clever to take it as Pelorus intended—it was always difficult to tell with Odysseus. In any case, he accepted uncritically the seer's judgment as to the difficulties he would encounter and the signs he must watch out for, and thus spent far more time puttering around the rim of the world than was strictly necessary. Had he been one of the *vagr*—as some heroes were, or at least seemed to be—he would surely have reckoned the wandering to which he condemned himself to be a terrible curse, but he was not. Whether he had secretly planned it that way all along, or simply rationalized it afterward, he made a cardinal virtue of the fateful delay. He proclaimed himself the first tourist, ever curious to see new wonders and face new challenges. "The word *odyssey*," he proudly pronounced, "will be an invaluable addition to any language intelligent enough to adopt it. It will become a benchmark of adventurousness and heroism, a prospectus for discovery."

When Odysseus finally did return to Ithaca to reclaim the bride he had earlier won by cunning he did not, of course, stay there for very long. *Vargr* or not, he had itchy feet. Pelorus met him several more times after the slaying of the suitors, but never knew for certain where or how he died, and thus was unable to comment on the very different stories which various historians later told.

As befitted the first tourist, Odysseus was a past master in the art of the traveler's tale. Whatever seeds of truth there might have been in the tale of the cyclops Polyphemus, the tale of the Laestrygonian giants and the tale of Scylla and Charybdis, were eventually lost in the process of exaggeration intrinsic to the business of endless repetition. It may have been true, however, that the gods went to some trouble in arguing over the great adventurer's fate. There is little doubt that Calypso really did offer him immortality if he would pledge himself to her, that Athene occasionally acted to protect him, and that Poseidon certainly did him more than one bad turn.

"If only I had been able to understand why the gods took such an interest in me," the ancient Odysseus confided in Pelorus, when they happened to meet in Egypt, "what a life I might have had! If only I could have figured out exactly what they wanted from me, I could have struck a healthy bargain with the most powerful, and really taken *control* of things. Had I known then what I know now I'd never have given up on Helen and used my wits to bargain for Penelope instead. I've always been too *reasonable,* you see—too willing to settle for *second best.*"

"But you turned down the offer which Calypso made you," Pelorus pointed out. "Why was that? Surely not because Tiresias had prophesied your death?"

"Immortality didn't seem such a good idea just then," Odysseus admitted. "What's the point of living forever if you have to do it in a cave, in the company of someone you really don't like all that much. She promised me wonderful dreams, of course . . . but I have this sneaking suspicion that if I'd been the kind of man who could settle for those kinds of dreams, I wouldn't have been the kind of man Calypso wanted for her own. She wasn't a bad sort, mind—she let me go, in the end, and helped me on my way. Why are gods like that, Pelorus? Why do they *court* us, and make bargains with us, and ask us for favors, when they could snuff us out like so many candles, or make us do exactly what they want? If only I could see the sense in it . . . well, it's probably too late now. Do you think Calypso would look at me now that I'm old, if I went back to Ogygia?"

"If the gods didn't *need* men," Pelorus told him, "they wouldn't ever have made men. As to what they need them for . . . most of them, I think, are just as much in the dark about that as you are, and even the one who did the making might not have been entirely sure of what he was doing. But you can be absolutely certain of one thing: if any of them *do* know, or if any of them ever find out, they certainly aren't going to tell us, for exactly the reason you've spelled out. They don't want us to be able to make our own terms when they come to bargain with us. They want to be able to seduce us, trick us and blackmail us into doing what they want us to do without our ever knowing what we might demand in return."

"Do you think there'll ever come a day," asked Odysseus, sombrely, as he looked into the depths of an empty wine cup, "when we've served our purpose? Will they one day decide that they've got what they want, and that the world they made for us can simply be scrapped—or, at least, folded up and put away until they need it again?"

"Oh yes," said Pelorus. "No doubt about it—that's the way it'll be."

"And will they condescend to tell us, even then, exactly what it was we did for them, and how, and why?"

"They might," said Pelorus, "but on the whole, I doubt it. It would be infinitely preferable, I reckon, if we could figure it out for ourselves. The sooner the better, in my opinion. It won't be easy, of course, but we really ought to give it a try."

"Well," said Odysseus glumly, "I've always considered myself the smartest man around—and I've certainly *been* around—but I really haven't got a clue. If I can't figure it out, who can?"

"One of the few benefits of being human and mortal," Pelorus observed, not without a certain twinge of envy, "is that each new generation has the ability to learn from earlier ones, without being too securely trapped by the forces of habit and the crystallization of dogma. The record of your exploits might become confused, and bits of it might get lost, but in the main it'll be remembered—and, of course, revered. It'll become part of an accumulating legacy, whose meaning and relevance might not always be obvious to its inheritors, but which will nevertheless remain available. It won't be the intelligence of any one man which finally penetrates the secrets of the gods but the accumulated wisdom of the race. With each new generation the legacy will grow and the hope will be reborn . . . and if the time comes when the gods want to put our world away, because it no longer has a function, they might not find it so very easy to do."

"Big ideas!" said Odysseus, his display of admiration tempered by one of his quizzical little smiles. "You're a pretty deep thinker, for a werewolf, aren't you?"

"Smarter than the average lapdog," Pelorus said, catching the mood.

"You did me a big favor on Aeaea," the hero recalled wistfully. "I've never forgotten that. That Circe . . . what a woman!"

"I steered clear of her myself," Pelorus admitted.

"And Nausicca, too . . . I sometimes think it was a great pity I'd become homesick by then. Penelope had aged quite a lot, you know, in those ten years—and I guess my memory had papered over a few of the cracks. Still . . . the one I *really* regret missing out on, even after all this time, is Helen. Now *she* was a peach!"

"Our paths never crossed," Pelorus told him. "Even werewolves can only be in one place at a time. I missed the whole of the war, you know. A pity, that—do you think there'll ever be another one to match it?"

"No chance," said Odysseus. "The sacking of Troy was the greatest carnival of destruction ever seen. Sheer madness. I'm just glad I was on the winning side. Never again."

"Still," said Pelorus, "who knows what the future will bring? Apart from Tiresias, that is . . . and the gods, of course . . . and the Cumaean sibyl . . ."

"Funny thing, life," said Odysseus, with a mildly intoxicated sigh. "Sex, death, the whims of the gods . . . it would have been nice to figure out what it was all about. Maybe you'll still be around when somebody finally does."

"Maybe I will," Pelorus admitted.

Part Three
The Web of Eternity

And I heard a great voice out of the temple saying to the seven angels, Go your ways, and pour out the vials of the wrath of God upon the earth.

Revelations 16:1

1

While the pain lasts, Mandorla is a wolf again. The pain which a wolf feels lacks nothing in intensity, but it lacks the meaning which pain has for a human; it is unconnected to the *angst* which haunts self-conscious existence, and it is so neatly stored in memory that it leaves no gaping psychic wounds. It is not so difficult for a wolf to join the company of the angels as it is for a human being.

Bodiless, save for whatever imaginary form the angels might lend to her, Mandorla cannot undergo metamorphosis into her human form, but her mind nevertheless recovers self-consciousness in time. The worst of the pain is over by now, but there is a lingering and irreducible discomfort which fills an interval of waiting.

When the waiting is over the discomfort remains, reinterpreted as mild but awkward physical distress. When she has collected herself she looks around. She has no difficulty recognizing the room in which she sits. She has been here before, or in the actual place of which this is a simulacrum. She knows, of course, that what surrounds her now is mere appearance. She has been drawn across the boundary of the world into the realm of the angels and that the ignominy and discomfort of her present position are insults casually heaped upon her by whatever contemptuous intelligence has charge of her.

There are two other persons present. The Clay Man is seated beside her, to her right. David Lydyard, or something which wears his appearance as a mask, is behind his desk. The image of Lydyard is thinner, more hollow-cheeked and more sunken-eyed than the real man from whom she was so recently parted, but that is not why she senses that this is a masquerader; the intuition comes from some deeper level of her wolfish soul.

In the actual world, she supposes, hundreds of David Lydyard's students must have sat in a similar position while they made what effort they could to concentrate on whatever the man behind the desk might be saying. They must have shivered periodically, as she now does, when the cool draught which blew under the ill-fitting door was delicately tainted by the sickly odor of preservatives and the barely detectable undertaste of dead human flesh. They must have scanned the shelves full of dusty books and the faded anatomical diagrams which hid the walls, as she does. Their eyes, like hers now, must have wandered to the high windows, marbled and begrimed, through which one might occasionally glimpse the blurred calves and feet of a passer-by—but could they ever have seen such an eerily flickering light outside?

The flickering light which shines through the high windows is less disconcerting than it would be were they less dirty, but it is puzzling nevertheless. It is as though night and day are alternating at intervals of less than a second—as though they and the room which contains them are hurtling into the future.

Why not? she asks herself. *We are recruits to an oracle, after all: an oracle of unparalleled ambition, if David was right.*

The room is also lit from within, by a single electric bulb whose translucent shade was once white but is now stained yellow. Neither the rapid alternation of night and day nor the discolored light shed by the shaded bulb can provide sufficient brightness to banish the army of shadows which gathers in the corners of the room, although there is light enough to display the massed cobwebs which march across the leather-bound spines arrayed upon the shelves.

Lydyard's students must have seen him as Mandorla sees his simulacrum now: as a tired and careworn man, his hands so crippled by arthritis that he can hardly draw a pen across a sheet of paper. They must have felt uncomfortable in the presence of his pain, his weakness, his effort, his dour determination. They must have thought him an alien being, apart from their own community of thought and feeling.

"There is a threefold path to be followed," Lydyard's simulacrum informs them. "Yours, I think, is the easiest way. Lydyard's is the hardest."

"Whose is the third?" the Clay Man asks.

"Your part is to foresee the future of mankind," says the person at the desk, ignoring the question.

The Clay Man will not put aside his curiosity. "If this is something more than a dream," he says, "where exactly are we, and what have we become? Have our souls been snatched out of our bodies? Have we left our flesh behind, sleeping or dead, while we have come to dwell with the angels?"

"The matter is not so simple," Lydyard's simulacrum replies coldly. "Minds are not so easily separated from their material envelope, and you could not simply leave your bodies behind to lie unconscious for a while. You have both undergone a kind of metamorphosis, more extreme than that which werewolves habitually undergo. You have been drawn out of the three-dimensional world into the many-dimensioned world of the angels. You have not become angels, but you have become entities which can co-exist with angels. Your experience is, of necessity, being translated into the kinds of representations your own senses habitually make. We have no alternative but to create false images of sight and sound, even though any such transfiguration is bound to involve a good deal of distortion. There is no way to describe what you must do except to call it a kind of dream, but it is not *unreal*. Like any other kind of dream, it may be polluted by your fears and hopes, but you should be able to see through them to the truth."

"Who are you?" Mandorla asks. "Why do you appear to us as someone you are not? If you are one of the angels, why not wear your own face?"

Lydyard's features become blurred, then shift to produce a mirror image of the Clay Man's face.

"Angels have no faces of their own," says the Clay Man's *doppelgänger* evenly. "I have another mask, which you might remember and recognize, but it was never my own. You know who I am."

"Machalalel," says the Clay Man immediately. "You are Machalalel, returned from the dead to make new demands of the chimeras he created in the morning of time."

"I am Machalalel," admits the *doppelgänger.*

"If you expect to find us grateful," Mandorla says acidly, "you will be disappointed. What do you think we owe you for the gift of life? It has been a mixed blessing, I assure you."

Machalalel contrives a wry smile. "It is I who stand in your debt," he says sadly, "but still I must ask more of you, promising nothing in return. Believe me, my children, I wish that we could meet as equals, knowing who and what we are and what possible fates lie before us, in order that we might settle our accounts. Perhaps we can, one day.''

"We are no longer your children," the Clay Man says, in a neutral voice, "nor your creatures, nor your slaves. We have long since set forth in quest of our own ambitions."

"You have changed," the *doppelgänger* says, "but you are what I made you to be. You, Clay Man, have been my eyes and my understanding. Through you I have learned a great deal."

"Pelorus was your will," the Clay Man observes. "But he is not here."

"Pelorus was and is my will," Machalalel agrees. "He too has his part to play in this."

"If the Clay Man is your eyes and your understanding, and Pelorus is your will," Mandorla says, "what am I?"

The duplicate Clay Man meets her eyes, and she feels the power within his gaze even though she tries with all her might to resist intimidation.

Machalalel smiles, though not in any mocking way, and says: "You are my heart."

In the beginning, all Anatole can feel is the pain, which fills him up and possesses him, tormenting him out of his true shape, his true form and his true identity. He has no mouth with which to scream, nor limbs to thresh; he cannot react in any way to the inexpressible agony. He cannot lose consciousness, and he cannot die.

It is a Hell of sorts, but it is not the terminus to which his wild adventure has brought him. He is certain of this; he *knows* that it is true. The knowledge helps him through the ordeal.

Eventually, Anatole's guardian angel enfolds him once again in its invisible wings; it has the art to soothe away his pain. It does not speak to him, but it takes him and makes him still and soft and *safe*. It lets him become aware that he is neither damned nor doomed, and that he is not alone. He is granted an interval of peace, that he might collect himself, and organize his thoughts. He begins the work of accustoming himself to his new existence as a ghost within the walls of the world: a phantom haunting the warp and weft of the fabric that is space.

While this peaceful interlude lasts Anatole has time to make such contact as he can with his companions. He can neither see them nor touch them but he can "hear" their verbalized and focused thoughts, and transmit his own to them. He and they have been given no spectral bodies, nor any virtual ground on which they might stand; such power of sight as they have been granted is directed to other ends. Anatole's new sight is magical in essence and in effect, but it is not entirely alien or unfamiliar to him. He has had dreams which have invested him—in his imagination, at least—with similar powers.

"Don't be afraid," Hecate says to him. "We have done something of this kind before, Lydyard and I. It hurts, but there is a kind of ecstasy in it too. Enlightenment can be elating."

"This oracle is not the same as the other," Lydyard says dolefully, "but the pain which we feel will be tempered by a better excitement, and one thing of which we may be perfectly certain is that the angels will do their utmost to keep us alive and sane. Their most urgent desire is that we may see, understand and explain whatever it is to which their sight gives us access. There is something which they desperately need—or, at the very least, earnestly desire— to discover by this means."

"I am not afraid," Anatole declares boldly. "This is what I asked of the Maid of Orléans when she offered me a miracle, and she has played fair with me. I will play my part."

Even as he speaks out, he feels the pain tearing at his formless soul like the claws of an enormous eagle—but then he sees the stars. He sees them in greater confusion than any man who ever looked up from the earth, for there is no atmospheric lens to filter their light. He sees them in all their hectic glory, and the sheer beauty of it all takes him aback.

As he fights to stifle the pain and concentrate his mind instead upon the light and the wonder, Anatole feels himself hurtling into the wilderness of space. As Hecate has promised, there is something about the sense of movement which is exhilarating. The exhilaration does not cancel out the pain, but it is compensation of a sort. He feels that he is flying faster and faster, as though he and his companions are not merely chasing beams of light but *becoming* beams of light.

"This is the ultimate odyssey," he says to himself carefully. "Godlike power I dared not claim when I was offered anything I might desire, but godlike sight I was not ashamed to demand. I go now to my reward: to occupy the throne of Laplace's Demon, there to taste omniscience."

Faster and faster they fly, while Anatole tries as hard as he can to focus his attention, to savour the experience—but no matter how fast they go, the universe whose panoramic appearance is displayed around them remains in all fundamental respects the same: magisterial; unperturbed; inviolate. It is only on closer inspection that he can see that appearances are not *exactly* the same. The objects distributed in the space through which they are passing seem distorted; they are slightly foreshortened. As their seeming acceleration continues, Anatole realizes—with all the force of supernatural revelation—that the world in which he has lived and believed is as much an artefact of his senses as something discovered and given. He realizes that the frame of time and space, which has always seemed to be the fundamental map upon which existence itself must be drawn, is as distorted a view of reality as the Mercator projection of the earth's surface, no less useful but no less artificial.

Anatole sees that it is *light* which provides the fundamental yardstick according to which all other things must be assessed, and that space and time are distorted so as to preserve the measurement of light's velocity for any potential observer. He realizes that the anthropocentric idea that light is *moving* may not be the only, or the ideal, way of conceiving of it. He tries to imagine—for he certainly cannot *see*—that every ray of light in the universe is still, and that apparently *stillness* is the most rapid movement possible, because all "movement" is a kind of *slowing down* . . . and his thoughts spin as they try to grasp the substance of the fantasy.

"One might as well imagine space as full and matter as empty," he says to himself. But when he has voiced the thought, it no longer seems such an absurd idea . . .

"If an observer were able to accelerate away from the earth until he achieved a relative velocity very close to the speed of light," Anatole says, trying to get a grip on the notion, "he would still observe light moving at the same speed, by virtue of the fact that his time-frame would be altered. To an observer on the earth the traveler would seem foreshortened, and time would seem to be passing more slowly for him. From the viewpoint of the observer on the earth's surface, the accelerating traveler could only get closer and closer to the velocity of light, but could never quite reach it or exceed it. From his own viewpoint, he could never get any closer. The velocity of light thus limits and determines the pace and progress of all transactions in the world of gross matter."

After a moment or two, he adds a further thought: "Where then, can Laplace's Demon possibly stand, in such a way as to see *everything* simultaneously? What can the word 'simultaneous' mean, in a universe of this kind?'' He remembers the enigmatic smile which crossed the face of the Maid of Orléans when he voiced his wish. He believed then that he was asking the impossible, but he could not have guessed how dramatic the confrontation with impossibility might be.

"This is only the beginning!" he exults. "Lydyard already knows more, understands more . . ."

It is true. So far, at least, Lydyard is seeing a drama whose theme and plot are familiar. This vision of the universe is by no means alien to his expectation, but it is become stranger all the while. Anatole continues to reap the benefit of their collaborative sight, and as he does so he senscs the growth of Lydyard's wonderment. His pain, it seems, is further eclipsed—as though it were, in fact, a collective pain shared out between the three of them.

Reality, Anatole realizes, is not three-dimensional. His own senses and the imagination grounded in them can only apprehend three dimensions, but borrowed angelic sight reveals to him readily enough that the universe has at least four dimensions, and probably more. Just as the Mercator projection distributes the three dimensions of the earth's surface upon a two-dimensional surface, inevitably distorting its form, so human perception maps the four dimensions of actual space within a three-dimensional conceptual space, with inevitable distortions. With difficulty—for even Lydyard is moving toward the limits of his prior understanding—Anatole sees that gravity, the force which binds all matter together with bonds of attraction, can be imagined as if it were a kind of *curvature* of space itself. He becomes aware, too, that mass and energy are convertible one into the other, as if mass were merely *frozen light*.

The flood of insight makes him giddy, and the sensation which seemed only a moment before to be soaring light now seems to be a precipitous falling. In the vertiginous panic which ensues he feels the great talon of his pain squeezing all the glad excitement from his soul. Had he a real voice he would certainly scream, but he has not, and the signal which he emits sounds in his own ears as if it were a mechanical siren sounding an air-raid warning.

"I am dreaming!" he howls. "Dreaming, dreaming, dreaming . . ."

It does not matter whether it is true or not, or what it might mean, for he has no alternative but to continue, no alternative but to exert every last fibre of his will to the task of evading Hell and finding Heaven . . . and he is profoundly grateful that he is not alone in the nightmarish realm at whose infinite vistas the luckless angels are forever doomed to stare.

Pelorus has woken from the long sleep many times before, sometimes in situations of dire discomfort, but it has never been as bad as it is now. This feels more like dying than coming back to life, although he is certainly moving toward consciousness and not away from it. He feels as if he is on fire, burning inside. His body is, alas, human.

Not for the first time, Pelorus wishes that he was the kind of creature that could die. Not for the first time, he is hauled into the world of light and sensation against the force of his own tiny, imprisoned will—knowing, all the while, that he is the helpless pawn of a more powerful tyrant. The fire dies slowly; it seems that he is racked by pain for far longer than any common clay could endure. In the end, though, he is able to open his eyes.

He is blinded by the light of a glorious sun, and covers his face with his hands. He rolls over, so that he faces the ground, and uncovers his eyes for a second time. He is lying on a carpet of green grass. His hands are unblemished by age; he is young again.

While he contemplates his hands a shadow falls across him; the gentle heat of the sun is eclipsed.

"I wanted Lydyard," says a sneering voice, ironically bitter with half-sincere disappointment, "not his lapdog."

Lydyard's lapdog? Pelorus echoes silently. *Is that what men have come to think of me?* He knows whose voice it is. He rises to his feet and glances around before looking the man in the eye. He and Jacob Harkender are standing in a meadow ringed with woods. It is not an actual meadow; it is a dream-meadow built by angels, lacking the depth and crispness of authenticity. There is no one else nearby, although he is certain that there were others close at hand during the mysterious interval which preceded his awakening.

"I doubt that Lydyard would find you congenial company," Pelorus says aloud, trying to match his companion for irony and casualness.

"*Congenial company?*" Harkender echoes contemptuously. "We have the chance to explore the outermost limits of the web of eternity—what fool would refuse on the grounds that he did not find the company *congenial?*"

"Not I, evidently," Pelorus counters. "But then, I never learned how to defy the will of Machalalel."

"Machalalel is a damned nuisance," Harkender says languidly.

"Had I the choice, I'd have taken anyone as a companion before you—which is, I dare say, why you were given to me. Well, so be it. Let Lydyard chase his truth to the dark and lonely edge of the universe and the end of time. Let him lose himself in irrelevance. The time will doubtless come when he will have to confront the proper produce of the oracle: the harvest which *I* shall bring from the farther reaches of possibility."

Pelorus looks around at the silent meadow and the bordering wood. It is all too orderly and too elementary, more like a preliminary sketch than a finished work of art. *A caricature,* he thinks. *If this is based in the angels' use of human eyes, they must be reckoned half-blind.*

"The magical woodlands of the Golden Age were by no means so lacklustre," he says aloud drily. "The angels had more imagination then."

"Your memories are false," Harkender informs him blithely, "and you might find that the future puts your fondly remembered mythical past to shame."

"This is a poor future," Pelorus observes.

Harkender smiles. "There are a great many futures," he says, "and I hope that the best of them have been reserved to us. Lydyard, I dare say, has set forth in search of the futures of destiny, little realizing how futile that kind of journey must be. You and I will hopefully have a very different spectrum to explore and analyze."

Shelving his pride, Pelorus says: "I don't understand what you mean."

Harkender's self-satisfied smile broadens, reveling in the good news. "Lydyard is a mere man of science," he says patronizingly. "Indeed, he has always been overwhelmingly *proud* to be a mere man of science. I pursue different ends. He has set out to take advantage of the gift of the angels as only a scientist could, and as only a scientist could possibly want to. He seeks to know, if he can fathom it out, what the true nature of the universe is, and what the true nature of the angels is. He does not realize, alas, that he is addressing all the wrong questions."

"Perhaps he is right and *you* are addressing the wrong questions," Pelorus says, as provocatively as he can.

"Consider this," Harkender says. "David Lydyard has devoted his life to the study of medicine—specifically, to the study of the nervous system and the mechanisms of pain. I dare say he knows as much about pain as any man of science in the world . . . and yet, he has been racked all his life by arthritis and a multitude of other minor ills. He *knows* everything there is to be known, in scientific terms, about what ails him, but that knowledge has not helped him at all. Men of Lydyard's stripe only interpret the world, my friend; the point is to *live* in it, happily and successfully—and beyond that, to *change* it to one's own advantage if one can. I have never cared a fig for the science of pain, but I have devoted myself very assiduously to a study of the *art* of it. I have never tried to bend my mind around the question of what the angels are, preferring instead to address the entirely pragmatic question of how best to deal with them. I have been a more useful instrument than he; consequently, I have fared far better in the world than he."

"He might disagree with that judgment," Pelorus says.

"His wife did not," Harkender counters triumphantly. "Nor will the angels, when the time comes for them to render their judgment of the world of men. Lydyard may be better able to teach them what kind of universe they live in, and what kind of beings they are, but what he teaches them will not bear at all on the question whose answer they devoutly desire to know, which is: what ought they to *do*, with themselves and with the universe over which they exercise dominion?

"Lydyard, you see, has no greater ambition than to tell the angels that they are *not really gods,* to prove to them that they are products of evolution, creatures not essentially unlike himself. It is probably true, but what can it possibly matter? The fact is that the angels have godlike powers, at least by comparison with merely human beings. In some ways, admittedly, they are naïve and uncertain, and thus in need of guidance—but the guidance they need is not the kind which Lydyard can provide, but the kind which *I* can provide."

"Which is?"

"The kind which tells them how best to use their godlike powers, for their own edification, and their own delight, and their own advantage. Pelorus, what your maker and his kin want from the men they have appointed to be their eyes and brains is not to be told that they are not real gods; it is to be told how to *become* real gods—and how, thereafter, to make full use of the privilege of godhood."

The light in Harkender's eyes is, in scientific terms, merely the glimmer of reflected sunlight. Pelorus knows, however, that it is also the light of ambition and anticipated glory. Harkender believes with all his heart that he can ask a price for teaching the angels how to be gods, and hopes to claim no less a reward than admission to their company.

"As I recall," Pelorus says, "you tried to educate them once before. Tallentyre forestalled you then—what makes you think that Lydyard will not outwit you this time?"

"This time," Harkender says sharply, "I am fully prepared. And we both know, do we not, that the vision with which Tallentyre bluffed my angelic ally was fatally flawed? Tallentyre frightened Zelophelon with a mere illusion . . . but Zelophelon knows now how little need there was to be intimidated. If you have been set alongside me to play Devil's Advocate, Will of Machalalel, by all means play your part to the full—but remember this: whatever answers Lydyard finds are answers to the wrong questions, and the angels will not be fooled or impressed. You had better hope that I succeed in convincing the angels that they have need of beings like us, for if I fail, *everything* might be lost."

2

While night and day continue to alternate rapidly the streets of central London seem deserted; people move too quickly to be perceptible. The inert buildings enjoy a curious half-life, even the most staid and stable changing the colors of their coats while others grow and die around them. Mandorla and the Clay Man are phantoms; the invisible people who move around them also move through them without either party experiencing any noticeable sensation. While time moves around them at such a hectic pace, stone walls are no solid barrier either, although movement through them involves a slight disorientation.

As time slows again, however, Mandorla's relationship with her environment alters. She remains a ghost, invisible and virtually intangible to living people, but the world recovers most of its solidity. She soon discovers by discomfiting experience that fast-moving humans pass through her without any significant hindrance, but that any such encounter is to her distinctly unpleasant. After suffering such collisions twice she has not the least wish to experiment with one of the lightning-fast motor cars which fill the street with black blurs. As the hours and the minutes wind down, approaching their ordinary paces, Mandorla finds a place to stand in a narrow alleyway, where she is unlikely to be forced to compete for space with what she cannot help but think of as the "real" people.

The Clay Man comes to stand beside her in his own time, delayed for a little while by the power of his fascination. "We should find a place which is not so busy," she says.

It is late evening and the twilight is fading as he speaks, but the

257

streets are still busy with unnaturally hurried pedestrians. Mandorla recognizes the Haymarket and wonders whether she would feel more comfortable were they to make their way south to St. James's Park or go along Northumberland Avenue to the Embankment, but the Clay Man shows no inclination to move. He is looking up at the darkening sky, which is gray with cloud, as though wondering whether it might be about to rain. Time seems to be normal now, and the people are moving normally, although their manner seems strangely sluggish by comparison with their recent mad alacrity.

The air is suddenly filled with the sound of some strident signal, which blares out from speakers mounted high on the sides of buildings or on lampposts. The clamor seems to Mandorla to be unnaturally loud and hurtful; in her attenuated form she is oversensitive to vibration and the sound cuts into her like a blunt knife. The effect of the signal upon the people in the street is instantaneous; they are gripped by a common panic, but they respond in a fashion which seems practiced. They begin to run, and to jostle one another wherever they form little crowds, but there is no real violence in their competition. The majority converge upon the north-west corner of the street, where there is a flight of steps giving access to the underground railway station which lies beneath Piccadilly Circus; the steps are soon jammed solid with people struggling to descend. The minority run instead to doorways, but the shops have already closed and the theaters do not seem to be open. Only a handful of doors are held open in order to allow refugees to take shelter within. Traffic vanishes from the street. A few motorists draw in to the curb, switching off their lights and locking up their cars before joining the anxious crowds filtering into their various hidey-holes.

A discarded newspaper lies on the ground near to Mandorla's feet, and she crouches down to look at the date. The street lighting is abruptly switched off, plunging the whole district into Stygian gloom, but she has time to see that the month is June, the year 1930. She has awakened many times before into a world which had moved on in time while she lay helpless in the grip of reversible death, but she never felt like a stranger before. More change has been crammed into her most recent lifetime than all the others put together, and she has changed too.

The sirens eventually fall silent; the streets are now empty of people. "Should we still be out here?" Mandorla asks belatedly.

"Why not?" says the Clay Man. "We are beyond the reach of any permanent harm."

Mandorla remembers how distressing it was when the body of a walking man passed through her own, and takes leave to doubt that she is beyond *all* harm. The immortality which she has in this dream-form might well be more efficient than the kind she has enjoyed through her earthly existence, but she can be hurt nevertheless.

Another sound has now replaced the soud of the sirens: a distant drone, faint enough at first to remind her of a swarm of bees, which gradually grows into something more raucous. Mandorla has difficulty judging the direction from which it is coming. The louder it grows, the higher in the air it seems to be. It is rapidly supplemented by the sound of distant gunfire. The darkness is interrupted by flashing lights which presumably derive from shell bursts, but the tall buildings on either side of the street hide the actual explosions.

The Clay Man has moved away from the shelter of the alleyway and Mandorla follows him. Searchlights reach up from the ground, but nothing is visible in their beams. The sound of approaching aircraft is much clearer now, but low-lying cloud still hides them. She judges that there must be dozens, if not hundreds. Gunfire on high tells her that a battle of sorts has begun in and above the clouds. A plane becomes visible, steeply descending, trailing smoke and flame. Another follows. They are not much like the ones she has sometimes seen above the fields of Kent and Sussex; both are monoplanes, and one is very much larger than the other. The inevitable bombs have already begun to fall; Mandorla cannot see them raining down but she can feel the shock waves of their impacts. The individual explosions are various, most seeming unexpectedly weak, but there are so many of them that their sound soon blurs into a staccato cacophony. The flashes and searchlight beams which illuminate the sky are joined by the ruddy reflection of numerous fires.

The effect of the few explosions Mandorla can actually see does not seem to be unduly devastating, but the blast of one which falls at the eastern end of Pall Mall is sufficient to send flying glass everywhere as it blows the windows out of the buildings at the southern end of the Haymarket. Mandorla winces and ducks down as a few shards of flying glass reach the place where she and the Clay Man now stand. She feels them slicing through her, but after the shock of the first impact the sensation seems no more bothersome than the shriek of the siren. The Clay Man bears the effects of the desultory cascade unflinchingly.

Mandorla sees something fall in the Haymarket itself, but realizes that it is not a bomb—not, at any rate, a bomb containing high-explosives. There is no flash as it fragments, but there is an audible hiss of gas. She wonders whether the primary purpose of the blast bombs might simply be to blow out windows, to aid the progress of the gas. This particular canister has presumably been wasted, but in streets full of tenements, where there is little or no shelter underground, similar missiles might be deadly. She has no way of knowing *what* gas is being dropped, but guesses that it is probably as far advanced beyond those used in the Great War as the aeroplanes delivering it.

A few more of the planes have been shot down, but none fall nearby. Far the greater number remain invisible, filling the sky so comprehensively with the sound of their engines and their machine guns that it is impossible to estimate the distribution of the fleets or the direction of their flight. The air close to the ground is less full of sound and fury, but Mandorla feels nevertheless that her frail and insubstantial form is the focal point of all kinds of tormenting disturbances. She stands firm and fast against the tumult, but it takes courage to do so.

"This must be a turning point in England's affairs," she says to the Clay Man, hoping that speech and concentration might take the edge off her discomfort. "No such destructive force can have touched this area before, and this is the very heart of the city. The people may have masks to protect them from the gas, but the mere fact that an enemy can strike *here* must signify that nowhere in these islands is safe."

"You sound less enthusiastic than I had expected," the Clay Man answers, peering at her oddly. "Does the wolf in you not rejoice in this destruction? Is this not the future for which you have always yearned?"

He is right, she thinks. *I ought to be rapt with delight. Has the human in me obliterated the wolf? Has David Lydyard corrupted me to such an extreme?*

"I have lost confidence in the idea that if only humankind might become extinct a better world might come into being," she tells the Clay Man, by way of excuse. "I know now that the destruction of mankind would not bring back the Golden Age. I have learned to see war as waste and madness, just as you do."

"I wish I could be sure that Machalalel thought likewise," he says contemplatively. "I remember a certain lesson he once tried to teach me, that war and progress are inseparable. The arts of offense and defense are powerful motive forces driving the quest for knowledge. Hatred and strife and the competition for limited resources are among the parents of invention. I once became convinced that men had found better motives for seeking knowledge, but I had begun to doubt it again even before the Great War broke out. If this is the true shape of things to come, perhaps Machalalel was right.''

"He is one of the senders of this dream," Mandorla reminds him. "Despite his calculated flattery, we are no more than toys to him, and he is playing with us. The world itself is no more than a toy to the angels."

"Do you not relish the idea that you might be your maker's heart?" the Clay Man asks sarcastically. "Would you not like to think that your feelings are his?"

"Machalalel has no heart," she replies. "If I have one, it is my own."

"I would like to think that the news I have brought him means *something* to Machalalel," the Clay Man says grimly. "I would like to think that what I have seen and understood has corrected the lesson which he bade me learn when the world was in its infancy. I have learned since then to place a high value on the finer products of the human hand, and was never able to find delight in their spoilation. I was premature in celebrating the birth of the Age of Reason in 1789, but I have lost my ambition to help in its midwifery. I would like to think that Machalalel might share that ambition." He does not sound confident. How can he, while they listen to the rain of bombs? He does, however, sound determined.

Should I share that determination? Mandorla wonders. *Am I, after all, on his side in this affair?*

The noise of the bombs slowly dies away, then the noise of the guns, and finally the noise of the planes; but silence never falls. Long before the sirens sound again, issuing a different signal, there are men and vehicles abroad in the streets, carrying hooded lanterns. The men are masked against the gas; they carry equipment to test the air, but set to work clearing the debris long before they dare to unmask. The minutes melt into hours as time accelerates again for Mandorla and the Clay Man. The doors which had earlier been locked are opening again, returning a steady trickle of fast-moving people to the streets. To begin with, all of them wear masks, but as time wears on and daylight dawns the masks are put away. The glass is swept away from the streets, and the traffic begins moving again, accelerating swiftly to near invisibility.

Mandorla glimpses a handful of dead bodies being carried out of the worst affected buildings, but only a handful. In this part of the city, at least, casualties are light. Perhaps, she realizes, this is not such a crucial turning point in the affairs of London or of Britain. Perhaps the raid had been long anticipated, and adequate preparations made. Perhaps the city can soak up a hundred raids like it, or a thousand, and not be destroyed or critically damaged.

"All citizens are combatants now," she says to the Clay Man. "They doubtless expect to come under fire, at any hour of the day or night. They know that bombing is something they must live through as best they can. War is simply a condition of their existence. I dare say that there has been no peace—no *true* peace—since 1914. Perhaps there will never be peace again. But life still goes on, and progress too."

"Progress *can* move all the faster under the spur of war," the Clay Man admits. "That I cannot deny, for all my foolish hopes."

"If we did not entertain foolish hopes," Mandorla says, not at all certain what she means, or ought to mean, by *we,* "progress would not move at all."

Anatole perceives, somewhat to his surprise, that the universe is not static. The appearances which are so carefully conserved at a local level by the relativity of time and space are, on a grander scale, far from placid and eternal. He sees that the universe, and the uncertain framework of space itself, is constantly expanding. The universe is involved in a process of growth and maturation so dramatic as to be reckoned explosive.

Anatole realizes that the star system which includes the earth's sun is one among many, and that the faint clouds which astronomers call nebulae are in fact galaxies of stars. With the exception of a few neighboring star clusters associated with the sun by the pull of gravity, all these galaxies are moving away, fleeing in every direction. It is as if the earth were at the dead center of a vast bomb blast—but he understands that observers in all the other galaxies would observe exactly the same phenomenon, each one with his own world, his own self, at the apparent center. The very fabric of space itself seems to be increasing in all directions, swelling up . . . with pride or lust?

Anatole remembers that he has had a vision of this kind before, when Asmodeus undertook to aid his powers of supernatural sight, but could not understand it at the time. The memory is oddly comforting, reassuring him as to the continuity and the wholeness of his experience, reinforcing in his lonely mind the hope that this dream will one day dissolve into the temporary adventure of a dreamer. It gives him courage to follow the current of implication which carries him on, deeper and deeper, into the mysterious profundity of the angelic revelation.

At some time in the distant past, Anatole deduces, all the matter in the universe must have been concentrated at a single point in space, in a single superdense mask, which disintegrated into billions of fragments as the expansion—the *explosion* of space—began.

No sooner has he formed this idea in the abstract than Anatole *sees* the explosive moment as though from some godlike vantage-point outside the universe. This, at least, he knows to be mere illusion, called forth by nothing more than a sense of drama, for the universe surely has no "outside," but he feels that there is something vital in this aspect of the vision, something which needs to be imprinted firmly upon his fugitive mind.

"Such was the beginning of time itself," he says reverently—but then he remembers the message which his guardian angel asked him to deliver to Lydyard, and Lydyard's explanation of the puzzling reference to the Clay Man's navel. This virtual image, he realizes, might be reckoned the navel of the universe: an implied point of origin which might in fact be an artefact of some later creation or metamorphosis.

There is, he realizes, another way open to him by which he might look back in time. The light which is even now arriving from the furthest reaches of the observable universe must have been emitted in the very distant past, and although he may not be able to see the primal explosion itself he can surely see its echoes.

When he tries to do this, he discovers another implication of what he has already learned. At a certain distance, he realizes, the relative velocity of the galaxies most distant from the earth's become nearly equal to the speed of light. These furthest galaxies appear to him to be foreshortened—flattened out into a kind of cosmic skin, like the surface of a bubble. To an observer in one of those galaxies, of course, the earth's galaxy would similarly appear to be a wafer-thin image at the boundary of the universe.

The implication of this is that although the universe is infinite in extent, it is finite in *size*; every observer in it must seem to himself to stand at the center of a vast sphere of definable diameter, and every observer must be able to observe the same echoes of the beginning of everything. Anatole exerts his supernatural vision to this end, and sees—or imagines that he sees—vast serpentine forms wrapped around the bubble-universe, writhing and squirming in ceaseless competition, open-mouthed and eyeless. The galaxies at the limit of vision appear as scales upon the bodies of these serpents, which are surely the angels themselves, perpetuating a contest as old as time; but what he sees is impossible, for they seem to be moving through one another rather than past and around one another, and their writhings contort into alien spaces which his sight—augmented though it is—cannot follow or comprehend.

Anatole is briefly overwhelmed by the concatenation of images, some of which are surely products of his own ambition to see *more,* while others are not yet graspable. He fights to restore some semblance of order and coherence to his sensations.

"Our senses," he reminds himself, "are only equipped to perceive three dimensions, but it seems that we may describe the universe more accurately if we introduce further dimensions into our model of it. We cannot *picture* this, but we *could* represent it mathematically. The true form of the universe might be a four-dimensional 'hypersphere,' which would bear the same relation to a sphere as a sphere bears to a circle—but even that might be an over-simplification."

This, he realizes, is an awkward stumbling block interrupting and confusing human understanding of the universe. Whereas humans can only conceptualize three dimensions, scientific explanations of the way the universe behaves are forced by the necessity of deductive logic to take in more. The angels, he suddenly understands, must be very different. To them, human sensation must be quite alien in its selectivity. It is entirely possible that for them the effort of imagination must proceed in the opposite direction. Whereas a human can easily say "I see" when he means "I understand," it is at least conceivable that nothing could be more foreign to the consciousness of an angel. For an angel, there might be nothing more problematic than the world of matter mapped by sight, or the mere idea of "sight."

Anatole "sees" the primal explosion again, in his imagination. He knows full well that there is no standpoint in space or time from which it could be "seen," but he can picture it nevertheless. The picture is a distortion, but a captivating one. In much the same way, he now admits, the idea of Laplace's Demon, able simultaneously to see and to know the position and velocity of every particle in the universe, is a captivating illusion. Whatever the angels are, no matter how magical their powers, they cannot take the place of that imaginary Demon. If he and Lydyard—and Hecate—are to understand what the angels truly are, they must work hard, not merely to see and understand everything which is set before them for sight and understanding, but also to escape the ready-made analogies which spring from the habits of their thought.

He immediately begins to raise questions. Were the angels "alive" when the universe began expanding? Did they emerge full-blown from that effusion, like proto-phoenixes newborn from primal fire? If not then, when? And how?

No answers spring to mind. Is this, he wonders, because the angels themselves do not know, or simply that they intend to keep certain secrets from their collaborators in this venture?

"They do not know," he declares boldly. "I really believe that they do not know. This is the process by which they hope to find out, and we are an essential part of it. They need us, in order that they may see themselves, perhaps for the first time in their history. We are their mirror, and their inquisitive eyes."

"Let us hope that they will like what they see," says Hecate.

The grass upon the shallow hills is a glorious shade of green; the trees and bushes in the woodlands are heavy with colored fruits; the sun shines brightly and the air is sweet and warm. The world is possessed by an uncanny quietude, as if it were balanced on the edge of sleep, but its peace is continually interrupted by rippling laughter and murmurous conversation, and by the whisper of turning cartwheels, just as the land is criss-crossed by rippling springs and numerous streams and silent shaded pools. The deer are tame; the birds are brightly plumaged; the honeybees are even-tempered.

"Where are we?" Pelorus asks, as he and Harkender walk along a deserted pathway. The road is well made, without potholes or deep ruts; like everything else here it is excessively artificial, but not in the same way as the place in which they first found themselves. Everything here seems brighter and more sharply focused than the actual world.

Harkender ignores the question.

The people who live here are handsome and gentle; they till their fields patiently, nourish their vines contentedly and speak to one another in friendly fashion. Most are aggregated in family groups, living in houses built of wood and stone; there are many children. Some, however, live in communities of a different kind, in towered monasteries whose low-toned bells sound the hours and whose libraries are full of illuminated books. All of these inhabitants ignore Pelorus and Harkender, although the intruders are neither invisible nor insubstantial.

Pelorus is possessed by an odd sense of the *familiarity* of everything which surrounds him. He feels that he knows all about this mysterious country, and feels a deep patriotic affection for its customs and its folkways. It is all illusion and fakery, but it is so very pleasant that he does not resent it in the least. He is content to wallow in the mellow calmness of it.

Harkender is less at ease but curiosity seems to be keeping his impatience at bay.

Pelorus has the impression that he has been in places not unlike this, but not for thousands of years. He knows how untrustworthy such ancient memories are, though, and he doubts that there ever was a place like this upon the dull earth. It is the Golden Age without the miracle workers, or the Age of Heroes without the warriors, or the Middle Ages without the feudal overlords, the heresy hunters, the plague, winter and all the abrasive attritions which perennially threatened to turn actual human existence into a wasteland.

"It is the land of Cokaygne," Harkender says contemptuously, when he finally decides on an answer to Pelorus's question. "It is the Utopia, or rather the Arcadia, of the common folk: the stupid, shallow fantasy of ignorant peasants incapable of wanting anything more than an end to pain. It is Heaven, but it is a Heaven for cowards. Not the worst of all worlds, perhaps, but one of the least likely: insane, ridiculous and unworthy. What possible business have we here?"

Pelorus cannot despise the world so thoroughly or so fiercely, but he cannot defend it either Because he is what he is, he knows that this world is designed for creatures which are neither wolves nor men. It can no more contain the innocent and conscienceless joy of the wolf than it can contain the vaulting ambition of reason. It is a world made up of negatives: an imaginary residuum left behind by the over-zealous banishment of ills. It is an experience to be treasured by the hour or the day but surely unendurable for an eternity.

They are passing through a little wood when an inhabitant of this world finally deigns to notice them. He steps out of a thicket into their path and awaits their approach, staring at them with patient brown eyes. Pelorus is mildly surprised to see that he is only half a man. There are horns upon his shaggy head, and the lower part of his naked body resembles the hindquarters of an extraordinarily stout goat. His enormous feet are shaped like cloven hooves.

"Not Heaven after all," murmurs Pelorus, "unless all accounts have been settled, and Satan forgiven."

Harkender smiles. "Heaven is exactly where we are," he replies. "Not quite the Heaven of the Orthodox Church, I fear, but Heaven nevertheless, built for the meek and the mild. This, if I am not mistaken, is St. Amycus himself: the sinless satyr baptized by a loyal but uncommonly liberal follower of Christ."

Pelorus is well enough acquainted with this particular heresy to see that Harkender is right. Carefully omitted from the Golden Legend, Amycus has flourished nevertheless as the patron saint of a patient order whose members have long devoted themselves to the distillation of a secret *gnosis* from meaningful dreams. But this is certainly not the Heaven imagined or desired by the order named for him, who consider matter to be an invention of the Devil and the intangible spirit the only part of man worthy or capable of salvation; this seems to be a realm which alloys devout Christianity with an Epicurean attitude to the sensual wealth obtainable from moderate indulgence in the pleasures of the flesh: a notion more accurately symbolized by the satyr-saint himself.

"It is a waste of time," Harkender tells the saint, without waiting for an invitation. "It takes more to humanize a faith than a dash of borrowed color. A Church is a very primitive instrument of social technology, whose sole useful function is to bind families together into a greater community of common feeling and common cause. All else is mere oppression, and no Church has ever shirked the nastier kinds of tyranny. Any dogma which sets out to circumcize the mean and quarrelsome aspects of the human mind is bound to end by castrating all desire and all ambition; it cannot be saved simply by reimporting a discreet measure of lust and a modest quantum of intoxication. This Heaven, like all products of religion, is counterfeit, and hardly fit for the substance of an idle daydream, let alone a powerful oracle."

"You are an unmistakable product of city life, Jacob," Amycus replies tolerantly. "Everything you own or desire is artifice, including your contempt. Your supposed wisdom is a wall which separates you from the world, serving only to secure your loneliness, your restlessness and your unappeasable vanity. It was the brutality of men that broke your heart, but it is the assaults of learning and self-loathing that have shattered your soul. You have sought to make a virtue out of the ability to hurt yourself when you ought instead to have sought solace and forbearance, and have thus estranged yourself from the pastures of Heaven. You should not hate or despise those whose desire is mirrored here; they are more fortunate than you, and have much to teach the angels.''

"This is a cradle-dream," Harkender counters, unperturbed by anything that has been said against him. "It is understandable in babes for whom paradise is sucking at the breast, and in simpletons for whom pleasure is release from the strain of conformity and the challenge of confrontation, but it is unacceptable in grown men. There is nothing *natural* in this kind of pastoral idyll; it is no less artificial in any respect than the greatest of cities or the most complex of machines. Everything that makes us human is a defiance of nature and a conquest of circumstance, even *you* and everything that partakes of your syncretic attributes. Let me tell you a secret, my dear Comforting Illusion. *There is no Heaven!* There are no Elysian fields for farmers nor Islands of the Blest for fisher-folk. There is no Valhalla for warriors and no Nirvana for mystics. But this is news which should make us all rejoice, for we are *human* beings, and there is nothing we ought to hate or fear as much as constancy and changelessness. It would be better by far to find a Hell beyond the world of life than to find a Heaven, for in a Hell there is scope for resentment and rebellion, and hence for progress. There can be nothing in Heaven to interest the angels.''

Can there not? Pelorus wondered. *We are here, after all.*

"Progress," says St. Amycus gently, "is merely the extrapolation of unhappiness into an endless, fruitless, joyless quest for a reward that would be better sought in another way. The truly wise man is one who can say *this is enough*; the truly good man is one who will. You carry Hell within you, Jacob Harkender; better by far to cast it out than to make every effort to extend it until it embraces the whole world.''

"You would have a better understanding," Harkender informs the satyr-saint, "if you had lived longer in the world. Even a wolf can learn what it means to be human, given opportunity and time.''

"A wolf which has been a man, even for ten thousand years, would be happier here than in any future *you* might find," St. Amycus remarks, amiably enough. "If only poor Pelorus were not the happiest executor of the will of Machalalel, I dare say he would prefer to stay here than follow you into the trackless wilderness of if.''

"Not so," Pelorus says, not without a certain reluctance. "I am too much the human now to be content with any mere Arcadia—and were I to be able to give up any part of my humanity, I would abandon it all. Better to be a man than a wolf . . . but better to be a wolf than half a man.''

The half-man, half-dream which is St. Amycus nods his shaggy head in polite recognition of the correction, but when he raises his liquid eyes again they shine as brightly as ever with the unbreachable certainty of faith.

"There is nothing else," the satyr says softly. "You may search the universe from end to end, but there is nothing to be found. There is burning fire and freezing ice, but no pleasant warmth at all beyond these horizonless hills. Be warned."

"I can't accept that," Pelorus replies; but when Jacob Harkender places a congratulatory hand upon his shoulder he can feel the fire and the ice eating into him, in a slow and merciless fashion which seems to signify something more profound than fear.

3

As time speeds up again and the world's moving objects dissolve into an untroublesome and barely perceptible flux, Mandorla and the Clay Man make their way down Cockspur Street to Whitehall. While they walk the length of Whitehall the alternation of day and night becomes ever more rapid, until it is a mere flicker, but when they turn left on to Westminster Bridge the flicker stabilizes.

Mandorla pauses on the bridge to look down at the Thames. The seaward flow of the river has become so fast that it seems, paradoxically, to be solid and still, although the ebb and flow of the tide import a subtler rhythm which is still perceptible. It is as if the river were a sleeping serpent, the pattern of light glinting from its scales slightly disturbed by feverish inhalation and exhalation. Mandorla is briefly mesmerized by the wondrous deceit, but her reverie is disturbed as time begins once again to slow. The Clay Man urges her to walk faster, and she obeys, although she has not the least conception why he should feel any sense of urgency now that time is disposed to do its own hurrying.

She glances back once at the north side of the river, where the skyline is in slow flux. Its principal landmarks remain stubbornly fixed, but other buildings fall and rise, as though London itself were a snake sloughing off certain worn-out scales and generating new and brighter ones to take their place.

From Westminster Bridge Road they pass into Kennington Road, and eventually turn into the meaner back streets of Vauxhall. This is a district in which Mandorla has hunted, but her human memory has retained no record of the grimy red-brick terraces clumped back-to-back, and she doubts that her wolfish eyes could ever have seen the newer blocks whose gray concrete faces look six or seven stories high. She presumes that these must have been built in order to gather large numbers of people together, but when time slows sufficiently to let her see the passers-by she perceives that the streets are not crowded. Many of the newer edifices seem all-but-deserted, their windows broken or boarded, their frames often soot-blackened. The older houses are more extensively tenanted than the modern blocks, but the terraces too are interrupted here and there by burnt-out shells. She is not surprised that the district bears such obvious wounds of war, but wonders why they have not been more speedily scarred over. There is little evidence of ongoing repair work.

When the flow of time becomes normal again it is inconveniently dark, but the electric street-lights are bright enough. The Clay Man points out to Mandorla that some of the doors of the terraced houses are marked with vivid yellow crosses, which must have been hurriedly painted in the recent past. Not to be outdone, Mandorla draws her companion's attention to the scarcity of motor cars—and, indeed, of any other vehicles. There are no horse-drawn carts at all; the few vehicles which can be seen are motorized vans, lorries and omnibuses.

The Clay Man kneels to look at a crumpled newspaper which lies within a pool of brightness cast by the lights within a shop's display window. It is dirty and has suffered the effects of more than one shower of rain, but it cannot be more than a few days old; the date can still be made out.

"October, 1947," he says to Mandorla.

"Such streets are always decaying," she said. "All I remember of the many occasions when I roamed them in wolf form, on far darker nights than this, is the dank odor of listless poverty. There is something else here now, though: a different fear, a different hopelessness."

While they stand on a corner, not certain which way to go, a high-sided van comes into view at the farther end of a short street. A siren mounted on top of the cab sounds a long plaintive note. The vehicle was once white, with a red cross marked on its side. After sounding its clarion call it rumbles to a halt half-way down the street and two men dismount, one from the cab and one from the rear. They are dressed head-to-toe in suits of some unfamiliar material; their hands are gloved and their faces are masked. The rear doors of the van have both been thrown back but Mandorla and the Clay Man cannot see what is inside from where they stand. Even as the Clay Man moves off along the street, though, Mandorla guesses what the van is. She has lived in London a long time, and she is able to read these particular signs. She follows the Clay Man, but not eagerly.

As they walk along the middle of the road, people begin to emerge from the houses to either side, carrying burdens wrapped in sheets or some kind of glossy black material. There are not very many— perhaps a dozen, from a street of sixty houses, the great majority of which are tenanted—but Mandorla can read the true magnitude of the tragedy well enough.

The Clay Man was not in London in the latter part of the seventeenth century, but he too has lived in the world of men for a long time. He half-turns to face Mandorla, and speaks just a single word: "Plague." Then he cocks an ear, having heard sound blaring from one of the houses whose door has been left open. He goes inside, curiously. This time, Mandorla does not follow him. Instead, she studies the faces of the men and women who are bringing out their dead.

Many of the carefully wrapped packages are small enough for a single person to bear; only a few are borne on stretchers. Most, Mandorla supposes, must be children or old people. The adults who bear them forth are mostly women. They wear the familiar stigmata of grief—their cheeks and eyes are hollow and haunted—but they seem oddly healthy themselves; there are no signs of emaciation and no evident sores on their flesh. The same is true of other women, often accompanied by unhappy children, who come forth from their houses to form a considerable crowd.

The crowd surrounds the masked attendants in a fashion which suggests suppressed agitation. Its members complain and fire questions in unanswerable confusion. Such replies as they receive are mostly given in gesture, but before closing the doors of the van upon its increased cargo one of the men fetches out a batch of leaflets and begins handing them out to the members of the crowd. Most of the women take them meekly enough, but some refuse, intemperately if not angrily.

For a moment, as those at the back push forward and the crowd presses against the sides of the vehicle, it seems that a scuffle might break out, but the moment passes and the crowd begins to disperse again. As the van drives off there are more expressions of anger and contempt, mostly from the few men in the crowd—shouts, raised fists and other gestures—but it is obvious that the people making them are well aware of their own impotence. They are railing at cruel fate, not at the men whose job it is to collect the dead.

Why are the sick not taken to hospitals? Mandorla wonders. *Where is the legacy of that modern medicine which David and others like him labored so long to produce?* She kneels down to read one of the leaflets, which has been casually thrown away. By the time she has finished the Clay Man has emerged again.

"It is a set of precautionary instructions," she tells him. "I dare say that most of them know it by heart. It suggests various hygienic measures, and procedures for treating the sick. There is a concluding paragraph which says that everything possible is being done to develop an immuno-serum, and that any new instructions will be broadcast immediately."

"There is a radio receiver within the house," the Clay Man says. "I expect there are few, if any, houses without one. I listened to a news broadcast, which mentioned the attempt to develop an immuno-serum against the disease which is decimating the nation."

"If this street is typical of the country as a whole," Mandorla says, "millions must be dying every week."

"Such plagues do not spread as easily in rural areas," the Clay Man reminds her. "In any case, London has presumably been targeted."

"Targeted?"

"This is but another phase in the war," he tells her dully. "The broadcaster made that abundantly clear, stating that resistance to the disease is resistance to the enemy, and that the dead are to be reckoned casualties of battle. He did not say who the enemy is—his listeners presumably do not need to be reminded—but it hardly matters whether it is Germany or Mars. The underlying progression is what matters: from chemical weaponry to biological warfare. No wonder there are so many deserted dwellings—and yet, the social order clearly remains more-or-less intact. The population is depleted, but it has not yet been sufficiently depleted to break down the intricate muscles and sinews of economic life."

"Nor, I dare say, has the decimation brought a final halt to your beloved progress," Mandorla says.

"The quest for an efficient defense against the newly fashionable weapons doubtless goes on as it always has," the Clay Man says, watching the defeated women retreat into their houses, closing their doors firmly against their neighbors, as though by doing so they might keep their microscopic enemies at bay.

"And yet," Mandorla says, "I see more reminders of the distant past than revelations of an unexpected future." She goes to the nearest window, so that she might look into the house. There is little within that seems unfamiliar: the furniture is much the same as the furniture she used when last she lived in London, and the wallpaper looks so old that it might have hung there unchanged since the turn of the century. The only inhabitant of the room is an old woman, who sits in a chair, patiently knitting, while a wooden box set on a table beside her gives out a constant stream of chatter. "Somewhere," she says, "huge armies are still in conflict. Even behind their lines the battle continues, but life stubbornly and stoically goes on. Children die and more are born. How long do you suppose it will be before an authentic climax comes?"

"I dare say we shall find out soon enough," the Clay Man replies.

Anatole discovers that the part in the oracle allotted to him and his companions is not restricted to the contemplation of space and time on the grand scale; their odyssey also involves adventure in miniature. When they are done chasing sunbeams and studying the limits of the universe, at least for the time being, it seems that they shrink to infinitesimal dimensions, in order that they might confront —in imagination, at least—the finest structure of matter and the grain of space itself.

This mode of experience, Anatole supposes, might be as commonplace to the angels as the other; but even if that is so, it might easily be the case that an understanding of what is to be seen here does not come readily to them. Unfortunately, it does not come any more readily to their human instruments; this realm is even stranger and more confusing than the other.

Atoms, Anatole realizes, are not simple entities. They are made of tinier "particles"—whose names, if they were ever to be given names, would perforce be legion—more complicated by far than the word "particle" implies. Nor are the forces which organize their structure and transactions simply arranged into smooth "fields"; their operation is associated with further particles which constantly come into being and disappear, most of them having lifetimes measurable in extremely tiny fractions of a second. Such entities as these, Anatole perceives, are not merely motes of dust too small to be visible, nor are they points in space to which properties such as mass may be straightforwardly attributable. Their reality is far more complex.

Anatole knows—because he knew it already, before he ever dreamed of Jeanne d'Arc on the battlefield at Chemin des Dames—that the behavior of light is complicated and confused. He knows that in some of its behaviors, as when it is reflected, light acts as if it were composed of particles, but that it has other properties, as when it is refracted, where it appears to be composed of waves. As an educated man, he has long known that the confusing conjunction of these different properties is parent to a fundamental difficulty in picturing the behavior of light, whose elementary constituents must be imaginatively pictured as "fluttering particles" or "packaged waves." He is already familiar with the notion that the behavior of light is describable mathematically, but that the mathematics becomes complicated because the wave properties of light can only be described in terms of sets of probabilities. Now, inspired by angelic intelligence, he "sees" all this in a more direct way. He sees that the same is true of all the sub-atomic particles: the heavier ones which make up atomic nuclei; the lighter ones which orbit those nuclei and the remainder of the vast legion.

Anatole realizes that this fundamental confusion of particle properties and wave properties is far more problematic than he has previously imagined. He realizes that although the energy "frozen" in matter is convertible into radiation, this conversion can only be accomplished in discrete steps, and that the minimum interval involved in describing these steps is as fundamental to the nature and structure of the universe as the velocity of light. The fundamental constant involved is a vital mathematical bridge relating particle properties to wave properties for all elementary particles. It is, however, a very awkward bridge.

Anatole has long appreciated the beauty of the notion that the behavior of all large-scale material objects is describable in terms of a mechanics whose basic terms are the positions and velocities of objects: a mechanics whose apparent universality led the great Laplace to invent his allegorical all-knowing Demon. At the microcosmic level, however, this simple and elegant beauty is quite lost. The discontinuities involved in the translation of matter into energy mean that it is not possible to map out a continuous spectrum of microcosmic "positions" and "velocities." Instead of changing "position" and "velocity" smoothly, elementary particles must "jump" from one state to another. The wave properties of matter and light arise because each particle has a number of new states to which it might "jump," and any calculation of its next state can only give rise to a set of probabilities.

Anatole grasps, readily enough, the fact that the equations which enshrine the laws determining the behavior of elementary particles are probabilistic. He finds no difficulty in understanding that whenever a large number of particles is involved—as, for instance, in all the transactions of gross matter—the probabilities translate statistically into a definite set of events. He ruefully observes, however, that if each microcosmic event is considered separately, the position is much less easily graspable. The question of exactly where an elementary particle is and what path it might subsequently describe through space remains essentially vexed. Here, as in the macrocosm, there seems to be no privileged point of observation from which everything about the behavior of a particle can be determined; any act of observation alters the system which is being observed because acts of observation require communication by means of elementary particles which enter into the transactions of the observed system.

Anatole realizes that the problems which Laplace's Demon would face in endeavoring to know everything about the macrocosm pale into insignificance by comparison with the problems involved in endeavoring to know anything at all about the microcosm. All that the Demon could know about the state of any elementary particle would be a set of probabilities unless and until some kind of measurement were made. He realizes that Laplace was wrong, and that his Demon could *not* calculate the entire history of the universe and the whole course of the future from simultaneous knowledge of the position and velocity of every particle in the universe, even if confusions about the meaning of simultaneity were removed, because the fundamental uncertainty of positions and velocities at the microcosmic level would surely introduce *some* uncertainty at the level of gross matter. He sees that the reliability of gross matter and its transactions is not absolute, and that the future is neither fully determined nor determinable. Even histories reconstructed from those echoes of the past which the present still contains are, he realizes, inevitably plagued by uncertainty.

"All history is fantasy," he quotes, "and all destiny too!"

As his thoughts drift he realizes that the interchangeability of matter and radiation makes it difficult, if not senseless, to speak of "empty" space. Space, he sees readily enough from his present viewpoint, is criss-crossed by multitudinous vague fields of force whose potential energy might in principle be made manifest as "particles" at any time. Its seeming emptiness is loaded with potential. He tries to comprehend this by picturing the reality which underlies space as a great ocean, and matter as the ripples upon its surface, constantly forming, decaying and re-forming. He proposes to himself that the seeming emptiness of space is an artifact of material being and human sensation. To alien beings like the angels, space might seem *full*, while matter might appear as a series of lacunae.

"Yes," says Lydyard, picking up his thread. "I had a sense of something similar in the course of the first oracle. I thought then that I had begun to understand what the angels must be. I think they may be creatures of oceanic depths which somehow *underlie* space. I believe they belong to an *implicate order* within ours, whose surface bears the map which our senses read."

This new analogy suggests to Anatole that the serpents he saw writhing about the walls of the universe might better be imagined as swimming eels, but he stifles the tempting confabulation.

"It would be understandable, if that were so," Lydyard continues, in his painstaking fashion, "that they might have some difficulty in making sense of the terms which we attach to the surface phenomena which make up the universe of matter. All that appears to us to be 'obvious' derives from the fact that our senses deal exclusively with the world of gross matter. The nature of our present dream assures us that the angels have access to the subtler realm of atoms and forces, where matter dissolves into a mist of might-be; they must therefore have a very different notion of 'the obvious.'

"The world of the very tiny—which seems to outsiders like ourselves to be inherently and utterly confusing, to the extent that it appears literally paradoxical—might to the angels be so plain and manifest that it is *our* perceived world which is sorely confusing and difficult to grasp. We have difficulty 'picturing' the transactions of the sub-atomic world; their difficulties might be complementary. When they borrow the sight of human eyes there must be a sense in which they see exactly what we see—but it is possible that it cannot and does not *make sense* to them as immediately as it does to us.

"It may well be that we who have long regretted that the angels would not consent to meet us face to face, have drastically underestimated their difficulty. Confabulation made our ancestors conceive of the angels as gods, but the way in which the angels have perforce conceived of *us* must also have been confabulation of a kind. All the bridges so far built between their kind and ours—and I do not simply mean their kind and *humankind*, for there may well have been other material species with whom the angels have made contact—have been fragile; such information as has crossed over has been tentative, incomplete and uncertain. It is possible, I suppose, that no better bridges can be built, but we must try. *We must try.''*

The huge ship ploughs its lonely furrow through the silent void, five light years from Earth and five from its first possible rendezvous with a habitable world. The ship itself will not make planetfall, even if the world in question is adaptable for human habitation; it will disgorge a hundred smaller craft which will carry the seed of Earth down to the surface: nanomechanical miners and large earth-moving machines which will collaborate in the construction of domes and hatcheries full of artificial wombs; self-replicating plaques of artificial photosynthetic systems for the manufacture of all kinds of organic materials; humans with legs, their bodies engineered for optimum adaptation to the particular physical circumstances.

Like the realm in which Pelorus and Harkender met Amycus, this one is so bright and sharp that its every surface seems to gleam, and everything is remarkably *clean,* but here the intensity of focus seems entirely appropriate. This is an artefact, a product of human engineering and human purpose. This is an actual future, not one which might lie, hypothetically, beyond the no-man's-land of death.

The humans who man the great ship have no legs; all four of their limbs are "arms" which bear manipulative hands. Such people never could and never would descend into a gravity-well; they will live their entire lives with the modest weights imparted by shipspin. Their lives are potentially endless. Like the inhabitants of the satyr-saint's Arcadia, though, they pay not the slightest attention to the alien visitors in their midst. Pelorus knows that there is a sense in which he and his companion are not really present, for he seems to himself to weigh just as much as he ever did; he cannot leap and soar as freely and as gracefully as the four-armed crewmen leap and soar. In a world not made for walking, he and Harkender must walk nevertheless.

The ship's velocity is limited; even light takes years to travel interstellar distances and the ship has perforce to take a longer time, although time moves more slowly aboard the ship than it does on the world which the ship left behind. Even so, the crew members expect to steer it to many star systems and many planetary encounters before they die, and only the youngest among them still require to learn the art of patience which will accustom them to the long intervals between events. The news which reaches the ship from home is always old but never stale, and its flow is constant; practicality sets a limitation on dialogue, but the inhabitants of the Earth system are also emortal—emortal meaning that they do not age, and might live for ever, although they may die by violence or by choice—and conversations of a slow kind can and do take place.

The exploration of the galaxy will take tens of thousands of years, but there are some among the starpeople who have already begun to speak of this as *mere* tens of thousands of years, and who are thinking ahead to the next stage in the Grand Plan. The majority, however, are prepared to tackle the task in hand first, and leave the planning of other adventures to a later day. The colonization of all the worlds in the galaxy to which human stock might be adaptable will take hundreds of thousands of years. It may well turn out to be a *collaborative* project undertaken alongside—or perhaps in competition with—intelligent beings born of other star systems, but these will surely have adapted their physical form for low-weight life according to much the same pattern that humans have used, with the result that all starpeople will meet as brothers, almost as mirror-images.

This world has shapeshifters of a kind, for there are some humans aboard the ship—and others in suspended animation awaiting the call to planetfall—who have limited metamorphic abilities, but Pelorus cannot think of them as kin. Unlike him, they have never been true wolves, and whatever they become when they change their shape they retain human intelligence and human self-consciousness. Like their fellows—but unlike Pelorus—they have conscious control over the phenomenon of pain, and are able to soothe or cancel any anguish at all by an effort of will. There are intelligences of other kinds too: minds evolved in neural networks based in silicon, whose bodies are only partly organic. These seem altogether alien to Pelorus, and sinister, in spite of the relaxed and comfortable way in which they communicate with the starpeople. They know no pain.

When they have had time to survey their new environment, someone comes to talk to them. Like them, he walks on heavy legs; he does not truly belong here, although this is an incarnation of his dreams and ambitions. It is, of course, Jason Sterling.

"This is the *real* future," Sterling tells them. "We are masters of our own being now. All flesh is subject to human dominion; neither famine nor plague can threaten us now, and no petty war—even though it blighted an entire ecosphere—could wipe out the human race. We have been truly born at last, emergent from the womb that was our world. No one now can set limits of any kind to the bounds of our empire. We may make of ourselves what we will."

Pelorus knows that in saying this Sterling is not ignoring the existence and power of the angels; he is declaring that this is the destiny of humankind, *if the angels will permit it.*

"Is this the best you can do?" Harkender asks him, with a sneer. "What real difference do you think there is between this dream and the Heaven which chimerical Amycus designed? What have your heirs done that is authentically new or praiseworthy? They have canceled out a few of the troubles and tribulations which afflict us. Death is inconvenient—let us have done with it! Disease is so unpleasant—let us wipe it out! Pain is so *painful*—let us refuse to endure it! Like the wards of the satyr-saint you desire a life of *ease.* Situated in the material world it may be, but this is a Heaven nevertheless. What do your swarming insects have that is any better than the sickly-sweet fruits of Arcadia?"

"We have infinity," Sterling replies calmly. "We have stars by the billion, and all the worlds which orbit them. We have the Protean ability to adapt ourselves to alien circumstances, to explore the limits of growth and form. We have curiosity. We have science. We have progress. We have everything. We have *enough.*"

"It is mechanical reproduction and nothing more," Harkender declares. "It is the human past writ upon a larger map, save only that the actors on this galactic stage are more securely cocooned against the vicissitudes of change. On what grounds is a galaxy full of cowards, or a universe full of cowards, preferable to a mere Elysium full of cowards?"

"You are ever enthusiastic to use that label *coward*," Sterling observes, in a tranquil manner, "but what does it really signify, except that you have accustomed yourself to pain, and earnestly desire to prove your superiority over those who have not? Even if that were authentic strength of mind and character—which I beg leave to doubt—what would it make you but a petty trickster? It is my people who have properly come to terms with pain, by conquest, just as it is my people who have properly come to terms with matter, space and time . . . by honest endeavor."

"This is a Heaven, and nothing more," says Harkender stubbornly. "And because it is a Heaven, it is worthless as a place for *men.* A wolf might find delight in Heaven, had it never learned to be a man, but this world of yours has done its utmost to rid humankind of the last echoes of the wolf which their ancestors preserved."

"Doubtless you are arrogant enough to believe with all your heart that you may speak for wolves as well as men," Sterling says, with a smile on his lips, "but you have a wolf beside you, who might see things differently. Could you not live in a world like this, Pelorus? Could you not be ambitious to help in its making? The Clay Man certainly could."

"The Clay Man is his own master," Pelorus replies uneasily. "The will of Machalalel commends me to applaud you, for it bade me watch over men, and to be their friend, and to protect them from harm as best I could. As for myself, I cannot tell. I am only beginning to understand."

Sterling is unperturbed by this half-heartedness. "We are all beginning," he says gently. "Better by far to be beginning to understand than to be confirmed in the mistaken faith that one has reached the end."

"You slander me," Harkender says quickly. "The advantage I have is that although I have been much further than you into the wilderness of if, I have not yet dared to begin to understand."

"You might never begin," Sterling counters, "while you are not coward enough to try."

As rhetoric, Pelorus thinks, this has a certain dash and verve; as argument it is so much hot air. He cannot help but wonder whether all this is a waste of time. *How does it help us to assist the angels?* he thought. *Even if a Heaven might be made for humankind, by one means or another, how shall we recommend it to them? How can we persuade them to care whether we are delivered into Heaven, or Hell, or mere oblivion? And yet . . . if they do not care at all, why are we here?*

"If the angels desire to find a better way to live than the one which nature gave them," Sterling says, as though in answer to his unspoken thought, "offer them this. Offer them the universe, and time enough for its exploration."

"If you think they would accept it," Harkender answers grimly, "you are ludicrously mistaken."

4

While the days and nights alternate at the pace of a pigeon's wing-beat, Mandorla and the Clay Man make their way south along the Albert Embankment and then into Nine Elms Lane. The city is changing much more rapidly now, at least in this district; its old skin has been sloughed and a new, much brighter tegument has taken its place. Huge buildings fronted with colored glass spring up on both sides of the river, whose silver-swift rush seems much diminished by contrast. Whatever depopulation London suffered in the Forties has been more than compensated; when the people and vehicles in the streets become visible again they have increased considerably in number, and the lengthening intervals of darkness are increasingly ameliorated by the multi-colored glare of bright lights mounted high on the surrounding buildings.

When time's pace eventually grants them permission, Mandorla and the Clay Man go into one of the tallest buildings south of the river, and are carried up to its pinnacle in a few subjective seconds by a soundless, metal-clad lift. When they emerge on to the roof subjective and objective time are once again in close correspondence.

It is a dark and cloudy night, but Mandorla sees immediately that two of the neighboring buildings have been badly damaged, presumably by bombs, although there was no evidence of any such damage before they entered the building; the damage cannot be more than two or three days old. There are no discarded newspapers here, but none is necessary. The Clay Man points across the river to a distant building which must be somewhere in the region of Victoria Station, which is topped by a giant sign obligingly displaying the date. It is the thirtieth of March in the year 1963. Mandorla goes to the parapet to look down into the streets below—which do not conform in any way to her memories of Nine Elms.

The people and vehicles far below are so tiny they look like insects. The people are only visible by virtue of the light which pours on to the pavements from windows and street-lights, but the cars and vans which crowd the street have lights of their own fitted fore and aft, and there are other vehicles which carry flashing blue lights on top. Many of the lighted signs which are ablaze at various heights above street level are also constantly flashing; many of the legends which they bear are continually changing. The city seems to Mandorla to be full of words, as though it is involved in a never-ending conversation with the night. The bomb-damaged buildings are shadowy lacunae in a great illuminated spider's web.

"This really is the future," Mandorla says, looking out over the Thames toward Westminster to the right and pimlico to the left. "This is what I was taught to expect when I was at last persuaded to invest a little hope in the human aspect of my soul."

"It is the world we left," the Clay Man replies, "more bloated and more garish but essentially unaltered. There has been no qualitative change—and the bomb-damaged buildings inform us that the same cancers are at work beneath the painted face."

"What would happen to this phantom body, do you think," Mandorla asks, "if I were to step over this guard-rail and leap into mid-air? Would I float down to earth like a gossamer thread? Can our guardian angels be trusted to make sure that my landing is soft?"

"Try the experiment, by all means," the Clay Man replies. "I shall be glad to observe its course. We have abundant experience of the angels' methods, have we not? In the course of our long and arduous lives we have been brought back from the dead again and again, but our maker has rarely been inclined to intervene merely to save us pain and indignity. You may be sure that the forgers of this oracle will not let us perish while they have some use for us, but I certainly would not trust them to preserve us from *all* harm."

"But what use are we, exactly?" she asks. "Why do the angels desire to map the future of London?"

"The French believed that the fall of Paris was the end of civilization," the Clay Man reminded her. "Perhaps the fate of London will measure out another phase of civilization's fortunes."

"But why should the angels care? They did not care about the fall of Troy or the fall of Rome."

"Perhaps they did," the Clay Man says pensively. "There is something about the human business of war which interests them. It is difficult to believe that they could have much interest in material weapons of destruction, but there is something in the escalation of destructive capacity which holds their attention."

Mandorla nods her ghostly head to acknowledge her agreement with the judgment. She does not doubt that they have been brought to this particular moment for a reason, and she strongly suspects that the reason has to do with some new phase of the war, but in spite of the visible bomb damage the life of the city seems to be perfectly healthy. The lighted sky offers no evidence of intimidation. It would be interesting, she thinks, to descend into the building and explore its multitudinous rooms and corridors, in order to see a little more of the conditions in which the people of the city live, but the desire is by no means urgent. She continues to study the traffic in the streets. Although time is flowing at its usual pace the unending stream of vehicles is oddly reminiscent of the hectically accelerated Thames which she watched from Westminster Bridge.

Some impulse makes her look up suddenly. Her keen eyes pick out a tiny gleam of red light high in the eastern sky. She draws the Clay Man's attention to it.

"Aircraft?" she suggests, uncertainly.

He shakes his head, partly in denial and partly in puzzlement. The red light has already blinked out, but something was most certainly there, and presumably still is.

Down below, sirens begin to well out a warning not unlike the one which panicked the crowds in the Haymarket. The gaudier lights begin to go out one by one, but the streets do not become dark. The columns of vehicles begin gradually to thin out, but it is evident that not everyone is running for cover. The city is not trying to hide, nor are considerable numbers of its people. Mandorla wonders whether this is because they know that the danger is slight, or because they know that there is no effective hiding place.

The sky lights up with some kind of gunfire, but it is impossible to see the guns or their targets. Mandorla is certain that she and the Clay Man are only two of thousands—perhaps tens of thousands—of observers trying to figure out the precise nature of the conflict. Anxious eyes must be pressed to windows throughout the city, watching the distant flares flickering in the darkness like Chinese fireworks. It is impossible to judge how the battle might be going. Meanwhile, the life of the city goes on, muted but by no means stilled.

The distant fireworks edge closer, but slowly. Any decrease in the violence of the firefight is marginal, although the flashes are more scattered as the aerial conflict spreads out to occupy a steadily increasing area of the starless sky. It seems to Mandorla inconceivable that such faint apparitions, so seemingly akin to twinkling stars, could have much effect upon the vast city, but she knows that these appearances must be deceptive.

As the battlefield extends its width the flashes of gunfire seem even more tenuous. Mandorla can see nothing at all to indicate what or where the targets might be, but it is obvious that they have not been turned back. She waits with eager curiosity for the first bombs to fall. She is not avid to see the destruction of the city, but she knows that something significant must be about to happen and the waiting is becoming bothersome. She is confident that she and her phantom companion have nothing to fear.

Without any warning, the whole sky explodes.

The darkness is consumed, from horizon to horizon, by a light a thousand times more brilliant than any she has ever seen before.

Mandorla knows that were she a creature of flesh and blood the flare would have melted her eyeballs and boiled her brain, but she is not; the blast cuts through her, and she feels its pain, but it cannot tear her apart or burn her to a crisp. She is whipped away from her coign of vantage by a great wind, and sent tumbling through the turbulent sky, but she is not allowed to die, nor is she permitted to stop observing what little there is to be seen amid the riotous confusion.

She sees the city ripped apart, its countless buildings shattered like so much matchwood, its heart scoured by an all-devouring fireball which descends upon it from above. Its remaining lights go out, but the entire sky remains redly ablaze for a second or two. The seconds seem eerily extended, although there is no angelic magic at work. Huge clouds of dust come billowing up from the ground to surround her while she hurtles through the air like an autumn leaf dancing on the wings of a gale. She falls, as though forever, still racked by unbelievable pain but still *seeing,* unable to switch off the unkind searchlight of her consciousness.

Time begins to accelerate long before she descends to the earth, but she is not immediately able to appreciate the mercy of its soothing effect. All around her, it seems, are the scouring fires of Hell, which have the power to destroy and cauterise everything material— except, of course, for her own phantom fire.

It is an illusory product of her own imagination, she knows, but she hears somewhere in the unimaginable distance the mocking laughter of angels.

Anatole finds that the end of time is not as easy to picture as the beginning. He knows that the primal explosion must have been a more complex affair than his feeble imagination is able to envisage, and it is by no means easy for him to understand the problematic nature of the "egg" whose pyrotechnic hatching gave birth to the cosmos, but the ultimate consequences of that beginning are shrouded in a different kind of uncertainty. The occult power of angelic sight reveals not one climax but several, and Anatole has no means of deciding which of the competing scenarios will be the actual culmination of the cosmic life-cycle.

In one of the overlapping images the expansion of the universe continues indefinitely. The galactic cluster which contains the earth—and every other cluster—becomes gradually isolated in a vast void, all the others having become so distant as to be all-but-invisible. In that lonely state each individual galaxy and each individual solar system gradually decays; all the stars in the universe burn out, their energy dissipated.

Anatole realizes that suns can only be temporary phenomena, decaying while they shine. Energy inevitably flows away from points of high concentration; all systems tend, by slow degrees, to a state of maximum disorganization which is also a state of energetic uniformity. The ultimate predestined fate of the universe—at least in this scenario—is a kind of energy-nirvana in which no further transactions are possible. Mass itself melts away into mediocrity, losing all variety.

In such a universe life too must be a temporary phenomenon, for life's creativity depends on the torrential flow of energy; life's capacity to build forms of greater and greater complexity is entirely dependent on the ceaseless flux of energy. The concentration, and subsequent dissipation, of matter in stars is a prerequisite for the existence of life. Indeed, Anatole sees now that the atoms that make up the molecules of life with which earthly evolution began are by-products of earlier instabilities, born out of the explosions by which over-energetic stars devastate themselves. Life is a phenomenon associated with second-generation stars.

Constant expansion is not the only possible fate which is imaginable with the aid of angelic perception. The force of the primal explosion which draws galaxies apart is counterbalanced, at least to some extent, by that curvature of space which is gravity; in an alternative scenario the trajectory which the galaxies follow will, in the end, bring them round full circle. Anatole can picture a time, therefore, when the expansion of the universe will reach a limit, after which the force of gravity will cause it to contract again, ultimately collapsing it into the same kind of entity from which it began. If this is the case, Anatole realizes, the end of time might also be its beginning. The cycle of causality might be closed, the cosmic egg which gives birth to it being the ultimate product of that primal eruption.

He struggles to come to terms with the notion of a universe engaged in a never-ending game of self-reincarnation. He wonders whether the cosmic egg formed by the ultimate collapse of the universe is necessarily the same cosmic egg which began its expansion, and whether, if so, it must give rise to a universe identical in every respect to the one which shaped it. Might it not, he wonders, be a subtly different cosmic egg which might give rise to a distinctively different universe, so that the closed cycle of time nevertheless plays host to an infinite series of variations? And even if the cosmic egg is *always* identical, will not the essential uncertainty of the microcosm ensure that there are subtle differences between cycles, and that there is in fact an infinite series of possible universes, not existing one after the other—for time is a closed circle with no "beforehand" or "afterwards"—but rather existing, as it were, *superimposed* one upon another, as a series of mutually exclusive yet parallel alternatives?

The sheer enormity of this idea intrigues him. The idea of a cycle of time which is always complete and yet always different has an intrinsic aesthetic appeal: a unique symmetry; an edifying sublimity; an inestimable grandeur. How many alternative universes might there be, contained within that single cycle? The answer to this question, Anatole immediately realizes, is stupendous in its magnitude: there must be as many alternative universes as there are uncertainties in the microcosm, which can pack millions of atoms into a space far too tiny for a human eye to see, while the macrocosm as a whole is far too large for a human mind readily to imagine.

There is more. Anatole's contemplation of these possible ends of time is elaborated and complicated by further data. He sees that the continuing process of expansion already plays host to small-scale processes of collapse. He sees that the exploding stars which scatter the molecular seeds of life leave embers in which matter can shrink to extraordinary densities. Many become energetic spheres of super-dense matter, whose atomic structure has been collapsed. Some reach a level of concentration at which the force of gravity becomes so strong that the curvature of space around the mass is closed off, resulting in an entity from whose surface nothing—not even light—can escape. These, he realizes, are essentially "holes" in the universe of space, and their surfaces are borders marking off "pocket universes" into which more matter is continually drawn.

Anatole cannot help picturing this process as a kind of predation by which universes feed off one another. He tries to extrapolate the ultimate consequences of this discovery. Can this simply be accommodated to the grander process of collapse which he has already envisaged? Is it merely part and parcel of the business of self-reincarnation, by which the universe consumes itself like a serpent swallowing its own tail? Is the cosmic egg merely the hole in space into which all other holes are ultimately gathered? Or is the constant formation of such holes a more ominous business, in which a series of independent parallel universes can be pictured, constantly feeding off one another, plundering one another's resources?

Even with the aid of angelic sight, Anatole cannot find answers to these questions.

"If the universe is fated to decay into mediocrity," Anatole says to his companions, "then everything will ultimately vanish. All material life will cease to exist, and whatever kind of life the angels possess will presumably suffer a similar fate. Even if time is a closed cycle, of course, everything is temporary and everything will perish ... but it is not inconceivable that what exists within one turn of the revolutionary wheel might influence the content of other turns. Even if we leave aside the godlike ambitions of the angels, it is not impossible that our descendants might entertain godlike ambitions of their own. Perhaps, in the fullness of time, it will be creatures made of matter—humanlike beings with brains and hands—who will find the means to play the part of cosmic architects. Who knows what human beings may one day become, if they can seize control of their own evolution? The angels have greater power *now* ... but what of the future?"

"You had better hope that they cannot believe you," Hecate says, with dour irony. "If their oracle were to show them a possible future in which human beings outstripped them and usurped the godly privileges they seem anxious to claim, they might decide that the career of humankind had best be ended forthwith."

"Unless, of course," Anatole suggests, "they require to keep us as instruments to do the work of cosmic engineering for them."

It is a mere conceit, and he does not believe it for an instant, but the secrets of the universe are displayed before him and even though he is not Laplace's Demon he is a mighty Demon of sorts, and—for the moment, at least—there is no heresy he will not entertain.

The world is light, and nothing but light. There is nothing beyond its boundaries but infinite emptiness and absolute cold, but what is beyond the boundaries does not matter; everything *within* is gorgeous color, welcoming warmth and vital energy. The inhabitants of this peculiar realm have form but are not weighed down by vulgar mass. Matter itself has been banished from this sphere of existence: what remains is a universe of souls and images.

The light which is the new reality is innately *loving,* and all those who fly within it are possessed by buoyant joy, perpetually exalted in spirit. All are "angels" here, but these angels are not at all like the creatures which men, for want of a better word, elected to call *angels.* These are not fallen angels, nor even guardian angels; they are only remotely kin to those beings which Pelorus has come to know, to fear and to hate. The inhabitants of this realm are the virtuous and generous white-winged angels of the religious imagination, forever bathed in sunlike light.

Pelorus readily recognizes this as the kind of afterlife which the dutiful philosophers of the Order of St. Amycus have long imagined: a world whose devil-made mask has been stripped away, purifying the divine fire which has always seemed to them to be the true essence of all consciousness, all conscience and all consensus.

Pelorus is interested to experience this realm, for it has always seemed to him that this is the nearest the human imagination has ever come to envisaging the innocence of animal proto-consciousness, the pure sensation of wolfish existence. The parallel is, of course, far from perfect—the philosopher-saints would not tolerate the *hunger* of the wolf in such a place as this, where lions are required to lie down with lambs—but it is close. Mandorla, he thinks, would surely argue that if merely human beings were able to shed the wearisome burden of thought this would be the condition they might attain: not perfect, but as near to perfection as the human mind could achieve.

Then again, there is something in this which recalls to Pelorus his false but personally precious idea of the Golden Age: a world of *potential,* from which solidity had yet to emerge by Creative magic;

a world full of hope, uncursed by disappointment; a glorious ocean of archetypal foam, awaiting coalescence by the penetrating mind and eye of the primal Observer.

Harkender, unsurprisingly, is far less impressed by it all. "The quintessence of stupidity," he says cynically. "The infantilism of intellectuals. The Heaven of the idiotic and the impotent, so embarrassed by the presence of their flesh and by the fact of life itself that they take leave to imagine a world from which all possible sensuality has been banished. This is the sickest of the Paradises we have been privileged to see—and, I dare to hope, the last. Surely we are wasting time here, when we could be doing valuable work."

"I thought you might approve," Pelorus answers, a little maliciously. "Have you not spent a lifetime emulating the saints of old, mortifying your flesh in order to escape its limitations?"

"I set forth as an explorer," Harkender informs him coldly. "My purpose was always to rip apart the veils of confabulation which made the voyage treacherous. The men who made *this* set out as little children in search of the womb, cowards in search of a magic fairyland where all would be well because everything threatening had been eliminated at the axiomatic level. The saints sought the Angel of Pain in order to appease her; they sought to win her favor in the hope that she would one day leave them alone. I sought the Angel of Pain in order to court her, to embrace her, to marry her and dwell with her in passion for all eternity. Do you think that these silly fluttering moths, which doubtless believe that they have metamorphosed into the flames which drew them while they lived, know *true* love?"

St. Amycus is not here, of course, because his name was taken in vain by the Order which adopted him as a figurehead, but there is nevertheless one who comes to meet them—or, rather, two, for this one does not come alone. Pelorus cannot recognize either one of them as they approach; while they are in flight nothing can be seen of them but their dazzling wings, which seem to move in more than three dimensions, trailing multi-colored wakes which whirl away into the golden ether. When they come to a halt, though, they take on something more closely resembling human form, and they put on faces so that they may meet their visitors eye to eye. Even then, Pelorus hesitates; he has seen them both before, but very briefly, and not in the world of men. It is not until Harkender speaks that he is certain of their names.

"My dear Gabriel," says Harkender silkily, "it is good to see you. I have often wondered what became of you. I should never have left you with the nuns—of all the foolish mistakes I have made, that was the worst. Even so, I am surprised to find you here, and even more surprised to find your companion. I thought that she at least had seen the error of her childish ways. Did you not leave the convent, my dear, to make your way in the wider world beyond its walls?"

"Poor Mr. Harkender," says Gabriel Gill kindly. "You should not be so quick to assume that the child is inevitably father to the man . . . or mother to the woman, or larva to the angel. I thought myself devil-possessed once, and did not know enough to be ashamed of it! Teresa thought herself Christ-possessed, and did not know enough to lament it; you, alas, have always been self-possessed, and have never found the wisdom to repent it. You have been too fiercely proud of all your faults, and have exercised your sophistry to extraordinary extremes in trying to make virtues of your sins. If only you could recover the innocence of the newly-born you too might find a Heaven—if not this one, then another—but you are too deeply enmired, unwilling even to attempt escape, in the fear and bitterness of the helpless child, for whom the ultimate horror is his own powerlessness."

"The proper answer to the discovery of one's own powerlessness," Harkender retorts, "is ambition, not submission. Whose love is it in whose fires you bathe, incidentally? Not your Creator's— I know that for sure. What angel has consented to be the captive of your need, condemned to motherhood forever? The angels I have met are not so patient."

Gabriel smiles, and his smile is naturally radiant. "The angels *you* know have fallen further than you think, and further than they themselves imagine," he says. He appears to be taking pleasure in the enigmatic quality of his reply. "They are right to regret their confusion, and to be impatient for salvation. What else can we offer them but the image of a Heaven fit for angels? What else can they possibly desire?"

"This is a silly dream," Harkender says dismissively. "It is a shallow phantasm, unworthy of our attention. It is a Heaven which elevates boredom to an enduring passion. I could not abide it for a week, let alone eternity. No one possessed of an enquiring mind could endure it."

"Are you so certain that your guardians have enquiring minds?"

Gabriel asks. "And if they have, are you certain that they would not give them up, in return for ecstasy?"

"It is evident that I think more highly of them than you do," Harkender replies, exercising his contempt to the full. "They have *power*, and this is a fantasy of the oppressed. It is no use to them— or to any being capable of thought."

"Pelorus knows better," says Gabriel Gill. "Pelorus knows the joy of innocence, the freedom of contentment. This might not be Heaven for the wolf in him, but it is Heaven for the man, is it not?"

Gabriel's liquid gaze is so frank and honest, and his companion's face so utterly gentle, that Pelorus is tempted to give a dishonest answer—but he decides that Heaven ought not to be polluted with diplomatic lies.

"No," he says. "It is built out of hopeful illusion; it rejects too much. I am no lover of the Angel of Pain, but I am beginning to accept that I would be lonely and incomplete without her haunting presence. Perhaps it is my own weakness and impressionability, but the more I hear of Harkender's arguments, the more I feel forced to agree with him. This is not what the man in me desires, Gabriel; an inferno of love and joy is an inferno nevertheless. The man in me no longer desires to be a wolf, but I am sure that it would be better to be a wolf than to be the kind of being which could dwell here for eternity."

"Poor Pelorus," says Gabriel, without a trace of resentment, before turning again to Harkender. "We will see you again soon enough," he says gently. "In the fullness of time, all will be forgiven. The angels, fallen though they are, are not eternally damned, and neither are you. In time, you will be able to accept that there is nothing worth seeking but joy, nothing worth having but love, nothing worth being but light. Never despair, Mr. Harkender. One day, you will learn humility."

"I already have," Harkender assures the child who was once his ward. "I learned humility long ago; the more difficult task is to learn pride, and to learn that it is not a sin at all."

"The fallen angels know better," Gabriel says. "Born on pride's wings they may fly to the end of time if they will, but nothing awaits them there except the wasteland which is Hell. This is the kind of world where they might truly belong, Mr. Harkender, and you cannot prevent their eventual understanding of that fact. In the fullness of time, the truth will become manifest."

"Indeed it will," Harkender retorts. "At least, we must hope so."

5

By the time Mandorla rights herself and comes to a standing position on the solid ground London lies in ruins.

Although the days and nights flow past more rapidly than they did during earlier intervals there is little evidence of change in the immediate environment. The buildings have been too comprehensively smashed to require much further settlement. The bridges over the Thames are broken, and are not rebuilt. The streets remain pitted and scarred according to a pattern which scarcely shifts, save for the slow accumulation of debris in drifts and heaps. It would be impossible to see people or vehicles, but she does not doubt that there are none to be seen.

When she is reunited with the Clay Man they begin to wander southwards. Clapham Common is recognizable by virtue of its emptiness, but there is nothing else to serve as a landmark. The fluttering of the days and nights continues long enough for them to cross five or six miles of wasteland, but Mandorla has not the slightest idea where they might be when the pace begins to slow again and the gears of time wind down to neutrality.

Their surroundings are virtually lifeless; few plants have been equal to the task of reclaiming the corners and the crevices, and the lichenous encrustations which are the most common seem more like leprous sores on the bodies of the flattened dwellings than the beginnings of an ambitious wilderness. What were once gardens have been reduced to patches of bare and dusty ground, scoured clean of grass and brambles.

There is a cold wind blowing, and it picks up clouds of fine dust which stain the borders of the sky with crimson. The whistling of the wind is the only sound to be heard.

"The dust itself must be poisoned," the Clay Man says. "Whatever wrought this destruction left a legacy behind to prevent even the most elementary healing. If there are humans left in England they must be far from here, in the rural areas."

But he is wrong. As they wander through the bleached bones of British civilization the silence is disturbed by a sound that is not the wind: the sound of a vehicle. The Clay Man immediately moves toward the sound, racing in the curious flowing gait of which dream-phantoms are capable. Mandorla follows.

The vehicle is a curious monstrosity, shaped like a bullet with wheels. It has a window of dark glass set in the front from which an invisible driver presumably looks out, but no obvious doors. It has the appearance of being hermetically sealed; there is no exhaust pipe to discharge waste gases. It is moving as rapidly as a galloping horse, but the Clay Man and Mandorla are able to keep pace with it as it heads eastwards.

As the mysterious vehicle skirts the northern edge of a desolate plain Mandorla realizes that the territory shows some signs of human activity, of clearance if not of reconstruction. The vehicle turns southwest along a road which is evidently not unused, and eventually draws up alongside a squat, cylindrical building resembling a pillbox. The concrete walls of the building are weathered but otherwise unscarred, and the huge steel doors let into its side are not significantly rusted. When the vehicle has halted here for several minutes the doors slide apart. No one is visible in the empty space within. As the vehicle moves into the space the Clay Man is quick to move in with it, and Mandorla dutifully follows.

When the doors slide shut behind them a light appears behind the dark glass of the vehicle's windscreen, allowing them to see the driver for the first time. His head is helmeted, his eyes shielded by a panel of dark glass which seems to Mandorla to be a miniature version of the window of the vehicle. The section of the floor on which the vehicle stands begins to sink into the ground, but there is space enough on either side to allow the two phantoms to accompany it.

The descending platform judders awkwardly and inconsistently as it sinks, as if the mechanism controlling its descent requires some minor adjustment. When it comes to rest again there is a brief period of inactivity; no doors open to allow the vehicle or its inhabitants egress. Instead, after a pause of ninety seconds or so, jets of water begin to blast the vehicle from all four sides. The experience is extremely uncomfortable but not in the least injurious to Mandorla and the Clay Man; real people would surely have been badly hurt. The water does not accumulate in the shaft; it drains away through arched exit-holes in the wall, positioned at what is now floor-level.

When the jets have ceased and the water has drained away a doorway opens in the side of the vehicle. Another opens in the wall of the shaft to allow its former occupants to pass through. There are three, all dressed in protective suits which cover their bodies completely. The doorway leads into another bare chamber where they pause and wait. More jets of water begin to fire, less violent than the ones which washed down the vehicle but no less prolific. Not until the entire ritual has been repeated do the people emerge from the interior of their artificial cocoons. They strip off the protective suits, stow them neatly in a cupboard set in the wall of the chamber, and then pass through a further door into a brightly lit corridor. They are clad in gray tunics and trousers, like military uniforms without insignia. Others are waiting beyond the door to greet them. Mandorla and the Clay Man follow them through into a network of corridors so crowded with people that they have difficulty finding a station where they are safe from the disconcerting encounters which their phantom state permits.

There are men, women and children here. Like people in crowds everywhere they move with varying degrees of purpose, taking little notice of their fellows except when they move in groups or pause to exchange perfunctory tokens of recognition. They are pale, but they seem well fed and healthy, and the expressions on their faces offer no evidence of any general misery.

"Life goes on, it seems," says the Clay Man. "Banished to an underworld beneath the city, but sustainable nevertheless."

"How do they grow their food?" Mandorla asks wonderingly. "They certainly have no fields up above—not within thirty miles, I'd wager."

"Evidently they have the means," says the Clay Man, who clearly does not consider it to be a question of any great importance. "They have light and water in abundance, so they may be able to grow plants here—or perhaps they have such technical command of the chemistry of life that they can manufacture adequate food without requiring actual plants as middlemen."

"They must surely be free now from the burden of never-ending war,'' Mandorla says, searching the faces of the passers-by for evidence of contentment and freedom from fear. ''With the crust of the planet itself for armor there is surely no weapon that can penetrate this kind of stronghold, and the task of moving armies over the kind of scorched earth we saw up above would be difficult.''

''Perhaps,'' the Clay Man replies. ''But we already know that men have found far subtler means of waging war than the ones they possessed before the end of the Nineteenth Century. Even if peace reigns for the present, it does not necessarily mean that old hatreds have been buried as deeply as civilization.''

The word ''if'' echoes in Mandorla's mind as she continues to scan the faces of the people of the underworld. There is no way of detecting the cause of the anxiety which shows in so many of them, and she knows full well that men can find anxieties aplenty whatever their circumstances, but she cannot help but feel now that the Clay Man has delivered his skeptical judgment that these people *do* still live in a world constantly under threat of destruction.

The Clay Man, meanwhile, is studying the various objects which some of the passers-by are carrying, and the fittings and fixtures in the corridors. There are abundant switches and control panels, but the most interesting artefacts are tiny screens bearing moving images of human faces or abstract symbols. ''This is the new Millennium,'' he murmurs, apparently having caught sight or sound of a date, or what he believes to be a date. ''The year 2000 has come and gone, and still the story goes on. If the pace of change has not accelerated, at least it has been maintained. What might machinery like this have made, had the city above still been habitable? What adventures might these men have undertaken, had they not been forced to live in warrens far beneath the surface?''

Mandorla has no time to echo his sentiments. Her phantom form, sensitive as it is to vibration, detects a faint tremor, which rapidly increases to the point where the people crowding around become aware of it. Their reaction is immediate, and although it is not quite blind panic she judges readily enough that they consider their situation hazardous almost to the point of hopelessness.

As the crowds seethe around her Mandorla presses herself back against the wall of the corridor, wishing that it might let her in and swallow her up, but the flux of time is too sluggish to render solid matter penetrable. It only takes a second or two for her to realize a further consequence of this fact, which is that she and the Clay Man must share the fate which will overtake the underworld as the earthquake—the *artificial* earthquake—brings down the rock which armors it.

Ghost though she is, she is not immune to pain and distress, and the crushing darkness which clasps her to its bosom is a terrifying thing. She wishes desperately, as she reaches out in the futile hope of catching the Clay Man by the hand, that she were capable of losing consciousness—or even of dying, like the luckless people who surround her.

Anatole and his companions undertake a quest through the wilderness of the Milky Way, proceeding from one rim of the great galactic wheel to the other, searching out life wherever it exists.

They have no difficulty in finding it; the fundamental molecules of life are absurdly common, in spite of their complexity. They exist in abundance in great gas clouds which measure many light years in diameter, but the self-replicating forms which exist in such diffuse and constant environments are very simple. Natural selection operating in such conditions, even at the full extent of its marvelous ingenuity, can produce nothing more complicated than a petty multi-molecular machine, a primitive proto-bacterium.

It is only on planets warmed by steady suns, in the presence of abundant liquid water, that life can progress to higher levels of complexity; but the aggregation of complexity is a difficult and problematic business. In the vast majority of cases such complexification is self-defeating; all but a few of the organisms thrown up by the hazard of creativity alter their environment so as to bring about conditions which destroy them. But this is not invariably the case; given time enough, almost any world which manifests appropriate starting conditions will ultimately produce progressive organisms which affect their environment so as to facilitate their own survival. Ironically, this facility can lead and often does to another kind of self-defeat, because many of these self-protecting systems are so adept in their self-protection that they rapidly reach stability. Such systems insulate themselves so efficiently from change that the progressive inspiration of natural selection is stifled. On the vast majority of planets which harbor life, bacterial proliferation and differentiation ultimately gives birth to an imperium in which a few species "discover" a sustainable equilibrium. Such equilibria can be recovered in the aftermath of any disruption insufficient to bring about their virtual annihilation.

Anatole soon realizes that it is very rare indeed for the kind of productive instability which produces many-celled organisms to be maintained in the long term. In the vast majority of instances where many-celled life does evolve, it quickly disappears again, unable to retain its viability in competition with relentlessly efficient single-celled creatures.

Gradually, Anatole builds up a general picture of the situation of life in the universe, and comes to understand how extremely unlikely it is that any planetary system will give rise to many-celled organisms which are capable of sustaining themselves for any length of time. When such organisms do succeed in maintaining themselves in the long term, they too face the almost inevitable prospect of reaching a fairly simple sustainable equilibrium, which damps down the pressure of natural selection to the point where the rate of evolution becomes a crawl. Anatole discovers that although life itself is very common, complex life-forms are very rare. It becomes clear to him that ecospheres varied enough and complicated enough to give rise to intelligence are so rare that no galactic cluster is likely to harbor two at the same time. Within a single galaxy they tend to appear at intervals of tens or hundreds of millions of years.

Once having understood this, Anatole has no difficulty in placing intelligent species in the general scheme of things. Intelligent species are, he realizes, very unlikely to act upon their environment in such a way as to secure their long-term viability. To the contrary, they exhibit a very powerful tendency to self-devastation—and, indeed, to lay waste the life-systems which produce them, often returning those systems very rapidly to a level where only the simplest many-celled organisms can survive.

The reason why the angels have taken an interest in human life now becomes a little clearer. Even if their lifetimes are measurable in aeons, and even if their sphere of influence takes in numerous galactic clusters, the evolution of humankind presumably provides them with a rare and ephemeral opportunity. Sir Edward Tallentyre's notion of a universe teeming with intelligent life was, after all, a hopeful illusion.

So much, Anatole thinks, *for my hope that our ultimate descendants might win such control over fate and fortune that they might entertain godlike ambitions of their own; where are the godlike descendants of the intelligent beings who evolved in the past?*

It is not only the distribution of life within the universe that interests Anatole. Viewing the phenomenon of life in such a broad context helps him to become more sensitive to the peculiarities of its nature. Looking at life through human eyes has accustomed him to thinking of living individuals as relatively stable entities, and viewing the Earth's life-system from within has allowed him to take its existence and richness for granted. Now he understands how very exotic its mere existence is, he also understands how absurdly precarious its richness is.

Life, Anatole realizes, is a product of the ceaseless flux by means of which energy constantly redistributes itself, always tending toward the ultimate mediocrity. As cataracts of sunlight rain down upon planets some tiny fraction of each energetic deluge is mysteriously whirled into that special kind of turbulence which is life. Life is not so much a by-product of the deluge as an aspect of it, and living organisms are themselves creatures of flux. Their seeming stability is, in part at least, an illusion of human sensation.

Like a many-jetted fountain, whose stable form is an artefact of the fundamental water pressure and the architecture of its channeling, a living organism maintains its form in spite of the fact that it is engaged in a careless interchange of matter and energy with its environment. New molecules are constantly flowing into the organism as old ones are discarded. Even when a life-form has reached the final phase of its own innate evolution—its *maturity*—it never ceases changing, and Anatole sees that the process of growth by whose mechanism it matures are more complicated than he had imagined.

Until now he has pictured growth as an additive process, a form of increase; now he is able to picture it as something more akin to sculpture, in which form is created by selective removal. He realizes that there is far more death in life than he had imagined. He sees that all living cells are not merely mortal but suicidal, and that their long-term survival and maintenance is the exception rather than the rule; the structure of an organism is generated by selectively insulating certain cells against their natural fate, so that the gaps between the fingers of a hand are generated by the death of the cells which would otherwise connect them.

Anatole has always thought of life as the normal condition, while viewing the threats which oppose it—disease and injury and aging—as alien and malign. Now, he sees that early death is the normal fate of all cells, and that the preservative forces which maintain and shape many-celled organisms might easily be regarded as a bizarre anomaly. Even within the living body of a complex organism the vast majority of cells have a strictly limited lifetime; even those which have vital functions to perform are constantly being replaced, and they are the survivors of a never-ending process of *internal* natural selection in which every specialized cell-mass is shaped and formed by the whittling away of an ever-burgeoning organic surplus.

Seeing life in this way, as a series of highly improbable and astonishingly intricate eddies in the thermodynamic flux which is the ever-dwindling legacy of the primal explosion, Anatole is moved to wonderment that *any* organisms exist, let alone that a few of the myriad worlds on which life finds a foothold should occasionally play host to a thinking being.

Why, he asks himself, does this turbulence occur? Immediately he sets the enigma further back, and asks why the flux itself exists. How is it, given the inbuilt tendency to energetic mediocrity which the universe has, that there are stars, and galaxies? Why was there a primal explosion which gave rise to this riot of confusion, rather than a primal silence which extended eternally in uninterrupted uniformity?

Anatole remembers that in the romance which his namesake wrote about a revolution planned—but not executed—by a rebel guardian angel the inspiration for the angel's rebellion was his reading of a particular book. Although unnamed in the text, the book was clearly the *De rerum natura* of Lucretius. In that book, which first popularized the claim that nothing existed but matter in motion, Lucretius suggested that in the beginning, all atoms must have been falling uniformly through empty space, in a universe devoid of design, until there was an infinitesimal random swerve in a single atom, which he called *clinamen*. From this single elementary event had sprung a spreading turbulence which had been further and further magnified, until in the end it led to the aggregation of matter in the radically discontinuous pattern now displayed to human observation.

This, Anatole realizes, is how the universe ought to be pictured. Somehow, there is within it a source of turbulence, of flux, of creativity. It may be something very tiny in itself, whose effects are self-magnifying, but it must be there—and if time is indeed cyclic, forever turning back from the ultimate decay into mediocrity, it must be preserved even at the extremities of expansion and collapse, ever able to renew the divine disorder out of which order might emerge.

"Jason Sterling once drew a similar analogy in trying to guess what the angels are," Lydyard says. "He has always been preoccupied with the capricious seed of order which lurks within chaos. He proposed that the source of the mutations on which natural selection works in making new species must also be the source of the magical power which the angels have to bend matter, space and time to their will.''

"If so," Anatole replies uneasily, "they might be more godlike than we have supposed, or dared to hope. If they are, in fact, the seeds of a turbulence which is responsible for the entire universe of matter, and for the phenomenon of life, are they not gods of a kind?''

"If the generators of such turbulence were sentient," Lydyard says, "they might conceivably lay claim to godlike status—but what kind of gods could they be if the turbulence they caused was neither planned nor controlled?''

"Blind gods," says Hecate. "Primary causes which know not what it is they cause, nor how. Gods who are ultimately all-powerful, and yet curiously impotent . . . unless and until they learn enough about themselves to begin the work of taking full control of what they have wrought.''

"If Hecate is right," Anatole says, "our own role in this may be a little clearer. If the angels began existence as blind gods not knowing what they did, or how, to set in train the great chain of creativity which is matter and life, they may now be seeking to discover how to take control, how to subject *clinamen* itself to the command of intellect.''

"And if we were to succeed in educating them," Hecate says, grimly satisfied with the compliment which he has paid her, "what then?''

The buildings of the city through which Pelorus and Harkender are moving are extremely tall, their faces as smooth as glass. The streets are clean and straight, and the vehicles which move through them are sleek and soundless. Beyond the city limits the streets broaden out into great highways which cut through the cultivated fields with great precision, never meeting. Where their paths cross they soar over one another upon huge pillared viaducts, which are intricately connected by slip-roads. The cloudless sky is criss-crossed with the vapor trails of gleaming aircraft, and by occasional columns of denser spume left behind by the rockets which drive upwards into the world beyond the blue.

The people who cross from building to building on walkways which bridge the streets are purpose-driven; they rarely pause for more than a moment and have little to say to one another except for the ritual exchange of greetings. There is no perfect uniformity in their style of dress, but there is an orderly set of different patterns, which seems to be correlated with different kinds of work and badges of rank. Pelorus observes that this kind of orderliness cuts deeper than mere matters of adornment. The people themselves have been tailored, no less variously but no less carefully than their clothes. The underlying uniformity of the human body has been modified in several ways in the inhabitants of this realm, most but not all of the adaptations being functional in terms of particular kinds of employment. Some are tall and muscular; others have additional limbs or modified teguments. Pelorus cannot tell whether their inward attributes—their tastes, their morals, their desires—are subject to a similarly careful categorization and adaptation, but he suspects so.

This is a world which has been very carefully planned, whose designs have been very carefully actualized; it is obvious, therefore, that it must have planners who enter invisibly into its pattern, but who nevertheless stand outside and above the scheme which is their handiwork. These planners are men, not gods or angels, for this is a planet which revolves around a sun, not some horizonless dream-realm, but they must possess a kind of godlike power over their fellows. Theirs is evidently the kind of aesthetic sensibility which produces order, symmetry and tidiness, and the kind of determination which opposes every disruption, every incompetence, every dereliction of duty. It is a realm which is very comprehensibly *ruled,* whose ruler enjoys an absolute monopoly on freedom.

Pelorus is not entirely surprised to find that the ruler in question is Luke Capthorn, no longer masquerading as Asmodeus. He is the grand planner, the director of directors, the man who has reshaped humankind.

"Has your gnawing appetite for evil really sunk to this?" Harkender asks him. "Have your lusts become so ordinary as to be fitted into this sort of straitjacket? I know that you were nearly incapable of learning, and entirely incapable of understanding, but I am amazed by your capacity for never ceasing to disappoint me. What possible pleasure or satisfaction can there be in ruling a world like a model railway, in which the destiny of everything is to go round and round forever on the same dull track?"

"What common men call evil," Luke informs him serenely, "is really a form of displacement activity. It arises out of frustration. Banish frustration from the world and you banish evil. The happily married have no need of lust, the friendly no need of wrath, the contented no need of envy. Avarice, violence, gluttony . . . all these can be rooted out at source. The human body and the human mind

are capable of refinement if only their chemistry is sufficiently understood. Men can be engineered for happiness, adapted to find joy in
all their allotted tasks. Society can be made in the image of a beautiful and efficient machine. There is no need of evil, and I have put
my own away with other childish things. I have absolute power now,
and need not be cruel any longer."

"How absurd!" Harkender exclaims. "You ought to understand,
Luke, that if *everyone* is a mere cog in a well-oiled machine, the
master-cog is no less a prisoner of the movement than all the rest.
If the one and only end is *order* the most powerful person in the
world is just as much a slave to the order as the lowest of the low.
You always used such power as you had in a pathetically stupid
manner, but at least there was a time when you rejoiced in a better
kind of freedom than this. To take pleasure in hurting others, in
torture and in rape, is in vilely bad taste, but at least it represents a
kind of self-assertion against the forces of adversity. To rule in *this*
kind of Hell is surely less rewarding by far than to rule the kind of
infernal empire you coveted before."

"You don't understand," says Luke, with patient good humor.
"You are confused, as I once was, between the futile exercise of
petty power and the wonderful privilege of authentic power. Those
who divert their energies into commonplace evils are rebelling
against their powerlessness. They seek to make the most of what
little power they have by maximizing its effects—which they can
only do by devoting themselves entirely to destruction. They rebel
against the constructive endeavors of those who have more power in
order to demonstrate that even those with no power to build have
the power to tear down, but theirs is a literally hopeless crusade;
they cannot heal themselves in hurting others. This problem cannot
be solved, of course, by giving more power to everyone, because
power is by definition power over others; but it can be solved by
reconciliation, by adapting people to *be content* with what little
power they have, to help them channel all of it into construction
rather than destruction. The man who succeeds in doing that has no
need to be a petty tyrant, ruling by fear and oppression; he has no
need to fight fire with fire, ever anxious to overwhelm little evils
with greater ones. He can, instead, become content with his own
power, and channel it entirely into construction. The ultimate exercise
of power is not evil but the *elimination* of evil. Petty power corrupts,
and becomes more corrupt with increase, but authentic power—truly
absolute power—transcends corruption. I have transcended corrup-

tion; I have no more need of rape or murder. In true dictatorship I have found peace and patience. I have learned to love power in itself and for itself. You must teach the angels to do likewise.''

"This is the voice of the beehive," says Harkender scornfully, "where the so-called queen, on whose behalf the workers supposedly labor, is really their slave, working tirelessly and without rest to secure the perfect reproduction of the whole. You cannot seriously expect me to recommend to the angels that they waste their godlike power like *this*! Are you quite mad, Luke?''

"No doubt you would do things very differently," Luke Capthorn says mischievously, "were you in my place, armed with my authority. No doubt you would allow your workers the luxury of their resentment and the self-lacerating fury of their despair. No doubt you would condemn them to the insanity of evil, so that they might ruin their own lives and those of others. You always were a crueller man than I, beneath your veneer of civilization and your affectation of politeness—but the angels are not made in your image. Like me, they have learned that cruelty is a meager meal for those with real authority.''

"Children play with mechanical toys as a crude preparation for the business of dealing with reality," Harkender tells him pityingly. "Only a very stupid child could ever believe that the proper way to be a god is to reduce the actual world to the status of a mere toy.''

"So you say," answers Luke. "But Pelorus is a wolf, gentler by far than a bitter man like you. Were you in my place, Pelorus, *you* would not visit your dependants with the curse of freedom, the horror of self-awareness. You would do as I have done, making the world happy, and tidy, and beautiful in its perfect order, would you not?''

"I am a wolf," says Pelorus. "Machalalel made me a shepherd of men, and a shepherd of sorts I have tried to be, but in myself I am a wolf and had I *true* power I would rule as a wolf among wolves.''

"And if you were a man?''

"I am not the kind of man that you are. Yes, I would curse the world of men with freedom, if I could. How, otherwise, could it be a world of men?''

"With evil, too?'' There is nothing diabolical about the arch of Luke's eyebrow, nothing Satanic about his smile. This is a man who has usurped the throne of the Prince of Evil, and no longer wishes to please anyone but himself.

"I would not wish to make evil impossible, even in Heaven,''

Pelorus replies stubbornly. "I would far rather men avoided it of their own will."

"Impossible!" says Luke.

"Impossible," agrees Harkender. "And that is why evil must be accepted, not in the narrow and foolish way that you once studied and practiced it, but in a braver way by far. What a waste of time this is! Why am I cursed to teach these children's lessons, when I might be extending the limits of the imagination?"

"Perhaps," says Luke Capthorn, "it is because you have underestimated the simplicity of those whose instrument you are. Believe me, Jacob, there is no better task for them to adopt but to *set the world in order*. That is work fit for gods, and *there is no other.*"

"It is work for fools," Harkender retorts, "and whatever the angels are, they are not fools." But Pelorus wonders, for the first time, whether a slight hint of doubt might have crept into his voice.

"Suppose for a moment that they *are* fools," Pelorus says. "What then?"

"Then we will have to educate them," says Harkender. "What do you think I have been trying to do these last fifty years?"

6

The acceleration of time liquidizes the rock which surrounds her, but Mandorla rebels against the force of circumstance, refusing to make any effort to return to the surface. The refusal is futile; she is soon born upwards by a breath of soulfire and rudely expelled from the dark womb of the earth, like a newborn child unwillingly thrust into the light. The Clay Man, who was always less inclined to revolt against his users, is waiting for her. Together, they wait for time to slow down. Eventually, they are abandoned to a bright noon and a cloudless sky.

A desert stretches from horizon to horizon. Its predominant color is white but it is streaked with various shades of gray and dappled here and there with reds and browns. There is nothing to inform the untutored eye that a great city once stood here, and that the scattered stone huts and crude shelters which nestle together in groups of ten or twelve are built from the debris of ancient edifices that were infinitely more imposing.

Mandorla's is not an untutored eye, and it is not so difficult for her to find faint signs of the lost past: the subtle lines which once marked the layout of streets; the shaped blocks of stone which once belonged to fluted columns and ornamental facades; brickwork corners; fallen lintels; neatly laid paving stones. When she kneels to touch the ground she sees that there are tiny things too, mingled with the drifting dust: pieces of glass and rusted steel; needles and cup handles; blobs of perished rubber. An informed antiquary armed with a trowel and a sieve might collect enough fragments in an hour or two to let him see a picture of life as it was lived here—how many years ago?

"I could believe that a thousand years had passed," she says to the Clay Man. "The Egyptians who lived beside the Nile left a greater heritage than this to the inquisitive diggers who came to explore their tombs and buried cities."

"Their immediate descendants had not such forces of destruction at their disposal," her companion observes wearily. "They had no sophisticated machines, but their rulers had the political power and the kingly ambition to organize tens of thousands of men in the work of erecting vast statues and vaster tombs. What is built by ten thousand pairs of hands plying simple tools cannot be torn down by a dozen pairs using those same tools. The men of the twentieth century built powerful mechanical slaves to do their work, but they built more powerful ones to undo it."

Mandorla and the Clay Man wander aimlessly, taking no account of their direction. The people who live in the crude shelters which have been raised from the corpse of the city are thin and ragged; they live as scavengers, descending into pits and shafts which give them precarious and hazardous entrance into the shattered underworld, which cannot have been entirely obliterated by the earthquake which trapped Mandorla and the Clay Man. The two phantoms make no attempt to descend into the underworld again; it is as dead now as the world above. The descendants of those who once lived there have become wild and savage; their heritage of knowledge is lost.

Mandorla and the Clay Man are given more time to explore this realm than the others they have visited. They have leisure enough to observe that the buyers who come from beyond the desert to haggle over the scavengers' produce come in ramshackle motorized trucks.

"I cannot tell what fuel it uses," the Clay Man says, after making an inspection of one such vehicle. "Imagine what its existence must signify. Somewhere—probably not so very far from here—there are workshops and factories, machine tools and skilled metalworkers. Craftsmanship is not extinct; progress has become unsteady, but it is not finished even now."

Mandorla is unimpressed.

The desert-dwellers have no trucks of their own, but when night falls the Clay Man rejoices in the discovery that each tiny cluster of shelters has an engine to produce supplies of electrical power. The production of light is not the only purpose to which the power is diverted; many of the stone shanties are mounted with shallow dishes directed toward the southern sky, which are connected by cable to boxes whose screens constantly display moving pictures. These machines, it seems, are reckoned among the necessities of life. As in earlier times, they provide a channel of information which gradually reveals to the patient Clay Man the state of the world, but the task is more confused than before because very little of the commentary is in English. The owners of the machines seem less able to cope with this than the Clay Man, who has learned to speak a dozen languages tolerably well in the course of his long life.

While the Clay Man pursues his researches, Mandorla moves away into an uninhabited region, where she can rest and look up at the bright, calm stars. She is able to sleep for a little while, but cannot dream.

The Clay Man tells Mandorla, when the next day has dawned, that the twenty-second century is not very old; only a few generations have come and gone since the last phase of their dream. He has learned that Britain and most of Europe have never recovered from the devastation which they suffered, and that North America has similarly been reduced to ruins, but that life goes on.

"The main centers of political and economic power," the Clay Man informs her, as he leads her back toward his listening-post, "seem now to be located in the Far East and in South America—which are, I fear, at war with one another. If I judge the situation rightly, tension between them is approaching its peak. Another conflagration is imminently due."

"Why else are we here?" Mandorla asks. "We are observers of the endless carnival of destruction, are we not? But a war in the southern hemisphere can hardly affect us here in the ruins of London. These people do not seem unduly perturbed by the news."

In the shelter which the Clay Man has used as his principal eavesdropping-station two adult males are busy cleaning and tinkering with objects recently brought out of the underworld, paying particular attention to a pistol for which they obviously have no ammunition; an adult woman is busy cooking food on an iron stove; two children are engrossed in petty bickering, simmering on the edge of violence. Mandorla halts at the threshold, having no desire to move into their midst.

"They feel that they are safe enough," the Clay Man explains, having had time enough to observe them during the course of his vigil. "More than that—they feel perversely glad about the troubles which afflict other people. They are utterly dependent on others more

fortunate than themselves, and they are envious enough to take pleasure in the hope that those distant nations which retain their prosper-
ity might suffer the same fate that their own forefathers suffered.
They know perfectly well that no one has any reason to attack them
or their near neighbors, and they are enthusiastic to see others reduced to their own level.''

"An admirable summary of human nature," Mandorla says drily.

"Their belief that they have no enemies is wrong," says the Clay
Man regretfully. "They have welcomed into their homes the worst
enemy of all: ignorance. They do not understand that even distant
wars might affect them. Look!"

The southern horizon is bathed with peculiar light. The thin clouds
which have gathered there are suddenly silvered, as though magically
lit from on high, and the air itself seems to come alive with
incandescence.

It is very beautiful.

The desert-dwellers emerge from their homes as the news spreads,
to watch and marvel. Whatever else they have lost, they have not
lost their sense of wonder.

"Poor fools," murmurs the Clay Man. "They do not know enough
to be afraid."

Time hurries on around them, accelerating as before. The wonderful brightness of the sky is a momentary phenomenon, immediately
lost, but the blueness of the sky is lost with it; the following days
are hardly distinguishable from the nights. The desert-dwellers fade
away like so many exorcised spirits. The stone shanties dissolve into
the ground like all the better buildings which preceded them; the
desert is complete at last, and now its lifelessness is no local phenomenon. The sun's path across the sky is an uncertain arch of dull red
fire, like a bloody wound engraved on the dark skin of an Arab or
an Oriental. The sullen skies release brief storms of hail and snow.

The sky soon begins to clear again; its colors fade from dark gray
to blue. The arch of the sun's path, waxing and waning with meticulous rhythm, becomes orange, and then yellow, and gloriously bright
as it flickers amid the boiling clouds—but the new dawn does not
reawaken the desert earth. The plain is gradually possessed by ice,
which creeps into its crevices to take up permanent residence, and
which grows by slow degrees into rivers and pools, and then into
mountains and glaciers.

"It is the winter of the world," the Clay Man says. "The heat of
the sun was interrupted for a while by the dust blasted into the higher

reaches of the atmosphere. The dust settled again soon enough, but the atmosphere and the oceans must have been permanently cooled. The plants whose photosynthetic activity maintained the balance of gases in the air were wiped out. Now the days are bright again, but the fundamental system of life has been disrupted beyond the limits of its tolerance."

They wait and they watch, but nothing changes. The ice-field is inviolate; it has conquered the earth, in these latitudes at least, and will not give up the spoils of its victory.

"Is the whole world dead?" Mandorla wonders. "Is the wound that men have inflicted upon its face so deep as to be mortal?"

"Not quite. Evolution must have been set back a few million years, but many single-celled forms will doubtless have survived, and a handful of many-celled species: a few worm-like creatures, a few insect species. It is an adequate foundation on which to rebuild an elaborate ecosphere, given a few million years, but whether the Earth will ever again play host to a creature blessed with self-awareness . . . . who can say?"

"Is angelic foresight incapable of such a determination?" Mandorla asks ironically. "Is angelic power inadequate to the task of ensuring it?"

The Clay Man shakes his phantom head. "I beg leave to doubt it," he says. "I think that this particular dream is finished."

"But we are still here," Mandorla points out. "I cannot think that we are doomed to haunt the derelict world forever; there must be something for us yet to see."

"Whatever it is," says the Clay Man, "it will not be human."

As he seems to drift in space, far from the Earth, uncertain whether to turn his magical sight toward the further reaches of infinity or the remoter depths of the infinitesimal, Anatole guesses that his silent partners are struggling. The angel which bears the three of them upon its tireless shoulders has run to the limit of its powers, or at least of its plans. He suspects that it does not know what else to show them, or how it should focus their attention. Like them, it awaits further inspiration.

Anatole tries, in his own fashion, to guide it. He stares outwards, in rapt contemplation of the shoalless sea of stars, hungry for further enlightenment. He makes every effort to savor the miracle of its existence, the *paradox* of its existence.

Existence itself, he now understands, is the product of conflicting tendencies. On the one hand, there is the implacable, eternal, ultimately irreversible tendency of energetic decay, by which the universe is winding down toward a deathlike state of absolute uniformity. On the other hand, within the ceaseless flow of energy which is the fundamental product of that unwinding there is turbulence, and wherever there is turbulence there is uncertainty. Within a turbulently excited situation even the tiniest hazard of chance might, in principle, be amplified into something very much greater—even into something unprecedented, something new. Because the universe began in a state so very far from the equilibrium toward which it tends, the underlying process of universal decay produces a near-eternal flux. This flux, in being vulnerable to turbulence, is the frame, if not the motor, of all creativity.

Even had he not been required to do so, Anatole would have discovered beauty in this: not the beauty of symmetry, of simplicity, of *order* but the subtler beauty of oddity, or profusion, of *novelty*. He observes, with the approval of one who despises all hierarchy and all oppression, that the universe is asymmetrical at every level: that life is constructed of left-handed molecules, that the world of matter entertains very little anti-matter, that the microcosm is prejudiced in favor of left-handed spins. He can take satisfaction now in the dethronement of Laplace's Demon and the clockwork universe which it was set up to observe. Time's arrow of irreversible decay seems to him to send forth a clarion alarm to all would-be tyrants, all champions of constancy and stability. He plays deliberately with the notion that death is not merely the price to be paid for creativity, but creativity itself: that Death is the great sculptor which carves anonymous matter into living, meaningful Art.

He tries to control his rhapsody, to become a careful man of science like Lydyard—that, after all, is what seems to be required of him. He tries to remove the element of intoxication from his discoveries, to make them sober, and responsible, and calm.

Even the very tiny uncertainties which affect the behavior of subatomic particles, he realizes, can and do have effects at the macroscopic level. He cannot see and tabulate all of those effects—even angelic sight is not so powerful as to reveal them clearly—but he can grasp the general principle readily enough. The overwhelming majority of chains of consequence are self-canceling, but some contrive to be self-sustaining through a whole series of orders of magnitude, each of which is a level of manifestation. The processes of natural selection which human senses can detect in their operation on living organisms and their natural species are simply a specific case of a much more general phenomenon. From the microcosmic level to the macrocosmic, self-protecting and self-reproducing systems survive amid a chaotic welter of dissolution.

Anatole realizes that it is not merely living organisms which are like fountains, preserving their form while remaining in flux. All products of the flux are akin in that respect; however stable they appear to be, however resistant to change, they are to some degree precarious. The durability of matter, he realizes, does not result from an absolute immunity to decay, but simply reflects the relative improbability that particular particles will decay within particular intervals of time. All structures, he realizes, are in essence *dissipative* structures, whose innate tendency to decay is temporarily counterbalanced.

All structure, Anatole realizes, is really turbulence. It is only in the eyes of human beholders that turbulence appears disordered and chaotic. True chaos is the kind of uniformity which would result were the winding down of the universe to run to its limit—which might not happen if the flux which is the parent of all creativity is somehow self-reproducing, moving drunkenly from primal explosion to terminal collapse and back again, endlessly repeating and yet never quite the same.

"The *real* beauty of this kind of universe," he says to his companions, "lies neither in its symmetry nor in its closure, but in the fact that it has no need of gods. In this context, there is no need of any ultimate planners or designers to generate order or to orchestrate evolution. The whole point about *clinamen* is that it might indeed be truly random, and there is no need at all to invoke the angels in order to explain it. As an argumentative move that is little short of fatuous, for it would simply require us to wonder how the angels themselves came to be. Do you not agree, Lydyard, that Lucretius was right; *clinamen* must be the ultimate explanation, the cause uncaused? All else, including the angels—including any and all beings, however godlike their powers or their ambitions—must be the products of its fount of creativity, hazards of its flux.

"The demand I made of the Maid of Orléans has been answered; we do indeed stand in the place of Laplace's Demon, seeing all that can be seen, extrapolating all that can be extrapolated. What we see is that the origin of all things is *clinamen*, and that the end of all things is mediocrity. There is existence solely because these forces are in some sort of balance. Eternity is the duration of that balance, and the cycle of time is the framework which contains the whole of the infinite wilderness of if!''

Lydyard is more able to resist excitability. "I like your idea of beauty well enough," he says, "but we were not brought here simply to discover or rejoice in the wondrous sublimity of the universe. Nor am I certain that you have leapt to the right conclusion."

"The angels are creatures of the flux, as are we," Anatole insists. "They are doomed to die, as are we. Whatever power they have to exert upon the course of cosmic evolution, they remain at the mercy of its perpetual turbulence. Creativity—the *true* creativity which springs by courtesy of the hazards of chance and spontaneity from the seed of *clinamen*—will overwhelm their petty magic and their hopeful *hubris*. They are not gods and they will never become gods, because the universe which we have seen by means of the combination of our different powers of sight is a universe which cannot and will not entertain gods." *How glad the angels must be,* he thinks, ironically, *that they thought to include a Frenchman in their oracle, and need not be content with the carefully unadventurous insights of a cold-blooded Englishman!*

Although the world into which Pelorus and Harkender have now come is an earthly paradise its factories are hidden away in the hills and forests. Its inhabitants live in multitudinous villages where no human hand is active. In this world labor is entirely reserved to machines, leisure to human beings. Even the vehicles which transport goods—and occasionally people—from place to place are self-directing. This is a world devoid of cultivated fields and livestock; even the processes of primary production have been neatly and comprehensively automated.

The houses of this world are more than half alive. Their roofs entrap and store the energy of sunlight, which is redeployed by synthetic neural networks as heat or light or power to energize the screens which serve the various media of communication. The roots of the houses draw water from the earth and purify it for the benefit of their occupants. The houses are self-repairing, although they can and do die eventually; then they decay, while their replacements grow from seed, elsewhere.

The architects and supervisors of this world are also machines, whose function is to react to the unprecedented in such a way as to restore and conserve the *status quo*. They are as tireless and as efficient as the mechanical hands which perform the simplest operations of all, but they are moral beings; their morality is written into their programming, and they are fiercely proud of their inability to do any wrong. Their prime directive is to maintain the world and its inhabitants safe from all possible harm, and no event short of a collision between the earth and a large asteroid would find them inadequate to that task.

This hyper-automation is possible because this is a world without growth and without evolution, a world where human history long ago reached its climax and its equilibrium. Like Jason Sterling's world, it is a world where no one ages, and where no one need die—but there is a fundamental difference between the immortality of this world and the immortality of Sterling's. In Sterling's world the aging process was halted in early adulthood; here it is halted much earlier.

The immortals of this world are children; they never reach puberty.

Pelorus expects Harkender to be more scathing in his criticism of this world than he has been of any other, for this seems on the surface to be the ultimate in what he has labeled *cowardice*. Here is a world of people who flatly refuse to become fully human, embracing immaturity as the preferable condition. He expects Harkender to be equally scathing about the underlying nostalgic assumption that childhood is a happy time. But Harkender is, as ever, unpredictable.

"It is honest, at least," Harkender allows, "and very ingenious, in its way."

"Surely you mean *ingenuous*?"

"I do not. Think—what is the chief deficiency of a world without labor or death?"

"The lack of any incentives, if I read your philosophy right. You feel that the absence of death or any other threat to well-being leeches all the purpose from the business of living. I am not sure that I agree, mind. There remains the pursuit of knowledge and education as a worthwhile process of self-development."

Harkender makes a rude noise. "Mercifully, we have so far been spared the spectacle of Heaven as the Library of Babel, where earnest scholars cultivate their minds *ad infinitum,* withdrawing by slow degrees into academic obsession and stagnation. Unless knowledge has some further purpose in application it is worthless; if the search for truth is a mere hobby, what can it matter whether one finds it or not?"

Pelorus shrugs his shoulders. "In what respect is this universal nursery preferable?" he asks.

"I do not say that it is preferable," Harkender answers. "I only say that it is more ingenious—that it clearly sidesteps the principal objection to all ideas of Heaven. Here, my lupine friend, we see the ultimate development of the one authentic foil against boredom which humans have: play. Here we see the recognition and shameless acceptance of an awkward and unpalatable truth: that Utopia is only fit for children. No one, save for an innocent child, is capable of living a life of endless ease and harmony."

"Are children truly innocent?" Pelorus asks skeptically. "I had thought it a myth generated by adult envy and regret."

"Innocence is *possible*," Harkender tells him. "Not easily won, and certainly not assured, but possible—in a child."

"Even in a child which lives for centuries, or millennia? These are children in body, to be sure, but how can they be children in mind?"

Harkender smiles, as he always does when asked a foolish question whose answer he knows. He spreads his arms wide, as though to indicate the breadth of his wisdom. "They have weak memories," he says. "They live entirely in the present, as only children can, without the burden of the past which adults must carry."

At first, Pelorus does not recognize the child who comes to speak to them. The child certainly does not recognize them. If they had still been in the world he knew, Pelorus would have judged her to be eight or nine years old. He is moved to wonder, as he briefly meets her curious eyes, whether there is any purpose to be served in their speaking to the child at all. Surely, he thinks, no debate will be possible here; or, at least, if a debate were to be possible, a more appropriate adversary would be one of the mechanical intelligences which fills the role of parent, catering to the children's every need.

Harkender, as usual, is one step ahead of him.

"Oh, Mercy, Mercy," he says, "how you have dared to dream! Where else but the inmost desires of a whore could one find such an extreme of innocence?"

"What are you?" asks the child. "I have never seen anything like you before."

"Nor will you ever see our like again," says Harkender, without derision "For this is a kind of Heaven, after all, forever closed to sinners like ourselves."

"What is a sinner?" asks the child.

"A mythical beast," Harkender explains. "A beast so rare and fabulous that even rumor of it must have been lost to a world like this: a chimera imprisoned by its own innate ambivalence, not knowing what shape it ought to have or what desires it ought to entertain.

Some species of sinners, including werewolves, parade their divided selves upon the stage of everyday existence; others, including human men and women, keep their divided nature secret even from themselves.''

"Is that a riddle?'' asks the child.

"Most certainly,'' says Harkender. "But I am no sphinx, and you do not have to answer it.''

"Would you like to play with us?'' asks the child. For a moment, reflected sunlight glistens in her eye in such a strange fashion that Pelorus sees—or thinks he sees—the fugitive legacy of long years of experience.

"No,'' says Harkender, firmly and without regret. "For monsters of my kind, play is best postponed for those rare intervals when there is no important work to be done.''

The child frowns, but only momentarily. Then she turns to Pelorus. "Would you like to play with us?'' she asks.

"Were I a wolf,'' he says regretfully, "I might consent. But were I a wolf, you might be in grave danger. Did you never hear the rhyme about the werewolves of London? One of its verses goes:

"Beware the coverts and courts, little maid;

Where walks the man with the coat of brown;

Though thou art abandoned, be not waylaid,

By the hungry werewolves of London Town.' ''

"Oh yes,'' says the child. "Everyone knows that. It's a nonsense verse. There's no such place as London, and no such thing as a werewolf, and no one is ever abandoned or waylaid.''

"I can't play with you,'' Pelorus says. "I would have to unlearn too much. A long memory can be a difficult burden to bear, but if I were to forget what I know I'd be laying down my life.''

A curious expression crosses the child's face. Just for an instant, the eyes of a middle-aged woman look out from the young head. It is as if they were the eyes of a gorgon: hideous, bitter, angry eyes which hate everything they see.

How magnificently noble! How marvellously brave! How ridiculously smug!

The unspoken words echo in his mind.

I have been a whore, of sorts, myself, he answers, *and all my sisters too.*

"We have seen enough,'' says Harkender tiredly. "If this is all that the collaboration of human and angelic imaginations has to show us, it is a poorer harvest by far than I had hoped to gather in. Either the angels have made a dreadful mistake, or I have.''

''What mistake?'' asks Pelorus.

''That depends whether it is theirs or mine. If it is theirs, I fear that what they hope to find by means of their intercourse with human minds is quite worthless.''

''And if it is yours?''

''Surely that is obvious,'' Harkender replies. ''I thought they wanted to be gods, not children. Because they are so very powerful, I have always assumed that they were capable of bravery and bold-ness—but all the puzzles which have arisen from their dealings with us might be easily solvable, if we accept instead that they are arrant and irredeemable cowards.''

7

When time slows in its paces again, Mandorla and the Clay Man find themselves stranded in a bright summer's day, standing upon a verdant plain from which the glaciers have long retreated. In the distant north there are purple hills whose ridges are capped with snow. There is a river nearby, which must be following a course not dissimilar to that of the ancient Thames. There are no substantial woodlands on the grassy plain, but it is not entirely treeless, and there are occasional clumps of woody shrubs. The grasses have not yet conquered every last bare patch of the once-poisoned ground; where they have not yet formed a carpet, clumps of spiky stalks bind loose dunes of gritty sand. There are no colored flowers, and no bright berries, but there are hints of pink and purple among the varied greens of the multitudinous stalks and leaves.

"Earthly life has conserved better foundation stones than I expected with which to begin its self-resurrection," the Clay Man says. "I judged too hurriedly, and forgot that even complex plants have single-celled seeds which can lie dormant in the ground for centuries. Those which require no insect or animal assistance to bring their pollen together with its receptacles have sprung up again to take full advantage of the ever-reliable wind. The decomposition of the atmosphere cannot have been extreme, and all these plants have inherited a cellular memory of the old equilibrium."

"Have we been brought here simply to observe that?" Mandorla asks. "It seems a disappointingly dull sequel to our earlier adventures."

"It is a beginning, not a conclusion," the Clay Man says. "All

321

bold adventures should end with new beginnings, as the best myths and fables invariably do. What is to be learned from any prophetic dream save that the cycle of growth and decay is implacable and eternal?''

Mandorla's phantom form trembles slightly, as if stirred by some vague internal malaise. "We were not sent here simply to savor the bittersweet taste of philosophy,'' she says acidly. She raises her slender arm to point. "Life may be reasserting its dominion over the humble earth,'' she said, "but *this* is what we have been brought to behold.''

The Clay Man comes to stand behind her, and she senses the turbulence stirred in his own spectral form as he murmurs: "It is, after all, but a dream. Here foresight ends and allegory begins again.''

Marching across the plain toward them is a company of phantoms even fainter than themselves. They march in a great column, at least a hundred abreast. The column has no end; it stretches to the horizon and beyond. The ghosts do not march in any military fashion; they march as slaves, chained together at the neck. They keep pace because they have no choice. Almost all of the chained figures—men as well as women—are carrying infants, and many are carrying more than one, but the ranks of the marchers include many children who can hardly have had time to learn to walk before they died. All the ghosts are naked, and the thin bodies they display are not so transparent as to conceal the scars, wounds and sores their bodies bear in profusion. All are whole in the sense that not one is missing an entire limb or a head, but some have legs which are bent or twisted, some have wasted arms which dangle uselessly, some have heads which are missing one or both eyes, and some have ripped bellies from which their entrails dangle dispiritedly. No matter what their size or condition, though, they march without pause.

On either side of the column masked riders can be seen, mounted on huge ghost-horses. These riders are humanoid in form, but they are covered from head to toe in loose clothing. Their faces are completely hidden by masks, so it is impossible for Mandorla to tell whether they are human or not. Each rider carries a long whip, but these are rarely cracked and never actually used to scourge the dogged marchers. None of the people ever glances sideways to see what the riders are doing.

The head of the column has drawn level with them now, and it begins to pass them by at a distance of thirty yards or so. Mandorla is not aware of any acceleration of time, and the measured tread of the marching ghosts does not noticeably increase, but within a short subjective interval the column stretches as far in the forward direction as the backward one. It would be easy enough to believe, now, that it has neither a beginning nor an end, but girdles the entire earth, unchanging in form in spite of its ceaseless movement.

"Had they flesh," says Mandorla unkindly, "they might be reckoned prey, but as mere ghosts they are infinitely tedious. If this is intended to compound my new-found sorrow on behalf of my precarious humanity, it has failed."

"Where are they going?" the Clay Man whispers, far more deeply affected by the sight than she.

"Where is there for them to go?" she retorts, with some asperity. "Oblivion. Nowhere. Into the deepest recesses of the memories of better beings, where they might lie dormant like your precious frozen seeds. They are gone—what does it matter now whether they were ever here?"

"It matters," says the Clay Man confidently. "Somehow, it matters."

Mandorla would like to say that he is wrong, but the words die on her lips. She feels it too.

One of the riders reins in his horse nearby, and looks down at them. He reaches up to his face in order to remove his mask. Mandorla is surprised to discover that there is in fact a face within, albeit a ghostly one, and that it is one she recognizes. She is not, however, deceived into thinking that the face is anything but a further mask, hiding an intelligence which has no face of its own.

"Luke Capthorn," she says derisively. "What strange imagination dictated that one such as you might ride while the rest of mankind is forced to walk?"

"Luke Capthorn walks with all the rest," the rider tells her, "as painfully as any. I am Asmodeus: the demon he aspired to be."

"Escorting humankind to Hell, no doubt," she says, taking care to display her contempt for this whole charade. "What a tedious task it must be—and how much more tedious it will be to entertain them once they are there! Will you dutifully warm them against the iciness of non-existence with the friendly fire of pain? Why take the trouble? Why take the trouble even to consider the possibility?"

"What else have humans ever asked of us?" Asmodeus replies.

"It is true," says the Clay Man. "For himself and a handful of loved ones, a man might request a Heaven—but what has any man ever requested for the limitless mass of mankind save for a place of torment and damnation? What have we seen in this torrid drama of the future but an unholy and unquenchable thirst for mass destruction?''

''We have seen the anger and innocence of angels,'' Mandorla says angrily. ''That, and nothing more. We have seen what angels see, and what men may see with angel eyes. You know that, Clay Man. You know how little we can trust such visions as this. Dreams are built from hopes and fears, and that perverse alchemical marriage of the two which insists that there is no possible end save for a new beginning.''

Asmodeus deigns to frown, but she cannot tell whether it is her manner or the content of her speech which has disturbed him.

''Tell me, Clay Man,'' the demon says, ''what you have learned from the story of humankind, carried through to its destined conclusion? What shall you tell Machalalel, when he asks you to justify your own creation?''

Mandorla does not wait for the Clay Man to answer. She has a powerful inclination to do her utmost to discomfit this ugly caricature.

''We have not been told the tale of humankind,'' she says. ''We have only been told the angels' tale in fabular form. What we have learned—and what we shall gladly tell Machalalel when he asks us how we have used the gift of life which was not a gift at all—is that the angels dread the future which lies in wait for them. What we shall reveal to Machalalel, and to his kin, is the one and only thing which he and they have sought to hide: that awakened angels cannot bear to face their fate, and have masked their faces against it, devoting themselves to cruel mischief in the fond but futile hope that they might thereby lessen or confuse the horror of their own self-appointed Hell.''

Asmodeus stares at her, but there is no expression in his bleakly handsome face. The Clay Man is staring at her too, in frank astonishment, not daring to whisper any comment or complaint. Eventually, Asmodeus replaces the mask upon his face. He extends the hand which holds the whip. so that the whole length of it may serve as a threatening extension of his arm. Mandorla smiles. Waking or dreaming, she is not in the least afraid of whips.

''You should not be saddened or angered by this vision,'' the demon says. ''You are not human—you are a wolf.''

''I *was* a wolf,'' she answers, ''but I am human now, despite that

I have struggled for millennia to resist that fate. Those who put on masks must be careful, lest their masks become in time their faces. You doubtless believe that Luke Capthorn was your ape, but it may be that you are his. His worship has ensnared your vanity, and you are in dire danger of becoming what he wanted you to be.''

The ghostly rider stares at her, his angry eyes like glowing embers. Then he spurs his horse with needless force, and quickly moves it to an intemperate gallop.

"Do you know what you are doing, Mandorla?" the Clay Man asks her, as the phantom host fades away into invisibility.

"No," she replies. "But I am sick of playing a meek and quiet part. Damn Machalalel, and all his kin. If the game is over, let us be done with it." And she looks up into the darkening sky, challenging her Creator to face her, or to dispose of her for good and all.

Anatole knows well enough that there is artifice in what he sees, and that the inferences which he draws feed back into his vision and pervert it. He knows, too, that his fancy is far less restrained than Lydyard's—but he is vain enough to hope that this might be reckoned a kind of boldness, and he does not repent of it. He is quite content to let Lydyard play the tentative skeptic while he accepts the hazards of their adventure in imagination.

He sees, as the vision unfolds toward its climax, that the universe as a whole *is* a whole, each and every particle having a part to play through its implicit connection with all others. The underlying mechanisms of material cause and effect are hewn in light, separated in time and space, but everything in the universe remains coherent and connected, dancing to an underlying rhythm which must have been imparted when it was still very tiny, compacted into the space of a single chimerical atom.

One of the key features of the turbulence which possesses the universe, he realizes, is that vast systems are capable of undergoing sudden changes of state. Such changes may be triggered by the arrival of some critical point in their affairs, or by the engagement of catalysts which promote change while themselves remaining unaltered.

Is that what we are? Anatole wonders. *Are we catalysts in the affairs of the angels, provoking changes on a vast scale while remaining relatively unaffected?*

When these large-scale changes of state occur, he realizes, it is as if all the particles involved, no matter how widely scattered in space they may be, act in unison. It is as though all of them are somehow "aware" of the condition of the whole system, without requiring information about it to be transmitted at the speed of light. Anatole realizes that this wholeness which the universe has—the unity which binds it, the rhythm which underlies and determines the choreography of the dance of matter, space and time—is in some ways analogous to a mind. He knows already that mind is not some magical elixir ordinarily contained in bodies but decantable therefrom. He knows that the way in which bodies incorporate minds is more closely analogous to the way in which printed symbols on a page carry meaning. Now he dares to hazard the guess that if only there is complexity enough, any ground at all might be mindful: not merely other kinds of matter than the organic but grounds that lie outside the realm of matter, in the implicate order whose surface the universe is. The universe itself is neither self-aware nor intelligent, but it provides a ground in which self-awareness and intelligence can exist and flourish: a ground which the angels might inhabit. It is easy enough to extrapolate the idea, to imagine that whatever ground plays host to the angels is a *battleground* where many might contend.

Anatole remembers that according to the deceptive memories of Machalalel's creatures—which presumably reflect something of the wisdom of the angels—there were far more than seven angels when the universe was younger. If they were born of the ceaseless riot of cosmic turbulence, they too must have been subject to rigorous natural selection, and their number might be fewer still in future. On the other hand, should the creativity of cosmic turbulence give birth to others of their kind there might be more: hundreds or millions more or numbers unimaginable. Perhaps the angels could create more of themselves, if they wished, or make room for more minds within the reaches of their own mindfulness. If the angels can play host to three human minds, Anatole reasons, they might as easily play host to *all* the minds of all mankind, and all the minds of all the species which grew to mindfulness on all the other worlds of all the other stars. In any case, there is nothing final or magical about the number seven, and it now seems probable to Anatole that it cannot long endure. Nor, given what he has seen of the true nature of the universe, can he believe that there is any path of destiny laid down for the angels to follow. All that is certain is that their future is uncertain.

He realizes, as he formulates this conclusion, that it is not what the angels desired to discover. He can only guess what the angels' secret ambitions were, and doubts that they had a clear idea themselves, but he feels confident in his judgment that the oracle has betrayed their fondest hopes and expectations. He suspects that they really were ambitious to be emperor-gods, and that they cannot welcome a vision of the universe which has no room for any ultimate tyranny.

"If men must look uneasily behind them lest they be shadowed by angels," he says deliberately, "is it not just that the angels have to look behind them too? Neither man nor angel has any right to be free from the fear of death and demolition, nor any right to be secure in the destiny which lies before them. Why should we be ashamed to tell them so?"

"It is not a matter of shame," says Hecate uneasily. "It is a matter of safety."

"When contact was first made between the minds of men and the minds of angels," Lydyard says slowly, "our ancestors gladly seized upon the hypothesis that they had found gods, who—if luck would only have it that they might be good and benevolent—might protect and cherish them. It is easy to understand why primitive men desired kindly and powerful gods who would assure them freedom from famine and disease, and victory in war, and were over-optimistic about the possibility of finding them. We have too long neglected to ask the corollary questions. What did the angels hope that *they* had found? What was their most fervent desire, which led them to take such an over-optimistic interest in us?"

"We may be certain," says Hecate, "that they had no need of prayers and sacrifices, or anything else they were actually offered."

"Perhaps," Anatole suggests, "they said to one another: *Here is a microcosm of our own existence, so very different and yet so strangely similar, from which lessons may be learned.*" Even as he says it, he knows that it will not do, but he indulges the flight of fancy by building in the theater of his consciousness a second universe of galaxies and stars and planetary systems, tiny enough to be held in the arms of an inquisitive man. He looks into it, and finds it teeming with life and with intelligence: a microcosmic multiverse; a glass of champagne whose foam scintillates with possible enlightenment. It is a dizzying prospect; for a moment or two he is able to pretend that he is no less than an angel himself—but then his arrogance collapses in upon itself like a pricked balloon, and he sees what a fool he has been.

He wonders, suddenly, how often this game of oracular adventure might have been played before by the angels, and with what result. None, apparently, sufficient to take the fascination out of it.

Another hypothesis comes into his mind. What if there is nothing at stake in this but mere dabbling and aesthetic distraction? What if the carnival of destruction is a carnival indeed, and the angels humble showmen, bent on nothing more profound than entertainment? The immensity of his vision, which has already filled him with a sense of awe, now fills him with a nightmarish suspicion of the *pointlessness* of everything he has seen or conjured up.

"Perhaps the angels already know," he whispers. "Perhaps they already know everything we can divine, everything we may venture to tell them. Perhaps they have heard it all a thousand times before. Perhaps this making of oracles is not their science but only their *sport.*"

"If it is true, we must act as if it were not," says Hecate. "If all this is theater, we must play our parts wholeheartedly."

"It is *not* true," says Lydyard, sounding sadly and uncharacteristically confident. "It might be better if it were, for when a play is done the actors may take up the threads of their other lives, and we may well be less fortunate. Yes, all this has happened before; yes, it may happen again, with only minor variations. I understand that now. I understand what kind of beings the angels are, and what they looked for in the minds of men. I know what mistake they made, and how we have corrected it."

"Show me!" says Anatole. "Show us all! Show us the faces of the angels, while we still have magical eyes to see." He looks again at the spherical wall of the macrocosm, finite in dimension but infinite in extent. He looks into the strange mist of galaxies which decorates that wall, and tries with all his might to perceive shapes in the mist: *anything* which might pass muster as a face or a form.

For a little while there is nothing to be seen but the sinuous, ever-shifting shadows which Anatole took for eels or serpents, coiling around one another in unsolvable knots, swallowing their own tails and devouring their own entrails. Then, with the tiniest shift of visual perspective, Anatole is able to dissolve that squirming confusion into a silver field which is almost uniform, and realizes that one might easily see it as a mirror.

The entire universe, he thinks, *is nothing but an all-inclusive magic mirror. The direction one chooses is quite irrelevant; no matter how hard one looks, the ultimate object is simply one's own staring eyes. What am I to the angels, then? Am I too a mirror? If I am, they cannot like what they see within its depths.*

"That is the beginning and the end of it," Lydyard agrees. "We are mirrors which allow the angels to see what they could not see before: themselves. When they put us away again, they will lose sight of what they are . . . and you are right, of course; they cannot possibly like what they have seen. But there is more, and worse. Like the first men who looked into mirrors they believe implicitly in magic, and are desperately afraid that the mirrors they have made will steal their souls away. That is the link which has always been missing from the argument: they fear that we will steal their souls.

"In a sense, alas, they are right to fear it. I wish it were not so, but they are right."

The valley is peaceful; the distant hills, patched with ploughed fields, are silvered with hazy morning light. There is a stand of poplars nearby but they are leafless. Their branches are stirred by a cool breeze. From this dubious vantage point it is impossible to detect the thirty thousand men distributed upon the flanks of the valley. They are hidden in trenches, and so are their guns, their batteries, their wagons, their horses and their stores. The telephone lines they have laid and the mines they have sown are invisible too, but the men who had laid and sown them are thus connected to command posts in the rear and thus defended against any advance from the other side of the valley. The landscape is deceptive through and through; wherever a clump of bushes rises, there also is a machine gun; wherever the leafless branches are tightly clustered, there sits a sniper.

A puff of smoke becomes visible near the crest of one of the distant hills; a second or two later a blurred booming sound reaches Pelorus's ear; after a further second there is an appalling crash as the shell arrives. Another puff of smoke follows; another muted roar; another explosion, tearing up the earth. A handful of uniformed men come briefly into view on the far side of the valley, moving like a column of ants. Their appearance is greeted by a desultory rattle of machine-gun fire, but the range is too great. They disappear into the ground as uncannily as they appeared.

Quiet descends again: the lull before the storm.

Suddenly, there are men everywhere: a host of gray-green figures vomited forth by the earth, running as if for their lives. The guns open up, from every ridge and every trench, from every bush and every covert. The earth heaves and belches; dirt flies in every direction; clouds of smoke and dirt erupt and merge. Men fall, then more, and more, but the headlong rush continues.

The valley floor is littered with corpses, and the explosions go on and on, as if they might go on for ever and ever, without end.

"Home again," says Pelorus quietly. "It was hardly worth going away."

"I don't think so," says Harkender. "Turn around."

Pelorus turns. He sees a city street, full of wagons and carriages, flanked by tradesmen's stalls. Night has fallen but the street is brightly lit by the glow of gaslights mounted high on metal stanchions, and one in every three stalls is dressed with an orange grease-lamp. Basket-sellers weave their way through the crowds while musicians play at every corner, each attended by his little corps of beggars.

He turns again, and sees . . . the congregation gathered in a church.

Again, and . . . nothing. He hears, instead, Jacob Harkender saying: "I see what I am to see. It is the world. Now make your point."

Pelorus turns again, and sees moonlit rocks, and great stone pyramids, scoured and pitted by wind-blown sand. He looks up, at the face of the sphinx. For a moment he sees it as it really was when last he saw it in 1872: the mere memory of a face, chipped and smashed and all-but-obliterated. Then he sees it differently, as the lovely, living features of a beautiful woman.

The living sphinx raises a huge paw, delicately using an extended claw to scratch her cheek.

"I cannot believe that the earth is Utopia, even to one such as you," Harkender says petulantly. "You have magic enough to grant your little whims, but what is *that* worth, really? How long can mere trickery stave off boredom? What satisfactions are there to be found in mere dabbling, mere *theater*?" He pronounces the word *theater* as if it were an obscenity.

"If you cannot find a satisfactory answer," the sphinx informs him lazily, "you might consider the possibility that you are asking the wrong question. If all solutions are to be judged false, perhaps the riddle itself is misconceived."

"Is *that* all we are supposed to have deduced?" Harkender says, in an aggrieved tone. "What a waste! Perhaps I was naïve to think that *any* oracle could rise above the banal and the tedious."

"Perhaps," the sphinx replies, by no means disconcerted by the insult. "Unfortunately, no oracle can reveal what its seers cannot imagine. Perhaps you should have chosen better accomplices."

"The choice was not mine," Harkender retorts venomously, "and I accept no responsibility for their ludicrous visions of perfection."

"Whenever any of your would-be architects of a better world have removed or ameliorated the ills that afflict mankind you have accused them of betrayal," the sphinx says, "or of reducing themselves to something significantly less than human. But if we are to retain humankind as it is, how shall we not retain all the vices of which human beings are capable? How shall we banish war, tyranny, oppression while retaining the human impulses that produce them? Can you think of any man who could have offered you a more convincing vision of the Age of Reason than those you have seen?"

"I doubt it," Harkender concedes. "But I had not the slightest desire to visit the insipid futures of the human imagination. What of the angelic imagination? It is *their* possible futures I was ambitious to explore. *Theirs* were the realms I desired and hoped to visit."

"Why should the angels listen to your judgment as to their potential, unless you can pass reasoned judgment on your own?"

A strange evasion, Pelorus thinks. *Harkender has a point. Are we addressing the wrong questions, extrapolating the wrong ideas?*

"Reasoned judgment was easy to pass," Harkender replies. "When will you show me something *worthy* of reasoned judgment?"

"You have rejected not merely the worlds you have glimpsed," the sphinx says, lightly enough, "but all the objectives of human progress which have so far been laid before you by their apologists. They have pleaded on behalf of peace, knowledge, innocence, transcendence ... but neither you nor your companion will have any truck with any of them. Very well—I offer you an alternative. I offer you the world as it is, and humankind as it is. I offer you pain, death, fear, and all the other challenges which you seem to hold so dear, but I offer you one thing in addition. I offer you a multiplicity of chances. I offer you the chance to begin again, every time you reach the end. Would you accept *that* as a preferable alternative to the world into which you were born?"

"Reincarnation!" says Harkender. "Is *that* all you have to offer? Which particular version do you favor? Is each soul simply recycled into a newborn body, or does each new station depend on the allotment of moral credit by some careful recording angel? Or do you propose, in spite of the apparent paradox, to send each soul back in time to the beginning of its own particular incarnation, which might then be lived over and over again in an infinity of alternative worlds, in the hope that its destiny might one day come out right? Of all human daydreams, none is more common than the dream of going back in time to correct one's mistakes; it is the simplest Heaven of them all.''

"Will you judge it the worst, on that account?'' asks the sphinx, seemingly unembarrassed by Harkender's reaction. "If it is the simplest Heaven of all, perhaps it is the one which reflects the deepest desire and most fervent hope of which the human mind is capable?''

"Perhaps it is,'' says Harkender, "but it solves nothing. If the reincarnated soul remembers nothing, there is no sense in which it can sensibly be said to be reincarnate, however it is reborn. If it remembers a series of births in different bodies, it will soon fall victim to a fatalism which urges it to be done with any present frustration by casting the die of rebirth yet again. If it is continually and knowingly reborn into an identical situation the restriction of that circumstance will surely come to seem oppressive. Like all daydreams, this one is idle; it is not properly thought through.''

"Then you reject it along with all the rest?'' The sphinx is as good-humored as most of those to whom Harkender had spoken, and Pelorus wonders whether they all expect to be judged less harshly in some other court.

"Of course I do,'' says Harkender.

"What, then, is *your* idea of a better world?''

"First of all,'' says Harkender, glad to have the riddle finally and forthrightly set before him, "I want no part of any world inhabited by men; I have had more than my fill of vulgar fellowship. Secondly, I want no part of any world from which *ills* have been eliminated; as my faithful enemy David Lydyard has observed but never fully understood, pain is a spur which urges us to see more clearly, and fear of death is what blesses life with purpose. I ask for eternal youth, but not for freedom from pain, nor for the certainty of revival after any and every death. Beyond that, I make no specifications; I have ever been a lover of mysteries and the hazards of the as-yet-unknown. The world in which I desire to live indefinitely is one in which the fruit of the tree of knowledge is bitter but nourishing, one in which every adventure in fascination and every battle against adversity could be won without ever putting an end to the quest or to the war. Such a world must also permit creativity on a scale far greater than the human, which means that in reach and variety it must be grander by far than any tiny ball of mud, with far more opportunity to find fascination and adversity than any mere *planet* could offer: a world fit for *angels* rather than men. That is what I ask of the angels whose pawn I have gladly been. I ask it for myself and myself alone. I could not care less what you choose to do with mankind, as long as I am not condemned to be part of it.''

The sphinx does not react in any way to this remarkable oration. Instead she turns to Pelorus, as if seeking support for her own offering.

''I have long enjoyed the benefits of reincarnation,'' Pelorus points out, ''but I have not found it any kind of Heaven. There is a certain glad security in knowing that one will always return to the world, but I have known Mandorla and the Clay Man far too well to think that mere security could ever be enough to make life sweet. The problem is that Mandorla's Heaven and the Clay Man's have always been poles apart . . . as have all the Heavens we have seen, or heard about. Few men, alas, could live in Heavens designed by others of their kind, but few—Jacob Harkender is, it seems, one of the exceptions—would gladly accept the burden of loneliness. It seems to me that if every human or other being that ever lived had a private universe tailored to its whim, even *that* could not be Heaven for long. If you really want my opinion, it is that Heavens are for wolves and their kin, not for men and theirs. You are better placed than I to decide where angels fit into the scheme.''

''Perhaps you are right,'' says the sphinx seriously. For her, it seems, this is an argument which needs to be weighed very carefully indeed. ''Perhaps that is all we know, and all we need to know.''

The Age of Irony

And I saw in the right hand of him that sat on the throne a book written within and on the backside, sealed with seven seals.

And I saw a strong angel proclaiming with a loud voice, Who is worthy to open the book, and to loose the seals thereof?

And no man in heaven, nor in earth, neither under the earth, was able to open the book, neither to look thereon.

And I wept much, because no man was found worthy to open and read the book, neither to look thereon.

Revelations 5:1–4

1

When James Austen lay on his deathbed, brought, after a lifetime of tolerance, to sore impatience and sour irascibility by the corrosive force of pain, the Clay Man went to see him.

"If you wish to say 'I told you so' you are quite welcome," Austen said. "You have every right. I tried with all my might to overcome what I took to be your delusion, that you would rise again from the grave, but here you are!"

"Am I sane, then, after all?" asked the Clay Man lightly.

"I have spent a lifetime trying to bring men to sanity," Austen answered, attempting a laugh but managing little more than a hoarse croak, "but I go to my deathbed not knowing what it is."

"Perhaps it is easier to say what we mean by madness," the Clay Man suggested.

"Once, I would have said so," Austen admitted, "nor would your lone example of my mistaken judgment have sufficed to make me doubt it—but as I have grown older and more feeble, I see so much evidence of madness around me that I am forced to wonder . . ."

He broke off, coughing. When he was fit to continue, he made a visible effort to pull himself together, and began again. "Most madness is mere exaggeration," he said. "One aspect of a man is magnified to the point at which it begins to crowd out all the others. Perhaps it is a single emotion, like melancholia or love—although we usually find the latter tolerable enough, provided only that the madness is short-lived. Perhaps it is the imagination, in which case we call it delusion. Perhaps it is a particular interest, or anxiety, or action . . . in which case we speak of obsession, of monomania, of

337

dementia. Seen in this light, madness is simply an excessive concentration of the personality, a narrowing of the field of thought . . . in which case, the task of the alienist is to dilute and broaden, to bring the whole man from behind the mask which has reduced him to a part. Except that . . .''

''I was never less than whole,'' said the Clay Man soberly. ''Melancholic, yes; deluded, perhaps a little; but . . .''

''That was not what I was thinking,'' Austen interrupted him, with the casual rudeness of one who clearly believed himself to be short of time. ''I was thinking that the world is full of supposedly sane men, pillars of society all, who are in truth mere parts of men, masked and veiled; it is simply that their narrowness fits the channels which the social order has laid down for them. They are well adapted to the way of the world—better, I dare say, than any *whole* man could ever be.''

The Clay Man considered such models of sanity, reason and intellect as Sir Edward Tallentyre and Jason Sterling, and nodded his head. ''Have *you* been a whole man, Dr. Austen?'' he asked, as politely as he could.

''I have tried to be,'' Austen muttered, a little resentfully. ''You had best ask my wife how well I succeeded, should you need a second opinion.''

''You were a good friend to me,'' the Clay Man said, ''and a better friend to the poor unfortunates at Hanwell than many of your predecessors. You have labored hard in the cause of enlightenment, by no means unproductively. I have known a great many men, and could not name a better one.''

''You always were a flatterer,'' said Austen gruffly. ''You wheedled your way into my home and my affections, just as you tried to capture the soul of all mankind with that brave and stupid book of yours. You told the proud and the pompous that they had attained the Age of Reason, when they had barely learned to button their own shirts. It did no harm, of course, to flatter a holy fool like me, but it might have been unwise to congratulate the common herd of madmen on their sanity.''

''As it happened,'' the Clay Man said, ''no one read my book. It would have made no difference if they had. The men who have ruled the world during your lifetime were fully adept in the dangerous arts of self-congratulation and self-flattery; they have never for an instant doubted their intellect or their virtue. You must admit that I was no

flatterer when it came to virtue—I merely hoped that victorious reason would in the end give birth to it.''

"It is a hope I shared,'' Austen said. "It was forlorn, alas.''

"I have not lost it yet,'' the Clay Man told him. "Given that we
have not, after all, seen the victory of reason, we may still entertain
the hope that it might be parent to virtue.''

"If the parent cannot come of age, the child can never be conceived,'' Austen retorted—but then he coughed again, and thought
better of his dark tone. "We have switched roles, you and I,'' he
pointed out. "I used to sit by your bedside, trying as best I could to
lift the burden of your pessimism.''

The Clay Man looked down at his hands. "We have done this too
often,'' he admitted. "We have too long made a game of it, and we
can hardly exchange a dozen words without slipping back into the
easy cut and thrust. Perhaps it is no bad thing . . . but tell me, Dr.
Austen, leaving aside if you can the wit and the deft rhetoric, *can* a
man really be whole, in the sense that you mean? Can he really
bring all the various facets of his mind into steady balance and sweet
harmony? In your expert judgment, is sanity *possible*?''

Knowing that it was a serious question, and one to which his
melancholically inclined ex-patient required a carefully considered
answer, Austen paused before replying. He took a drink from the
glass of water that was on his bedside table, then set it down again
with punctilious care.

"No,'' he said, in the end. "Steady balance is possible, perhaps
. . . for a while. Sweet harmony is perceptible . . . now and again.
But we must never forget that the wholeness of the mind, like the
wholeness of the body, is a phantom of flux, always approximate,
always changing. Day by day we must take in food and water to
replenish our bodies, so that new cells may constantly be born while
old ones die . . . and in the end, we cannot overcome the creeping
forces of decay no matter how bravely we make our stand. Whatever
we mean when we speak of *ourselves* we cannot mean anything fixed
or coherent. Self-consciousness is born of conflict and chance, of the
bitter and beautiful necessity of *choice*. We are not wolves, Clay
Man; we have no wholeness. Unlike the companions of your immortality, we have not even the memory of wholeness to which we might
cling. But if we could not *aim* for balance, if we could not occasionally hear the sweetness of harmony, and regret its fading, we would
have no hope at all. We are madmen, condemned to the asylum of
life, but we know how to be better, to win free of the heaviest

shackles that hold us down and earn the respect of our fellow men. It is because true, permanent sanity is impossible, but at the same time so valuable, that we must strive with all our might to win it, and never rest content while it evades our grasp. Do you not agree?''

"Wholeheartedly," the Clay Man said.

"Good," said the doctor, lying back upon his pillow. "Now, perhaps, I can die in peace."

2

When Sir Edward Tallentyre lay on his deathbed, facing death with the same fortitude that he had shown against all adversity, the Clay Man visited him, in order that he might enjoy one last discussion regarding the cruel and unfortunate way of the world.

"Are you writing another book?" Tallentyre asked him wryly.

"Yes I am," the Clay Man admitted.

"Will it be another *True History of the World,* four volumes long, and as dull as ditchwater?" Tallentyre smiled as he spoke, to take the sting from his teasing.

"Not this time," said the Clay Man. "This time, it will be an admitted fantasy—and a comedy of sorts."

"All history is a kind of fantasy, and a comedy of sorts," said Tallentyre. "The opposite is also true, alas; all fantasy, however comical, is in its own fashion a kind of history."

"I have already quoted you more-or-less to that effect," the Clay Man told him. "And you may be sure that my fantasy has no less truth in it than my history had."

"Am I in it, then?" asked the baronet, evidently not displeased by the prospect.

"We are all in it," the Clay Man answered. "This very conversation may end up reproduced in its pages, provided only that it be true enough, and fantastic enough."

"I will do my best to make it so. Will your new book also deal with the whole story of mankind, from its ill-remembered beginnings to its hoped-for destiny?"

"Oh yes—but I have changed the titles of its parts. Instead of *The*

Age of Gold the first part is called *The Age of Fool's Gold;* instead
of *The Age of Heroes* the second part is called *The Age of Fallen
Heroes*. I have not finished the third part, but it will not be called
The Age of Iron. I am considering *The Age of Rust* but I have not
yet made up my mind. I have become cynical, you see, now that I
have belatedly begun to grow old.''

''So you have,'' said Tallentyre. ''What of the fourth part—the
part which deals with the future? Will that be called *The Age of
Lost Reason?*''

''I have not even begun to think about a fourth part.''

''Will you sign yourself Lucian de Terre again? No one will believe that the same man could write two books more than a century apart.''

''I will use a different name,'' said the Clay Man. ''Lucian de
Terre was a *nom de plume* appropriate to the writer of a true history,
but for an acknowledged fantasy I will need a name in a different
vein: a name suggestive of steadiness and reliability, but with just a
hint of liquidity about it. I shall think of something apposite when
the time comes.''

''No doubt. I wish that I might read it, but even if there were but
a handful of pages yet to write, I do not think I could promise to
wait for the end. I am not in much pain, thanks to the morphine, but
I am all too conscious of the ravening beast which is consuming my
organs. My doctors call it by a different name, but I call it Chaos:
an upswelling of the inchoate filling up my inner spaces with a
profusion of crude, non-functional cells. To know that I have such
potential for growth still in me, turned to such imbecilic and destructive ends! One day, Clay Man, we will be masters of our own flesh,
and it will be the reasoning mind which says to the cells of the body:
Divide! Differentiate! Dissolve! Such powers should not be at the
beck and call of mere decay.''

''In spite of all that you have learned about the reality of angels,
can you still believe in the perfectibility of man?''

''It is not a matter for belief,'' Tallentyre told him sternly. ''While
the future is yet unmade, there is hope that we, and not the wretched
things that think themselves gods, will be its makers. We must do
our best, even though we might fail. What more can we do?''

''I have heard several accounts of what happened when you faced
one of the angels,'' said the Clay Man soberly, ''and all of them
agree that you won the confrontation very cleverly—but I do not
think the angel was a *wretched* thing even then, and it is wiser now.''

"While it remains intimately involved with Jacob Harkender," said Tallentyre, with some asperity, "it will never become wise, and there will always be a certain wretchedness in its view of the world."

The Clay Man was not so certain, but he knew better than to press the point. Even a man as bold, as brilliant and as skeptical as Sir Edward Tallentyre was vulnerable to the effects of old age, and some few of his ideas had set so hard within his white-capped skull as to be immovable.

"Do you still believe," asked the Clay Man quietly, "that the vision which you showed Harkender's angel was true in every detail? Do you not fear that future discovery might show the vision of nineteenth-century science to be one more phantom of the human imagination?"

"Again you speak of *belief*," Tallentyre complained. "But I will answer you anyway. I do not doubt for a moment that future discovery will have a great deal more to say about the nature of the universe. The vision which I showed the angel in 1872 is already out of date. How could any such vision possibly be final, given that our knowledge of the universe is still in its infancy? But how should that make me *fear*? The vision of the universe which I possess is at best a partial truth, but I know it for a partial *truth,* and no mere phantom. Future science will make it more elaborate, and perhaps more bizarre, but it cannot do otherwise than make it *truer,* because that is what science is, and in making it truer it cannot help but make it better, and finer, and more beautiful. You say that Harkender's guardian angel has grown wiser, but the best of men have grown wiser too, and they have the safer method of acquiring wisdom. If there are to be other confrontations, when David Lydyard or his son may have to stand in my place, they will be better armed than I was, and they will make their advantage felt. Can you doubt that, Clay Man?"

"No," said the Clay Man. "You are right, of course." *Except,* he added silently, *that wisdom might not be enough. According to Pelorus, a barbarian with a sword slew Archimedes while he contemplated a theorem scratched in the sand. Whatever they lack in intelligence, the angels make up for in sheer brute power. Were they not so apprehensive of one another, any one of them might send the Earth tumbling into the Abyss, and all mankind with it, upon a momentary whim.*

"What a shame!" said Tallentyre. "If I am right, *of course,* then nothing I have said is fantastic enough to warrant reproduction in the pages of your book.''

"Better, finer, *and more beautifully,*" repeated the Clay Man ruminatively. "Does the last sensibly follow? I had not thought you a disciple of Keats.''

"All truth is beautiful," Tallentyre said. "That is what we mean, or ought to mean, by beauty—whether we realize it or not. Beauty resides in the eye of the beholder because truth is something which has to be both apprehended and *known*. Without a beholder, there is no beauty, and there is no truth. Science is the most beautiful thing in the world, as even painters know, although most of them can no more bring what they know to the level of conscious statement than a bicycle-rider can explain the dynamics of balance or a sharpshooter the science of ballistics. Is *that* fantastic enough for you, chronicler?''

"I believe it is," said the Clay Man.

3

Cordelia was still in the prime of life when the Clay Man went to see her. She had been in the prime of life for many years; she was sixty-five years old and looked twenty. There was not a blemish on her face, which would have been perfect save for the slight tightness of her lips as she studied the Clay Man.

"You've begun to grow old," she said, with no more than faint amazement. "Has your guardian angel relaxed his care?"

"It seems so," the Clay Man admitted. "I had hoped to finish my new book at a leisurely pace, but I'm beginning to learn impatience—at long last, some might say."

"What have I to do with your book?" she asked. "You would do far better to talk to my husband. He is the one who is party to the secrets of eternity."

The Clay Man did not think it diplomatic to comment on the fact of her calling Jacob Harkender her husband, nor on her description of him as a man party to the secrets of eternity. Given the sensitivity of the questions he had come to ask, it seemed sensible to avoid any other remarks which might annoy her.

"I have humbler aims than that," he said politely. "I'm trying, as best I can, to understand the inner workings of the minds of men. I shall not pretend, this time, to oracular wisdom; I have promised myself to be content with subtler implications, lest I overreach myself."

His amiability made no apparent impression upon her. "I don't see how I can help you," she said.

"I was with your father when he died," he said softly.

"I would have been with him myself," she retorted swiftly, "had I been welcome in his house. I cannot believe that his dying words contained any message for me. Had he been inclined towards forgiveness he would doubtless have let me know sooner; he was always an orderly man."

"There was no message," the Clay Man agreed. "But I am certain that he was thinking of you, in his last hours."

"Did he tell you how unlucky he was to be cursed with a daughter?" she asked, in a bitter voice. "How 'sharper than a serpent's tooth' it must have been for a man such as he! At least poor Lear had two which pretended to love him. At least poor Lear could convince himself that he had love to waste on *them.* Sir Edward never could."

"I think you mistake him," the Clay Man said. "His disappointment never destroyed his love."

"There was none to destroy," she insisted. When the Clay Man inclined his head in disagreement, she added: "None, at least, that could outweigh the hopeful tenderness he had for his substitute son. I dare say he had a loving message for David, had he not? Or was David there too, laying down his pain and his anguished tears as tributes to his petty god?"

"David never leaves World's End," the Clay Man said. "He has become something of a recluse, I fear. Even Pelorus sees him rarely."

"He was ever enthusiastic to be a recluse. He is doubtless very happy there, playing the martyr. It's a role of which he never tires. Nell assists him in it, or so I'm told. What a beautifully doleful pair they must make!" The waspishness in her voice was half-hearted, as if she were playing a part in which she could not wholeheartedly believe.

"It hurt him when you left him," the Clay Man said, this being the tender issue he could not shirk. "It redoubles his misery to know where you are."

"Do you think I don't know that?" she said. "Are you laboring under the delusion that I did it because I couldn't understand how he would feel? Is *he* laboring under any such delusion?"

The Clay Man was glad that she had framed the question herself. "David does not understand why you left him," he said quietly. "He can list reasons which he would find plausible enough in someone else, but he cannot understand how they were ever adequate to move a woman who loved him. He judges love, you see, by the strength of his own.''

"He judges everything by his private standards,'' Cordelia replied. "No doubt that was why nothing in the world could ever make him joyful, or hopeful. I never doubted that the pain which he felt was as intense as he claimed, or the gloom as deep, but in the end I found it too much of a burden to share. Doubtless he thinks I came to Harkender for shallow reasons, and I won't deny the force of those reasons. Why shouldn't I claim eternal youth, if it's offered to me? Why shouldn't I delight in making love to a beautiful man, just as men delight in making love to beautiful women without reference to their marriages? Did you know that my one and only daughter was named after my father's favorite mistress instead of my mother— and that I was never told until I came to Jacob? Did his mistress Elinor love him, do you think, as much as Jacob Harkender undoubtedly loves me? Did David love me any more than that? But that's not all. There were other, deeper motives. Even if the intensity of David's love were taken for granted, why should any amount of austere and prisoning love be considered equal to the enthusiastic, open-hearted love which my husband has? You say that David doesn't understand, but that's because he *won't* understand, and never will. I only wish that I admired his stubbornness a little less.''

"It can't have been easy to do what you did,'' the Clay Man observed, taking care to be as sympathetic as he honestly could.

"It wasn't hard,'' she said, in a voice which carried less than total conviction. "I was always a rebel against expectation. My head had already been turned by Mary Wollstonecraft and the suffragettes— and I fled, after all, into the arms of a man whose principal delight has always been the flouting of every convention, the violation of every rule. I haven't escaped the old conventions and sentiments entirely, though. I miss the love and approval of my children—and of my first husband too. I won't say that I sustained no loss . . . but I don't regret what I did, and I won't concede that I had no right to do it. I honestly wish that David could be less unhappy than he is, but I won't take the blame for it.''

The Clay Man said nothing, and there was a brief interval of silence before she spoke again. "Is that all you came for?'' she asked, as though she did not quite know whether to be surprised or disgusted. "I wouldn't have thought that you, of all people, could interest yourself in such trivial matters. Surely Machalalel designed you for more serious enquiries.''

"Machalalel made me inquisitive about everything," the Clay Man said ruefully. "He didn't make me emotionless, but it's hard for me to put myself in the shoes of a mortal man. I want to understand, you see. I want to understand the workings of the human heart. In my *True History,* I called the modern era an Age of Iron; in my new fantasy, I shall call it an Age of Irony. In pursuit of that end I must try to understand the intimate machinery of the flesh, in all its complexity and waywardness."

"And your new account of the coming era," she said acidly, "will doubtless be called *The Age of Treason.*"

"I had not thought of it," he said judiciously, "but I shall certainly take it under consideration."

Part Four

The Atom and the Crystal Light

And I saw the dead, small and great, stand before God; and the books were opened; and another book was opened, which is the book of life; and the dead were judged out of those things which were written in the books, according to their works.

Revelations 20:12

1

When Nell took her place on the throne beside Hades—becoming, as she supposed, the Queen of the Underworld—she fell into a kind of trance, and lost all consciousness of time. She could not fall asleep, and certainly could not dream, but she entered into a peculiar state of mind. She felt as if her mind had lost touch with her phantom body; she was incapable of any physical action. Most of the time her body remained perfectly still, as if it had turned into a statue made of thin glass, but there were occasions when she felt her lips moving. She knew that she was speaking, but she could not hear what she said.

She felt cheated. She had volunteered, as boldly as her father or her grandfather would have done, to play her part in this monstrous ritual, but the angels would not even let her listen to her own words. They had placed her at the very center of their oracle, to be its focal point, but at the same time they excluded her from its providence, from its secrets, from its implications. It seemed terribly unfair, and for a while she thought it a fate akin to that of Tantalus, but the resentment faded away and left her possessed by a dull uncaring calm.

There were no external signs by which her staring eyes could measure time's passing, nor had she any kind of internal clock within her rigid spectral form. She had no heart to beat, nor blood to flow, nor hunger nor thirst to undermine her patience with unease. Save for the sluggish but ceaseless flux of thought and imagination, she had no map on which to trace the extension of her being, and she soon became a past mistress of the cold arts which were necessary to this mode of experience: the gelation of thought and the glaciation of the imagination.

She *was* haunted by tedium at first, while she still wished that she could at least hear what her captive body was saying, but the tedium did not last. Boredom, she came to realize, was merely the dark companion of haste, and ought to be incapable of troubling the properly balanced mind. She adapted her mental outlook to the fact that the burdensome pressure of everyday time had been lifted, and eventually arrived at a state of mind which was devoid of any urge to seek distraction or entertainment. She was glad to attain this state, which seemed to her once she had mastered it to be a special kind of maturity.

Her grandfather, in one of his rare flights of fancy, had once suggested to her that such mental phenomena as boredom and the sense of beauty were of relatively recent evolution, adaptations or curses called forth by the particular features of a culture founded in ambitious, progressive, restless individualism. "When the peasants of the Dark Ages had nothing to do," Sir Edward had suggested, "nothing is exactly what they did. What we call boredom they must have called bliss, for the sensation of having nothing to do must have been an infinitely precious release from their daily round of labor and their eternal riot of discomfort. What other Heaven could they imagine but a Heaven of emptiness, given that their unenlightened minds had not the visionary force to dress the world with bright delights? Unrepentantly illiterate, they had no medium of communication capable of fostering the habits of private thought, and had not the means to live an inner life. For all their latent intelligence and technical skills, such men must have lacked all but a few of the aspects of what you and I think of as *human nature*. When modern men try, imaginatively, to place themselves in the shoes of their remote ancestors they are guilty of an anthropomorphic folly." It was, of course, one more way of saying *all history is fantasy*. All her grandfather's cleverest arguments tended to come, in the end, to that dictum. By slow degrees it had driven all the other bees out of his once-busy bonnet.

"So boredom and the sense of beauty are evidence of our mental advancement?" she had said at the time, knowing even then that he had some further rhetorical ploy up his sleeve.

"That's only one way of looking at it," he had replied. "The whole evolutionary history of man is a gradual exaggeration of neoteny—which means, of course, the preservation of traits associated with immaturity into adulthood. The Medieval peasant who knew neither boredom nor beauty was actually more mature than we are; he had shed a greater part of his childish innocence. In a sense, therefore, our so-called advancement is a kind of enhanced infantilism. If it were not for the threat of boredom and the lure of beauty, we could not take such heady pleasure in the vexed and difficult business of living and learning, growing and wondering.''

But this, Nell now thought, *is the Underworld: the world beyond life. Here, if anywhere, we have our chance to become truly mature, properly finished. Perhaps I am in the process of becoming more fully human—more fully human than anyone ever can be who is doomed to die at threescore years and ten.*

Although she could not turn her head toward him, Nell could see Hades out of the corner of her eye. He too was unmoving, but it did seem to her that the expression on his face was subject to subtle changes. From the very beginning he seemed thoughtful, anxious, sorrowful and generally troubled, but as time went by it seemed that these implications became more exaggerated, more deeply engraved upon his stony features. She suspected that even though he appeared to be snug and safe here in this ultimate bunker, he was incapable of any release from the war in which he was engaged.

She had no idea what the expression on her own face was.

Freedom from tedium was not the only unexpected mercy which Nell came to enjoy during her long sojourn in the Underworld. The anticipated curse of loneliness also failed to affect her in any marked degree. She had always thought of the human animal as an essentially gregarious being, and would have nominated eternal loneliness as a kind of Hell had anyone asked her for a list of unbearable torments, but in the event she came to find isolation rather congenial. She observed the companies of shades which were occasionally visible in the distance without regretting their reluctance to approach. Her curiosity was sometimes teased when an unusually large crowd came into view, filling the twilit horizon completely and conspicuously, but she never felt regretful about her inability to leave her throne. She deduced from the existence of such hosts that it was possible for millions to die on earth in the space of a few fleeting hours, but there was no real sense of amazement or tragedy in the conclusion.

When, after an immeasurable lapse of time, the crowds of shades thinned out, and eventually disappeared, she was neither alarmed nor distressed.

Having attained the terminal state of patience and reconciliation which, she supposed, all the immortal dead must eventually achieve, she was by no means delighted when she ceased to give voice to words she could not hear. When she found that she was free to move again, and to speak on her own behalf, she did not know what to do or what to say.

She was initially incapable of any motivation whatsoever, but in the same way that she had adapted in time to her condition as a helpless medium of communication she adapted herself by slow degrees to self-repossession. She slowly formed the desire to ask a question—*any* question—of her captor and erstwhile partner, and eventually selected one.

"Why do none of the shades ever come near to the Seat of Judgment?" she asked. "Is not the whole purpose of the Lord of the Underworld to call men to account for the sins which they committed while they were alive?"

"The majority of men have long since ceased to believe in the divine right of kings and other overlords," he told her sadly. "Most have withdrawn their consent to be judged by anyone. As for the rest—let them judge one another. Why should I be required to do it? I have my own concerns. There are more than enough members of their company avid to do the job in my place, and I am perfectly happy to let them."

"I doubt that they do a good job," Nell told him wryly. "In my experience, the men who are most anxious to serve as judges are those least likely to deal justly and humanely with their fellows."

"Should I care about that?" Hades demanded witheringly.

"Perhaps you should," Nell answered. "You're not a real god, and you're only an angel by virtue of our inability to discover a better label, but still you have the power to determine the fates of men. Perhaps that power would carry no corollary responsibility if you had not chosen to intervene in the affairs of humankind, but you *have* taken a hand in those affairs, and ought in consequence to accept a certain moral obligation."

"Your father and your grandfather asked nothing of us but to be let alone," Hades pointed out. "It was Jacob Harkender who demanded that because we could be gods we *should* be gods—guided, of course, in the arts and measures of godhood by no less a counsellor than himself. Do you take his side now?"

"No," said Nell. "But I do say this: for your own reasons, which I don't pretend to have fathomed, you've interfered in the history of humankind; you have a duty, it seems to me, to make sure that the result of your interference is to leave humankind no worse off than it would have been had you not interfered.''

"You make it sound very simple," Hades said.

"It is—in principle," she replied. "In practice, I admit, it might provide a very knotty problem."

"Less knotty than you might think, as things have turned out," he said cryptically.

"Do you not feel that you owe us *something*?" she asked. "We are useful to you, are we not? With our aid, you are able to pursue some end which you could not reach without us—and for some of your projects, at least, you need our consent, our willing co-operation. Are we not entitled to expect some *quid pro quo*?"

"There is a certain justice in your claim," he admitted. "We *can* understand the elementary principles of justice. But it is sometimes difficult to be grateful to a messenger who brings such bad news."

As these words were communicated, Nell felt an odd thrill of sensation—which was all the odder because she had almost forgotten what sensation was. It seemed that there was a deeper chill in the air, a deeper darkness in the somber twilight.

"Is the news bad?" she asked, awkwardly conscious of having been the innocent deliverer of the most recent, and perhaps most vital, news which the angels had received from humankind. But how could he hold that against her, when she had not been able to hear what it was that she had said?

"Yes," he said sorrowfully. "The news is bad. It always is bad. I had forgotten, but I remember now. I dare say your grandfather would never have accepted it, but there really are things it is better not to know."

"Is it *all* bad?" she asked. She was genuinely concerned on his behalf. Was he not her only companion, her only friend, her only protector? Should she not be terrified at the thought of his loss, his peril, perhaps his extinction?

"No," he said, "not all. The awareness that one must die, and must be less than one desired to be while one lives, is inevitably tempered by the extra edge it lends to the experience of life. Human life, human hope and human pain have a certain . . . shall I call it a *piquant taste*? It is, alas, something that can only be experienced from without, and you are always within. We are not entirely incapable of empathy, nor of pathos, nor of a sense of tragedy; perhaps it would be better if we were. But we are what we are. It's not your fault that the news is, at bottom, bad. Those who desire to hear the music of the spheres have no alternative but to hear it as it is; it would be foolish to complain about the quality of the composition.''

"The music of the spheres?'' she queried. "Is that what I have been relaying to you? You might have found a better Orpheus— I never learned to play an instrument, and have no singing voice at all.''

She stepped down from the throne, and went to stand before the angel, so that she could look him directly in the face. It was, she knew, a borrowed or invented face, but it was still *his* face, and no one else's.

Tears were visible at the corners of his eyes. It seemed to Nell that they were not tears of pain but emotional tears.

"The story of Orpheus was a wonderful invention,'' said Hades, "but it was all hope, all folly. If only it could have been true, what a Golden Age men and angels might have made together! Alas, you cannot begin to imagine how little harmony there is in the world which we inhabit, and how incredibly difficult it would be to bring the smallest measure of harmony into it.''

"I'm sorry,'' she said. "I truly am.''

"I know you are,'' he replied. "So am I. I say again, we are *not* incapable of sympathy and generosity. Our gratitude will last for a little while yet. Trust me, Nell—the carnival of destruction will pass you by, for now. I can promise you that much. I honestly wish that I could promise more, but time is against me and I cannot long maintain this mask.''

"I don't understand,'' she said.

No explanation was forthcoming. Hades simply raised an arm to point into the wasteland behind her. She turned to follow the direction of his finger. Another shade was coming toward the throne of Hades: a single shade, alone in the vast and desolate landscape. She did not immediately recognize the person whose ghost it was, but when he was close enough to reach out a hand to her she saw that it was Anatole Daumier. He looked much older than when she had last seen him, and perhaps a little wiser.

"Come with me, Nell,'' he said. His English was as quaintly accented as ever.

She did not immediately take the proffered hand. Instead, she looked back at the false and purposeless god who sat on the imagined throne of an empty empire.

"Was it worth it?'' she said, knowing that she would be allowed no more questions after this.

"It was worth it," he told her, "for the living and the learning, the growing and the wondering. It was worth it for the *beauty*. But it's over now; there's only one way to resist the destroyer, only one road that can lead the likes of angels to any kind of Heaven."

The form which had been Hades changed, and became female. The woman he became seemed to be much younger than Nell, and would have been far more beautiful in the flesh. Nell easily guessed that she was Anatole Daumier's vision of the Maid of Orléans, and that whatever else the angel had to say would be addressed to him.

The Maid had not much else to say. As Anatole's hand closed upon Nell's, imperiously claiming the authority to determine her immediate future, the lonely figure on the decaying throne was overcome by what seemed to be a tremor of absolute anguish. It seemed to require a superhuman effort for her to form just three short words before she dissolved into sinister shadow.

"Don't look back," she said.

Nell had not the slightest idea whether the words were meant literally or metaphorically—or whether, in her present condition, there was any sense at all in trying to draw a distinction.

2

It seemed to David that he passed easily from one unearthly dream into another. It was as if his consciousness, disembodied for an interval which might have been a few hours or a few centuries, was abruptly and cunningly decanted into a new vessel. He knew before he opened his eyes that his form was human, and that it had every semblance of solidity, but he did not doubt for an instant that he was still dreaming. This was not the body which had provided his habitation at World's End; nor was it a replication of any body he had ever possessed in his youth. It was not merely pain-free but possessed by an altogether unnatural and impossible sense of well-being, and it felt as if it were no heavier than an air-filled balloon.

Better an illusion as kind as this, he told himself, *than a reality as unkind as the one I left behind. Even if I were truly to wake up I could never be sure that I had not simply slid into a new phase of the unfolding nightmare. There is every reason to be grateful for a dream of pleasant sensation, and every reason to savor it to the full. I must not compromise the gift by too strenuous an exertion of the levers of skepticism.*

He opened his eyes, and found that he was lying on his back in a narrow bed, in a narrow room which had no furniture except a second bed: a platform jutting from the wall, devoid of mattress or blankets or any attachment save for a dangling strap. The bed was empty, but the man standing awkwardly beside it could not long have risen from it.

Not such a pleasant dream after all, he lamented. *It seems that I am doomed to inhabit yet another of the angels' caricature-environ-*

359

ments, and that the company in which I must take my place is de-
signed for disputation rather than congeniality.

The other man was Jacob Harkender. He was as young and handsome as ever, although he was very lightly dressed in what looked
absurdly like a suit of underclothes. He had watched David carefully,
evidently having anticipated the moment of his awakening.

"Welcome back to the real world," he said, with affected casualness. How typical it was of the man to greet his enemy with a
lightly ironic jest!

David tried to sit up, but could not do it. The effect of the frus-
trated action was very peculiar, filling his unfamiliar body with unprecedented sensations. He found that he was being held down by a
strap exactly similar to the one which dangled from the other bed.

"You must be careful," Harkender told him, revelling in his advantage although he probably had not had more than a few moments
to acclimatize himself to this perverse dream-arena. "We have very
little weight here, but collisions can hurt. Be very careful in your
movements once you have released the strap."

The catch holding the strap was of a kind David had never seen
before, but it was a simple mechanism and he released it easily
enough. He did indeed seem to be virtually weightless, and he clung
on to the bed as he maneuvered himself into a sitting position. He
was dressed in the same absurd manner as Harkender. He looked
around, not wanting to give the other man the pleasure of explaining
anything that he might observe for himself.

The walls of the room had a uniform metallic sheen, but were
multi-colored and haphazardly decorated with abstract designs. The
wall above each bed had several blank screens inset into it, each
with a control panel to the right hand side. There was only one door,
which had no handle or any other obvious mechanism by which it
might be opened. The uncarpeted floor was very slightly curved, as
though it formed part of the arc of a vast circle. The light that filled
the room was diffuse, tinted with just the lightest hint of yellow. A
single rounded window some three feet across was set in the wall
opposite the door. It looked out on to a field of darkness spangled
with innumerable stars.

Although he had never seen anything remotely like it, none of this
seemed of much immediate consequence to David. It was, after all,
mere illusion—and in any case, his mind was preoccupied with unexpected internal sensations. He felt possessed by a grotesquely exaggerated awareness of his own corporeality. He had not the slightest

difficulty in hearing the pounding of his heart and the susurrus of blood in the veins close to his ears and the oceanic stirrings of his unhungry gut.

When he tried to stand up the tentative force which he exerted with his feet was sufficient to propel him forward much more hurriedly than he had hoped. He managed to avoid Harkender but when he impacted with the windowed wall the force of the collision shook him from top to toe, and made him gasp with shock—but the pain faded very quickly, and was soon gone. He was able to make himself still again, but he had to cling hard to the narrow ledge beneath the window in order to keep himself steady.

A reflection in the window confirmed that his appearance in this world had been completely rejuvenated. His face was recognizable as his own, but his skin was smooth and unblemished and he had the appearance of a man of twenty-five.

The panorama of stars which he could see behind his phantasmal image informed him that this imaginary locale was not supposed to be located on the Earth, nor on any world with an atmosphere. It was somewhere out in the wilderness of space, presumably within some structure far too tiny to reproduce the Earth's gravity.

He was pleased with himself for being capable of these deductions. All angelically inspired dreams were, in a sense, puzzles to be unraveled, riddles to be solved. He knew that the most significant question about the present stage was not "Where am I supposed to be?" but "*When* am I supposed to be?" He looked at his companion, spitefully hoping that Harkender had no more idea than he.

"The angels never cease to surprise me," he said sourly. "I would have thought that they could have designed a more convenient space to hear our reports on the revelations of the oracle."

"Is *that* what you think this is?" said Harkender, with a calculated disdain which David took to be false. "I doubt that they require to hear *reports*. I think they know by now what we discovered on their behalf. I only wish they had been bolder and cleverer in planning our enquiries."

The door opened before David could formulate any retort. It slid noiselessly back into a hidden cavity to one side. The man who came in, moving with what looked like practiced ease, looked similar to the Clay Man but not so very similar as to be mistaken for him. Had he been a real human being he might have passed for the Clay Man's brother—or, if the Clay Man's last appearance were taken as a benchmark, his son.

"I am Machalalel," the newcomer said, as if he expected the news to cause astonishment.

"Of course," David said, with reflexive irony. "I knew you immediately. We have met before."

"Not like this," the other said. "This is not a mask, nor an apparition, nor am I a possessive spirit speaking through a golem. I am Machalalel. The Age of Miracles is dead and gone."

This was a peculiar speech, but David was well used to the fact that characters in dreams did not always speak in readily comprehensible ways. "I don't understand," he said acidly.

"I think he means," Harkender said, so carefully that it had to be a deduction, not something he had previously known, "that he is all that is left of Machalalel. He means that the entity which was once an angel—the least of the angels—has decided to become material, and nothing but material. It seems that Jason Sterling was not so ludicrously mistaken after all." His tone of voice suggested that he did not approve.

David still did not understand, but refused to say so. *Concentrate on the pleasantness of inner sensation,* he advised himself. *This is a good dream. There is enough in it to render it enjoyable. You have done your duty in regard to fierce concentration and deduction; relax now and let the imagery drift by.*

"The choice was made under the spur of necessity," Machalalel said evenly. "I have studied human beings for a long time, but I never learned to love them. I understood only too well, though, how close I was to extinction. There are no rules, you see, in the conflict of angels, and hence no cunning strategies by which the weak might overturn the strong. In spite of all your scepticism, Jacob—for which I am properly grateful—this seemed the preferable alternative, for all of us."

"*All* the angels have become human?" David said incredulously. *This is a dream indeed!* he thought. *This is naked wish-fulfillment.*

Machalalel smiled, very faintly. "Of course not," he said. "I mean all of *us.* All that remains of *human*kind. Jacob played his part in the oracle far too well even to tempt my erstwhile brethren. I am glad of it—had any other followed my example, this might not have qualified as an escape."

"This was not the end I sought to reach," Harkender said bitterly.

"Of course not," Machalalel said. "You sought an escape in the opposite direction, for yourself at least—but no such escape was ever possible. David proved that. He will explain it to you, if you care to ask.''

Harkender clearly did *not* care to ask, at least for the present. David was not sorry, because he did not believe for a moment that he could provide the requisite explanation. "You have *chosen* to become incarnate?" he said. "You have undergone an irreversible metamorphosis into human form? Is *that* why the angels took an interest in human affairs? To decide whether or not they ought to remake themselves in *our image*?"

"Not at all," said Machalalel, turning away from Harkender to face David, exposing the melancholy gray of his eyes. "The primary purpose of the oracle was rather more banal. It was a means by which we hoped to understand ourselves, and to understand the possibilities which the future held for us—which is, in essence, the same thing. You played your part as well as Jacob played his, David, with Anatole as your imaginative counterweight. You have a fine sense of beauty to direct your sight. I doubt that we have ever encountered better, although it is very difficult to be sure. We have problems with memory, as you now understand. My adversaries will soon have forgotten everything. They will no longer be angels—they will be what they *truly* are, and must remain."

"Then what on earth was it all *for*?" David complained, wondering what the hidden meaning of this conversation might be. "If your erstwhile companions will forget what they have learned as soon as they cease to parasitise our ephemeral intelligence, what has *anyone* gained?"

"*You* have gained the gratitude of an angel," Machalalel said. "You should not despise that, no matter how much trouble you have suffered in winning it."

"We helped you to design a bolt-hole to escape the endless war," Harkender said, "and you have graciously preserved us in order that we might share it. Is that really gratitude, or simply fear of loneliness?"

"We cannot escape the endless war," Machalalel answered mildly. "It is everywhere; it is existence itself. We may designate ourselves as non-combatants, and hide as best we can from its turmoil, but it goes on regardless and we can have no possible guarantee of long-term survival. We could be annihilated at any moment by forces beyond our control. It is no different for the creatures which were briefly appointed to be angels. That is the lesson which you taught them so cleverly—or at least recalled to their fugitive minds. Their world, in its entirety, could be destroyed just as easily as the planet where men once dwelt.''

The last words, spoken so very casually, reminded David of the first question he had thought relevant to the deciphering of the dream, implying an answer that would have been horrific had all this been real.

"What year is this supposed to be?" he asked. "Into what era have you pretended to awaken us?"

Machalalel's calmness seemed contemptuous in itself, although there was no trace of malice in his eye and no trace of venom in his voice.

"There is no supposition in it, and no pretense," he said. "This is not a dream, David. This is a real place, securely present in the world of matter, not some phantom planted in your mind or a borderland like Zelophelon's mock-Hell or Hecate's false Eden. From now on, David, there will be no more magical dreams and no more miraculous interventions in the world of matter. All this is real."

David glanced at his ghostly reflection in the window. Even that small movement made his feather-light body giddy. Real! Was it not the dearest desire of every figment of a dream to claim reality, thus to establish its illusion as the basal reference point of all experience?

"Very well," he said, not trying too hard to mask his insincerity. "I will rephrase the question. What year is this, into which you have kindly awakened us?"

Machalalel smiled, in apparent acknowledgment of the irony of David's concession. "Were there any men awake to count," he said, "they would reckon this the thirty-fourth century after the supposed birth of that other incarnate angel. The oracle in which you recently took part, unlike the first to which you contributed, was by no means momentary; it lasted longer than a thousand years. The angels dwell in time, as you do, and their explorations must proceed at a measured pace. All life on earth is extinct, alas, but one tiny atom of community survives and it is that which will provide our refuge. The human story is not yet concluded, and we have a part to play in carrying it forward."

"*All* life on earth is extinct, you say?" Harkender challenged him.

"All," Machalalel confirmed. "The human species and many others were extinguished by the war that finally ended war, and the thousands of species which survived that devastation were destroyed several hundred years later when the earth collided with a wayward asteroid. The impact of the collision cracked the planet's crust, re-

leasing vast floods of molten magma whose heat sterilized the biosphere. At present the world is nothing but a cinder. Given a billion
years or so, it could be reseeded and renewed, but that is of no
relevance to us.''

''Is it not?'' asked David sarcastically. ''Are we immortal, now?''

Machalalel addressed the question with perfect seriousness. ''The
kind of immortality the werewolves had, and the kind of miracle
which brought about your own incarnation, are no longer possible,''
he said. ''While the angels were everywhere it was not so very
difficult to build bridges between minds, or to conserve minds when
bodies were smashed or burned, until they had been regenerated, but
the last of those bridges is broken now. We three and all the others
here have emortality—which is to say that our bodies will not age
and have inbuilt defenses against all diseases—but we can be destroyed. Should you or I have the misfortune to die here no friendly
angel will be on hand to bring us back from the dead. We must be
careful now. With luck, we might live for a very long time, but
not forever.''

''Where have the angels gone?'' David asked, although he knew
as soon as the words had escaped that it was a foolish question.

''It is not a matter of *where*,'' Machalalel said, as though stating
the obvious. ''You know what they had to do, in order to resist the
destroyer, for it was you who revealed and explained it to us. The
conflict goes on. Our present environment will not long remain constant, no matter how placid it seems now, but we have a firm and
trustworthy promise that this tiny atom will be left in no-man's-land,
unharmed and unspoilt. When the coming battle is over there will
be time enough for us to flourish after our modest fashion, even
though the war will go on eternally.''

When Machalalel said ''our present environment'' he moved his
right hand, almost negligently, to point to the wilderness of stars
which filled the vistas spread before the huge window. David looked
out, reminding himself how deceptive such images were. The light
which arrived from the nearest of those stars had been travelling for
years; the light arriving from the faintest nebulae had been travelling
since the dawn of time. The stillness and consistency of what he saw
with his feeble human eyesight was an artefact of his own in-
adequacy.

Six angels, he knew, had power enough to rip that whole picture
apart, even if it were in fact the reality of the material world—and,
if they were disposed to do it, would neither hesitate nor feel the

slightest pang of regret. But that seemed irrelevant. What was going on *here*? What was the purpose of this new phase of the oracular dream? What could the angels possibly want from him, now that he had penetrated their secrets to the extent of knowing what kind of beings they were?

For the first time, he wondered whether this might not be a dream after all, no matter how absurd it all seemed. Perhaps, in either case, he ought to pretend that it was real, and act as if it were. Suppose that the revelation which he had vouchsafed to the angels really had persuaded them that the only way to resist the depredations of the mysterious seventh—the destroyer—was to sever all contact with humankind. Suppose that one of the six, Machalalel, really had reached the conclusion that its only chance of any kind of survival lay in becoming incarnate—having obtained some kind of safety warrant from its erstwhile companions. It was not entirely unthinkable—one thing he had learned in the course of the oracle was that the angels were cowards all. It was not impossible to believe that when the present crisis in their affairs was over, and a precarious balance restored, they would all retreat to lick their metaphorical wounds. It made sense. As a *story,* at least, it made sense, and if the dream dictated that this was now to be the narrative of his life, the fable in which he must exist, should he not be prepared to participate fully in its unfolding?

How many times, he wondered, *has this happened before? How many times might it happen again? Can anything fundamental ever change, in the dream, or in the actual universe?*

The answer to the last question, he knew, was *yes.* In time, anything and everything could change—but for the moment, the news was all bad. Dream or reality, the carnival of destruction would go on, and on, and on.

If I had but one wish, he thought, *it would be to live in a world—in a universe—where there could be no such things as the entities we have called angels, in which a man could always know for certain that he was awake, and that his choices really mattered.*

He found that he had a single tear in the corner of his eye. He was appalled by the discovery that he could shed no more, even in a dream, for the fate of his world and all the teeming life to which it had once played host. *I have learned angelic indifference,* he lamented silently. *I am so far lost within the maze of myself that I can no longer connect myself to any exterior world, real or imaginary.*

"What is this place?" he asked. "How many people are here?"

"We are a station built in the interior of a hollowed-out plane-toid," Machalalel told him. "It had another name before men first came here, but those who were left when the earth was destroyed renamed it Pandora—it was, I suppose, a bitter joke. It is now home to seventy people, and an unimaginably numerous host of clever machines."

"Shall we go to meet the others now?" David asked, feeling suddenly claustrophobic, as if the narrow walls had drawn in around him while he clung to the window-ledge for fear of floating away. He remembered a throwaway remark his father-in-law had once made to Nell, to the effect that Hell might consist of being locked in a narrow room for all eternity with all the people one had ever loved.

"Unfortunately," said Machalalel, "that will not be possible. There is one awkward problem, you see, which no preparatory mira-cle could have overcome. If we are to live for a very long time—as I think we must, if we are to find any kind of permanent refuge—there are certain sacrifices we have to make."

Of course, David thought. *We are living a legend now, are we not? We are prisoners in a mythical tale, in which many secret meanings are hidden. We have studied our reflection in the mirrored walls of the universe, and have visited the denouements of time itself. How could there not be conditions and sacrifices and fateful warn-ings? We are fallen heroes now, living amid the decadent ruins of the age of fool's gold, waiting for an age of enlightenment which can never arrive.*

"You had better explain everything," he said, wearily contenting himself with the duty of having to listen.

3

Machalalel explained, in leisurely fashion, that the station in which the chief participants in the oracle were now reincarnated had been built in the last few years before the self-immolation of that part of the human race which dwelt on the planet's surface. The people who had built it had feared that the final war was coming, and had made what preparations they could, but they had known that they could not long maintain the kind of life they were used to living.

The architects of the station had emortality, by virtue of swarms of tiny machines which dwelt within their bodies, assisting the innate processes of self-repair, but they nevertheless remained creatures of the flux, requiring a constant input of energy to maintain them against the ravages of entropy. They had the means to harvest the energy of the sun, even at a relatively remote distance, and they could recycle almost all the water and the greater part of the organic and inorganic materials they used, but without constant sources of supply they could not meet their needs indefinitely. The station had been established with a view to its becoming the kernel of an independent and self-sustaining colony, but the scheme was in its infancy when the last war came; the resources were simply not in place for the station to become a self-sufficient world in its own right.

The occupants of the station had a clear view of their predicament. They had the means to move the planetoid, but very slowly. Any journey which it undertook within the solar system would take years; any journey without would take centuries. The meager harvest of energy and materials which they were able to reap from their immediate environment was inadequate to sustain the kind of life which they were leading, but they had another recourse. They had been engaged in the development of a technology of suspended animation, which they had intended to use in equipping starships which would set forth from the solar system to explore the worlds orbiting other suns. They had developed a means of reducing the metabolic rate of their bodies very considerably: a kind of artificial hibernation. By this means they could reduce the energy requirements of their bodies to a minimum, while maintaining essential processes of cell-repair and cell-replacement. In effect, they had a technology which could greatly extend their lives, while greatly reducing the demands they placed on their environment—but the cost of its use was that all but a few of them must remain permanently asleep.

"The crew of the station drew lots for the right to occupy the available life-support chambers, which numbered sixty-nine," Machalalel told David and Harkender. "The remaining personnel did everything possible to ensure that all would be well for the sleepers. All but seven then committed suicide, leaving the remainder to take charge of the movement of the station and the scavenging of further supplies. Their calculations suggested that the life-expectancy of the sleepers would average several thousand years, although some lives would certainly be lost much earlier and a few might exceed that by an order of magnitude.

"The remaining crew members originally intended to exchange places at regular intervals with the sleepers. They hoped that they would be efficient enough in their scavenging not only to maintain themselves but gradually to accumulate a heritage of wealth, but these hopes were futile. They could not go to the one place which might have provided an abundance of useful raw materials—the surface of the earth—because they had no way of transporting themselves back and forth, nor could they visit any other body of very considerable mass. Their equipment was inadequate and their number too few for them to do anything effective, even though they had so much time in hand that it seemed limitless. They could not agree among themselves as to the wisdom of leaving the solar system behind and setting forth on the long voyage to another star, and never did.

"The history of the seven who remained awake continued to follow the pattern set by all previous human history. Their quarrels grew gradually worse. They left no record of their individual fates for us to read, but in the course of a few decades their number was steadily reduced by murder and suicide. A few others must have been awakened in order to maintain their numbers for a while—several of the life-support chambers were empty when I came here—but they must have come to the conclusion that such a policy was self-defeating. The waking crew-members accepted the rate of attrition, even when it reduced their numbers to two, then to one, and eventually to zero.

"The remaining sleepers were safe and comfortable, and could have remained so for a very long time, but with no one to wake them they would eventually have died, one by one, never knowing that the station no longer had any active crew or any hopeful destination. Had I not needed a refuge of some sort their only hope of release would have been that visitors from some other solar system might arrive here and find them. You and I, David, know how very forlorn that hope was."

What a pretty parable, David thought. *Seven human beings instead of seven angels, damned by their inability to put aside their petty disputes and live together. What other end could the likes of Machalalel possibly imagine for their humble instruments? So this is the way the human world is destined to end—or would have been, had it not been for the other war and the oracle its warriors made. What a delicate picture to paint upon the fantastic stage of history: Humankind reduced to a mere handful of patient dreamers, waiting quietly and purposelessly for a rescue which can never come. What would the Clay Man have called this, had he ever had the chance to complete his second true history of the human world? The Age of Dreams? The Age of Eternal Peace? How would the sphinx have incorporated this culmination into her ever-evolving riddle whose answer was always "Man?" What is it that begins life dreamless in a womb designed by nature, and returns in the end to a womb designed by a far more cunning architect, having only briefly awakened to walk upon the surface of the good earth, and having recklessly indulged that pride which inevitably leads to self-destruction?*

Jacob Harkender seemed to have been thinking along a very different line. "How many of the chambers remained for *your* use?" he asked. "Or had you no scruples regarding the dispossession of the living?"

"There was accommodation enough for those who stood in my debt," the fallen angel replied. "The Clay Man is there, and Pelorus, and Mandorla. Anatole Daumier is there too, and Nell Lydyard with him, in answer to a promise made by another."

"What about Sterling?" Harkender asked. "It would seem churlish to exclude him, given that you seem to have ranked his Heaven far above the rest in designing your conclusion."

"No," said Machalalel. "Not Sterling. It is too late for you to plead on his behalf, alas; I have no more magic now. Hecate is here, awake—she is the only other not presently asleep—but she is as merely human as the rest of us. There are two chambers still unoccupied; we must somehow decide between the four of us which of us will stay awake, and with what purpose. I shall, of course, take charge of this little world, and I dare to hope that more than one of you might condescend to keep me company—but if none of you wishes to do so, an exchange of places with one of the sleepers would be easy enough to arrange. You insult me, though, with your accusation that I *designed* this conclusion. It was designed by a fate in which I had no hand; we are here because there really is no alternative refuge."

"It seems to me that the dead have the better parts in this shabby melodrama," said Harkender contemptuously. "What purpose can there possibly be in living for a thousand years—or ten thousand— cradled and asleep? And what purpose can there be in remaining awake to nurse an army of patient sleepers, with nowhere to go, nothing to do and company as dull as this?"

Dull, am I? David thought. *Well, perhaps—but he did not even ask after Cordelia! I can hardly believe that he could be so callous, even as a figment of my dream.*

"The body which you have is quite robust, thanks to the ingenious machines which crowd its interior," the fallen angel told him, equably. "It might endure thousands of years awake, perhaps a million asleep. A great deal might happen in a million years. If nothing else, a man might enjoy a plethora of pleasant dreams."

"Or nightmares," Harkender retorted.

David could not keep up with this deluge of information concerning an incredible adventure in an impossible world. He was too far removed from the work into which he had been born, and in which he had almost served the full terms of his allotted threescore years and ten. This fantasy was far too alien and far too peculiar to make much sense. It was not easy to find a sensible point of contact to grasp, or a thread of meaning with which to forge a connection. Unlike his odyssey to the limits of space and time, this was a venture into some absurd realm which lay beyond life, beyond sense and beyond intelligence. However solid the walls of this world might seem to his dream-persona, it had no ring of authenticity. For the moment, he could not follow the intricacies of the situation that was being described to him, nor could he writhe on the horns of the dilemma which was being extended like a snare to catch and confuse him.

I too might be reckoned an incarnate angel fallen out of Heaven, he thought. *I suppose that I have lost all hope or opportunity of making any further distinction between waking and dreaming, reality and fantasy. For Machalalel, the adventure of incarnation would be simply one more magical move in a career which had always followed the logic of dreams, so he can play his part with enthusiasm regardless of all the implausibilities in this fantasy which he is trying to pass off as human history. I wonder—can there any longer be any essential difference, for one such as me, between real and virtual worlds, between the material and the imaginary, between the bruising experiences of the flesh and the phantom caprices of the sleeping soul?*

He said nothing aloud, content for the time being to let the figment of his dream which masqueraded as Jacob Harkender do the talking.

"I cannot believe that you have brought us to this," Harkender said vitriolically. "It beggars the imagination that you studied the human species far longer, and more cleverly, than any others of your kind, and could make no more of destiny than *this*. Could you not have saved the earth, if you intended to be human? How great a miracle would it have required for you to stifle the destructive power of war, or to deflect the asteroid which crashed into the planet?"

"Not so very great," Machalalel admitted mildly. "Perhaps we could have prevented the war which eventually consumed the earth, if we had only seen reason enough to interfere. We could indeed have deflected the asteroid which destroyed the life which remained—but we did not foresee the collision, and although we can play certain tricks with time, one thing we cannot do is turn back the clock to unwind the chain of cause and effect. I repeat that I did not *contrive* this end; nor did any other of my erstwhile kind. At the worst, we simply stood aside and let it happen. If you had only been able to show us a reason for doing so, we might have extended sufficient protection to humankind to have permitted a better kind of survival, but you could not. You and David were collaborators in the oracle we made; if we found no reason there to act in favor of your fellow men, perhaps you should look to yourselves for an explanation of that failure."

So this is the Day of Judgment after all, David thought. *The aveng-*

ing angel calls us to account for all our sins of action and omission, and asks us: Why did you not save your race and your planet? Why did you not succeed in persuading us that you were worth moving heaven and earth to save? Why were you not cleverer, braver, more virtuous? Why were you not gods, capable of using the powers of angelic sight for the benefit of those you loved? Why were you Satan pinned to the floor of Hell? Why were you a prisoner in Plato's cave, so utterly accustomed to shadows and firelight that the true light only blinded you? Why were you stupid, confused and merely human?

What can we possibly reply, but guilty! guilty! guilty! Have we not been punished enough already?

"Why have you brought us here to share your fate?" David asked, innocently enough. "Have we not served our purpose, like the poor half-men you made to be your agents? Why did you not simply throw us away, dissolving our borrowed angelic consciousness into the empty darkness of the void?"

"My long acquaintance with the human mind has taught me the meaning of gratitude," Machalalel said.

"And the meaning of solitude," said Harkender with naked disgust. "You have not yet abandoned *all* hope of performing as a petty god, it seems. I am only surprised that you have left your former slaves asleep while you let Lydyard and myself have our say. You surely know what to expect of us."

"You are not required to be grateful in return," Machalel said, with an all-too-human shrug of his shoulders, "but this is what is left of the world of men, and we must live in it as best we can, if we are to live at all." Having said this, he turned and went out through the door which had admitted him. It slid shut behind him, smoothly and soundlessly, with all the deft efficiency expectable in a device of the imagination.

"It seems," Harkender said to David, without any evident awkwardness, "that the kind of gratitude he has learned is the kind which princes have. It is understandable, I suppose, that a demigod who decides to become a man would become the kind of man who thinks of himself as a demigod."

"I wonder, then," said David, "that he chose to wear the Clay Man's face, and not your own. Or are you really Zelophelon in disguise?"

Harkender smiled, as though the sarcasm were an unexpected compliment. "If only you had come to me at Whittenton when I first invited you,'' he said, with a calculated sigh, ''we might have become friends. If we had only been able to combine our resources, we might have become a force to be reckoned with in this sad affair. I never meant to do you harm, David. You can never believe it, I know, but I loved your wife more fervently than you, and she never ceased to love you even though she loved me more. I am sorry to have lost her.''

David felt tears rising irresistibly into his eyes—more tears by far than he had shed for the human race considered in its entirety—and was too ashamed to show them. He turned away, but he knew that turning would not suffice to hide his shame, and he quickly pushed himself away from the window, with a reckless disregard for his inability to deal with the alien conditions. The door opened as he approached it, and somehow, he passed through it without hurting himself.

It slid shut behind him, as cleverly as it had before.

4

The station was huge, empty and seemingly quite dead. David had not imagined, before leaving the room from which the stars could be seen, how large the artefact that now confined him might be. He could not have begun to imagine how claustrophobic and desolate a thing of multicolored metal and glossy plastic could be. He wandered for hours, slowly getting used to the tiny weight which his lumpen body now possessed, without coming across another window, or anything which moved or glowed, and without encountering a single speck of dust. He could not help comparing and contrasting the experience with one of the most persistent of the recurrent dreams with which his guardian angel had afflicted him in former times: a dream in which he had wandered through the mazy corridors of an ancient house containing an implausible number of mirrors and clocks. In that place there had been dust everywhere; the very air had been thick with it.

Throughout his life David had estimated the age of neglected human artefacts by measuring the progress of recognizable processes of decay and infestation: by the accumulation of dirt, by the softening of rot, by the decoration of cobwebs—but none of that was applicable here. Everything remained perfectly clean, solid and bright. No vermin had ever taken refuge in these walls, which were devoid of nooks and crannies, and there had never been a spider here to spin a futile web. Here, it seemed, human artifice had at last won free of the endless and arduous battle which it had had to fight on the surface of the earth. There was neither wind nor water to erode the designs of the human hand, which retained their virtue long after their desertion by the living.

In the recurrent dream of his true youth David had passed from the infinite house into a landscape of Cyclopean ruins, over which he had flown by miraculous means until he reached the pyramid where Bast—sometimes green-eyed and sometimes amber-eyed—had waited for him, surrounded by pampered cats. What would it be like, he wondered, to float like a mote of dust above the desert surface of planetoid Pandora, beneath the glorious arch of the Milky Way?

It appeared to David's wandering eyes—which were, by slow degrees, becoming *wondering* eyes again—that every switch and circuit in this hollowed-out worldlet was ready to spring into electrical life, spurring every graceful machine to enthusiastic action; but experiment soon showed that this was an illusion. There was diffuse light everywhere, but there was only light, not movement. The station in all its myriad colors, all its incomprehensible complexity, was like a newly embalmed corpse. Some mysterious central power-source had been damped down to a minimum level of activity, and the vast majority of the switches were dead. Long after he had abandoned hope of achieving any significant effect, however, David continued to flick switches and press buttons. It became a ritual of hopeless interaction, a continuing testament to the fact that he did not belong in a dream of this madly futuristic kind, displaced from his own time and his own heritage.

He knew that in his heart he was a ghost, in spite of the fact that a generous and grateful angel had granted him the delusory reward of superhuman flesh.

There was, David felt, a terrible irony in the fact that he had travelled to the edge of the universe, to the beginning and the ends of time, and returned safely to an exceedingly comfortable prison of imperishable flesh, only to be told that he must go to sleep forever, or spend eternity in a not-so-narrow space with a handful of people whom—with the sole exception of his daughter—he did not even love.

What a marvelous capacity we have, he thought, *for turning dreams to nightmares!*

At times, as his reverie unwound and he began to adapt himself to the parameters of his new situation, he wished that he might have been spared the moment of marvelous sight which had told him how rare a thing life was, and made him realize how extremely unlikely it was that other living beings would ever visit this fantasy to discover the last pathetic remnant of the human race. At other times, though, he could not even regret that. Enlightenment was, after all, enlightenment. He had seen what other men had never had the chance to see—and had not Anatole Daumier been brave and clever and *right,* when given one wish on the point of death, to demand that he be granted *enlightenment*? The truth had to be reckoned precious, and beautiful, however little sweetness it contained.

All my life, David thought, *I have asked that an angel might condescend to meet me face to face, and answer my questions frankly. My wish is granted now, at least in the imagination; Machalalel has condescended to become incarnate, and has offered me all the time in the world to question him. But what can I ask him, now, and what can the answers matter? What possible significance is there in any explanations he might give me? Does he understand any more than I do, given that I was the one who told the angels what they needed, but did not want, to know?*

It was not Machalalel he met, eventually, but Hecate. As he passed through a narrow corridor he met her coming the other way. She too seemed to be wandering aimlessly, exploring the last remaining monument to human ingenuity. Her face, although it was as plain as ever, was lit by an inquisitiveness he found strangely touching.

"There is something sad about an empty stage," she said.

"The earth," he observed drily, "is doubtless emptier and sadder."

"Doubtless," she agreed, without any evident distress: "Have you seen Machalalel?"

"Yes. He lodged me with Jacob Harkender in a room which had a window that looked out upon a riotous field of distant stars spread upon the airless void, and came to tell us what that panorama signified. If the earth was visible, I could not tell it apart from all the other feeble and futile points of light."

"He pointed out the earth to me," she said. "I suppose I must have been awake a little longer than you. Have you seen the chambers where the sleeping people are?" she asked. "I have been looking for them, but I have not found them yet."

"No," he said. "I dare say Machalalel will show them to us, in time. He is human now, but he has not done with meddlesome games. If I want Nell awakened, I suppose I must ask his permission—but it might be kinder to let her sleep, and dream her own dreams. This particular fantasy is a poor and tawdry thing, is it not?"

She looked at him strangely, as if she could not fathom the reason for his bitterness. "This is not a dream, David," she told him. "This is the real world. Everything which has happened has happened. Nothing can be undone—not even by magic."

It means nothing, he reminded himself, *that a figment of a dream should claim reality.* But there was doubt nagging at his stomach.

"It is a dream," he insisted.

"There are no more dreams," she told him. "It was *all* real. We are beyond the reach of illusion now."

He thought it best to change the subject.

"Can you be content, do you think, to stay awake for centuries with such companions as Machalalel has provided?" he asked her. "Or will we inevitably fall to fighting, as our predecessors did?"

She understood that the questions were a mere diversion, and did not answer them. "We are both the same now," she said to him, as though it were a matter of considerable wonderment to her. "We are monsters, with nothing but cold darkness in our souls. But we have magic of a kind inside us, apparently. Each of us is a universe, so I am told, full of little mechanical microbes which will labor tirelessly to preserve us and keep us safe. If they were sentient, would they think of us as gods?"

"We are not gods, and cannot hope to be," he told her. "We are what we are, and I see little hope of becoming anything else, even if Machalalel succeeds in piloting this imaginary worldlet across the void to the estates of some other sun. It would be ludicrously optimistic to expect to find a hospitable world there, which we might remodel into a second earth. If we are indeed beyond the reach of magic this must be our terminus, and I cannot see that it matters much whether we spend a hundred years awaiting death, or a thousand—or whether we spend the time awake, or in dream-filled sleep."

"It makes a difference," she pointed out. "All the difference in the world. You cannot say that it does not matter, when it is the only thing which does. In any case, we have more than ludicrous optimism to help us in our quest for a second earth."

"How could we know for certain if, in fact, we were not dreaming now?" he retorted. "We sprang into being fully-formed, as though by some mere trick; are we not fully entitled to reckon our seeming flesh a mere delusion?"

She shrugged her shoulders. "I am certain," she said. "This is Machalalel's drama, and we are playing the parts which he has allotted to us, but it is no mere dream. His is the stagecraft, his the plot, and he alone will dictate the conclusion—the *deus ex machina,* if you will—but we are real, and must operate as independent beings, making our own choices and creating our own opportunities. His kinfolk are done with us for good and all; we have not helped them to avert their orgy of mutual destruction, even if we have helped them to see its armaments and strategies more clearly. Perhaps we have only served to catalyse their own processes of self-immolation—just as they served, after their fashion, to catalyse ours.''

"Perhaps we have," David said, wondering whether it might conceivably be true. "If so, perhaps we can claim not to have lived in vain.''

She did not smile. "I am glad that I was able to participate in the oracle," she said evenly, "even if I contributed little enough to the process of understanding. I am not too proud to be grateful. This may only be a game, but if so, it is better to play than not to play, better to be a pawn than nothing at all. Does it help to be bitter?''

"In much wisdom is much grief," he quoted, "and he that increaseth knowledge increaseth sorrow." But his voice was dispirited rather than bitter, almost apologetic. She was right, of course. He had not the means to be a player in this kind of game, and ought to be grateful for the opportunity to be a significant pawn. Whatever was left of the world, he must live in it as best he could. Was he not heir to the intellectual estate of Sir Edward Tallentyre?

She was right. This was real. Even if it were not, it had to be lived as if it were.

"Why are you afraid?" she asked softly. "You have died a hundred times already, and have endured more than a lifetime's pain. The world you knew is irredeemably lost, and that is worth mourning, but there is nothing more to be afraid of. From now on, it ought to be as easy for you to be brave as it has always been for me.''

"It isn't fear that troubles me," he told her. "It's simple disappointment. I had hoped for a far better end than this.''

"You still have a choice," she pointed out.

"To stay awake or dream forever?" he said, trying—hopelessly—to match Harkender for contempt. "Should I accept the end of my world, and the utter dereliction of everything I once was, everything I once believed in, everything I once hoped for, provided only that my sleep will be favored with pleasant dreams?''

"You should not underestimate the value of dreams," she said. "I never have.''

"You always were a figment of a dream," he told her. "You have always had the power to work petty Acts of Creation; the world in which you have lived has never been inflexible. I have only been the *victim* of magic, and have learned too well to hate it. The human world would have been a better place by far without its interventions.''

''You misremember my history,'' she told him, seemingly pained by his carelessness. ''I think you once saw what I was before I came into my inheritance. Believe me, David, the world of aristocratic privilege in which you lived, albeit on its fringe, was an incarnate dream envied without hope by millions less fortunate. Never tell me how courageous you were to live in a godless and unmagical world, or how dearly you long for it now. You have endured more than a lifetime's pain, I know—but you have no notion, even so, of the real potential which a human lifetime has for the provision of suffering. Harkender always understood that better than you—in fact, even Mercy Murrell understood it better than you. It is too easy for a man like you to wish that there were no such things in the world as werewolves and witches. Don't preach to me about the folly and cowardice involved in being a figment of a dream. I know what I have been, what I am, and what I might be. I doubt that you ever have.''

She squeezed past him then, and went on her way.

He watched her retreating figure until a closing door cut off the sight of her. He went on his own way then, in a slightly chastened mood, still not having the least idea where he might be going or where there was to go.

5

David had no idea how much time had passed by the time he encountered Jacob Harkender again. There was nothing in his surroundings to offer the slightest evidence of change and duration and he did not know how far he could trust the biochemical clocks within his reconstituted body. He had become hungry and thirsty, but there was nothing urgent about either feeling; indeed, they seemed as strangely remote from his consciousness as the subdued and polite pain which attended the occasional collisions caused by his clumsiness. For this reason, he was able to hesitate over the question of whether to join Harkender, who was making a meal of sorts. He did not like the idea of breaking bread with his enemy, and the "bread" which Harkender was patiently devouring did not seem unduly appetizing. It was a pale lump bordered in dark brown, shaped into a mere caricature of a loaf.

Harkender was eating standing up; the table at which he stood was a square panel let down from the wall. The loaf was resting directly on the flat surface rather than on a plate, but there was a single item of cutlery to hand: a knife secured close to the rear of the board by a metal clip. Harkender was drinking while he ate, but not from a cup; he was sucking the fluid from a sealed container through a hollow tube.

When he saw David come in, Harkender silently reached out to take up the knife, and used it to cut a fresh slice from the loaf before him. The knife must have been razor-sharp; it cut cleanly through the dark rind and glided through the paler meat. Harkender did not

touch the piece which he had cut, but merely gestured toward it with
his free hand. The pantomime was polite, but slightly mocking.

"The taste is much better than the appearance," Harkender said.
"The people of this mechanical world reduced eating to a mere
function, but they took care not to eliminate *all* pleasure from the
experience. The nectar is even more pleasant." He replaced the knife
very carefully in its holder, adding: "It is necessary to be careful
when handling sharp objects—they weigh almost nothing, but they
are capable of doing a deal of damage."

David came forward, and picked up the slice which had been cut
for him. The crust was firm and dense but the lighter material it
enclosed was more delicate in texture. "What is it?" he asked.

"I refuse to call it ambrosia," said Harkender. "The food of gods
it is not. Manna might be more appropriate. I presume that it is
carefully concocted to supply all the nutritional needs of our reconstituted bodies—not a technically difficult feat, I gather. It seems that
Jason Sterling was the most apt prophet among us, despite that his
Heaven proved as unattainable as all the rest. Our descendants might
have reached a world like his, if only they had not destroyed one
another with such ruthless efficiency."

David did not care to ask Harkender to explain his remarks. Instead
he broke off a fragment of the "manna" and placed it in his mouth.
Its taste and texture were indeed far better than he could have
guessed. It was not sweet, but was slightly reminiscent of a good
mild cheese. Strangely enough, the engagement of his sense of taste
gave him a much greater sense of the solidity and reality of this
bizarre world than anything he had seen, He was not prepared to
trust the conviction yet, but he knew that he had to work on the
assumption that all of this was, indeed, real—and might indeed prove
to be the ultimate destination of his long odyssey in exotica.

Harkender pressed a second button, and the wall, by some remarkable process of eversion, extruded a plastic bladder filled with liquid.
As David reached out to detach it from its station it stubbornly
retained a connecting thread which, when he snapped it, became a
thin hollow tube. A small spurt of liquid jetted out just as Harkender
said: "Don't squeeze it yet!" The expelled droplets gracefully followed a languid descending arc to the floor, where they bounced
around in a most peculiar manner before finally coming to rest as a
chain of pearly droplets.

The liquid was, indeed, far sweeter than the solid, but not in the
least intoxicating.

"Do you know what I mean by Sterling's world?'' Harkender asked him curiously. "Did you see the Heaven which his imagination made, through the lens of the oracle?''

"I saw nothing of that kind,'' David said warily.

"This oracle was unlike the first,'' Harkender said. "The first time, the entire vision was shared. This time, our angelic partners were more reserved. I understand that you and Hecate became lost in the world of stars and atoms. I had a very different experience, among visions of possibility born from the dreams and desires of human and other beings. I wish I could say that they had done their work well, but I fear that the angels decided—and rightly—that there was nothing in the myriad Heavens of humankind to tempt them, or to show them a better way to live. I could have done far more for them, if only I had been trusted.''

"I dare say that I could have done far less for them,'' David told him wryly, "if only I had been trusted less. I suspect that they were very careful, attempting to conceal themselves from my understanding even while they used my sight to secure their own, and I hesitate to trust my intuitions fully . . . but I think I understand well enough, now, what they are.''

As he said it, he was able to meet Harkender's arrogant stare with sufficient confidence. Harkender, he was almost sure, did *not* understand what the angels were.

"And does it help,'' Harkender enquired, "to be able to guess what they are made of, and what alchemical processes underlie their powers? Can you now make demands upon them which you could not make before?''

"We never could make demands,'' David said flatly. "What they needed from us they could simply take, without offering anything in return. The protracted youth which you obtained was not given as a fair price for services rendered, but merely on a speculative whim. Whatever dreams you entertained of entering their world and joining their company were always hopeless.''

Harkender did not contradict him, but David knew that the other man's silence did not signify an acceptance of what he said. It seemed that Harkender had not yet discarded all his delusions of grandeur; perhaps he believed even now that if only the angels had listened to his advice, he could have instructed them in the art of becoming and being gods.

David patiently chewed the manna which the storehouses of planetoid Pandora had provided, and sipped their nectar. He tried to imag-

ine the millions of tiny machines at work in his body, sharing his
blood with all the ingenious molecular forms devised by natural selection for human use.

In my own day, he thought, *we had begun to feel puny and weak
by comparison with the fiery behemoths of steel which we had built
in our factories. We had all but lost respect for the cleverness of
our own flesh. The people who inhabited this little artificial world
must have thought themselves veritable giants: macrocosms filled
with the artful products of their genius. They must have thought
themselves far superior to the angels, if they knew of the existence
of the angels—for the angels have no technology at all, and no
intelligence save for that which they borrow from entities like us. In
terms of magnitude and crude magical power we are infinitely less
to them than insects are to us, but they are more like insects in the
broadest metaphorical sense: sucking parasites and reflexive predators. When Harkender imagined Zelophelon as a monstrous spider
he was nearer to the truth than he knew!*

He had to wait a long while before Harkender finally said: "Will
you tell me what you learned?"

"Why not ask Hecate?" David countered, out of sheer perversity.

"Hecate has not your educated mind," Harkender said, patiently
enough in view of the fact that he knew that David knew it already.
"She was a passenger in your shared adventure; she has hardly begun
to understand what she saw."

"Machalalel then," David suggested. "He is—or was—an angel."

"Don't play with me, David," Harkender said, attempting to be
disarmingly frank. "You may hate me, if you wish, but we are here
together. Our adventure continues, and we have no choice but to be
members of the same company. Let us be courteous, at least. Tell
me, please: what did you learn?"

In truth, David was longing to share his conclusions. He was uncomfortably aware of the extent to which they relied on guesswork,
and he had never had the kind of arrogant faith in his own guesswork
that a man like Harkender effortlessly achieved, but he was as sure
as he could be that he had discovered as much of the truth as would
ever be known.

"In the Clay Man's *True History,*" he said thoughtfully, "it is
alleged that Machalalel, having discovered humankind, tried to duplicate the feat of their Creation but could not quite manage it. He
made immortals incapable of the kind of reproduction which permits
evolution, all but one of which were werewolves. The *True History*

represents this as an ironic failure to duplicate the essential tawdriness of merely human flesh, but it was not. Like the gods of legend, Machalalel made man, in an important sense, *in his own image.* If you want a metaphor to help you grasp the nature of the beings we have stupidly called angels, you must look to the werewolves—perhaps, above all, to resentful Mandorla.''

Harkender made no response, but simply waited for him to continue.

''You must understand,'' David went on, gradually warming to the task, ''that it is an error of emphasis to think of the werewolves as *shape-shifters.* In their own way of thinking, the physical aspect of the metamorphosis is secondary to the mental; in their own estimation the change which overcomes them is a change in their *state of mind.* Humans undergo changes of mental state too, when we move from wakefulness to dream-states; in that respect, we have a little of the werewolf in us—and a little of the angel. If we are to understand the angels' history, particularly the history of their association with humankind, we must concentrate our attention on changes of mental state rather than on the metamorphoses of matter which we think of as their magic and their godlike creativity.''

David paused again, but again Harkender had no question. All he said was: ''Go on.'' He was hooked by fascination, like a fish on a line.

How like an angel, after all! David thought, smiling at the irony of it. Then he settled into his work.

6

"I do not know for certain even now," David said, "*exactly* what the angels are made of, or what matrix they inhabit, or when they first came into being, or how they evolved. I know, though, that they are not material, and that the world of matter is alien to them. They do not know themselves very well, for they have no mirrors in their own world which might display what they have instead of physical forms.

"The angels exist in what might be called the *implicate order,* which you may best imagine as whatever lies *beneath* or *behind* the surface which is the ground of matter, space and time. It may help you to picture them if you think of spiders spinning multidimensional webs which extend across vast reaches of the universe in which we live—except that the webs are not inert products; they remain a vital aspect of the spider-angels' being. The number of attachments they make, and the number of connections thus formed, are extremely large but finite. The angels have been spinning themselves out into these webs for a very long time, growing all the while, but they are in constant competition with others of their kind. Sometimes, one web will overwhelm and incorporate another; at other times one will partially displace another, injuring and reducing it.

"I think there was a moment in my vision when the angels did believe that they might have been gods of a sort, or might have the potential to become gods. When they fed me a vision of the primal explosion in which the expanding universe was born they became hopeful that they might have been involved in that event, perhaps to the extent of shaping its aftermath in order to produce a universe hospitable to their kind—but they saw, with the authority of our

combined sights, that it was not true. Like material beings they are
products of the energetic instability which is the ultimate creative
force in the universe. Like material beings they are temporary phantoms of the flux: walking shadows which will strut and fret their
hour upon the universal stage and then disappear in a catastrophe of
sound and fury. The webs which they spin are truly wondrous cre-
ations, doubtless very beautiful to those capable of glimpsing them,
but they are in the end mere artefacts . . . tales told by idiots, signifying nothing.

"Although these webs extend through the implicate order, and
give the angels marvelous powers to interfere with the world of
matter which is founded in that order, they are not the skeletons and
sinews of the cosmos. No matter how well they are spun, or for how
long, or how magnificently they grow, they can never give their
spinners the power to decide the fate of this universe or to reshape
any universe which might emerge by metamorphosis from a collapse
of space-time and the sealing of a great circle of causality. The angels
are humbler beings by far than they had hoped to be—just as we
humans are humbler beings than our ancestors' delusions of grandeur
once led them to hope.

"There are seven angels whose webs have—or recently had—
attachments within the earth. There were more in the distant past,
but in the course of time some were swallowed up and integrated
into others. The seven angels whose webs bridge the earth maintain
a similar presence in many other places, some so distant as to be at
the very limits of the observable universe. There are undoubtedly
other webs which intersect and interact with theirs in those regions,
although they have no anchorages hereabouts. The total number of
the angels remains a mystery to me, but I suspect that it might be
very large.

"I am unsure as to the exact scope of the angels' power to manipulate the matter and space in whose underworld they work. They could
probably manufacture matter out of raw energy if they ever found it
necessary to do so, but it is infinitely less effortful for them to deal
in *metamorphoses,* and they undoubtedly find living flesh a more
obliging clay than inert stone or metal. They deal easily with the
faint material transactions which constitute the sensations, thoughts
and visions of material being; far the greater fraction of their effects
on human consciousness are illusions of some kind. Because they
can do this so easily, those humans who have encountered them and
have been influenced by them have tended to credit them with great

cleverness, tending toward omniscience—but that is the greatest of all the mistakes we have made in trying to figure out what kind of beings the angels are.

"In this matter, too, it might be productive to draw an analogy with animal species. In what might be described as their native state the angels have no more intelligence than spiders, or worms . . . or wolves. What they do have, by virtue of their capacity to build human beings into their webs, is the power to *appropriate* and *mimic* the intelligence of other beings. By material association with intelligent beings they can acquire the trick of becoming intelligent beings themselves, although the intelligence they acquire is inevitably made somewhat in the image of the beings whose example they are following—not in their *physical* image, of course, but in their mental image. In association with men, the angels acquired certain key attributes of the human imagination.

"When they are not linked in a particular way to human or other material minds the angels' state of mind cannot be so very unlike the mode of experience which Machalalel's werewolves have when they are in wolf form: they are presumably conscious, after a fashion, but their minds are empty of organized thought. I am tempted to assume, although I cannot be absolutely certain, that the state of consciousness which Mandorla thinks of as 'wolfish'—with all its fierce appetites and exalted joys—does not resemble the mind-state of an actual wolf nearly so much as it resembles the mind-state which an angel has when it is disconnected from the human intelligence it otherwise mirrors.

"Mandorla's long-maintained preference for the wolfish mode of being is testimony to certain actual advantages of that way of being— and her eventual partial reconciliation to the human aspect of her nature is testimony to a partial reconciliation which the angels themselves have experienced, *to their cost.*

"For the angels, you see, intelligence is as much a curse as a gift, as much a dangerous trap as a marvelous opportunity. There is grave danger in the kind of experiment on which they tentatively embarked when some of their number first came to consciousness as a result of building human minds into their webs—danger which became critical as soon as six of the seven had fallen prey to temptation and had gorged themselves on the fruit of the tree of human knowledge and imagination.

"Their association with humankind was by no means the first adventure in intelligence which these angels have had, but in their native state they have hardly any memory with which to carry information forward from one encounter to another, and so they have preserved none but the dimmest recollection of those earlier encounters. One might be able to detect relics of that dim recollection in the myth systems which were formed in collaboration by angels and primitive men, but it would be difficult to isolate the traces of memory from the welter of confabulation, and impossible to purify them. One thing, however, is certain: those earlier encounters ended catastrophically for the angels and for the species whose intelligence they borrowed.

"Some angels were undoubtedly injured by their fellows in the aftermath of such contacts; some were probably destroyed. Some, threatened with injury and almost-certain extinction, may have done what Machalalel has done, subjecting themselves to a remarkable metamorphosis and becoming incarnate within the world of matter—but that must be an extraordinarily desperate move for an angel to make, no matter how perfectly it has become reconciled to the particular features of its second-hand mentality.

"You probably have not seen the bewilderment of the werewolves on those occasions when they awake in human form but cannot immediately recall their human selves; I have; it is an oddly pathetic sight. The angels, I think, must always be like that when they first encounter intelligent beings. Insofar as they are mental beings they live under the curse of constant rebirth—or *reawakening*—and they are constantly having to learn new identities. I am certain that they find their linkage with thinking beings intrinsically uncomfortable, perhaps as painful in its way as our linkage with them tends to be. In spite of its discomforts, though, there is something about the link which attracts them powerfully, as flames attract moths. The pain itself seems to fascinate them, to secure them all the more firmly. Perhaps for them *all* conscious sensation is marvelous and intoxicating—the more intense the better.

"Can you wonder, given these circumstances, that the angels' gratitude to their human instruments is limited, and that they are inclined to meet us with such a curious mixture of condescension and unkindness? The fundamental ambivalence of their attitude to beings of our kind helps to explain the awful perversity of their dealings with humans. The worst difficulty which the angels suffer by virtue of being associated with intelligent material beings is, however, of a far greater order of magnitude.

"You and I naturally tend to think of intelligence as a great gift and an unparalleled advantage in the earthly game of natural selection. We recognize that intelligence made men the undisputed overlords of our own petty creation, and in spite of our anxieties regarding the human tendency to collective self-destruction we persist in thinking of it as a source of limitless opportunity, a pathway to glory. I dare say that in spite of all our differences, you and I have felt equally free to pity and despise Mandorla and her fellow werewolves for conserving the ambition to be rid of the burden of reason, and equally vainglorious in respect of our superior intellect. For the angels, on the other hand, intelligence—in spite of the seductive appeal which it has for them—is no pathway to glory, and no advantage in the game of natural selection. If intelligence had been an unalloyed advantage to beings of their kind, I presume that the angels would have evolved it for themselves under the pressure of natural selection; the fact that they have not is eloquent testimony to the awkwardness of its disadvantages.

"I am a little unclear about these matters because the angels did not care to expose them fully to my oracular gaze, but I am fairly certain that association with intelligent beings inhibits the angels' powers of self-extension. Perhaps it is simply that their attention and activity become too narrowly focused—that contact with intelligent beings leads to a kind of obsession or mesmeric fascination—but it may be some more deeply seated inhibition. At any rate, there is some crucial weakening of the vitality of the webs which they are ceaselessly spinning. This is why they have a tendency, once having built bridges to intelligent minds, to become quiet and cautious in their dealings with those minds. Perhaps it would be better for them if they never forged such links at all, but reacted with horror every time they encountered intelligence. Perhaps some of their kind do, in much the same way that some humans react with horror if they catch a glimpse of a spider. But some, at least, find it impossible to resist the force which intelligence exerts upon their comatose minds; like Narcissus they become entrapped by the process of reflection which reveals and subtly changes them.

"I suspect that when the angels are in their native state they are better able to co-exist with one another. They may not have the solidarity of a pack of wolves, but they are able to *ignore* one another: to be blissfully unaware of the extent to which their webs intersect others. Consciousness changes that relationship; it intensifies the competition between them, making them into enemies. It also gives them the opportunity to make pacts and treaties, which is reparation of a kind—but that too seems to have its inherent dangers. There is something in the business of strategy which is addictive, to the point at which petty deceptions and feints may become an end in themselves. The angels can easily become fascinated with rules and rituals—as, of course, humans often do. It is possible that the long and puzzling history of human entrapment by rules and rituals is a consequence of the angels' involvement in our affairs, but I doubt it; I suspect that it is an unfortunate tendency to which all intelligent beings are prey. In any case, the webs of intrigue which the human-influenced angels knitted into their own forms incorporated a kind of weakness, which made them perilously vulnerable— because, rather than in spite of, their fragile alliances—to the one angel which did not fall prey to temptation: the Destroyer.

"I do not mean that when the angels are in their wolfish state they live in harmony, or that they are altogether unready to absorb and digest one another, but the acquisition of individuality, of identity, of *personality*, inevitably makes them more urgent and more fearful competitors. They become afraid, and in becoming afraid they become more aggressive—but their fear and their aggression are enemies within themselves. Conscious angels become planners, but the element of strategy which enters the business of self-extension and self-complication does not work to their advantage, and the general diminution of their powers of self-extension puts a steadily increasing burden on the ingenuity of their strategic thinking.

"It is a limited allegory, I know, but it may help to picture what I mean by imagining a population of spiders which, by some magical means, acquire quasi-human intelligence and a quasi-human sense of beauty. These gifts enable the spiders which have them to spin ever-more-intricate webs, into which are woven wonderful portraits. Unfortunately, the spinning of these enhanced webs is exhausting, and the webs cease to function so efficiently as traps for flies, with the result that the spiders grow weaker, to the extent that they become attractive as prey to those of their kin who have never been cursed with the gifts of artistry, and are eventually devoured. The parable has many weaknesses, but I think it captures the gist of the angels' problem. Six of the seven which were connected to the earth became locked into a curious dance of mutual suspicions and muted hostilities, keeping one another at bay with intricate strategies of growth and extension . . . with the final, inevitable result that the overcomplicated structures they had built were attacked by the more fortunate seventh.

"The six angels which had involved themselves very intricately with earthly life and human intelligence really did gain, in the end, a much better understanding of themselves and their situation in the many-dimensioned world. I would like to think that the oracle of which I was a part might have shown them more than any other oracle they have ever built, anywhere in the universe, but that is probably mere vainglory. What it revealed to them in no uncertain terms, however, was the magnitude of the threat which faced them, individually and collectively. The one thing which was, in the end, abundantly clear to them was that they could not fight effectively while they remained tied to us, fascinated by us, and imprisoned by the limitations of our imagination.

"They had a choice of sorts, but as Machalalel has admitted, his was was the choice of absolute desperation. The only decision which the others could sensibly make was to shear their links with human intelligence and become . . . what would you rather call them, Harkender? Spiders? Wolves?

"Anything, I suppose, except *angels*."

7

Jacob Harkender had long since finished his meal, and had carefully crammed the litter left behind into an orifice mounted in the section of wall exposed by the lowered table. He let a few seconds go by before responding to what David had said, and David revelled in the respectfulness of that silence.

Of all the people to whom he might have told this story, he realized, Jacob Harkender was the perfect audience. In accepting and believing it—which he had no alternative but to do—Harkender would have to admit that it was David, not he, who had made the better use of the angels' oracle, and the better use of the gift of human intelligence. David was startled, but not ashamed, by the extent of his exultation at the thought that he had *won*.

"They lied," Harkender said finally. "Zelophelon told me nothing but lies. It gave me youth, and strength, but it would not tell me as much of the truth as it knew."

"Much of what it led you to believe was simple misconception," David reminded him. "Much of the rest was optimistic confabulation. But yes, there were lies too. We were used, and not very scrupulously. On the other hand, the spider-angels did make themselves in images we provided. If they lied, they learned the trick—and the necessity—from us. And in the end, we learned the truth—as much of the truth as was capable of revelation, given that they and we exist in different conceptual universes, separated by a great gulf of incomprehension."

"Now that we are castaways in this distant time," Harkender said, "when the world which gave us birth is lifeless, what good has it done us to learn what we have learned?"

"What good would it have done not to have learned it?" David countered, not having realized until Harkender provoked him to say it that it was true. "Would you rather be a thousand years dead? Doubtless the angels must have wondered, before they severed their ties with us, what they have gained by sharing the mindfulness of a species doomed to self-destruction. What good could any such adventure do them, save to remind them yet again that they are condemned by fate to be creatures of instinct, for whom enlightenment is simply a road to Hell paved with noble intentions?"

Harkender permitted himself a wry smile, although his features were still clouded with bitter annoyance. "You were right, were you not," he said grudgingly, "to cast your own guardian angel in the image of one of the gods of ancient Egypt, half-man and half-animal?"

"And you were right, were you not, to see yours as a spider?" David said, finding himself able to be a little gracious. "How easy it is in retrospect to penetrate the enigmas of our supernatural sight!"

"Very easy," Harkender agreed sarcastically. "What a great gift hindsight is! We should be proud of it—after all, it is not one for which we have the gods to thank."

"What did you learn from your part in the oracle?" David asked, in a neutral tone.

Harkender was not grateful to be asked. "I learned that I was wrong," he said dismissively. "I told Pelorus that you would be addressing all the wrong questions, but it was in fact the angels which were addressing all questions. They sent me on a fool's errand, because they did not know until you explained it to them what fools they were, and because I did not know that the explorations I desired to carry out for myself lay beyond the limits of their parasitic imagination. I fear that I have been guilty of *hubris*."

"So have they," said David quietly—and not by way of consolation.

"I wonder if they really did contemplate becoming incarnate, as governors of some human-designed Heaven?" Harkender said. "Or were they simply *savoring* the reach of the human imagination, in all its bewildering complexity and all its comical perversity? Was I merely their hired guide, their educated cicerone?" It was obvious that he found the notion insulting and humiliating.

"We did what we could," David said. "I think, with the aid of hindsight, that we did as well as could be expected. Better, at any rate, than our fellow men, who could not wait for their allotted doom to fall from the skies, but had to visit premature destruction upon one another. Is our failure any greater than the failure of the angels, do you think? After all, if I am right then they are doomed to fail again and again, always forgetting the lesson almost as soon as they learn it. Being angels, they can only live vicariously—but we are men, and can live for ourselves. Perhaps Machalalel's choice was not so desperate after all. Perhaps he is the only wise angel there has ever been.''

Harkender smiled again, just as bitterly as before. "And we are still here, are we not?" he said. "The human story goes on, as the story of the angels does . . . although the narratives will now diverge. We have lost a world, but we have gained an atom: a narrow coffin in which to dream the dreams of death. *All* hope is not gone.'' He did not sound as if he believed it.

"No," said David, less sarcastically than the other. "Not all.'' But he remembered, then, that this was his enemy. He had done what he came to do; he had demonstrated his superiority, and won his private war. This aftermath had brought them too close to an implicit common cause and commonwealth of feeling. He turned away from the table, saying: "I must find Hecate now; there is something she said to me which requires clarification, although I was too preoccupied with another matter to realize it at the time.''

Harkender did not ask him what he meant.

David glanced back once as he moved toward the door, to find that his enemy was watching him go, with a dark, bleak and dolorous look in his eyes. He was glad to take the expression as a grudging but honest compliment.

8

He found Hecate looking out of a window. The window was far larger than the one in the room where he had first awakened, taking up almost the whole wall of a room twice the size of that one. He could see a little of the surface of the planetoid, although the window was eccentrically tilted and the horizon was only a few hundred yards away. The landscape did not look as desolate as he had anticipated. It was full of the evidence of human presence and activity: hatchways, shaped cavities, machinery of various kinds.

Not even a worldlet, properly speaking, he thought. *Merely a huge and complicated box. A narrow coffin where the near-dead might dream of life . . .*

It was just possible, by standing at an odd angle, to see his reflection in the curving window.

"You were right," he said to Hecate. "This is the real world. A thousand years and more have passed, the earth is but a cinder, and it is no arbitrary nightmare; it is all true. I can face the thought of it now. I can almost face myself, stranger though I am."

"Good," she said. "Can you face the thought of living here, awake, for another thousand years and more, while Machalalel formulates some plan for our further destiny?"

It was an awkward question. "It would depend on the company, I think," he said eventually. "The prospect of living another dozen lifetimes is by no means unwelcome, even if I must spend them in a place like this . . . but the thought of seeing Jacob Harkender's face and listening to his voice day by day is another matter. I wonder how Machalalel plans to organize the rotas of his crew. Or is our

401

fragile company a democracy of sorts, now that you and he have no magic to command?''

''I wonder,'' she said quietly—and then flinched as a sudden flash of light struck her eyes.

The sun was rising over the planetoid's horizon. Because the horizon was so close the sun seemed for a moment to be close as well, but as soon as David's eyes had adjusted to the brighter light he realized that this was an absurd mistake. In fact, the sun was much further away than it had been from the earth; its disc was very much smaller than the disc to which he was accustomed.

It took less than a minute for the whole disc to become visible above the horizon, and David tried to calculate how fast the planetoid must be turning—but as he was attempting to marshal the relevant figures the sky began to change more dramatically. The sun's disc began to grow, and the uneclipsed stars close to the edge of the window began to fade into darkness.

It is an optical illusion, David told himself. *It cannot be the motion of the sun which produces the effect, because the sun cannot be approaching us so rapidly—nor can it be the movement of the station toward the sun. And the stars cannot be "going out," for their light was emitted years, or hundreds of years, or hundreds of thousands of years ago. The glass in the window must be darkening in response to the brightening of the sun's light, so that the stars only seem to be fading . . .*

He realized almost immediately that this process of deduction must be at fault, and that he was failing to make sense of what was happening. The transparent window *was* darkening rapidly enough to hide the greater number of the stars, but the sun continued to grow far too rapidly for its growth to be any kind of optical illusion, and the stars which shone outside its expanding rim were *moving* now— and not in unison.

It was not the station that was tilting; the stars really had taken flight. Either the sun was approaching very rapidly or . . .

Or the sun was exploding.

The brightness of the expanding star was uncomfortable, but not unbearable. David could look into its white heart without being blinded. But the explosion of the sun, however melodramatic it might be and however menacing to the tiny planetoid, was not the marvel which captured his attention. The stars which danced around and behind the sun, cavorting in a seemingly random fashion, challenged him with the impossibility of their action.

To look into space, as David now knew very well, was to look into time, and he had already reminded himself that the light which was now arriving from those stars had been radiated years, or hundreds of years, or hundreds of thousands of years ago. They could not be dancing together in a jig which extended from one edge of the universe to the other. It was flatly impossible.

"What's happening?" Hecate asked. She seemed more curious than alarmed, too astonished to see the implications of it all.

"I don't know," David said.

If the stars could not be dancing, he realized, the space through which their light was transmitted must be distorting. Something was warping the fabric of local space, making it *appear* that the stars were dancing. Was the slow explosion of the sun an appearance too? Or. . .

"It's the war between the angels," he said, as the tattered net of his consciousness suddenly caught hold of the only possible explanation. "It's the fight against the destroyer, the disconnection of all their attachments . . . the tearing of their webs!"

If the earth had not been destroyed before, he knew, it would certainly have perished now. He could not see the planet, and doubted that there would have been much to see at this distance had he been able to, but he could picture in his mind's eye the material result of the angels' shearing of their anchorages.

It was not so very different, really, from trying to picture the retreat from Mons, where Simon had been killed. Destruction was only destruction, after all. Creativity was complicated, always producing *new* things which challenged the imagination and the sense of wonder, but destruction was simple. Creativity was the better and truly beautiful face of turbulence; destruction was a mere carnival, a ragged chain of tawdry sideshows. Destruction, even on this cosmic scale, was a petty and passionless firework display, an inartistic matter of pulling things apart, a tantrum of smashing and shattering and splintering and crushing and devouring and . . .

The sun filled half the sky, now, and the bigger it became the faster its expansion appeared to be proceeding—though that, at least, was surely an optical illusion . . .

"It will destroy the whole system," David whispered. "We're only a few light-minutes away. The explosion will simply swallow us up, sublimating us into a lick of flame and a wisp of smoke. It's all over. There's no salvation at all, not even for this little box of dreams!"

What a fool Machalalel was, he thought, *to put on flesh, knowing that this must happen!* But then he remembered what Machalalel had said when he welcomed his last guests into his hidey-hole. *"Our present environment will not long remain constant, no matter how placid it seems now, but we have a firm and trustworthy promise that this tiny atom will be left in no-man's-land, unharmed and unspoilt."*

"But perhaps not," he said to Hecate, who seemed now to be transfixed by alarm. "They owe us something, after all. They owe us *something!*"

Their field of view was completely filled with white light now, but there was nothing else. The station did not lurch, nor did it show by any other sign that it was under threat. The light grew no brighter, and there was no perceptible heat. It was as if the planetoid sat safely in the eye of a great cosmic storm, or as if it drifted patiently in a tiny lacuna at the heart of a huge crystal.

David seized upon the latter analogy, hoping that it might be true: that a spherical shield, hard as diamond, had been thrown up around them, so that whatever else might be smashed and obliterated, the last tiny remnant of mankind would be safe.

"They certainly owe us that much!" he said again. "If they have not the gratitude to do as much as that . . ."

"If they will not do it for us," Hecate muttered, having caught up with his train of thought, "they will surely do it for Machalalel."

"Oh no," he countered swiftly. "They will do nothing at all for Machalalel. He is—or was—their rival, and the moment they began to put on masks he became their enemy. He is hiding behind our skirts. If the angels which have known us are disposed to spare us, it is because of you, and Anatole Daumier, and David Lydyard . . . and even Jacob Harkender . . . but it is *not* because of Machalalel."

Nothing changed. The light grew no brighter. The planetoid continued serenely to spin about its axis and follow its own proper movement, respectfully obedient to Newton's first law. The crystal of still and silent light which contained and protected them was perfect and inviolate.

"Do you know what it is they're doing?" Hecate asked. "Why are they wreaking such destruction?"

"It isn't deliberate," David said. "I doubt that there's anything controlled or directed about it. The six angels *might* be trying to deploy what they learned through the medium of the oracle about the underlying nature of matter and energy, but I suspect they've moved beyond the realms of knowledge and strategy by now. It's more probable that the intersecting patterns which are the angels' implicate forms are moving reflexively, as if to drown one another out or pull one another apart. At best, they'll only succeed in producing new patterns; at worst they might unravel. I don't think any of them can win the battle—not even the destroyer—and I doubt that any of them can survive unchanged. This is a fundamental aspect of the evolutionary process according to which the angels live and change. Perhaps it's an essential element of whatever passes for progress in their world, or perhaps it's just a destructive curse under whose painful spur they have to exist. Either way, whatever imprint their temporary association with humanity has left will be disrupted and erased. They'll come out of the battle mere creatures of primal instinct, with hardly a trace left of their hard-won intelligence.''

The crystal expanse of light shimmered suddenly, as if a series of ecstatic tremors were passing through it. It was a temporary turbulence: a ripple crossing the face of existence. The angels were, after all, merely creatures; as their excitement died, calm returned.

The white light filled David's eyes as the ripples died, and it seemed to him that they filled the whole infinite space which was the private universe inside his head, illuminating his soul.

I have come to the mouth of the cave, he thought. *I am here, alone and unafraid, looking out into the light of truth.*

No sooner had he thought it than the white blaze became colored, and some inner eye at the core of his being perceived moving shapes within it. He saw the Web of Fate, spun not by the three bickering sisters cheated of their silly treasure by Perseus but by a host of brightly bejewelled spiders with eyes like yellow diamonds and green emeralds, and legs of jointed crystal. He saw the Angel of Pain, soaring upon the ecstasy of her sensation, blissfully unaware of her cruelty. He saw the werewolves of London, running like the wind in pursuit of some hapless prey. He saw Satan rising triumphantly from a nest of liberating fire, tearing loose the nails which had pinned him to the floor of Hell. He saw Pandora's paradoxical box opening to disgorge . . . all that it contained, *and miraculously more.*

And behind all these figures, in the depths of the mirror which was the lighted wall of the universe, saw himself, rapt with fascination, staring at the dance of *clinamen* which was the fount of all creation, all novelty, all beauty, and all thought. He saw himself at the center of his own mental web, in his narrow room in the bowels of the hospital, surrounded by dusty books and the odor of pickled human flesh. He saw himself as a creature of blood and bone, hand

and eye: the product of billions of years of the drunken progress that was evolution. He saw himself as a creature of mind and memory, imagination and confabulation: the product of an adventure in fantasy every bit as deceitful and every bit as honest as the Clay Man's navel. He saw himself as a man, within whose microcosm was inscribed the whole history and potential of humankind, and he realized—for the first time—what a responsibility he carried by virtue of that fact: a responsibility to judge and to learn, to follow strategies and rituals, and to discover the beauty of the world.

Why did I need the angels to show me this? he asked himself. *I should have known it anyway.*

The light became white again, and perfectly even. It began to fade. After half an hour or so it was possible to see the stars again. They were almost at rest against the velvet darkness of the void. The magisterial processes of cosmic change had become patient again.

There was no sign of the sun, but a soft haze lay across the center of their field of vision.

"I suppose that was an apocalypse of sorts," Hecate said, when she was sure that it was over.

"So much has changed in a thousand years and more," David said, "that we are perfectly entitled to consider it one more in a series of petty and haphazard disasters. There never can be and never will be a final end to the cosmic process of which it is a part, even though the angels will one day become extinct."

"Ah!" she said, remembering. "That is what Anatole saw, is it not? I caught a glimpse of it while our sensations overlapped. He saw—or imagined—time folding back upon itself, renewing its potential by magical contortion. He dared to hope that although chaos will always threaten, it will always be aborted; that on the largest scale of all there is only change and more change, evolution and further evolution . . ."

David took up the sentence for her. He too was remembering Anatole's tendency to rhapsody. "And perhaps—just perhaps—progress and further progress. We are not gods and the angels are not gods, and we might dare to hope, if we care to, that whatever might eventually emerge from the melting-pot of eternal flux and re-Creation, *nothing* will ever have the power to impose rigidity, destiny and finality on the shape of things becoming."

"It was a fine oracle," she said. "I am glad that I was able to ask Anatole to include me."

"You were a contributor, not a mere observer," he told her. "We all played a part in the picturing. It was colored by *all* our hopes, and all our ambitions too.''

"So it was," she said. "And here I am, with a minor part still to play, and a chance of sorts to shape the end of this infinitesimal drama."

While they were speaking, David looked out of the window at the vast and trackless wilderness of stars. The light of the explosion had died away now, and the residual haze was fading to a glimmer. The conflagration which had raged through the solar system had left Pandora untouched. As David had anticipated, the wrathful light of the angels' disengagement—the visible echo of their latest adventure in fascination—had dwindled almost to nothing, and now the stars shone through again: a majestic panoply whose fundamental order would always reassert itself, and whose joyous creative light would not be put out for a very long time.

A door slid open, not quite soundlessly. David did not turn immediately, but when he heard Hecate gasp in astonishment he looked behind him.

Jacob Harkender stood before the closing door. The absurd clothes he wore were spattered and half-soaked with drying blood.

In his left hand he was carrying a severed head.

9

David had seen a severed head once before, but not through his own eyes. He had shared Mercy Murrell's consciousness of the moment when Hecate first achieved conscious control over her angel-donated powers. He remembered that Harkender had played a part in that particular melodrama too. The three of them had watched the head, magically suspended in mid-air and slowly dripping blood, with horrid fascination.

The severed head had worn a terrible expression: an obscene mask of horror. This one had no magic to hold it up; it dangled ignominiously from the fingers which Harkender had carelessly tangled in its hair. The expression on its face was not horrified; it was not even surprised. It would not have been allowed on stage at the *Grand Guignol.*

"He told the truth," Harkender said, negligently parading his contempt for their astonishment. "He could be killed. No matter how carefully a mortal man may stock his flesh with protective machines he remains a *mortal man.* There are certain accidents of fate whose effects cannot be set aside."

"Accidents of fate!" David repeated mechanically, his senses numbed by dreadful amazement. *Surely this is a dream!* he thought. *It is a nightmare, and we need only awake to find the welcoming world.*

"In the broadest sense," Harkender said, in a mocking fashion. "I do not mean to imply, of course, that this was not deliberate."

David's lips began to form the word "why," but the murderer was ahead of him.

"He was still ambitious to be a god," Harkender said flatly. "He had failed as a wolfish angel, and so he elected to become a man, but he had no intention of being a *mere* man. He intended to be our captain, our navigator, our commander. He intended to be the architect of our future. He was not entitled to that. He came to us from a company of liars, betrayers . . . devils in disguise. We have had our fill of angels, David, have we not?"

David was dumbfounded; he could not reply. *But it is not a dream,* his internal Devil's Advocate informed him. *It only seems like a dream, because it is so strange. Act your part, by all means, and set the horror aside for later indulgence, but remember that you must live with every consequence of all these vital moments.*

Hecate was not as squeamish as David; she found her voice readily enough. "He told me that this station once had a crew of seven," she said, not needing to spell out who *he* was. "Seven men and women, whose task it was to protect a precious cargo: the future of the human race. They could not do it. They could not control their petty hatreds and fits of wrath, and in the end they could not resist the pressure of despair. They left no exact record, he said, but it is not too difficult to figure out what happened to them. They could not live together in such a narrow space, and so they died. I said that the space did not seem particularly narrow, and he replied that the narrowness was of the mind."

"According to the Clay Man," Harkender said, "he always had a certain penchant for wordplay."

David was ready to take part now, even though he knew that the head was real, and not the produce of some visionary melodrama. "Who will be next, Harkender?" he asked bitterly. "If our first commander is dead already, how long can the next expect to live? Usurpers always sleep uneasily, do they not? How many more of us might you have to kill before you feel safe in our company?"

"You misunderstand me, David," said Harkender lazily. "You always have. I have no quarrel with you, nor with any other *human* being aboard this flying coffin."

"You had no quarrel with Machalalel," David replied. "He saved your life. He brought you to this world."

"What did he expect?" Harkender sneered. "*Gratitude?*"

"I think he did," Hecate said softly. "I think he expected that and more, and thought himself entitled to it."

"According to the lore of scripture and legend," Harkender said, "false gods have always expected gratitude *and more* from those who were victims of their lies and impostures. If this is to be a new beginning, it is best that we start with a clean slate.''

A clean slate! The words echoed silently in David's head as he flinched from the stare of Machalalel's dead eyes.

"Perhaps he was ambitious to lead us to a promised land," Hecate said quietly. "Perhaps he did assume that he was entitled to be our commander, the architect and founding father of our new world. Who, after all, is now to take his place? Do *you* know how to operate all these cunning machines?''

"Any one of us can do *that*," Harkender replied offhandedly, "provided that he or she will only take the trouble to learn the necessary skills. We have all the time in the world—and if we need tutors there are more than fifty men and women asleep who know how to determine exactly what resources the station has, and how best to search for more. For myself, I have no ambition to be captain of this ridiculous life raft. It does not matter to me who does the job, so long as it is not *Machalalel.*''

As he pronounced the name he threw the head away, in the direction of the window. It moved in a manner which was no longer unexpected, but nevertheless seemed quite uncanny. David did not try to follow its careering progress; he kept his eyes on Jacob Harkender.

Harkender reached out to him, offering him the bloody knife, handle first. "If you are afraid for your own life," he said, "you only have to eliminate the danger. You are a surgeon of sorts, are you not? If I am a cancer within the body of this little atom of community, you have only to cut me out and cauterize the wound. If I am a seed of evil which must be destroyed for the good of that fearful herd which is mankind, do what you must.''

David stared at him incredulously—but he reached out and took the knife. It was the one Harkender had used to cut the loaf of manna which they had shared.

"Good," said Harkender. "Try me; judge me; condemn me. Strike here, if you will, between these two ribs. Puncture my heart precisely—but you must be careful of the fountain of blood which will erupt, for this strange world plays tricks with jets and cascades.''

David made no move to obey.

"What are you waiting for?" Harkender asked, meeting his stare squarely and fiercely. "Have I not played the villain throughout the long and tortuous narrative of your life? Am I not everything you hate and despise? Did I not steal the only thing you were ever able to love, after your crabbed and cautious fashion? Am I not a murderer, almost a deicide? I am Cain and I am Judas and I am Satan himself—I confess to all my crimes and plead guilty to all your charges. If you have any doubts, simply ask yourself what Sir Edward Tallentyre would have done—that is how you have managed your life and your affairs, is it not?''

There was no doubt in David's mind as to what Tallentyre would have done, but he did not think that he had ever been guilty of mere mimicry. Nor could he help remembering that enigmatic message which had come from Simon after he had died at Mons, slain for a cause which had come to nothing in spite of the best efforts of St. George's phantom bowmen and all the angels in Heaven. *Tell him that it does not matter that my grandfather was wrong,* Simon had said, *because he is the one with the finer sense of beauty. Tell him that it is not necessary to love his enemies, provided only that courtesy is an adequate shield against hatred.*

Silently, David handed the knife to Hecate. She barely glanced at it before handing it back to Harkender. David could see the expression of triumph in Harkender's eyes—the expression of a man who had turned a bitter defeat into a kind of victory by blatantly unfair means—but his resentment was not beyond control.

''He was only a man,'' David said. ''A mortal man, like you, returned from the dead for the last time. We too are revenants, with no more right to be here than he had. You should not have hurt him in the name of revenge. But the killing, the destruction and the waste have to stop somewhere. Now is the only time left to us, and we are the only ones who *can* stop. If we fail, there is no one to come after us.''

''And we must not fail, must we?'' Harkender said derisively. ''We have work to do, decisions to make. We have a choice, it seems, between eternal sleep and the patient execution of a tedious, meaningless and probably hopeless mission. How ironic it is that the human story should end, after all, with a choice between a Heaven of dreams and a Hell of tedium. How doubly ironic that I, of all people, should be forced to prefer the Heaven!''

He did not wait for any further response, but turned and left. No one had told him that he had missed the destruction of the sun and the salvation of Pandora.

The quiet efficiency of the doors was beginning to get on David's nerves. While the one through which Harkender had gone slid shut he turned to Hecate, remembering that she had once posed as Eve in a paradoxical Eden outside the world. *Eve is innocent,* Simon's message had said. It was a pity, David thought—feeling ashamed of the thought even as he framed it—that Hecate's face was so utterly plain. Eve had been prettier by far, as befitted the mother of an entire species.

"They do dream, don't they?" she said, although she must have known that he could hardly be expected to answer with any certainty. "The sleepers, I mean. They have their dreams, their private Heavens. They must."

"I suppose they must," he said. "Are you also determined to find out?"

"Oh no," she said. "For the time being, at least, I must play my part in steering this problematic ship. I am the only one who knows which way to go, am I not?"

"*Do* you know which way to go?" he asked, remembering at last why he had sought her out. "You hinted that you did, but I wasn't sure. During the oracle, when we explored the distribution of life within and without the galaxy, I was concerned with generalities, and with the *meaning* of the vision . . . and so, I think, was Anatole. It was our role, our vital function—but you had different interests and priorities, did you not? You took care to remember the location of a world which might support us. Did you know then that we would emerge from the experience into a situation like this—or had you merely dreamed it long before, when you had a witch's magic to guide your dreams?"

She smiled. "I wish I could take credit for the knowledge or the inspiration," she said, "but all I can honestly claim is the luck. Still, I'm ready and able to serve as your navigator, if you will be captain of the ship."

David returned the smile as best he could. "You do not need me," he said. "Better to have the Clay Man as a companion. He might have been made for the task of playing Adam to your Eve."

She shook her head. "That's not a game I wish to play," she told him. "If I am to be captain now, I'd rather have a Pelorus than an Adam. He has the reputation of being an excellent navigator. The Clay Man told me once that he guided Orpheus into the remotest depths of the Underworld and out again—or remembered it, whether it actually happened or not."

"According to his own rumor," David said, "Hannibal could never have crossed the Alps without him, and might have gone on to take Rome save for the sad results of advice given by counselors

less wise and less wolfish than himself. But he is no longer the will
of Machalalel.''

How like a dream this reality is! he thought, as he finished this
peculiar speech. *How easy it is, now that we have so little weight,
to set aside shocks which would otherwise make cowards of us. These
clever machines inside us, which have led humankind to the conquest
of aging, disease and pain, have made us far better than we were
before!*

"If the time should come when I must take my turn to sleep,''
Hecate said, "Pelorus will see us safe, whether or not he has the
will of Machalalel to prick his conscience. It may seem foolish, but
I am not in the least afraid.''

"Nor am I,'' said David. "Foolishly optimistic I may be, but I
am not afraid of what we will ultimately find when we reach our
destination, nor of the dreams whose bridge will bring me to that
end.''

Hecate stepped sideways, and picked up Machalalel's head from
the place where it had finally come to rest. She looked into its bleak
eyes. The expression on her own face was unfathomable.

The apprentice gods are dead and gone, David thought. *Far better
for humankind had they died a long time ago, before they ever had
the chance to snare us in their labyrinthine nets.* He wondered what
expression Mandorla might have worn had she been confronted with
the severed head of her maker, and felt unreasonably confident that
it would not have been triumph, nor loathing, nor predatory glee.
She learned to be human, in the end, he told himself. *She learned
empathy, she learned pity, and she learned the meaning of tragedy.
When she wakes, she will be as beautiful as she ever was, and not
without a heart.*

"It will not be an Age of Gold,'' Hecate said, referring to the
destination which awaited them, hundreds of years in the future. "It
will be an Age of Toil and Trouble. To build a world, we must forge
the tools, and then provide the labor. It will be arduous, and tedious,
and there will be no magic to help us.''

"It will be an Age of Iron,'' David said mildly, "but it will also
be an Age of Heroes and an Age of Reason. Who among us, now,
would have it any other way?''

Epilogue
The Age of Enlightenment

And I saw a new heaven and a new earth: for the first heaven and the first earth were passed away; and there was no more sea.

Revelations 21:1

1

The bed was hard but not uncomfortable; the sheets were drawn too tightly across his supine body, but they were warm. His leg was doubly uncomfortable because of the splints and the bandages, but the hurt *inside* was not so bad. His head was also bandaged, but it did not hurt at all. His thoughts were sluggish with the aftereffects of some opiate, but there was no ache in his brain. His throat was dry, but not so fiercely dry that he felt in dire need of water.

He lifted his right arm, to prove that he could do it. It moved easily, and he looked long and hard at the upraised hand, expecting to recognize and thus put a name to himself.

I am Anatole Daumier, he thought, with wonderment and satisfaction. *I am Anatole Daumier, not dead after all.*

He did not call out, but a nurse came to his bedside, perhaps having seen him raise his arm.

"Be calm," she said, in English. She was older than he, but not quite old enough to be his mother, and her pleasant face was lit by an astonishingly charming smile.

"Where am I?" he asked, in the same language, looking anxiously up into her face. "What day is this?"

"This is the field hospital at Villers-Cotterêts," she said. "It's June the twelfth."

"The twelfth! Has Paris fallen yet?"

She seemed surprised. She shook her head vigorously. "Indeed it has not," she said. "The German advance was halted at the Marne. The American second and third divisions and the French fifth army are holding firm."

417

For a moment or two he was confused, but only for a moment or two. The Americans had come! *Of course* the Americans had come! Wilson's soldiers had been pouring into France in their hundreds of thousands, as fast as it was possible to land them.

"It was a diversionary attack," the nurse said. "A new offensive is expected to begin in the north any day now. Even so, there is a widespread feeling that the tide has turned. The new American troops are fresh and recklessly hungry for action—tales of their bravery are putting new heart into the French and the British. The Germans have shot their bolt—everyone thinks so." She sounded excited, and thoroughly confident.

"I was at Chemin des Dames," he said in a puzzled tone. "The Germans overran us."

"You were very lucky," she said. "Soldiers from the British ninth corps trapped behind enemy lines on the Californie plateau came west by night along the Chemin des Dames, while the Germans were still pressing forward. They found you in a shell-hole, raving with delirium because of the bullet in your head. Common sense should have made them leave you there, but they would not. They improvised a stretcher, and carried you as far as Soissons, where they handed you over to your own thirtieth corps. The surgeons there removed the bullets from your head and your leg, but you were still desperately poorly when you had to be evacuated by ambulance because the Germans had laid siege to the town. You were brought here more dead than alive; I don't think you can possibly imagine how hard a fight you had to wake up again."

"If Paris is safe," he whispered, "*civilization* is safe."

"Not quite yet," she answered, with a small indulgent laugh, "but nearly—very nearly."

He studied her face more carefully. She was not pretty in any conventional feminine way but she was remarkably *handsome*. She seemed marvelously cool and collected—as if nothing short of the apocalypse could jolt her out of her courageous optimism.

"Where are the Britishers who brought me out?" he asked.

She laughed again, as though it were a silly question. "Returned to the action," she said. "There is a great deal of work still to be done."

It was only to be expected. He tried with all his might to remember being carried from the place where he had fallen to Soissons, but all that came into his mind was the sound of someone whistling a tune while someone else sang the words of an obscene song in a curiously hushed and melodic voice.

It must have been a memory, but it seemed more like a fragment of a dream. He must have been dreaming while he lay so long unconscious, carried sleeping through a veritable riot of adventures. What dreams he must have had—and what a pity it was to have forgotten them so soon!

The nurse had turned to go, but he reached out and caught her left wrist in his right hand, imploring her to stay. "What's your name?" he asked.

"Elinor," she said. "Elinor Lydyard."

The surname sounded vaguely familiar, but he could not place it. "The Americans have really come," he said to make perfectly certain that he could believe it. "The Germans are retreating."

"Oh yes," she said. "The man in the bed to your left was hurt at Belleau Wood, but the wound has not affected his voice or his spirit. He will certainly tell you all about it, if you ask him."

"And the tide has definitely turned? We are winning?"

"Everyone thinks so. It is far too soon to be certain, but everyone thinks so."

"I have a family in Paris," he told her. "My youngest brother, P'tit Jean, is only six years old. I do not want him to grow up only to be used as cannon-fodder in a never-ending war—I would as soon he were given directly to the Devil."

"There is no danger of that," she assured him, in a soothing tone. "The tide has turned, and it cannot be turned back."

He knew that she was humoring him, trying to calm him. That did not matter. She meant what she said, and he felt in his tired bones that it was true.

"Are you a Communist, Miss Lydyard?" he asked.

She laughed, and shook her head. "My mother's father was a baronet, I fear," she told him. "My father is a mere man of science, but the blue blood is in my veins nevertheless. I am part of the *ancien régime* which has yet to be swept away by the great revolution."

He tried to smile. "There is nothing *mere* about a man of science," he told her sternly. "Men of science are the makers of the future, and the venous blood of every one of us is blue, until it is shed. As a nurse, you should know that."

"I do," she said.

"We are all made of common clay," he insisted, obscurely determined to make his point, and to make her understand that he was perfectly serious, in spite of the good humor which they shared.

"Not so," she told him, becoming perfectly serious herself. "I have been a long time in this dreadful war, and have been witness of the shedding of a deal of vivid red blood. If there is one thing I have learned it is this: that we are each and every one of us made of *uncommon* clay, of a rarity and preciousness we have not yet learned to value as we ought or might."

Having said so, she gently detached his hand from her wrist.

"My name is Anatole," he said. "Anatole Daumier."

"I know," she said. "I will not forget it, never fear."

"I have been through Hell, have I not?" he said, with a sudden catch in his voice.

"Don't look back," she told him. "Look forward. Always look forward, and Hell can never claim you."

She left him then. While she went about her business he stared up at the cracked ceiling of the ward, and breathed in air that was pungent with disinfecting fluid.

The odor was sharp, but the fluid had been perfumed, and the florid combination of scents reminded him of a grove of syringas where he had walked with his father and his mother one summer long ago, when he had been no older than P'tit Jean was now.

For no reason at all, he suddenly thought of the Maid of Orléans, and her heroic defense of France against the British, who had taken their revenge by having her burned as a witch. She was a saint now, and would doubtless have forgiven her erstwhile enemies, but he was an atheist, and had previously never seen any need to do likewise . . . except that some Englishmen whose names he did not know and whose faces he would not recognize if he were to see them had carried him for miles along the Chemin des Dames, all the way to Soissons, almost every inch of the journey being behind German lines.

What an adventure that must have been—what a brave, stupid, heroic adventure!

"*Merci,*" he whispered. "*Merci bien.*"

It seemed woefully inadequate, but thanks were all he had to give, for the present. In future, he was certain, he would be able to do much more. If the war really were ending at last, there was no limit to what enlightened men like himself might some day achieve.

2

There was once a man who was caught in a terrible fire, and died.

There was no *justice* in his death; it was not a punishment inflicted by Heaven or the judgment of any avenging angel. It was simply that there was no one to save him.

Half a dozen servants, reinforced by men from the neighboring village of Whittenton, tried ineffectually to fight the flames with water borne in buckets from a nearby stream, but they might as well have tried to turn back the tide of time. The only useful task which unkind fate had been left for them was to keep the fire from the stables, at least until the horses had been led to safety.

Several witnesses said afterward that the strange dome built above the attics of the house was lit for several minutes from within like some great bauble—a Hallowe'en lantern or a child's toy—before its panes of colored glass were blackened by the smoke or shattered by the heat. No one knew the real purpose of that eccentric decoration, but it was widely rumored to be instrumental in the occult researches of the man who died, and there were some among the witnesses who claimed that the fire which briefly lit the panes from within was no *natural* fire but a visitation from the prince of Hell. They were, of course, quite wrong.

So far as could be ascertained, only one other person died in the fire in addition to the master of the house: a young boy of some nine years, who had until recently been lodged with the Sisters of St. Syncletica at Hudlestone Manor. The boy was said to have been the bastard son of the man who died, borne by a one-time whore taken from the house of a notorious brothel-keeper—but there was no evidence of this save for the fact that the man had paid for the boy's keep and had eventually come to take him away from the nuns, into his own care.

One of the witnesses—the vicar of the parish—reported meeting a woman who had apparently emerged from the house after the fire started, although she was not a member of the household. He claimed that she seemed very confused, offering as evidence to support this judgment the contents of the brief conversation which followed his enquiry as to whether the owner of the house had managed to escape.

"Not in the way you mean," she replied. "But he has ever regarded the human condition as a prison, and life a Bedlam worse by far than the asylum at Hanwell. Like you, he has faith in the immortality of his soul, and he undoubtedly thinks that his adventures are only now beginning."

"If his reputation can be trusted," the vicar said unhappily, "I fear that he may not find it easy to gain entry to Heaven—but I dare to hope that he was able to repent his blasphemies at the last, and make his peace with God."

"He did not," the woman told him. "He has set forth on his journey as a bold explorer, with neither fear of Hell nor hope of Heaven to guide him, in search of territories of which the human imagination knows nothing. That is the only salvation he could ever believe in, and the only one he could ever desire."

"I hope that you are wrong," the man of God informed her dutifully. "Who are you, who knows the mind of a diabolist so well?"

"My name is Mercy," the woman replied, and said no more.

The man who died went largely unmourned, even by those in his employ, although he had never been an unduly cruel or parsimonious master. He had no true friends and there were many among his casual acquaintances who disliked him thoroughly, on the grounds of his overweening arrogance and evil reputation. It is entirely possible that no one could have been found to declare that the world would be a poorer place without him. Even so, and notwithstanding the rumors which charged him with sexual perversion and active diabolism, the Sisters of St. Syncletica decided to hold a special mass in his memory, and to pray most earnestly for the eventual salvation of his soul.

3

William de Lancy's delirium had faded now. The murmurous babble which had spilled incomprehensibly from his lips had almost ceased. The low-slung hammock no longer rocked back and forth as its occupant trembled and writhed about. Father Mallorn's anxiety abated, and he was able to reassure himself that all would certainly be well. The snake which had bitten the man had, after all, been very small—much tinier than the cobra which had earlier wounded David Lydyard—and the lethality of its venomous dose had evidently been in true proportion to its size.

Mallorn was very glad to see the crisis pass. He felt himself to be responsible for the stricken man's predicament. It was he who had persuaded de Lancy, Tallentyre and Lydyard to leave the route planned and approved by Thomas Cook in order to accompany him into the Eastern desert, in search of more ancient relics of Egyptian civilization. He had appealed, of course, to their intellectual curiosity, but Mallorn knew in his heart of hearts that his motive had been a cowardly one. He had been afraid to venture alone into the angry wilderness. He had always been ashamed of his easily awakened fear, which never seemed to let him alone for long. He sometimes wondered whether the vocation which had committed him to the Society of Jesus had been anything more than a sublimation of his anxieties.

Latent fear made Mallorn start as the tent-flap was roughly pulled back. Sir Edward Tallentyre came into the tent. The baronet's eyes caught the yellow lantern light, so that it seemed for an instant that a fire had been lit within him. His dark hair was, as always, precisely combed; he was a man orderly to the point of severity.

"How is he, Father?" Tallentyre asked.

"Better," Mallorn said. "Much better. I think he will be well again by morning—but it would not hurt to say a prayer for him."

There was just a hint of ironic malice in this last statement, for Tallentyre had made not the slightest effort to conceal his atheism from the Jesuit. The baronet had been born and brought up a Catholic, but had lapsed in adolescence, and he displayed the zealous fervor typical of all converts. In spite of the fact that Sir Edward considered him a victim of superstition, Mallorn could not help but like the man; apostate though he was, Tallentyre had a stout heart and an authentic desire to do good in the world.

"I wish we had not come here," Tallentyre said. "There is little enough to see—not enough to justify a dangerous expedition."

"I did not mislead you," the priest said defensively. "I did not promise you huge pyramids or carven sphinxes—only shattered mastabas and rude rock-hewn burial chambers, which is what we have found. They are pre-dynastic relics, older than the great pyramid. If Lepsius is to be trusted they were made four thousand years before the birth of Christ."

"You knew that the guides we hired would not come here," Tallentyre said. "You knew that they would be afraid."

Mallorn shrugged. "Superstition," he said, casually turning the baronet's favorite dismissal against him.

Tallentyre shook his head. "Danger," he said, instead. "Not curses left over from antiquity, but real danger. Snakes, bandits, dust storms."

"We are civilized men," Mallorn reminded him. "We understand that the venom of serpents is not a kind of witchcraft. We have guns to defend ourselves against bandits. We have tents in which to shelter against storms of all kinds." *And we have prayers,* he added silently, *to armor us against the failures of our own resolve.*

"You are right, of course," Tallentyre said, passing his hand across his sweating brow. "I apologize—de Lancy's injury has disturbed me. I feel responsible for him, in a way. He is only a little older than David, although he seems so much more the man of the world—a mere boy, in truth. To hear the terror and the madness of his delirium was . . . upsetting."

To a man like Tallentyre, Mallorn knew, anything which threatened order and mental discipline was repulsive. The baronet was a man of science, who desired everything to be safe and sane, and would have preferred it were there no such things as dreams, let alone nightmares. He was utterly intolerant of the notion—which Mallorn found strangely comfortable—that the world was vulnerable to divine Acts of Creation, and might at any moment acquire the substance and logic of a dream. Mallorn would have liked to continue their running debate, but he recognized that now was not the time.

"Go back to your tent, Sir Edward," he said. "I will keep watch over the boy, although I am sure that no mortal harm can come to him now."

The baronet nodded, and did as he was told.

Although it was nearly midnight, David Lydyard was quite content to sit in the open, beside the dying ashes of the fire, looking up at the quiet stars. The air was so clear here that the great arc of the Milky Way was more like a ribbon than a necklace of jewels. One never saw stars like that over London, whose air was now so polluted that stinking sulphurous smog was a permanent curse afflicting the winter nights.

David loved the tranquil light of the stars, whose imperturbability testified to the essential permanence and safety of the world. Generations of men might pass across the face of the earth like phantoms, leaving nothing behind but a few paltry hand-hewn relics which would quickly dissolve into the desert, but the stars endured—and now that men knew for certain that they were not little lanterns lit by God, but distant suns orbited by worlds of their own, it was possible to have the fullest confidence in their endurance, and in the majestic beauty of the cosmos. To know the truth of the universe was to feel very tiny indeed, but David was not intimidated by that feeling of tininess, nor did it make him feel insignificant. To understand the true magnitude of things was, in a curious sense, to share in that magnitude, to participate in the majesty—whose beauty was, after all, in the eye of the beholder.

David felt closer to the universe of stars here in Egypt than in any other place he had been. It was not simply the clarity of the sky that made him feel that way, but something about Egypt itself and the ancient objects he had come to see. The pyramids had been built by thousands of men working to a single end, and although that particular end—the voyage of a dead king to continue his reign in some imaginary land of the dead—had been a mere mirage, the planning and execution of the task had proved beyond doubt the awesome capability of the human hand, working in harness with the human imagination, to transform the world.

When he confronted the sphinx, David had imagined her face made whole and beautiful again, and had pictured her painted eyes looking out approvingly upon this marvelous promise. He knew well enough that the Egyptian sphinx was not quite the same as the Greek sphinx which had asked its riddle of Oedipus the parricide, and which Francis Bacon had made into the symbol of science, but he was nevertheless prepared to hypothesize that the mind behind those imagined eyes had found the pyramids a satisfactory answer to the riddle of how the future of the earth was to be shaped and the Age of Reason brought eventually to term.

None of David's companions was yet asleep. Both of the tents were illuminated from within and he could see shadows moving within them both. Father Mallorn clearly intended to watch over de Lancy all night, and his own guardian seemed to be keeping some private vigil, maintained in his alertness by the discipline of his undoubted genius. David knew that he ought to join Sir Edward, but some unspecifiable reluctance held him back. It was as though the crystal light of the stars had caged him, and made him prisoner.

David had done his level best to be worthy of his adopted father's love, by shedding every last vestige of the superstition which his early life had inculcated in him. He no longer believed in God or in ghosts—but as he looked around the valley slopes he could not help but feel that there was something in the glamor of the starlight which whispered of arcane secrets lost hereabouts for a very long time— but not quite forever.

Perhaps, David thought, *there are more mysteries in the world than a man like Sir Edward could ever concede.* It was not so difficult to believe it on a night such as this, when the valley was so elaborately dressed in moon-shadows.

He was abruptly seized by a tremor of unease. Were those shadows moving?

He knew they could not be moving in reality. The movement of the moon and the stars was imperceptible, and the rocks were immovable, so the shadows in the mouths of the tombs could not be moving. The apparent movement must be a trick of his own eyesight: an optical illusion or a self-induced hallucination.

It is only a dream, he told himself firmly. But then a new thought burst upon his consciousness with a dreadful giddiness, and he found that he could take no comfort at all from the notion that it was *only* a dream, because that was, after its fashion, the most terrifying notion of all. He realized that he *was* dreaming, and that the dreamer of the dream was . . .

David stood up abruptly, and watched the ghost emerge from the Stygian gloom of one of the empty tombs.

She was dressed in a sleek white gown, exactly as he had imagined she might be in the long-gone days of his childhood, when he had first heard the well-known nursery rhyme about the werewolves of London. She was very pale, and had remarkably beautiful silver hair, and her shining eyes were violet in color.

Though thou art forsaken be not beguiled, he quoted to himself, and knew it for good advice.

"You never loved me, David," Mandorla said. "You never made love to me, no matter how I pleaded."

"I could not," David replied regretfully. "I could not, and I never can."

She came to stand before him, close enough to be touched—but he dared not reach out his hand, because he knew only too well that it would pass through her. She was only a trick of his own eyesight, a dream within a dream.

She looked up at the stars: at the wonderful godless firmament which inspired him with such wonder and such hope. Obediently, he followed her gaze. "Is there comfort in this?" she whispered. "Is there joy? If you could only know what it is to live as a wolf, and be free!"

"I am a man," David said. "That is all I can be, and all I need to be, and all I desire to be."

"You should have loved me," she complained again. "What shall you do now, my poor darling? Will you go to England, and marry your faithless Cordelia, and suffer the racks and rents of your disease, and study pain but receive no comfort, and die all over again, knowing nothing but what you have learned and forgetting even that?"

"Yes," he said. "That is what I shall do."

"You could have had my love," she told him. "You still can."

"There are four good reasons that bind my fate to Cordelia's," he told her by way of a rebuke.

"One will die screaming in the blood-stained mud of Flanders," she told him. "One will wither as an old maid beneath the burden of the duty which you will impose upon her. The first-born will forget you, as all ungrateful children forget their progenitors. Men are not wolves, after all. They do not know true love, or true joy, or true hope. Are those three reasons good *enough*?—and is the fourth any better?''

"I love her," he said, referring to the fourth. "Perhaps the day will come when I no longer do, but I cannot think of that. What can I say, Mandorla? I am a man, and only a man. If the world were to acquire the substance and logic of a dream, still I would have to live in it, and understand it as best I could—*as a man,* Mandorla, not as some creature of legend, some whim of fancy, some demon's pet.''

He flung his arms wide, as though to embrace the vastness of the sky, and all it contained. "This is the world, Mandorla!'' he cried. "It is the world as I desire it, the world I have discovered as a man: my home, my refuge, my reward!''

"And by your uncompromising decree, it is a world which has no place for me,'' she complained bitterly. She reached out with her own delicate hand as she spoke, and stroked his cheek. Her hand did not pass through his solid flesh. He was able to feel the caress, but it was not like the touch of a human finger; it was as if a delicate cobweb had trailed across his face, catching briefly in the stubble of his uncleanly shaven beard. "Of all the men I ever met,'' she told him, "you were the only one I loved, if only for a little while.''

He knew that it was a lie, a temptation, and a vengeful compliment, but he liked it anyway. "Of all the ghosts I ever met,'' he assured her, "you were the only one I desired, if only for a moment.''

She smiled, showing her delicate, pearly teeth. "You forget the Angel of Pain,'' she said coquettishly.

"Oh no,'' he said, with all due sincerity. "I do not, and never will—not, at least, while I am capable of dreaming.''

When David came into the tent his guardian looked up curiously from the book which he was reading.

"Where on earth have you been?'' he asked. "I had begun to fear that you had been waylaid and carried off. I was about to come searching for you.''

"I was perfectly safe,'' David assured him.

No sooner had he spoken than the night was rent by a blood-curdling howling, which began with a single cry and continued in a host of eerie echoes.

Tallentyre leapt to his feet and thrust himself through the tent flap into the open air. David followed him. The Jesuit had emerged from his own tent, and seemed more alarmed than either of them.

"For the love of God," said Mallorn, "what was that?"

"Some animal," Tallentyre answered, having already regained his composure.

"It was only a wolf," David said negligently, "summoning her pack, and receiving the obedience which is her due."

The moonlight was bright enough to show David the expression of astonishment on his guardian's face. It lingered only as long as it took Sir Edward to conclude that he could not be serious, but even after reaching that conclusion Tallentyre could not resist the temptation to say, "There are no wolves in Egypt."

"There are wolves everywhere," David replied, although he no longer knew exactly what he might mean by it. He did not wait to hear Sir Edward's response, but went back into the tent. He sat down on his bunk, and began to unbutton his shirt.

His eye was caught by an amulet he had bought in Cairo, which was hanging negligently upon a hook set in one of the tent poles. It was of the kind which the Egyptians called an *utchat,* symbolic of the inner eye which could look into the realms of the supernatural. It stared at him, mutely.

It would, he supposed, continue to stare—with a gloss which sometimes gleamed amber and sometimes gleamed green, according to the whim of the lamplight—long after he had laid himself down and closed his own obedient eyes, intent on dreaming of Cordelia, and of love.

Acknowledgments

The shape of the project whose third volume this is was determined partly by Robyn Sisman, the editor to whom—in the autumn of 1988—I showed an outline for a single volume (of approximately 250,000 words) entitled *The Wolf and the Fold*. As I initially envisaged it, that work would have had four parts set in four different periods of past and future history, narrative continuity being provided by a group of immortals; Pelorus would have been the central character. Robyn proposed that 250,000 words was too long for one volume, and suggested that I split the project into two. As the four parts could not be evenly divided I decided to expand part three and embed the residuum of parts one and two within it; this move necessitated making David Lydyard the central character instead of Pelorus. On seeing the revised outline, Robyn suggested that it might be more productively marketed as a trilogy, so I devised a second sub-climax and laid out the plan of the work as it now exists. Things worked out a lot better this way than they probably would have if I had followed my original plan, and I am appropriately grateful for Robyn's input. I am also grateful for the continued support given to the project by her successors, Maureen Waller and Martin Fletcher.

The vision of the universe contained in part three of the present volume includes several key ideas, phrases and metaphors borrowed from *Order out of Chaos* by Ilya Prigogine and Isabelle Stengers. I also borrowed one nice phrase and one neat analogy from David Bohm's *Wholeness and the Implicate Order*. I am grateful to Jon James for the loan of useful research materials, and to Philip Tung

431

Yep for showing me his own attempts to extrapolate such notions into the realms of scientific romance.

In constructing the alternative history which begins to diverge sharply from our own in the early months of 1918, I made considerable use of John Toland's *No Man's Land.*

Sir Edward Tallentyre's ideas regarding the philosophy of history, briefly elaborated in *The Werewolves of London* and aphoristically cited in the present volume, owe a good deal to arguments which I first encountered in R. G. Collingwood's *The Idea of History.*

I owe apologies to Sabine Baring-Gould and Henry Mayhew, for falsely quoting them as authorities in establishing the (wholly invented) mythology of the werewolves of London, and to René Descartes, for falsely crediting him with an (entirely imaginary) alternative version of his first meditation.

Literary influences on the work have, of course, been very numerous and varied. My debt to the tradition of British scientific romance, which I had occasion to analyze in some depth while writing my book on *Scientific Romance in Britain, 1890–1950,* is very obvious. Although the title of the present volume is taken from George Griffith, who initiated the preoccupation with the impact of technological progress on the business of war which became central to the genre's concerns, the development of the narrative owes more to examples set by the visionary fantasies of John Beresford and Olaf Stapledon. The one explicit mention of Anatole France included in the present volume (there are two supplementary references to his novel *The Revolt of the Angels*) is insufficient acknowledgment for the debt I owe to the tradition of "literary Satanism" which he brought to abundant fruition; it was in his work that I discovered St. Amycus. The other story which Anatole remembers having read is by Catulle Mendès.

Although there is no connection between the contents of *The Werewolves of London* and Warren Zevon's excellent song "Werewolves of London," nor between the contents of *The Angel of Pain* and E. F. Benson's fine novel of the same title, l was conscious of the coincidence in each case and am duly grateful for the inspiration.

The translation of Dante's *Inferno* quoted in *The Werewolves of London* was made by S. Fowler Wright. The passage incorporates one minor correction which Wright made in his own copy of the published version.

I am greatly indebted to my wife Jane for all the hard work she put into proofreading the three volumes, and for her stout moral support on occasions when my confidence in the progress of the project wavered. Her contributions to the contents of the work have been many and varied; the vision of God included in David Lydyard's deliria and some of the Heavens visited by Pelorus and Harkender were based on suggestions of hers.

Brian Stableford, Reading, May 1993.